The Malandrine

a novel

DONALD GRECO

The Malandrine
Donald Greco
Published April 2026
Little Creek Books
Imprint of Jan-Carol Publishing, Inc.

ISBN: 978-1-970471-30-4 (Paperback)
ISBN: 978-1-970471-31-1 (Hardcover)
Library of Congress Control Number: On file

You may contact the publisher:
Jan-Carol Publishing, Inc.
PO Box 701
Johnson City, TN 37605
publisher@jancarolpublizshing.com
www.jancarolpublishing.com

The Malandrine

a novel

Also by Donald Greco

Youngstown Quintet Series:
Abramo's Gift
Tommy the Quarterback
Dracaena Marginata
The Ghost Hawk

For Young Readers
What Ever Happened to the Smooth-Tongued Cats?

To Angie,

forever

Part I

The Magic

IN THE OLD GOTHIC GYMNASIUM, an oval colonnade undergirded an indoor track that ringed the great room high above the floor. Around the track, leaded windows, dirty and cracked, let afternoon sun in to cast symmetrical slant shadows of banister spokes across the floor. This was now a storage place for odd things Spring Common College never threw away: ornate dark wood cabinets, ugly brass lamps, broken desks, old pianos, three-legged chairs, mirrors with cracked gilt frames, boxes, paint cans, and yellowed drapes—everything in a shroud of dust, all of it old, all of it unnoticed and forgotten high in Crandall Hall.

It was four flights of stairs to the old gym. The elevator had broken long ago, and for almost everyone, the stairs weren't worth the trip. A young man paused on the landing a moment to catch his breath. Three large sets of double doors confronted him. The one nearest him had a broken lock; he knew it.

Inside the gym, the old floorboards creaked under his weight. He walked slowly, remembering earlier times when life had filled the room with crowds and players. With each step, he imagined hearing ghostly voices as he turned to the four corners of the gym. So few memories had faces; all he dreamed were shouts and movements—blurs of eye and ear.

How strange it was to see his footprints following him in the dust. How long ago had anyone else been there? He paused, determined to quit his dreaming. Behind a large crate was a roll of canvas tarpaulin. He moved the tarp to the side of the crate, grunting as he did, to find a soft, thick rope he knew was hidden beneath it. He stood on the tarp and boosted himself to the top of the crate, cursing softly as he tore a small hole in his shirt. Moving quickly and silently, he secured the rope to one of the thick knurled spokes of the banister that bordered the track overhead. He knotted the rope and tugged it once again. It slipped easily around his neck; the knot beneath his chin was neat and tight. After a long, deep breath, he stepped off the crate. For an instant, with the tightening of his muscles, he seemed to stand suspended in the air. But then he fell. Only a faint snapping noise disturbed the tranquility of the gym.

The long gold conduits of early spring sun bent through the windows into the gray silence of the room—across the banister, across the lifeless, bloated face of the young man, and across the footprints patterned behind him in the dust.

Youngstown was a city of the children of immigrants. The third and fourth generations of people who settled in the Mahoning River valley at the turn of the century—the children of laborers, foremen, truck drivers, and policemen—were now the lawyers, doctors, teachers, engineers, and businessmen who ran the city.

When the mills were gone and the skies were clear instead of smoky and grimy with the soot from blast furnaces, the town grew quiet and small. Many of its children had gone on to other cities.

All three of Luigi (Lou) Bellanca's children lived out of town: Amy in Pittsburgh, Jack in Boston, and Dom in Chicago. Guarino (Rino) Bellanca's children were less remote: Frank, his wife, Jean, and their two children, Libby and Larry, lived with Rino in Youngstown; Nancy lived in Warren; and Jerry lived in Akron. James, Rino's youngest son, died in the Gulf War in 1989.

Rino and Lou's elder sister, Concetta (Connie), told them truths they didn't want to hear. They didn't exactly fear her, but they often squirmed in the face of her sensible and outspoken indignation. She had two children: Joe, an accountant, and Danny, a lieutenant in the Youngstown Police Department. Connie never liked the odds she faced against her brothers. She could never divide and conquer them, though she'd tried for 60 years.

One Sunday they were together at Connie's house, and she was annoyed by Lou's cigarette smoke. "How's Jerry's house, Rino?" she said testily, waving the smoke out of her face with her hand and glaring at Luigi.

"Still the same. If the carpenters' strike isn't over soon, they won't be able to move in till spring."

"Did they sell their old place yet?"

"No, but Rita doesn't want to stay in it anymore," he said disgustedly. As he answered her, he left the room. Connie turned to Lou, who knew what to expect next.

"What's the matter with him, Lou?"

"Nothing. He's okay."

"You always say 'nothing.' Is he sick?"

"No."

"Did he have a fight with Jerry?"

"Connie, please! If you want to know something, Rino's over there. Go ask him."

"You're both crazy, you know that? You retire and you still work. You look tired and you don't rest. Do you know neither of you have been here in two weeks?"

"We don't come over here because you drive us crazy with your goddamned questions," said Lou wearily. "I tell you Rino's gonna be all right. He just feels..."

"What?"

"He feels lonely."

"But we all feel lonely, Luigi. He has to start getting used to it."

"His loneliness is newer than ours; it's harder for him."

The Italian Day festival at Barber Park was always the first Sunday in August. The Ninth Ward Political Club brought forth its politicians, great and small, office holders and heirs apparent, poll watchers and chauffeurs. This was the day for grandchildren and great-grandchildren, a day for carrying a statue of the Madonna through the streets, a day for bands, parades, and outdoor Masses. Then, at night, there was a bazaar and fireworks... Chinese lanterns, beer and wine, sausage, lupini beans, raffles of Cadillacs, crap games, poker, and roulette.

The parade and the Mass were for those who were assured a place in heaven, for the self-proclaimed saints and the pious frauds who made grand gestures such as pinning hundred-dollar bills onto the blue silken robe draped over the statue of the Madonna. Rino and Lou both sneered as the band passed and the train of paper money floated back on the midsummer breeze.

The brothers were looking for the officials' booth, next to the wine and beer booth. Over the years, the functionaries had learned that to press the flesh, to store up good will, and to deal for support in the next election, they had to be in the way of all who passed through the festival. And everyone passed the wine and beer booth. Rino and Lou moved through the crowd and the noise, being shoved and crushed, nodding hello and muttering greetings to others passing in the flow against them.

Big Paolo's huge body was the easiest to spot. He was an official greeter at the main booth, a giant with a reddened, pockmarked face and a great thick mustache, graying on the edges. Lately he was stooped a little more, and the asthmatic wheezing and tortured breaths cracked and hoarsened his deep voice.

"Hey, guys, how about some house wine? Rino? Lou?"

"I don't want any wine, Councilman," Rino grumbled.

"Hey, I ain't running for anything. Come on. Have some wine."

"Never mind, Polly," said Lou, looking scornfully at Rino. "I'll have some, and my whore of a brother'll have some, too."

Rino gave him a sullen look. Paolo brightened a little and dove into the crowd of bartenders behind the booth to get some good wine.

"Why the hell do you have to talk to Polly that way?" Lou muttered to his brother. "He never did anything to you."

"I was joking," said Rino.

"Then smile when you're joking, asshole. You know he's sick. And you know he wouldn't hurt a fly."

Both men stood together, nodding to acquaintances and talking to friends. Paolo returned with two plastic cups of wine.

"Thanks, Polly. Where are Pete and Marty?" said Rino in a friendlier tone.

"Haven't seen them, Rino. I think they're coming later."

Rino went to the lupini booth to get some small bags of the salted yellow beans. He stood in line, waiting and looking through the moving mass of people. Suddenly Lou was at his side again, and Rino frowned instinctively. "What do you want, Lou?"

"Look, Rino, there's Andrea Manasseri."

"Where?"

"Over there. Look. What a woman, huh?"

Both men watched Andrea move through the crowd. Her son was on one arm, and she was talking to her sister as she walked.

"Go say hello to her, Rino," said Lou with a gleam in his eye.

"You must think I'm crazy, Lou."

"Crazy, hell. She's a nice lady. Say hello; that's all. You don't have to tear her goddamned clothes off."

"No."

"Rino, you bastard, go say hello to her. I know what's wrong with you, and so do you. You haven't talked to a woman since Mary died. Go on!"

"Forget it, Luigi. I'm not doing it."

"Rino, when are you gonna decide what to do with the rest of your life?" Lou muttered.

Rino didn't answer him. Instead, he turned and bought two bags of lupini beans and handed one to Lou.

"I got it. You're just gonna stand here and eat fucking beans and let the whole world pass you by, right?"

Rino stood silently, watching Andrea as she talked to Vito Rinaldi, the Ninth Ward councilman. She was slender and rather tall. Her eyes were dark, and her skin was clear and light. Her long, gray-and-black hair was pushed up neatly upon her head.

She always seemed aware that people were looking at her. She had the kind of aloofness that made men fear her yet be attracted to her. *Why should she be so inaccessible?* he thought. *Why did she seem so high class?*

Maybe it was just that she felt herself to be high class, and that intimidated everyone. She hadn't been an extraordinary beauty when she was young. Yet, as she grew older, she began to develop a mysterious aura, an attractiveness that made all men notice her. Maybe because they didn't turn her head, she became more of a challenge.

He started moving toward her against his better judgment, fascinated by what her reaction to him would be. He was stopped by some friends and tarried too long; Andrea had moved on. Then he saw her again, waiting near the Saint Luke's Church booth. Someone was probably getting her a lemonade. Her sister had gone to talk to other friends.

She caught Rino's eye across the stream of people between them. She knew he was going to stop to talk to her. And she was uneasy because she knew that he would ultimately be embarrassed. She couldn't consider herself available again; she couldn't make herself put men at ease. She just didn't want the word to be out that she was approachable. She wanted her husband to be alive and other men to leave her alone. She wasn't lonely; she had her own children and their children. And this man who was coming toward her wanted what they all wanted, what she couldn't give them.

"Good evening, Andrea," said Rino.

She hesitated for a second as she observed him closely. He was a strange man, square and muscular, more handsome than most who had approached her, younger-looking and more vital. There was even something vulnerable about him, and that was pleasing. And she felt troubled because she knew this man would be harder to resist than all the others. "Good evening, Rino," she said softly.

"How have you been?" *Damn,* he thought. *It was so hard to say the simple things that would make these moments easier.* "I mean, I hope you're doing well."

She smiled. "Yes, I'm doing well."

Rino looked around uneasily. No one was watching that he could see. "And your family?"

"They're all fine. And yours?"

"Fine, fine. Uh, this day is much nicer than the one last year, isn't it?"

"Yes, I've heard that. I wasn't here."

They suddenly found themselves staring at each other and not speaking. They broke their gaze when Rino said, "Andrea, how do you spend your days now?" His formal tone upset him, but he couldn't feel at ease not using it. Still, he was getting closer to what he really wanted to say: "Can I court you and spend time with you?" But he couldn't yet—not yet.

"I spend time with my grandchildren. I live with my son, as you do."

"My son lives in my house, as yours does with you," Rino said emphatically.

"Ah, yes," she said, sighing. "But I'm a woman, and I have to depend upon my sons to help me... as my husband once did."

Invoking her husband's name was not the best thing for Rino's concentration. "Yes, I understand," Rino said. "Andrea, I've come across all these people not just to say hello to you. I've no way of ever seeing you. I don't go to church much; I don't play politics." He was laboring. What he had thought he might say easily, he was blurting out with no style or grace. And it was having the opposite effect of what he had expected. He was scaring her, showing her what an oaf he was.

"Andrea, would you... I know you still care for your husband... as I do for my wife... but... would you permit me to call upon you at your house?" There. It was finally out. Awkwardly and too fast, but finally done.

She tensed, and her face blanched slightly as she looked away from him. "Other men have asked me the same thing, Rino." She hesitated, noticing that her son was coming toward her. "But my answer is always the same. Thank you. You honor me. But I'm not ready to be called upon by other men. My husband's memory is—"

"Andrea, there are a lot of days and nights we face without the dead."

"I understand what you're saying, Rino. But I'm not the same as other women. I just can't. My children want me to cherish the memory of their father."

"Here it is, Ma," said her son. "It took me 15 minutes to get through that line of kids at the stand." He nodded unsmilingly to Rino, obviously displeased that he could hardly leave his mother for a few moments without some eager old man coming after her. "Where's Aunt Tina? Can't she stay with you even a few minutes?"

"Carl, you remember Mr. Bellanca, don't you?" Andrea said, seemingly ignoring her son's irritation.

Carl looked coolly at Rino for a moment, displeased with his mother for forcing him to acknowledge the older man. "Yes, I think so. Bellanca?

Didn't you used to work for my father sometimes?"

He was good at subordinating people, and Rino understood the tone and implication of his words. "No, my son did, a few summers back when he was in school," Rino said. He huffed softly and looked one more time at Andrea, despite her son, searching for some special return look. She returned a polite and noncommittal glance. Rino bid them both farewell, and her son nodded with pleasure knowing that, once again, he had helped his mother rebuff an eager suitor.

Rino returned to the booth where Lou and Paolo were still standing. "You gonna stand here all night?" he said to his older brother.

"How did it go, Rino?" asked Lou quietly.

"How are the lupines, Polly?" said Rino, ignoring his brother.

"Goddammit, Rino, what did you say to her?" said Lou.

Rino spoke softly but emphatically: "I said it quietly and with respect. I asked her if I could come to call on her. She said no, for the memory of her husband is fresh. And that her children want her to honor him by being a virgin again. Okay now, Lou?"

"She didn't say that," Lou said skeptically.

"I added the virgin part," said Rino.

"Maybe you broke it too fast," Lou said, more to himself than to his brother.

"Forget it, Lou. That was my chance, and it didn't work. Her son made me feel like a dog sniffing after his mother."

"A little more wine, Rino?" said Paolo.

"No, Polly. Thanks. I'm tired. I think I'll go home."

Rino had waxed and buffed all the corridors in Stilton Hall and had fixed leaks on two fixtures in the lavatories. He was tired, not because he had done anything unusual but because the heat of the day and his own melancholy had drained the vitality out of him. His old Ukrainian buddy, Joe Potokar, called out to him as he walked through the workers' locker room, a long, shadowy corridor lined with dull-green painted lockers.

"Hey, Rino, are you going to the union meeting?"

"Not tonight, Joe, I'm tired."

"How were you gonna vote on that raise?"

"It's about all we're gonna get without a strike. It's gonna pass, right? So I'd be tempted to vote no just to keep the bastards honest. I'm better off going home."

Joe laughed at Rino's perverse logic. "Rino—I almost forgot—the dean of education wants to see you before you leave this afternoon."

"Me? What's he want with me?"

"I don't know, but he asked Sammy to send you up... special."

Rino sighed. "I probably left an ashtray full of butts on one of the office desks."

He walked slowly across the lovely green mall to a large, redbrick, Georgian-style building: Crandall Hall. He seldom took elevators, but the stairs this day seemed like mountains, so he did. The secretaries hardly noticed him as he walked alongside the pool of three rows of four desks each. It wasn't just that they didn't notice him; they didn't see him. The more they stayed at the college, the less they saw of people. They saw only deans and department chairmen and important professors and one another—no students, young instructors, workers, or visitors—no one who didn't sparkle with the iridescent dust of academic authority.

As he went into a smaller hallway, administrators' row, he was passed by several hurried-looking men and one secretary. They looked at him as they did all other custodians, with indifferent tolerance, as he trudged slowly by. The dean's office was at the end of the corridor.

He knocked and was ordered to come in from behind the closed door.

As Rino entered, the dean looked up from what he was writing to nod at him. "Sit down, Rino," he said, motioning to a chair on the other side of his desk. Rino sat down warily, wondering what good could possibly come from his being there.

"You must be wondering why I've sent for you," the dean said.

"A little," Rino said.

"Well, Sammy told me—when I inquired—that you knew Dr. Reese and that you helped the police the day of the... uh, unfortunate incident."

"My youngest son took a class that he taught. I met him a couple times," Rino said, eyeing him suspiciously.

"Well... Rino... uh, since the incident, many professors would feel awkward meeting his wife again, so we need someone to deliver these things." He pointed to a large cardboard box on a table at the far end of his office. "They're some of his personal effects, some books and papers we've accumulated since he died. We've been remodeling those few offices. Anyway, I'd like you to take that box over to his widow. Sam said you could take time off early to deliver the package—he'll sign your timecard out at the regular time. I'd greatly appreciate it."

"Is that all you want me to do?" said Rino.

"That's all," said the dean nervously. "Here's the address."

Rino thought for a few seconds, uneasy because they were asking him to do something that a professor wouldn't do. "Okay," he said finally, "I'll pick it up tomorrow afternoon."

The next day Rino didn't eat lunch, so at 2:30 he picked up the box and loaded it into his station wagon. The ride wasn't too long, and he enjoyed the freshness of the air as it blew through the car. It was nice to be off work early, especially on a Friday.

The apartment was in a small fourplex of beautiful gray and white brick. The place looked comfortable and expensive, clean and well kept.

Inside, a wide lobby separated the downstairs apartments as a wide hallway separated those upstairs. The sky was changing, probably for rain, and the dull light through the draped and curtained windows made the upper hallway dim. He knocked at the door once, and then in a moment, knocked again.

The door opened, and a young woman answered. "Yes?"

"Mrs. Reese? My name's Rino Bellanca. I'm from Spring Common, and I've brought you this box—"

"What's in it?" she interrupted.

"Well, some things that belonged to your... husband."

She looked at him suspiciously, and her voice became cold and unfriendly. "Take it back; I don't want it."

Rino hadn't expected that kind of reception. "But these things are yours, miss—his papers, books, even the nameplate from his mailbox."

"I've forgotten all those things. I don't need them anymore."

"Look, miss, how about if you keep them just for a while? In a week or so, if you still don't want them, then call me at school, and I'll come to take them back. Okay? Ask for Rino."

Though she still eyed him coldly, her features began to soften. "Oh, all right," she said. "Bring it in... over there on the couch."

Rino smiled. "Thanks." After setting the box down, he turned quickly to leave.

"What did you say your name was?" she said to his back.

"Bellanca... Rino Bellanca."

"If I don't want them..." She spoke her words nervously.

He examined her face for a few seconds. He felt sorry for her. She was the lovely young debris from some discarded dream of great promise. If she were his daughter or niece, his own heart would ache for her. But she was a stranger, and no matter how pathetic she was, he wasn't close enough to help ease her grief.

"I'm sorry I spoke to you that way," she said. "Would you like a cup of coffee?"

Rino shook his head to indicate refusal. "Thanks," he said. One last time before going, he looked back at her, and this time he caught a sight that moved him. The young woman was standing 10 feet from him, in the middle of the room, with her eyes closed and tears rolling down her cheeks.

"Miss?"

She didn't answer. Instead, she seemed dazed and unaware.

He walked over to her and gently touched both of her shoulders. "How about if you sit down, huh?" He guided her into a chair behind her, handed her his handkerchief, and sat in another chair opposite her, waiting silently. She had lowered her head and stayed still for several minutes. Then, as time passed, she began to wipe away the tears and compose herself. When she looked up, Rino was staring at her, and she seemed embarrassed.

"Thank you," she said in a soft voice.

He waved his hand, palm down, in response. It was a curious Italian gesture that seemed at the time more expressive than words could have been; it meant many things, but here it meant that she had nothing to be grateful about. He felt awkward now that she had stopped crying.

"I'll take that cup of coffee, miss, if you're still offering," he said finally.

She seemed surprised. "Yes, I'll get some."

They made small talk as they drank the coffee. "What's your name?" he asked her.

"Leila," she said. "But most people just call me Lee."

"Can I help you in any way?" he said. "Maybe you're still not feeling..." He let his voice trail off, not wanting to put his train of thought into words.

"I'm okay most of the time," she said. "But sometimes, like when you brought those old things back, I wish I could never have been through it all. Did you know my husband?"

"Slightly. My youngest son took a class that he taught… and they played a few games in intramural basketball."

"What's your son's name?" she asked.

"It was Jim," he said. "He was killed in the Gulf War."

She shook her head. "I'm sorry to bring that up. This just doesn't seem to be my day."

"It's no problem," said Rino. "Really."

"Are you Italian?" she asked.

"Yeah. Are you?"

She smiled. "No, I'm Swiss and French."

She asked him more about himself: about his family and how long he had worked at Spring Common College. He answered in his own fashion, a combination of blunt cynicism and humor. They talked for almost two hours, and Rino had two more cups of coffee. Always she steered the conversation toward Rino and away from herself. She became composed and friendly, smiling often, sometimes even laughing softly. Finally, Rino began to realize that he had spent the last hours in a way he never thought he would do again, talking to a lovely young girl who, for her own reasons, seemed interested in him. Yet he had a sixth sense about overstaying any welcome. "I'd better get going, miss," he said.

"Lee," she said.

"Lee. It's been nice. The coffee was good."

"Thanks for talking to me," she said. "You made me feel comfortable for the first time in a long while."

Yeah. At my age, I make women feel comfortable, he thought as he left the apartment.

About a week later, Rino worked into the evening. The whole custodial crew was painting before fall classes started. And since it was easier to make scaffolds then, they worked on summer nights when no students were around. The night had been hot and windless. Rino was glad to be done with work.

On the way home, the traffic was unusually heavy. Someone at a stoplight told Rino that there was an accident on the square, tying up traffic through downtown. Rino was feeling grouchy and hot. Maybe he would stop at the Tre-Sette for a beer before he went home. He found himself passing near the apartment building where the Reese girl lived. There was a light on inside her apartment. He stared at the light for a second in a kind of dim awareness that an animal has before it does something and doesn't know why. Impulse. Stop the car. Go up there and ask for a cup of coffee. God, he was getting crazy in his old age.

But he found himself climbing the stairs. He paused a moment before the door of the apartment and stepped back to see if he could see a light beneath it. He couldn't. He knocked, quietly at first, and then more firmly.

Lee opened the door slightly, as much as the night lock would permit. She seemed surprised to see him. But in a second, she closed the door, released the lock, and then opened it again.

"Hi," he said. "I was just going by. I wondered if you had any coffee left."

She stood aside to let him in. "Yes, I have some. Come in." She seemed friendly enough, as though he were familiar.

Rino was frightened. Sooner or later, he was going to have to explain why he had come back to see her. But he didn't know how. He had done what he wanted to do, on the spur of the moment. He was there and talking to her. And it was a lot more pleasant than a beer down at the Tre-Sette.

Her legs and feet were bare. All she had on was a short blue robe that tied at the waist and ended above her knees. Her hair was not pinned up, as it had been the other day.

"Please sit down. I'll make a fresh pot," she said.

"No. I didn't really need—" he stammered.

"Really, I'd like a fresh cup," she said, interrupting him. "It's no trouble."

The television was playing softly. As Rino watched it, he caught glimpses of her as she walked back and forth across the kitchen door. *Her legs were beautiful and tan*, he thought. But his daughter and daughters-in-law and nieces had slender, tan legs, too. Yet she seemed different. How could all those muscles be so perfect?

She opened a cupboard for something and stood on tiptoes. God, he was too old to look at legs like that. Maybe blood makes all the difference. He saw Nancy and Jean and his nieces in their houses and at the swimming pools, and they were young and clean and lovely. But they weren't exciting.

Lee was quiet as she walked about the kitchen. *How much of a fool have I made of myself? What's she thinking?* Rino wondered. *Will she try to get rid of me? Will she do something perfunctory and mechanical just to get me out of here? But what's she thinking? Will she change her clothes? Or will she sit across from me and talk? And notice me looking at her legs? My God, I'm going crazy. What if Lou or Polly could see me now? Why is she taking so long? Is she sorry she let me in? Afraid to come out because she thinks I might be some kind of nut?*

He could hear the coffee percolating. The smell of it was familiar and pleasant and gave him a sense of well-being. Then she walked out with a tray, and their eyes met for the first time since they had met at the door 10 minutes ago.

They spoke awkwardly at the same time.

"I hope I'm not bothering..."

"Did you work..."

She smiled. As she walked, he noticed her grace. Her feet were slender and tan, toenails and fingernails painted translucent pearly white. As she bent over to set the tray down, he marveled at the play of sinews, the firmness of the muscles in her calves, and the momentary dimpling in her skin as the muscles of her calves and ankles pulled slightly in the bending motion—all of it in an instant. Yet she made no move to change clothes or cover herself.

"The coffee will be ready in a minute," she said.

On the tray were cinnamon roll slices, butter, and cookies. Maybe she really didn't want to get him out after a quick coffee. She went back to the kitchen for a couple of minutes. Rino was still uncomfortable.

She returned with a tray of coffee and held it in front of him until he took a cup from the tray and put cream in it. Then she held the cookie tray in front of him. Neither of them spoke.

Rino took a slice of the roll. She took a cookie and sat down, one foot under her and the other tiptoe on the floor, resting on the ball of her foot. One golden leg to torment his sight.

"I saw the light in the window," he said by way of explanation.

She took a sip of coffee without looking at him. "It's nice having a visitor. Other than my family, no one ever comes to see me," she said. Rino didn't respond, so she continued, "Having someone over for coffee... I haven't done this since..." She stopped. There were a few seconds of silence.

"This roll is good," Rino said. "Can I have another one?" He reached over to the tray as she nodded. Then he settled back into the chair.

She knew that he didn't want the roll, but in a nervous, instinctive way, he kept her from dwelling on something depressing. "What do you do nowadays?" he asked.

"Not very much, I'm afraid," she said. "Someday I'll probably move."

"Out of town?"

"Maybe... probably. I'm going back to work full time."

"Did you go to college, too?" he asked.

"Yes, I have a degree in library science from Indiana University. That's where I met Ted."

"A reader, huh?" he said.

"Yes. And I watch old movies on TV. And talk to my mother and sister. And shop. And work at the Rogers Library two days a week. Not very exciting, is it?"

"Not much is exciting about living," he said.

"Are you coming from work?"

"Yeah. Usually I quit at five, but we've been painting. And when we paint, we do it late. Anyway, there was a wreck down on the square, so I came this way."

She studied his face silently for a moment. "I'm glad you stopped by," she said, not changing her gaze.

He hesitated a few seconds, as though he couldn't believe that this venture had happened without a foolish or embarrassing moment. As they continued to talk, she grew more animated, and Rino grew more relaxed. She laughed a few times, rather a gentle laugh, and he loved the music of it. Sometimes she would change her position on the couch and both legs would be visible, and then she would change again and only one bare, silky limb would tantalize him. He would look at her in passing glances, sometimes looking out into the room and then back at her. But with every change he saw her legs.

It seemed funny to Rino that she was so relaxed and poised, sitting there with so little clothing on, in front of a strange man old enough to be her father. Occasionally at first, she had seemed tense and awkward as she spoke. But she didn't feel self-conscious at all about the clothes that covered her so incompletely. *Kids are different nowadays,* he thought.

He kept asking her questions about herself, her family, school, and her future. And this time he avoided saying much about himself. He drank more coffee. And listened more. Until he got the feeling that he should be on his way before the charm of the evening would fade and he might somehow say the wrong thing.

"I have to get going," he said. "Thanks." She smiled and stood up slowly after he did. After all he had ventured tonight, he felt he could say one more thing: "Are you gonna be okay?"

She was touched by his fatherly concern. Without thinking, she reached over to kiss him on the cheek. "Yes," she said softly, her eyes clouding, "I'll be okay."

"If you ever need anything–some help moving, something painted, a faucet leaking, anything. Just let me know, okay? It's my line of work."

He turned and headed for the door. She followed him silently. Then he turned back around toward her. "Take care of yourself," he said, knowing that there was no rational reason for another visit, no rational reason for a 62-year-old man to think about seeing this young woman again. God and nature didn't want such things to happen. He opened the door and stepped outside, pulling it closed behind him.

"Rino," she called. He stopped and then stood facing her in the doorway. The sound of her calling him by name was strange and musical. No one had ever called his name and looked the way she did. Ever.

"Thanks for being concerned for me," she said. "Do you often work late?"

"Once in a while–a couple times a month."

She shrugged. "You can stop here for coffee. I mean... well, I usually don't go out nights, and it's nice having coffee over long conversations. I miss..." She caught herself before finishing the reference to the past. "Well," she stammered, annoyed with herself, "I always have coffee."

He shrugged and nodded at the same time. Another way of saying maybe. Then he closed the door.

The next day, Rino was troubled by what he felt when he looked at Lee. What in hell had made him go there? Out of all the women in the world, he was drawn to a girl young enough to be his daughter, a girl whose husband he had helped cut down from his own gallows.

This was the girl who cried from the memories she saw in the box of her husband's things, whom he had tried to cheer and divert, who had been in his arms crying, and whom he had comforted as a father does a daughter. But this was also the girl whom he desired, whose legs were tan and slender and lovely, whose body was a soft mystery shielded behind a brief robe, and who moved so easily and gracefully as he watched her stretch and walk and sit. She had become a dream he wanted to look at, to talk to, and to touch. A dream to touch.

But it was sinful. He was thriving on the loneliness and pain of a young widow. Had he come to that? He had to stop. The real world only brings heartache at the end of such dreams.

That night, at home, his daughter-in-law Jean walked around the kitchen making supper. Rino watched her moving back and forth to the table. She was slender and attractive at 39—gentle, clean, sure of herself, sure of Frank's love, sure of her children, sure that if she worked hard enough, her world could be just as she had planned it.

But he didn't see in Jean's eyes the inner anguish that he saw in Lee's. She had something that made him burn inside and, also, something that he didn't understand. Maybe it was pain or guilt over her husband. Whatever it was, it made her different and more complex than Jean.

After supper, Rino took the newspaper into the living room to read it. His coffee tasted good after the meal. It was going to be easy tonight: a good movie on TV, a day off tomorrow, a long weekend. Maybe he'd talk Lou into going fishing.

As he read the sport pages, he was subliminally aware of Frank answering the phone and speaking softly. *Maybe the Browns would finally be good this year*, he thought.

"Pop," Frank called quietly.

Rino didn't look up at him but answered, "Yeah, Frank?" as he tried to finish his football article. Frank didn't answer. In a moment, Rino realized that his son was standing before him. He looked up from the paper to see both Jean and Frank.

"What is it, Frankie?" Rino said, suddenly afraid of what he would hear.

"That was Agee Mancuso on the phone." Frank had the same pale look he used to have when, as a boy, he had done something that he didn't want to explain. "Pop, Big Paolo just died," Frank said, almost in disbelief. He nodded again in response to Rino's doubting look. The one and only Big Paolo. No mistake. "He just had a heart attack over at the Cavour Club. Agee said he was dead before the ambulance got there."

The paper had fallen from Rino's hand. He sat hunched over, staring at the scattered mess on the floor. "Does Uncle Lou know?" he said.

"Agee's going to call him now," Frank said.

Rino stood up, looking at both Jean and Frank. "When Uncle Lou calls, tell him I'll be right over to pick him up. I'm gonna get ready."

"Dad, maybe you... are you gonna be okay? Frank can drive you," Jean said.

Rino smiled at her, then shook his head. "It's all right. I'll let you know what's going on after I get Lou. Bad business, huh?"

The next weekend Rino felt strange, just the way he did when Mary died. Something changed the complexion of every thought he had, the way one missing note would change a song and leave it incomplete. Why

Big Paolo? Why are the good things in life so fragile? He could have been nicer to Polly, could have passed up all those sharp remarks. Polly was so childlike, so gentle, so easy to tease.

And now, just when things seemed to be going okay, Rino had to worry about people dying again... about himself dying. Nothing ever leaves you at peace. Mary didn't have to die; she had everything to live for. She had security; she had the peace of knowing that her kids were all right. She had him. She didn't have to die.

Rino was glad to go to work Monday morning. The weekend had been a dreary two days of finding things to do: fix the basement sink and the downstairs toilet, put a shelf up in Larry's closet. Down at the Tre-Sette, everyone had been subdued and moody. The poker game Friday didn't run—not enough people. A pinochle game lasted two hours on Saturday, and then everyone went home.

Work was welcome relief. Joe was on a week's vacation, so Rino had Crandall Hall all to himself. He had to move some offices, Sammy told him. Sammy was his foreman: a young, chubby man in his early 40s, just about as old as Frankie. He even bowled against Frankie in the church league.

"Hey, goombah," Sammy said, gesturing for Rino to come closer. "You ready for work today?"

"Yeah, I'm ready, Stash."

They had a nice, easy relationship. Rino was Sammy's resource man. There seemed to be nothing Rino couldn't figure out how to fix at the college. Sammy liked him because Rino always did the jobs he gave him quickly and well and then cleaned up after himself. Sammy never heard any complaints about him. If he wanted something done right, he sent Rino.

"You're Hunky of the Week, now that Joe's gone," said Sam.

"Hunky I can handle. At least I won't have to be Polack as long as you're here," Rino said.

"How many times do I have to tell you? I'm not a Polack; I'm Croatian."

"Right. Croatian... kielbasa eater and Croatian. I'll have to remember that."

Sammy took a mock swing at Rino's gut as the eight o'clock bell tower chimes went off. "Okay, goombah, here's what you do today: you have to move two offices. You know who Chandler, the rich prof, is?"

"Is he the slick guy who drives a Mercedes?"

"Yeah. They just had some kind of blowout in education. Dresner resigned Thursday after the department meeting. So, Chandler's the new chairman, and Dresner goes down to the empty office on the second floor. Might as well get started now."

Dresner was downcast. He had lost, had been finessed by a young Turk. It was gratuitously insulting to be moved down to the second floor with all the associate and assistant professors. But his colleagues had turned on him, and when Chandler made his power play, Dresner couldn't call in enough markers to hold Chandler off.

Rino, knowing what had happened, was sympathetic to Dresner even before he went to his office. Yet, Dresner, too, was hard to like—naive, remote, and formal. To him, Rino was a primitive life form whose nerve endings were not sensitive enough to understand the plight of the "professoriate," as Dresner often referred to his calling. He was not glib or mockingly friendly as was Chandler, but he wasn't warm or helpful, either. He brooded and sulked, and Rino got one-syllable answers out of him every time he asked directions on how his goods were to be moved.

Dresner was everything Chandler was not: dumpy, short, balding, nondescript in every way, a company man who had been screwed by the company. Chandler was polished: tall, slender, a casting director's version of a young professor on the way up. But while one was a harmless, stuffy apple polisher, the other was aggressive and dangerous.

Dresner thanked him for moving his office so carefully. He was formal but polite. Rino nodded welcome as he maneuvered the flat out of the room into the corridor. He took the elevator up to the third floor to pick up some trash he had left in the storeroom. He wanted to end the day with this unpleasant job totally done and with nothing of it to do tomorrow.

Tomorrow, he had to paint. Jesus, he hated to paint. Too bad Joe had to take these two weeks off, just when Sammy was getting on a painting kick. And with Joe gone, he had to work every day. Man, part-time was better. You do something today and then take a day or so off. That was the way he liked it.

That afternoon, after lunch, Rino pulled the loading flat on his way to Chandler's office. The door was open, and inside was a man dressed in brown wool slacks, brown loafers, and a white button-down, long-sleeve shirt rolled up at the sleeves. Rino was impressed with the casual expensiveness of his dress. His shirt had a sheen on it, Rino thought. It looked like the Parisian silk shirts he had seen during the war. Chandler had sandy-blond hair and wore large, wire-framed reading glasses. *An all-American*, Rino thought. *Young, wealthy, and good-looking.*

"Dr. Chandler?" said Rino.

"Yes?"

"I'm supposed to move your office today."

"Well, sure, you can move it. But it won't fit on that cart, friend."

Rino snorted, trying to act pleasant. He didn't need any wise-ass remarks today. He walked inside, and Chandler said after the fact, "Come in," as Rino surveyed the room. Rino was getting irritated, so he turned to look at him directly, in an exaggerated gesture, so that their eyes met. "This is the right room, isn't it? You're going to move down to the corner office?"

"Remarkably perceptive. Are you sure you're not a philosopher posing as a custodian?" said Chandler. Whenever he spoke, he always seemed to be addressing an imaginary audience to which he could make smug and witty asides as in a Shakespearian play.

Rino ignored his remark and just concentrated on the job. "If you're not using them right now, I can move your books first. That way you can still use your desk."

"That'll do," said Chandler, not willing to engage Rino further.

Rino took the books from each shelf and carefully set them in boxes on the flat. Chandler ignored him most of the time, often staying out of the office for long periods. But when Rino would ask him something about what he wanted moved and how it was to be set up, Chandler's answers were curt and unfriendly.

Occasionally other professors would come to the office. Rino listened as they talked, and he grew increasingly scornful of Chandler's posturing and condescension. *What a bastard*, Rino thought. God help them now that they've given this man power.

Slowly the office was being moved: all the books and cabinets and papers and equipment. Chandler collected frogs: paintings, caricatures, clocks, knick-knacks, pencil holders—all very cute. *The great man was into frogs*, Rino thought. Then he had a moment of perverse inspiration: "Dr. Chandler, you don't want these little frog things in the chairman's office, do you? I can put them in the trash tonight."

Chandler bristled, but he kept his composure. "These are mementos and gifts," he snapped. "And yes, I do want them in the chairman's office. Do not—repeat—do not use your limited mental resources to decide one goddamned thing. All you do is deliver, stock, and sweep."

Rino felt smug and showed it with a slight smirk. He was glad he had been bold enough to irritate the new chairman. The work went on, and finally the move of Chandler's office was complete.

Rino, as he took a coffee break, was getting tired. It's dreadful enough when bad people get ahead as though they were good, but when it's hard to tell the good guys from the bad guys, the whole place seems cursed and misbegotten. He just wanted to punch out and go home.

After coming off the elevator, he moved the flat slowly and quietly down the hallway past two classrooms. Both had open doors, and he could hear professorial tones coming out of each door in a garbled clash of noises that he never paid any attention to.

Suddenly as he passed, he heard a sharp call. "Janitor!" It seemed to come from one of the classrooms he had just passed. For a moment, he thought of going on but decided to go back to the source of the noise. Hesitantly, he peeked into the first room. The professor was writing something on the blackboard, and the students were copying diligently. As he turned to walk toward the second door, he heard the voice again. "Can't you hear, janitor?"

It was Chandler. And Rino was instantly angry.

"I thought you told me you'd done all the moving?" Chandler asked imperiously. He was standing outside the doorway of the classroom.

"I moved every bit of stuff from your office," Rino said.

"How about the rest of the books?"

"What books are you talking about?"

"Those in there." He gestured into the classroom. Rino looked inside and saw two large bookcases full of books. All the students looked bemused and smiling, enjoying Chandler's grandstanding at Rino's expense.

"You could have told me they were in here," Rino said to Chandler after he had stepped back into the corridor. "How was I supposed to know that?"

"Why didn't you ask?" said Chandler.

"You weren't in your office the last two hours," Rino said.

"Well, take care of it, pal. I need them moved today."

Rino sneered at Chandler as he walked past him. He had made an enemy, and it would be hard to stay out of his way, he thought; Chandler thrived on pain and power.

Rino told Sammy about Chandler's game, and Sammy asked him to stay overtime to move the books when the class was over. Rino waited until six o'clock. Then he carefully moved the books from the classroom into Chandler's new office. He used the master key to get in; Chandler had gone home.

When he was done, it was dusk, and he was weary. He never liked to work when he was angry or tense; it made him all the more tired. Yet he didn't feel like going home. Maybe he'd shower and change and then go down to the Tre-Sette for some hot dogs and beer. Maybe he could sit down and talk to somebody—and unwind.

The first preseason football scrimmage game was being held at Spring Common Stadium that night. The main entrance to the college was jammed with cars, and even now the back entrance was becoming clogged. There was only one quick way off the campus for Rino: the delivery entrance behind the power house. Rino drove behind the building and saw lights on through the windows. He stopped his car, got out, and knocked a few times on the back door. No answer. He knocked again. "Yeah?" a gruff voice said as the door opened. "What the hell you want, Rino?" said the big man who now stood before him.

"Hey, Peewee, how about opening the gate? I'd like to get out of this place."

Pewee looked at the line of car lights on the far side of the campus. "You should stay, Rino. Be dedicated like me." He was smiling as he fumbled for the key chain clipped to his belt.

"Your two buddies are in there, right, Pee? Cigars, the coffee smell...

You bastards are in there playing gin."

Peewee chuckled. It was a combination of laugh and cough and choke around the cigar clenched in his teeth. "Dedication, paesan. Some of us have it, and some of us don't. Greasers don't."

Peewee waved as Rino drove out the back way. He went over a small bridge on the river that ran alongside the campus and then along the gravel road that led through the woods. He'd be bypassing downtown again, going the long way. Rino growled to himself, cursing his fate. *What a hell of a day*, he thought. He hadn't seen Lou all week, and he'd be in Pittsburgh until Sunday. What a hell of a day.

He drove by instinct, possessed of his own thoughts, half listening to the muted radio music in his car. This way home seemed so much longer, with all its stoplights, but it was better than fighting that football traffic. He had been here before. The girl's apartment was just a slight deviation from this headlong journey. A deviation. Slowly he eased the car into the right lane and turned right at the next intersection. *Will her light be on?* he thought. Somehow, just knowing she was there would satisfy him tonight.

But the light was on, and he wasn't satisfied. He stopped alongside the curb in front of the apartment building where she lived. It was a pretty place with small gardens front and back, full of flowers, evergreens, and ferns.

But should he go in? What in God's name could ever sanction this madness? But he wanted to look at her and hear her talk. He wanted her to be in that short robe and barefoot so he could watch her calves dimple as she stretched her legs. It had been a bad day. Not much worse could happen. Maybe she'd just slam the door in his face and call him a dirty old man. Maybe that would finally wake him from his mad dream. But he had to see her.

But maybe she'd be scared; it was already 8:20. Maybe she'd forgotten who he was. Maybe now she'd see him as a foolish, pathetic old man, drooling over the body of a young woman.

He rang the doorbell, not even conscious of having climbed the flight of stairs to her apartment. But no one came. Then he rang again, fearful now of being too insistent. This time the door parted a few inches, the length of the night chain. Rino stood there, never feeling so vulnerable in his life. When she saw him and their eyes met, he said "hi" helplessly.

But she smiled, closed the door, released the latch, and opened it again. "It's been a long time," she said as she stood aside for him to come in.

"A few weeks, huh?" Rino said.

Her hair was wrapped with a towel and was still wet. Small beads of water trickled down her temples onto her cheeks. "I just got out of the shower. Did you ring very long?"

"No, I just rang twice," he said uneasily, looking around the room as if expecting someone else to be there.

"Come and sit down," she said as she walked toward the couch. He sat in the chair he always sat in. She sat on the edge of the couch. She had on jeans, a blue cotton sweatshirt, and a pair of gold, backless slippers. How easily he noticed everything she wore, he thought. He was never like that with anyone else, not even Mary.

"I was going to make a snack," she said. "You came just in time." Somehow the ice was breaking between them. "Uh, could you spare me a few minutes? I'll put the coffee on and go dry my hair—"

"If you're busy, I can go. I just—"

"No. I'm not going anywhere or doing anything," she said emphatically but gently. She was also smiling, which made her words easier to believe. "You just sit here, and I'll be right back. Would you like to watch TV?"

"No, thanks," Rino said. "Is this today's paper?"

"Yes. Will that keep you until I get back?"

"Yeah, this'll be fine."

Again, he caught glimpses of her through the kitchen doorway. Only this time, her legs were covered. Still, with the tight jeans folding over every curve, he could imagine the wonder of her legs as she reached into the cupboard. She was also preparing something else, just as she had done before. Then, without a word, she was gone. He could hear the dryer from a room down a hallway behind him.

Rino tried to read the paper. The Browns had lost another defensive lineman to an ankle injury. It was going to be a long season. He tried to read about the mayor's newly disclosed slush fund, but he couldn't. He couldn't handle anything that made him concentrate too much. Finally, he began slowly paging through the newspaper, reading only headlines.

But then, after a few minutes that seemed like days, he could hear her back in the kitchen. It was funny that whenever she made coffee for him they never talked, even though they could have easily heard each other. Maybe each was trying to think of what to say when they were together in the same room again.

"I've got some nice rolls here," she said. "I think you'll like them."

She put the tray on a coffee table in front of Rino, handed him a cup, and then went back into the kitchen. When she returned, they both awkwardly moved to put a cup and the coffeepot together. Suddenly she put her hand on his to steady the cup so she could pour. "We'll both get burned if I spill it now," she said. The soft feel of her hand electrified him.

Then she poured her own cup and grabbed two cookies. In one quick and easy move, she slipped off her slippers, tucked her legs under her, and sat cross-legged on the couch, facing him.

"You must bake a lot; these things are really good," he said.

"I do a little, but my mother and sister bake all the time, and they always have something for me when they come."

"What side of town do they live on?"

"They don't live here. My mother lives in Canton and my sister in

Akron. One of them manages to get over here about once every couple weeks since... Ted's death."

Again. Life for her had separated into those events that came before her husband's death and those that came after. Her reference to her husband chilled the atmosphere for a few seconds. Neither of them could think of what to say. Finally, she broke the stillness. "I didn't think you would ever come back."

"Ah, I didn't know if I should. Maybe I'm making a pest of myself."

"Pests don't get fresh coffee and sweet rolls when they come here," she said. "Did you stop by to see how I was doing?"

"Yeah."

"I'd hoped you liked talking to me, too," she said somewhat playfully.

"Well, I did. But maybe I'm horning in where other people should be."

"All I have is my sister and my mother," she said. "So I don't mind your checking up on me." She paused, looked down at her coffee, and said, "You stayed away a long time."

Rino felt his anxiety lessening and all his strangeness dissipating. Suddenly it was perfectly natural talking to her, being in his usual chair in her living room. The taboos he seemed to fear, the restraints that seemed to bind him from deep within his psyche, were loosened. This girl, with a few words and actions, had put him at ease.

"I felt funny coming back," he said. "I thought you might..." He shrugged as he talked. "I was just afraid you might think I was a weirdo or a dirty old man."

She laughed softly, and for Rino it was the best thing she could have done. "I know you're not a weirdo, but are you a dirty old man?"

He looked at her, took a sip of coffee, and then chuckled. "Sometimes, maybe."

"Well, now that we've established that, tell me what you've been doing for almost three weeks. I haven't seen you since the beginning of August."

"I'm not sure myself. A good friend of my brother's and mine died a few weeks ago, and it took me a while to get over it. We've been busy at work painting, which I don't like."

"Was his death sudden?"

"Well, we knew he was sick. His heart was bad a long time. But then when it happened, knowing that didn't help."

"Do you feel better now?" she said.

"Yeah. It's just tough getting old and seeing people die around you. Crazy, huh?"

"You don't have to be old to have people die around you," she said. He nodded in agreement, knowing what she meant. "But you once came here to comfort me. Maybe I could have done the same when your friend died. Sometimes it helps to talk."

"I guess I didn't feel I had the right to bother you. I mean... well, I thought you'd rather talk to people your own age and not a guy as old as me."

She got up to pour him another cup of coffee. "Will you do me a favor?" she asked. "Next time you come here, will you not mention your age, or being old? By the way, how old are you?"

It hurt him to answer. "62," he said.

"Okay. You're 62, and I'm 33. And from now on, no more talk of age. Now. Tell me more about your family. All we ever seem to do is talk about me."

They talked a long time. Rino told her about Lou and Connie and his kids. It felt strange talking so much about himself. "When did your wife die?" she asked.

Rino was surprised at her question, but still he answered it. "About three years now. She had cancer, and we never knew it until almost the end. She found out she had it, and nine weeks later she was dead."

They continued talking about their jobs and how they spent their days.

He glanced at the large, curved, walnut mantel clock as it chimed 12:00. "It's late. I'd better go."

He stood up and started for the closet where she had hung his jacket. She walked ahead of him to get it and held it for him to put on, but he grabbed for the coat. She resisted and held it for him. "It was nice talking to you," she said.

"My pleasure. You make good coffee."

"Don't stay away so long," she said. Then, in the next breath: "When do you think... No. I don't want to know. You just come whenever you want; I should be here. It doesn't have to be just when you work late, you know."

Rino was thrilled to hear her ask him to come back. "Goodnight," he said as he turned for the door and went outside into the hall. But she held the door open as he stepped outside.

"Rino," she said softly. "Do you think you could come Sunday night?"

"Uh, sure I can," he said in amazement.

"Well, it's just that Sundays are lonely around here," she said. She smiled and said, almost to herself, "You can come before then, too. You don't have to wait till Sunday."

The next day, Rino was euphoric and preoccupied. He mopped the third floor of Crandall, emptied trash from all the offices, and cleaned the storeroom. Everything went easily and smoothly. After work, he and Lou played nine holes of golf and then went to the Tucker Cafe for a fish dinner.

The Tucker was a Wednesday night ritual. The best card players, golfers, bowlers, and liars met to eat and drink and tell stories.

"By the way, where'd you go last night?" Lou said. "Frankie came over to pick up my fish cooler, and he said you weren't home yet."

"I had some coffee with a friend," said Rino uneasily.

"Who? Some guy from work?"

"No, not from work."

"Someone I don't know?"

"Yeah."

Lou asked the waitress for another beer and then waved to one of their friends who had just come into the café. But he was still thinking about their conversation. "Well, who is this guy? Do I have to drag it out of you?"

"Why do you have to know everything, Lou? Can't I have any secrets?"

"Well, kiss my ass," Lou drawled. "I was just curious. You don't want to tell me? Fine. I should be eating instead of talking, anyway."

"It was a woman," Rino said after a few seconds.

"A what?"

"You heard me. What's so goddamned strange about that?"

"Andrea Manasseri?" Lou asked hopefully, suddenly very animated.

"No. You don't know her. Hell, I just got to know her."

"But what's she like? Nice? Good looking?"

"Both."

"Well, I'll be damned."

"Enough questions, okay? I'll tell you about her someday."

The next day was paint day. Rino had a headache most of the morning, but later in the afternoon the sun started shining, and he began to feel better. Maybe he'd go see Lee tonight.

After work, he went home for supper. Jean was in the kitchen alone when he got home; Frank had taken Larry to work at the market.

"Hi, stranger," she said, looking up from her work at the sink.

"Hi, yourself. Smells good."

"You here for supper tonight?" she said, smiling as she teased him.

"If the food's up to it," he said with a wry smile on his face.

"How have you been, Dad?"

"Hanging on. How about you?"

"There's nothing wrong, is there? Nothing Frank or I have done?"

"Nothing wrong, kid. You still can't make spaghetti without it tasting like sauerkraut, okay?"

She laughed and put her arm through his. "You know we don't want anything to happen to you."

"I'm all right," he said, giving her hand a kiss. She, Connie, and Libby were the only ones he was the least bit demonstrative with. Usually his affections were reserved, more so than Lou's, though neither of them was a charmer. "Libby home yet?" he said.

"No, she had cheerleading tryouts tonight."

"I'm going up to take a shower. When's supper?"

"5:30."

"I'll be down," he said.

When Frank came home he said to Jean, "Where's Pop?"

"Upstairs taking a shower," Jean said.

"Now? Is he going out?"

"I don't know. I'll bet he does."

"You know, he came in past midnight a few times recently."

"It's strange that he's going out during the week so much," Jean said.

"He almost never went out like that except to see Uncle Lou. I wonder what's going on."

"I tried to pump him a little," Jean said, "but he just said he was fine."

"Maybe he feels bad about Libby and Larry being so busy. They're hardly ever around anymore, and they're his favorite grandkids."

"Or maybe Paolo's death bothers him more than we think."

Rino left the house about eight o'clock. It seemed strange going to Lee's house directly from his. Before, he had always come from the college, preoccupied and weary, almost stumbling upon her place. But this was different: for the first time, he felt good about going, unashamed and unselfconscious. He knew the attraction was only one way; she certainly couldn't be attracted physically to him. But he enjoyed being with her. And she was lonely yet not threatened by him. They both got something out of it.

He rang the doorbell and waited. *She was probably in the shower again*, he thought. But she opened the door quickly and unlatched the night lock. "Hi," she said, standing aside to let him in. She was just as she had been the other time: in a short robe and barefoot, with part of her auburn-brown hair loose and soft across her forehead and the other part held behind her ear with a barrette. *She was so stunningly beautiful*, he remarked to himself. She almost took his breath away. He desired her so much, he ached.

But he couldn't think about it. He had to be a friend who would treat her with kindness and respect, to take their relationship for what it was worth on the surface—a young widow and an old widower who could do a little bit to help each other get over their loneliness.

She smiled but seemed more subdued. Her eyes seemed a little red, he noticed, as she tried not to make much eye contact with him up close.

"I'm glad you came," she said, "but I'm surprised."

"You said I could come before Sunday," he said.

"I did, but I didn't think you would." She hesitated as if to say something else and then deciding not to.

"Are you sure I didn't come at a bad time?"

"No. I said I'm glad you came," she said with just the slightest edge in her voice. "You know, you ask me that every time."

"I do, don't I?" he said, and then he hesitated for a moment. "I guess I can't believe you enjoy seeing me."

"Really. I'm glad you're here," she said.

"Okay," he said, unconvinced.

"I'll put the coffee on." She got up without looking at him and walked to the kitchen.

He sat in the chair and waited as he always did, occasionally catching glimpses of her walking past the doorway. But suddenly he got out of the chair and headed for the kitchen, stopping at the doorway. It was his deepest incursion into her apartment since he had known her.

"Bad day today, huh?" he said.

She nodded assent while not looking at him. "Lonely, confused day," she said.

"Do you go out every day, see some friends, family?" he said.

"I usually go out every day—shopping, the library..."

"How about friends?"

"I don't have many friends anymore. Some call occasionally, but after Ted died, they all felt so awkward around me that... we just drifted."

"So you just don't see people anymore?" he said.

"That's right," she said, still not looking at him but staring at her hands laid flat upon the counter, almost for support.

"How often do you go to Akron or Canton?" Now he was feeling fatherly. She was answering painful questions, and he was probing, trying to find out where he could help.

"Every few weeks," she said.

"When are you going again?" Now he had moved into the kitchen and was standing close enough that he could have reached out and touched her. But he stood at her back, subconsciously not wanting to press too much or hover over her.

"I don't know," she said.

The coffeepot had shut off. She moved to the refrigerator and took out a small, covered glass butter dish. Then, from a wooden box on the counter, she took out some sweet rolls, which she put into a microwave oven for a few seconds. Neither of them spoke. Occasionally she would glance at him and catch him staring. She'd smile but avoid his gaze, seemingly intent on fixing the snack.

"Lee?" he said, feeling a strange exhilaration at having spoken her name directly to her for the first time. It was as though, in that small way, their relationship had reached a new stage of familiarity. He could speak her name aloud. It wasn't a dream this time. And for all the turmoil of his conscience, she was there, had heard him, and would answer.

She turned to face him. In a strange way, that one word had reified the relationship between them, making it real where it had once been uncertain and illusive.

"You asked me to come here Sunday night. Would you..." He faltered. Jesus, what an unreal thing all of this was.

She didn't respond. Instead, her eyes showed that she was waiting for him to complete his thought. Would she what?

"Would you be ashamed if..."

"Ashamed? Ashamed of you?" she said.

"No, not me. Well, yes... of me... of... What if you have dinner with me Sunday night? Out... at some restaurant. I mean, it'll be a nice place and all... If you don't take me wrong, no disrespect, I mean..."

"Ashamed, Rino? God, how could you say such a thing?" Her eyes clouded, and she put her arms around him and rested her forehead against his shoulder.

Rino, for a moment, didn't touch her. But then he carefully put his hands behind her and locked them behind the small of her back. She stayed in his arms a few minutes. He didn't move, because, in a way, he was afraid. Never had he felt anything like this; she was warm and soft and pliant, almost conforming to every contour of his body. It was as if she fit there, exactly where she was, a perfect fit.

Then she looked up at him, still not letting go, her cheeks stained slightly by tears, her hair askew, yet she was smiling. "No, Rino Bellanca, I won't be ashamed."

Suddenly she moved away, holding him at arm's length, her hands on either side of his elbows. He didn't move; he just looked at her skeptically. "What will I wear?" she blurted out, seeming to be talking to herself. As she held him for that moment, Rino seemed like a small, uncertain boy whom she could have completely shattered in an instant. Yet she wouldn't; she couldn't. How could she be so attracted to him? She seemed to be as captivated by his warmth and goodness as he was by her hair and her eyes and her body. But that was silly. He was an uncle to her, an old man she was kind to. She stared into his eyes for a long moment.

He smiled and took a deep breath, wondering if he had forgotten to breathe those last few minutes. She took him by the hand, led him back to the couch, and gently sat him down. She sat next to him, cross-legged and sideways, facing him. She had become a little girl again, and he seemed dazed by his good fortune.

"Well," she said, her eyes sparkling, "where are we going?"

"Any place," he said. "The restaurant you like best... or maybe you want some out-of-the-way place?"

"No! I don't want any 'out-of-the-way' place," she scolded. "I want an in-the-way place, but someplace quiet and relaxed."

"Pick it."

"Chinese?"

"Fine."

She squealed softly. "But what shall I wear?" she said again.

"Anything you want."

"What do you want me to wear?"

"What you have on now is good enough for me," he said.

She pushed his shoulder in a halfhearted punch, smiling at his teasing.

But she wondered about what he had said. Was he really conscious of her physically? He looked at her often and did seem to notice what she wore and how she looked.

"Now, I have to go to a family dinner at my sister's Sunday afternoon," Rino said. "Dagos eat early, so I'll just have a salad and slide out while they're watching the Browns game. How would it be if I picked you up around seven o'clock?"

"Seven's fine. Is it a special occasion at your sister's? We don't have to go out this Sunday. Next week, maybe?"

"No. Sunday night—and don't worry. I'll be glad to leave there."

"What will you tell them when you leave?" she asked, wondering how he was perceiving their dinner engagement, how he would tell them what he was doing.

"I'll tell them goodbye."

"Are you sure you want to do it? I mean, we could just stay here, and I could make us supper."

"No. It's my invitation, remember? You said yes, so now you have to go along with it. Now. When are you going to see your mother?"

"I don't know. Soon, maybe," she said.

"Go this week," he said casually.

"Why this week?" she said.

"Because you should see your mother. Because it'll be good for you to get out."

"One date, and you start ordering me out of town," she teased.

"It's not good for you to be alone here all the time."

"You come to see me," she said.

"Yeah, but an old man dropping by once in a while isn't enough company for you."

"Oh, Rino, you are not an 'old' man. I thought you said you weren't going to talk about your age anymore."

"I'm talking about you seeing you mother, Leila," he said emphatically.

She changed the subject. "Rino, I have to ask you a question."

"What?"

"What did I wear Tuesday night?"

"You mean the night I was here? Don't you remember?"

"Of course I remember. Do you?"

"Why do you ask me something like that?"

"Tell me!" she said, tugging at his arm playfully.

"You wore jeans and some sort of blue sweater. I'm not good at this. Tight jeans, sweatshirt, and slippers."

He was teasing her, she knew. But what he saw was what she'd hoped he saw. He didn't see a niece; he saw her. He saw a woman in tight jeans; he even saw her slippers. God, what a crazy thing this was! Ted had been dead 10 months, and she was wondering whether someone else found her attractive. But then, Ted had been gone from her long before he died. She hadn't dressed for a special man in years.

But she was dressing for a 62-year-old man. God, she was attracted to a guy older than her mother. Crazy. When he was there, he might as well be 30; his reactions to her were no different. Instead, there was less pretense. It's as though he has never done this before, she thought. Maybe when he was getting married they didn't have time to fall... Maybe they didn't have time to play. Maybe life and earning a living were too serious for fun.

Maybe that was some of the wistfulness, the sadness that she sensed in him. Her own was obvious, but his was deeper beneath the surface. Maybe he had never done this, had never had fun meeting a strange girl and getting to know her. Maybe it was just fatherly kindness and reserve. *Maybe he feels sorry for me because of Ted*, she thought. But do uncles notice what you wear? He had said "tight" jeans and slippers. He noticed everything, top to bottom. "Good memory. I was testing you," she said. Then she tried to change the subject again with small talk. "How long has Frank been a junior high principal?"

"About five, six years. I don't think he'll ever do anything else; he loves it."

"And Jerry?"

"He's our money man, the go-getter–an orthodontist who drives a Cadillac and lives in a big house in Akron. I think he likes the Cadillac more than his wife." He chuckled.

She smiled. "And Nancy?"

"Her husband's a painting contractor in Warren. Big outfit, has about 20 painters. They do stores and offices mostly."

"Then Frank's the only one who lives in Youngstown?"

"Yeah. After Mary died, he and his family came to live with me. I like having the kids around. Libby's a sophomore at Thorn Hill High, and Larry's a freshman at Spring Common."

"What's Libby like? Is she cute?"

"Yeah, but then I'm prejudiced. We sure have a lot of young guys calling and coming around lately."

They talked until past midnight. It had all become easy and spontaneous. They seemed to be able to tell each other secret thoughts, things they would tell no one else in honesty. That was the kind of bond that was forming between them.

Throughout it all, he sat facing front and turned slightly toward her. She still sat cross-legged on the couch, facing him. She was so close to him that he was often distracted. With his eyes, he traced the outline of her legs as they tapered into her feet folded under each knee. What perfect muscles, he thought. Sometimes, as she talked, she would wiggle her toes, and the light would glisten off the lacquer on her toenails. Her fingers glistened at the tips with the same pearl gloss that she had on her toes. She wore no ring.

Even the smell of her was different. It was of powder and cologne. But it was she whom he breathed in along with all the balms and talc. She had a wondrous scent that made the powder and cologne and soap and shampoo come together to be her. Jean was familiar; he knew the scent of her, and it was light and pleasing. But Lee was different; her scent was opiate for his brain.

Once, while he talked, she took his left hand in hers, studied it as she listened, and held it between her two hands for several minutes. Their warmth excited him, and his mind began to wander back to her and away from what he was saying. When she went to get more coffee, he moved his hand away so she could get up.

Rino seemed to be learning about the world anew each time he was with her. He was sensing something for the first time: muscles, softness, and the wonderful smell of her. *I'm going crazy*, he thought. *Hell, if she doesn't throw me out, I might never leave.* Here was a girl talking to him the way he saw kids talk to one another at the college. They talk, but they can't bear the closeness, so they touch. But he couldn't touch this girl. He was afraid. He was probably reading himself wrong, let alone her. *Face it, Bellanca,* he told himself, *it's all about an old man driving away loneliness.*

But she was the one who had called it a date. *God, could she be just toying with me?* he thought. *How in the hell am I going to handle it when she gets tired of me? And some young guy on the move comes by and takes her away?*

She returned with the coffee and sat on the floor in front of him on her haunches, her legs beneath her. She poured the coffee and handed it to him.

"Would you miss me if I visited my mother next week?" she said softly and childlike, looking up at him.

"Yes," he said.

Later, after almost another hour, he stood up to leave. "I should have left here hours ago, you know," he said. "What would people think?"

"I have a hard time caring about what people think anymore," she said, looking down at her cup.

He reflected on that for a moment. "Yeah. You're right. Well, I'll see you Sunday night, okay?" He began putting on his jacket.

She was going to ask him to come sooner than Sunday, but she didn't.

"I play cards Friday. Been doing it since the Flood. And Saturday, I have to go to a wedding. My goddaughter is marrying a rich kid." He looked into her eyes. "If I didn't do those things, would it have been all right to come here one of those nights?"

"I'd want you to come both nights," she said.

His heart beat faster. "Well, I'd better go. Damn, it's late, huh?" He chuckled to himself. "See you Sunday."

"Okay," she said. But before he got to the door, she put a hand on his arm, stopping him. He turned to her, and she reached up to give him a kiss on the cheek. But it was not like the kisses he got from Jean or Libby or Nancy. This one was soft and lasted longer than a second. "Goodnight," she said. "Hope you won't be tired tomorrow."

It was 1:30 when he got into his house. On Rino's way upstairs, Frank was coming out of the bathroom. "Pop? You just coming home?"

"Yeah, Frankie. Goodnight."

"Everything okay, Pop?"

"I'm fine. See you in the morning."

Frank went back to bed troubled. What in God's name was his old man doing? He wasn't drunk; it takes more than anisette and coffee to do that. *I hope he was with Uncle Lou*, he thought. What a life! Not only did he have to worry about Larry growing up and driving too fast and Libby now that she was built damn near like a grown woman, but now his father was acting funny. He tossed and turned for a while and finally fell back to sleep.

In a way, work was relaxation for Rino. But it was better when he could leave it every so often. Working every day was a bother. He had done too much of that for 40 years. He'd be glad when Joe came back. One more week of this.

At lunchtime, he went to the cafeteria for a coffee and a hamburger. As he sat at the custodians' table, he watched two girls come in, set their books on a table, and walk to the cafeteria line. One had low-slung, full hips, and the other, a bit taller, had narrow, almost boyish ones.

They wore jeans as tight as Lee did, he thought. Why not, if you have the body for it? Yet Lee looked different somehow. The girls moved slowly through the line and walked back to their table. The girl with the low-slung hips was fuller-breasted. *Nice*, he said to himself as she walked by.

He started thinking about Lee again. What were her breasts like? Jesus. Amazing, he guessed. She always had a robe or loose sweater on. He looked at her legs so much it never occurred to him that the rest of her wasn't just as beautiful.

Some boys joined the girls, and they all seemed to be talking at once. *How much do they know about what life is really like?* he thought. One thing was for sure: they don't know anything about feeling old.

But when you look and feel like they do, how can you think about getting old? How can you think about what kids do to your wife, or what work does to you? How can you think of being tired, tired for days, no matter how much you sleep? Hell, these kids get eight hours, and they can run for two days. How can they think about what the pain of someone dying does to you?

Where did they get such self-assurance? They go through life so easily, so confident, never scared. Nobody's shy anymore. You let it all hang out; that's what they say. There are no strangers. You talk, you relate, you move in and out of affairs, in and out of marriages. How did kids get so sophisticated? How could they be so sure of themselves when he seemed unsure of every step he took?

After work Rino went home for supper. He took a shower and got ready for poker. They played in the back room of the Tre-Sette. Agee made sure they didn't have to leave the table if they wanted drinks. He even made sure they had something good to eat after midnight. It had all started in the days when Friday was a Catholic day of abstinence—no meat. So they would wait until after midnight to have a meal. Agee saw no reason to change the custom just because the church had changed canon law. Some things were even more sacred than religion.

Tonight's game started about 8:30. All the regulars were there. Rino and Lou always tried to sit at different tables—there were usually two games going—to save them both the trouble of having to explain how one of them could have a miraculous lucky streak. Mortal poker players seem too willing to believe that not only God but fraternal collusion was the cause of a streak. Rino and Lou had managed to play without suspicion for almost 40 years, so their idea must have worked.

But Rino was not doing well. He won some big pots early, on sheer luck and good cards. But his skill games weren't so good. His concentration would wax and wane, and his big lead began to dwindle. He was about even and losing ground.

"Hey, Rino, you all here tonight?" said Pete.

"Yeah, I'm here. Win some, lose some, right?"

They chuckled. It was about 11:15, and Rino needed a break. "Hey, guys, I'm gonna get up and stretch my legs a while. Deal me out a few hands. I'll be back." He left the room, feeling his brother's gaze riveting his back as he left. He turned around and winked at Lou.

It was 11:30. *It's late*, he thought. *I wonder if she's still up.* "Hey, Agee, how about if I use your other phone?" Rino motioned to the small private room that served as Agee's office. Agee nodded, knowing that Rino could be trusted in there.

Rino looked in the phone book for the number. It was under "Leila Reese." He dialed hopefully. After two rings, she answered. "Lee," he said, "this is Rino. Were you asleep?"

"No. Just watching a movie."

"How was your day today?"

"Much better. I'm looking forward to Sunday night," she said.

"Me too. Did you go out?"

"Uh-huh. I spent all afternoon looking for something to wear."

"Did you find it?"

"I think I found something you'll like."

"Me? Hell. I know I'll like it. Lee, you're gonna look so much nicer than me. Are you sure about all this?"

"Oh, Rino, your age again? Do you think I'd spend five hours shopping for an outfit I think you'd like if I didn't want to be seen with you?"

"Uh, sorry. I can't get used to the idea, that's all."

"I've noticed," she said. "Are you winning or losing?"

"About even now. Fading a little, though. You know I won't be able to call you tomorrow night. It'll be a madhouse, and I might be a little lit up. Okay?"

"Okay. Have a good time. Can't wait till Sunday."

Rino lost money the rest of the night. He went home at two o'clock feeling tired. No need to worry about meeting Frankie in the dark; Fridays were always late nights.

The wedding was loud and boisterous and plenty of fun. Rino and Lou had just the right amount of whiskey in them to dance with people they had known for years: nieces, sisters, friends, and cousins.

After one dance, Lou came over to Rino and said, "Andrea Manasseri's here, Rino... over there."

Rino looked over to where his brother was pointing and saw Andrea in a navy-blue dress, formfitting on top and pleated from the waist. She looked serene and dignified. Her dark eyes shone under the long lashes; her hair was black and streaked with gray in long silver strands that were swept up on the crown of her head. She was talking to Marty, one of the Tre-Sette gang.

"Go ask her to dance," Lou said to Rino.

"Leave me alone, Lou. The woman doesn't want my company."

"Goddamn, I don't want you to fornicate with her. Just ask her to dance."

"You're a pain in the ass, Lou."

"Go on, Rino."

Why do I get myself into these things? Rino said to himself as he made his way across the dance floor. Still, she looked beautiful and slender as he approached. She was almost as tall as Rino—tall, at least, for an Italian woman.

But she always made him nervous. Something about her intimidated him. Even when she was young, few guys ever tried to put the make on her. And then when her husband died, she didn't become eligible again—ever.

"Hello, Andrea," Rino said. "Hi, Marty."

"Hello, Rino," she said quietly and with a slight smile.

Maybe it was her intelligence, Rino thought. *Maybe she scares people because she seems smart.* Marty talked to them for a few minutes. Then he said, "Well, I'd better find my wife. I have to dance one more time with her before the night's over."

When he was gone, Andrea motioned to a seat. "Would you like to sit down?" she said.

"Uh, okay," said Rino. "Nice wedding, huh?"

"Yes, very nice... and loud."

"Whose family do you know—the bride's or the groom's?"

"Well, I know them both," she said. "But I've known Rick's mother for years. We're good friends. And you?"

"Lucy's my godchild. When Carl died, Mary and I kind of looked after the family. Helen and Mary were good friends."

There was a momentary silence between them. To break it Rino said, "I really came over to ask you to dance. Would you?"

She hesitated a moment and then said, "All right." He had not seen her dancing with anyone else.

Rino stood up and let her lead him out to the dance floor, through the tables of sitting people. When she reached the floor, she turned to face Rino. In a quick movement, she raised her hands to accept his in the dancing position. The music was one of the rare slow pieces the band played. She would only make eye contact with him briefly and then always look out to other people. She was a good dancer and felt light and graceful in his arms.

"Are your children here?" Rino asked.

"Only Bobby," she said. "Greg's out of town, and Nick's at a reception for the new bishop; he's on the diocesan council."

"Oh," Rino said. He didn't like her kids. They were courteous enough, but they were aloof and condescending—more like their father as Rino remembered him.

"How's your family?" she said.

"Oh, they're fine. All but Jerry's here."

"Your daughter is very attractive," she said.

"Thank you. You also look very nice tonight."

She seemed to recoil slightly from his compliment. "Thank you," she said, half swallowing the words.

As she looked out at people around the room, Rino studied her from his close vantage. Her neck was slender, and her most compelling feature, her eyes, were dark and oval shaped. Her complexion was fair, with some small wrinkles near her mouth and eyes. Her mouth was thin, and her nose was straight and slightly prominent. She was, in the soft light, a very attractive woman.

But as they danced, he thought of Lee. Though they were both reserved in public, Lee was so different from this one—smaller, lighter haired, slender, yet fuller bodied. Lee was the kind that made his juices flow: tan legs, firm muscles, dark-brown eyes that glistened in their depths. Lee was someone to watch and desire. Lee, he wanted to touch. With Lee, he began to sweat. With Lee, his mind was at rest. It was his emotions and glands, his breath and his hands that vibrated.

With Andrea, it was his mind. He felt like autumn days and cool wine. Andrea, even when she was young, couldn't sit next to a man cross-legged and do to him from the distance what Lee did so easily. Andrea would never open a door barefoot in a short robe. Never—not even for her husband. Andrea was sobriety; Andrea was restraint. Andrea couldn't play.

Andrea never looked messy and always cared about it. Lee never did. Lee wasn't self-conscious, and Andrea was. Lee enjoyed being attractive and seductive because she didn't have to try. Lee was visceral, and Andrea was cerebral. Lee's heart was part of her intellect; Andrea's was not. Lee would probably look less elegant in later years than Andrea did now. But always she would be more desirable. Andrea would have men look at her and want her but never desire her, never sweat.

"You're staring at me, Rino," she said uncomfortably.

"I'm sorry," he said.

They danced in silence. When the song was over, they walked back to their table. "Andrea, I'm sorry. I was thinking about something as we danced. I didn't mean to embarrass you."

"It's all right, Rino," she said in a tired, patronizing voice.

Another encounter had gone awry. Rino was irritated—first with himself, then at her, and then at Lou for getting him into these messy encounters, and he was tired of it. "You know, Andrea, every time I come near you, you make me feel like I'm trying to degrade you somehow," Rino said.

She seemed startled. "I'm sorry you feel that way. I didn't say anything to give you that impression, did I?"

"No, you didn't say anything," he said in frustration. They were both very uncomfortable now. "But you didn't have to dance with me when I asked. I can take no for an answer."

She looked away, flustered, but retained her outward calm. Then she turned back to him, trying to find words to answer what he had said, but the words weren't there.

"Thanks for the dance, Andrea. Goodnight." Rino walked away angry, especially with himself. He was fed up with people who wanted to be angels apart from the human race.

"How was the dance, cowboy?" Lou said.

"Like dancing with a nun, okay? Face it, Lou, there's got to be something wrong with her. Nobody could stay married to that asshole, Jack Manasseri, all those years and still be right. Look at her, like a goddamned china doll. Look but don't touch. Who needs it?"

That night, Rino was tired but couldn't fall asleep. He felt his heart beating as he lay in the still darkness of his room. Only the faint glow of streetlights shone through the windows to cast a few vague shadows. What a strange thing life is. Never did he think his autumn years would be like this. He thought once that when the toil of his youth was done and his children were grown and taking care of themselves, then he and Mary would have a long, comfortable old age. But the turmoil of life never stopped. Just when he thought things had settled down, Mary died. And they were cheated of what they had worked for and saved for and hoped for.

And even after she died, he couldn't grow old quietly and follow her in peace. He had to face himself and the life around him, and it was hard and full of lonely gaps. Trying to find peace—or just a way to live, let alone be happy—seemed as hard as any work he'd ever done.

He knew he was crankier and gruffer than he had once been. But now, when time was short, with more years long behind him than ahead, he saw fools and weaklings, liars and cheaters, hucksters and phonies, and couldn't pass them off, couldn't be mellow and resigned, couldn't forget that they represented the injustice in life. That his wife, Mary; his son, Jimmy; Lou's wife, Terry; and Big Paolo were all dead, and other vipers still lived.

But then there was Lee. It was as though God enjoyed playing give-and-take with him. He thought about her constantly, and she was fading Mary's memory for him. Lee was part of his turmoil now, because she made him dream impossible dreams; she made him dream of a warmth and pleasure he had never known, something she alone could give him yet something he could never hold.

He awoke that Sunday to the noise of the wind and to clouds that promised chilly rain. At breakfast, he gently scolded Libby for neglecting him. He and Jean and Frank talked of mundane things, and the closeness felt good. It occurred to him that he should talk this way to these, the closest of his children, more often.

He read the paper slowly but not with much enthusiasm. Then he watched the Browns pregame show on television and remained disgusted with their tolerance of sloppy play in prior games, bumbling in the last minutes of games that cost them losses. Frank, who had been out for two hours, was back now, talking to Jean in the sitting room. Rino decided to let them in on his plans.

"Kids, I'm gonna leave Aunt Connie's after supper. Maybe before then if Joe and Carol decide to get there late."

"Dad, aren't you going to tell us something?" Jean said. "How could we ever contact you if we need you?"

"Contact Uncle Lou, okay? Uh, look, if I don't eat much at Connie's, don't make a big deal about it. I'm going out to dinner later."

"Pop, I don't understand this," said Frank.

"Look, I behave myself. For once in my life, I'm leaving my sister's house before supper. That's all."

Frank had, by now, developed a perpetual shrug of exasperation. It was no use. His father had a newly discovered knack for evading all his questions.

Connie put her arm around Rino when he arrived at her house. "Haven't we met somewhere before?" she said.

Rino chuckled and kissed her on the cheek. "Putting on a little weight, huh, Con?"

She laughed and shoved him into the kitchen. "Where are Frank and Jean?" she said.

"They're coming. They were right behind me."

"In their own car? Are they going somewhere after?"

"No—I am."

"Where're you going when you haven't seen me for a month?"

"Two weeks—and I have to meet somebody," he said. Connie had her usual sharp and skeptical look about her, but Rino knew she was feeling hurt. "Look, I'm sorry, kid. But I have to leave around five tonight. I won't stay away so long again. I promise."

"You know, Mary must have been a living saint, Rino, to put up with you," she said.

Suddenly, it jarred him to hear Mary's name. He didn't want to think about her. "Who's here, Chub?" he said.

"They're all in the living room. Get the hell out of my kitchen." She was smiling despite her annoyance at him.

The first person Rino saw was his nephew, Danny, Connie's youngest son. "Hi, Uncle Rino."

"Oh, the law is here, huh?" said Rino. "How's business, kid?"

"Winning some, losing some," said Danny. "How are you, Uncle Rino?"

Rino liked his nephew. As a boy, he always seemed to be over at Rino's house to play, especially when his father was sick. There were whole summers that he lived as one of Rino's own children and slept with Frankie in the upper bedroom. Connie had two children, Joe and Danny. Danny was not as well off as his older brother but not as phony or estranged from people, either—a perfect kind of cop, a rare and humane man.

"I'm okay, Dan. How's Kaye?"

"She's fine. She'll be here later. She had to take Danny to a gymnastics meet."

In all, 16 people were there at Connie's. And the time spent was full of loud talk, laughing, cards, beer, coffee, and cookies. There weren't any quiet moments, and there weren't any tense ones, either. Everybody there made an easy, good time, a nice party just for a dinner. As usual, Joe and Carol were late, so the meal didn't get started until nearly five o'clock.

Rino was getting nervous. How could he leave gracefully? No easy way. He had to say goodbye—simple and fast. When Connie went into the kitchen, Rino got up from the table and followed her. "I'm leaving, boss," he said.

"But you didn't even eat anything, Rino," she said plaintively.

"I'll be fine, kid. See you this week."

He went back into the dining room and said goodbye to the group, just a simple, "Goodnight, everyone," and left. All but a few of them were astounded. But Lou came to Rino's defense after he left. "He had to go see an old friend. It's an appointment he's had for a long time."

Rino went back home to shower and dress. *He didn't look so bad in a dark suit,* he thought as he looked at his reflection in the hallway mirror. *If I could keep my mouth shut, I might pass as a banker.*

It was almost seven when he got to Lee's door. As soon as he rang the bell, the door opened. His heart seemed to falter a beat when he saw her. She was in a stark, black-and-white, wool dress, black nylon stockings, and black heels. She had been ready for a while.

He stood without talking for several seconds. Finally, she said, "Hi. Are you coming in?" It was more of a greeting than a question. Rino walked in without speaking, still not taking his eyes off her. "You're the most beautiful woman I've ever seen," he said.

She huffed softly in disbelief. "Thank you," she said. "I like being flattered—even if it isn't so."

They left her apartment as soon as he helped her on with her coat. The restaurant wasn't crowded; Sunday nights were usually not busy. They were seated in a booth that was lit by a flickering candle enshrouded by a red glass shade that played strange and illusive images across her face. The dining area was dimly lit, and the place was quiet except for some soft, nondescript background music. "I never saw you dressed up before," he said. "No, I take that back. The first time I saw you, you were."

"I had been out that day," she said, looking down at her hands.

"You remember, huh?" he said.

"I remember that I was nasty to you," she said, still not looking at him.

"You were never nasty to me. You were just upset by all those things, those memories."

"What did you think when you first met me? Did you like me?"

"I liked you the minute I saw you," he said. "How about me?"

"I hated you for the first minute," she said. "But you didn't act or sound like one of their messengers, so I listened to what you said, and I liked it... and you."

There were some long pauses between their conversations. "You know, Lee, it's really nice visiting you all these nights. Sometimes I wonder what I ever did when I didn't know you."

She reached for his hand. "I don't ever want you to stop coming to see me," she said.

"Someday I'm going to have to, you know," he said.

"Why?" Now she held both his hands.

"Because I..." he said. "Someday some young guy is not going to want an old fogey like me hanging around two, three nights a week."

"I know all about young guys, and I've had grief from too many of them. No good for me? God, Rino, I wait to see you all day, hoping you'll come. Why do you think I'm always home at night lately? I may not have many friends, but I still can find something to do with my evenings." He sighed and squeezed her hands, interlocking his thick fingers with some of hers. "Please don't stop coming, Rino," she said.

"I have a hard time, Lee," he said. "Hell, half the time I don't know why I come over to your place."

She arched her eyebrows, and her look sharpened. Yet, somehow, she seemed to know that he didn't mean he didn't care for her. "Don't you come to look after me?" she said.

"Yes..."

"Don't you come because we talk, because we're a man and a woman who are getting to know each other?"

He nodded but added, “An old man and a woman.”

“And because you’re lonely, aren’t you?” she continued. He just looked back without answering. “But don’t you see? I’m lonely, too. And I like to talk. I want this to happen. I get as much out of this as you.”

“Not quite,” he said without elaborating.

The waitress asked if they wanted drinks. Lee shook her head. Rino ordered whiskey and soda. They also ordered their food. Lee chose moo goo gai pan for both of them. Since he had never eaten Chinese food before, she was delighted to order something mysterious for him. When the waitress brought Rino a drink, he took a sip.

“Could I have some of your drink?” she said.

“Sure. Did you change your mind? I can order you one.”

“No. I just want some of yours,” she said.

He handed it to her, and she took a sip.

The waitress returned quickly with the soup: a clear, thin chicken broth that had a few spare vegetables floating in it. “Jesus. No wonder the Chinese are so skinny,” Rino said as he valiantly used the strange soup spoon they had given him.

“What does ‘not quite’ mean?” Lee asked.

“What?” said Rino, wishing he had never said it.

“You said ‘not quite.’ What did you mean?” she asked.

“I don’t remember,” Rino said, still slowly eating the soup and avoiding her question.

“Rino?”

“It was nothing. I shouldn’t have said it,” he said.

“But you did, didn’t you, Rino? Look at me.”

“I get more out of these visits than you. You’re being nice to an old guy…” She began to arch her eyebrows and contradict him, but he stopped her. “No. Let me finish. My life is on the wane, and yours has only begun. This deal is better for me.”

"And that's it? Our ages again? Just that, Rino?"

He shifted nervously in his seat. "And I like to listen, to look at you."

She didn't respond for several seconds, turning her gaze out into the restaurant. Finally, she said, "I know you do."

"What?"

"Did it ever occur to you that I want you to look at me? That I enjoy it?"

The waitress brought the moo goo gai pan, a large mound piled on a full plate of white rice. "I won't eat all of this," Rino murmured, shaking his head.

"Well, I'm going to pig out on mine," she said, feeling good about the forthright and honest tone of their conversation. She had a warm feeling inside her that she couldn't describe. He had really noticed her—not her mind or her heart or her personality. He had noticed her body, her legs, her eyes, her skin. He finally admitted it. She was filled with the satisfaction of knowing that she had brought it out in a man who had tried to fight it, out of respect and decency, but who couldn't withstand her presence.

"Rino?"

"What?"

"I wanted you to look at me. I wanted you to want me."

The conversation was becoming a little too forthright for Rino. He wasn't used to any girl, especially this one, talking openly about his desire for her.

"But I can't," he said unconvincingly. "It's not right."

"Shouldn't you and I decide what's right, instead of everybody else out there? I care about you, Rino, and it is right."

"Lee, I'm a fossil from another time—"

"Rino, do you care for me? Do you want me?" She talked in barely a whisper, so that he couldn't hear her if she were not close. "Rino, please answer me."

He didn't answer. This time he searched the outer room for a way to avoid her gaze.

"Rino?"

"Of course I care for you," he said. "I wouldn't come around if I didn't."

"That was only part of it," she said. "My question was, do you want me?"

She waited, knowing he had to answer. She had gotten to know him all these weeks and had learned that he desired her.

He looked at her helplessly. "Yes." He sighed.

She smiled and said nothing more about it. The meal was long, and they ate slowly and talked more. Occasionally her hand would touch his, and he would marvel at the softness of her. Somehow, those few tense moments, when they had gotten their feelings into the open, were forgotten.

As Rino talked, she watched him. *How will I ever get to know all about this man?* she thought. Strong yet gentle, careful, respectful, unpretentious, and realistic. It was a combination that neither Ted nor any man she had ever known possessed. And beyond it, he had a need within him for someone. He could give love and accept it by instinct. Somehow that longing was there, flowing in his veins, without his realizing it.

But why did she want him? He was hairy where Ted was smooth, square and solid where Ted was slight and tall, old where Ted was young. What was it? Maybe because when they were together she wanted to do things for him—serve him coffee, make him happy, make him play. She liked knowing that he could be lonely for her. She could sense his hunger when he looked at her but thought he couldn't touch. She wanted him to need her.

And she knew, as she watched him—the tan, weathered skin on the handsome, square face; the thick white hair with faint streaks of brown; the large brown eyes; the thin lips; the deep, heavy beard shaved as close as it could be yet still rough in spots; the square shoulders; the straight, powerful neck—she knew that his heart could have her in it.

The world was complicated enough, and cruel enough, so that she never worried about social taboos anymore. The outside world had never known her pain when Ted was alive and never understood her anguish after he died. No. The days when she worried about what other people thought were over. Now she was looking inward, and no one from a distance mattered. Wherever her happiness was, she would cherish and protect it. All of it was Rino.

When the waitress returned with the change on a small tray, they left the Green Peacock. Rino looked self-consciously from side to side as he walked through the restaurant. Things were different leaving than they had been when they came in. And Rino didn't know what would come of them.

Outside, Lee tried to lighten his spirits. "I really like your car. Are you rich, Rino? This is beautiful." She was trying to tease him. For ages, she had not been this happy.

"I always drive a nice car. It's my favorite vice."

"I've only seen your station wagon before," she said.

"That's because I usually came from work. The wagon's my work car."

In the car she said, "So you don't like Chinese food, huh?"

"It was okay... really. I just had some other things on my mind."

She didn't sit close to him in the car, and they didn't talk much. When they arrived at her apartment, she said without looking at him, "Put your car in the garage. Mrs. Berning won't be here all week. She's in Toronto."

He hesitated for a moment and looked over to her. She was still facing deliberately ahead. Then he slowly drove into the garage.

As he followed her upstairs, he gazed at her glossy, black-stockinged calves as she took each step. He was frightened. When they entered the apartment, she took his coat and hung it up as he walked over to a chair. But she stopped him before he sat down. "Will you sit on the couch? I want to sit with you."

He sat on the couch. She sat next to him, kicked off her shoes, and turned toward him. "What's wrong?" she said. He shrugged and shook his head. "Don't you want to be here?" she asked.

Looking into her eyes, he almost lost his train of thought. "You know I want to be here. I can hardly stay away."

"Then why are you like this? I don't care about our ages. I told you that."

He snorted. "Would you believe I've never done this before?"

She giggled softly. "What haven't you ever done?" She shifted her hips so that her left foot was gently stroking the side of his knee.

He chuckled. It felt good to relieve some of the tension that was so palpable between them. "I've never been with a girl like you."

"Like me, Bellanca?" she said in a mock-threatening voice she had come to use on him in playful times. She was smiling, but he realized how awkward it must have sounded.

"I mean who looks like you... who does this to me." She waited for him to continue. "I'm just afraid..."

"Afraid of making love with me?"

He made no move in response; he just kept looking at that magical face. She leaned over to him slowly. He was still. She kissed him on the mouth with her lips slightly parted. He kissed her back gently, and as he did, he felt his heart pounding in his chest, and he felt the stirring of his penis as the blood flowed to his groin.

Never had he felt anything like her lips. They were warm and wet and soft. He couldn't imagine anything in the world as wonderful. His whole life had passed, and he had never had this, never had the fire, the churning feeling in his whole being, the feeling that she wanted him as much as he wanted her.

This one was so different from Mary; every drop of blood coursing within him knew that this one was just right. His arms went around her as their lips met and lingered. When they finally parted, she said breathlessly, "That wasn't so bad, was it?"

He took a deep breath. "Not bad."

"Really?" she said brightly, with a big smile. "Want to do it again?"

"Maybe if I do it a few dozen times, I'll get the hang of it."

She thrust herself into his arms, this time pressing her upper body against his. The kiss was just as warm and moist as the first one, and this time he held her tightly to him. Then he pressed his lips to the hollow of her neck. She luxuriated in his embrace and smiled to herself as he held her. *Never before for me, either, Rino,* she thought. *It's wonderful.*

When they parted, she was disheveled. A hair barrette she had been wearing was loose, and her earring had snagged on his tie. They laughed like children as they tried to come apart. Her dress had ridden up her thighs, and the top part of it was twisted on her upper body. She looked so flushed, so luminous and beautiful, that Rino could hardly keep his hands off her.

Suddenly, she stood up and walked over to an étagère. From within two small doors, she took out a single cordial glass and poured a few drams of B&B into it. Then she returned and held the glass out to him as she stood before him. He took a sip of it and then handed it back. She put it to her lips and took a sip.

"Why don't you take off your tie and jacket?" she said.

"It would be more comfortable," he said as he stood up to take them off. As he did, she loosened his tie and slipped it off. She took the jacket and tie to the closet and returned to him. He was seated again.

"Be right back, okay?" she said. As she did, she reached for the liqueur and then took another sip. She handed it to him to drink again; he did. All the while, their eyes were meeting. The drinking ritual had some symbolic meaning for her, he mused.

She quickly walked down the hall and back into her bedroom. After a few minutes, she was in the bathroom, and then she returned to the living room. She had changed her clothes; the black stockings were gone; her legs and feet were bare. She had on the same blue robe that she had worn so many other times when he was there. She faced him as he sat looking up at her. Then she knelt in front of him on the floor, her eyes peering into his.

"You've seen this robe before, haven't you?" she said. He nodded. She continued. "But tonight, it's different. There's no nightshirt under it. All I have on is this." He was sitting forward on the couch, his face a few inches from hers. She talked very softly and slowly. "Rino, I never want to be without you again. I want to care for you, to love you, to be life to you." Rino wasn't sure if he was dreaming. He couldn't believe she was with him, let alone saying those words. "Take my robe off, Rino," she said.

He hesitated. "Lee, what if I..." She touched his lips with the tips of her fingers to silence him. He bent forward a little more. Hesitantly, he reached for the tie, undid it, slowly undraped the robe from her shoulders, and let it fall onto the floor behind her.

Her body was small and spotless. Her breasts were perfectly proportioned to her body, not large, but full and firm. Her skin, which still showed faint, pale lines from her bathing suit, was a warm, creamy color, her nipples small and light brown, a perfect complement to the brown of her hair. Yet as slender as she was, as athletic and firm, there was a lush fullness about her thighs and her belly. Her belly indented slightly at the navel and tapered down smoothly into the dark patch of brown hair at her groin. He gazed at her with a sense of wonder. There's nothing in the world he could have done to deserve this.

As he watched, transfixed, she stood up and held out her hand. He stood up and put his hand over hers. Without a word, she led him out of the room and down the hall into her bedroom, a large, cozy room that made her double bed seem small. The curtains, the rug, the furniture—all reminded him of her. It was orderly and clean, yet warm and comfortable.

She stopped beside the bed and turned toward him. Without a word, she began to unbutton his shirt. He undid his trousers. She stood aside a half step to let him take off his shoes and socks and all the rest of his clothes. When they were both naked and standing side by side, she put her knee on the bed, pivoted on it, and lay herself back, still looking at him. She stretched her arms outward, welcoming him to her.

It was as though he had never known softness. He had never held anything in his arms that seemed so small yet seemed to engulf him. Every part of him felt her, her legs, her breasts, her hands, her belly. He kissed her again, more confident now. His penis had thickened and hardened and was throbbing to the beat of his heart. *She's not afraid or ashamed of this*, he thought. *She cares for me. She doesn't want to be anywhere else now but right here with me.*

He kissed her face, her neck, her breasts, and felt the erect tautness of the nipples at his mouth. He lingered there, burying his face in her breasts. All the while her hands caressed his shoulders, his hair, and his neck. She let him do whatever he wished and constantly encouraged him and responded to him.

But as her own heartbeat increased, she felt him, too, growing more excited. His breathing grew heavier, his kisses and touches more insistent. Finally, as they kissed, when she felt the warm slickness of her labia and the wetness all around her crotch, she easily guided his rigid penis into her. She wasn't just guiding; she was joining. Every sensation she felt told the difference between him and Ted. She ran her hand across his back and felt the warm, damp, heavy muscles. She felt her fingers digging into his forearms as his thrusts grew in intensity.

They hadn't said anything to each other. But now she placed her hands on either side of his face to fix it before her. "I love you, Rino," she said. "I love you." In a few moments, she was ready for orgasm, and at the same time he responded, feeling the pumping in his loins, feeling the surge of his sperm entering her, the last movement in a long symphony of lovemaking.

Afterward, they lay on their backs side by side for several minutes without speaking. He lay at an angle so that part of his back shoulder rested against one of her breasts. "I love you," she repeated without looking at him.

"I love you, too, Lee," he said softly.

She sprang upward to a sitting position, looking down at him. "You do?" He nodded. "Then why didn't you tell me?" she asked excitedly.

He chuckled. "I was busy." She threw a soft punch at his shoulder. "No. That wasn't it... just the same old thing. I think I'm cheating you. Life is tough enough without falling in love with someone old enough to be your father."

"You know that this is different for both of us, don't you?" she said.

"I know, but nobody is going to care much about that."

"We'll show them," she said, laying her head back down.

"I have to go soon," he said.

"Oh no. Please. Can't you stay here tonight?"

"This is Sunday, Leila. Tomorrow's a workday."

"Then stay here until morning. You can shower here, then go home to change. And I can make breakfast for you."

He thought about it. "It'll be early," he said.

"That's okay. I'm leaving too, remember?"

He grimaced. "No, I forgot. I'd have never told you to go see your mother if I'd have known we'd..."

"Be in love?" she said.

He snorted and smiled. "Yeah, that, too."

He grabbed her wrists before her hands went to his throat. She giggled as he pulled her on top of him. "You know, I was afraid I couldn't do this," he said thoughtfully. "It's been a long time."

"I knew you could if you just thought of me," she said. "You were only thinking of me, weren't you, Rino? No one else?"

"No one else, kid. You take up every minute of my life."

"Me too," she said.

"When are you coming back?" he said.

"Thursday afternoon. Should I stay home?"

"No, go ahead. This will give you time to think about how you're going to fit an old man into your life."

"I've already fit you in," she said, "old man." Then she kissed him, her tongue lashing in and out of his mouth.

Finally, they grew quiet. She lay her head in the crook of his arm and put one of her legs over his and cuddled up snugly.

At work, Rino began his last week as Joe's stand-in. He hated it when Joe took his vacation; he hated working full-time. Sammy called him into his office. "Hey, goombah, have a seat."

"What's up, Sam?" said Rino.

"Nothing. I just want to talk to you."

"You and me... just talk, right?"

"Okay, okay. I hear Chandler didn't like the way you moved his office."

"Who told you that?"

"That's the word I get from the dean's secretary."

"Did he complain to the dean?"

"No. He just made a few comments about all of us, and he made sure he mentioned your name." Rino snorted. "You know, Rino, he's a real prick. He came here about seven or eight years ago, and I've watched him operate. He's one of those guys with nice hair and teeth who'd cut his own father's balls off and sell them if he thought it would do him some good."

"But there's no complaint, right?"

"Nothing. But watch out. I don't think he likes you, and he never forgets. Understand?"

"Yeah, Sam. Thanks."

Rino was glad to leave work that night. He missed Joe because they worked well together. Joe was always his partner on big jobs, and all the time they worked, they talked about life and kids and wives and working.

When Rino got home, Libby was the first to meet him, as he was putting away his coat. "Grandpa? How are you?" she said.

"Fine, babe. How about you?"

"I haven't seen you much lately. You staying for supper?"

"Yeah."

"Me too."

She was so much like Jean that he sometimes forgot who he was talking to. She had big green eyes, blond hair, and Jean's slender body. Her mouth twisted some words the way her mother's did, just a little play of her lower lip, not a lisp, but almost—still something different in the way she talked. She had some of Frank's personality too: orderly, gentle, unpretentious, and hopeful.

"Gramps, can I ask you a question?"

"Yeah, Lib, what's on your mind?"

"Did you stay out last night?"

"Yeah," he said, untying his shoes, trying to look busy.

"Mom and Dad were nervous wrecks when they got up and realized you weren't home," she said.

"It was my fault, honey. I should have called earlier, but I didn't get around to it. It was dumb of me to make them worry."

"Did you stay with Uncle Lou?"

"No, somebody else," Rino said, reddening slightly.

"Grandpa, is there someone you like, more special than other people?"

"You mean like that dark-haired kid who has lunch with you every day at school? The one Mom and Dad don't know about?"

She giggled, and her eyes widened. "How do you know about that, Grandpa?" Then she whispered to herself, "Gross!"

Rino chuckled and then made a sinister face. "I have spies everywhere, Lib. Remember that. Now how about getting me a beer?"

After supper, Rino went to Lou's house to pick him up. They were just going to stop at the Tre-Sette and play pinochle. When he got there, Annie's car was in the driveway. He knocked, and Lou answered the door. "Annie's here, huh?" said Rino.

"No," said Lou disgustedly. "My car's over at Hugo's shop. I'm using hers until it's done."

"I told you that U-joint was squeaking," said Rino as he sat down in the living room, staring out the large window. He was quiet for a few moments, and then he said, "Let's stay here a while tonight, Lou."

"I thought you wanted to go down to Agee's," said Lou.

"Not yet. I have something to tell you."

"You better not cancel out on that Canada trip, you bastard."

"No, it's not that. Sit down here."

"It's about the woman you're seeing, huh?" said Lou gleefully. "What time did you get home last night?"

"6:30 this morning," said Rino with a grim smile on his face.

"Jesus, Rino, I'm gonna get one of those phone calls from your son now." But Lou knew there was still something yet to be told that disquieted Rino. "So? What's the problem? This woman's married, right?"

"No, nothing like that."

"Well, what, then?"

"Well, she's young."

"How young?" said Lou, now showing a slight concern.

"33."

Lou didn't answer for a few seconds. He just stared at his brother. "This is no joke, right?"

"No joke," said Rino.

"How much do you care for this girl, kid?"

Rino sighed. "A lot, Luigi."

Rino looked so forlorn that Lou felt sorry for his brother, the one person whose feelings mattered most to him in the world.

"Look, kid," said Lou. "You don't have to put yourself through this. Don't tell me anything you don't want to."

Rino shook his head in disagreement. Finally, he mustered up the words, "I love her, Lou. And, honest to God, she loves me. Isn't that something?"

Lou searched his brother's face for any hint of foolish infatuation or insincere belief. "Rino, you never hurt anybody in your life, so you don't owe anybody any explanations. If this makes you happy, then go with it. Hell, life's short enough as it is, and there isn't all that much happiness in it."

"You mean that, Lou?" said Rino.

"Of course I mean it. But I don't want you to get hurt, either."

"Yeah, I know, I know. That's the first thing everybody's gonna think."

"Who is she? Do I know her?" said Lou.

"You don't know her."

Lou knew Rino well enough to read him when he talked like this. "Well? What else now? Does she have two heads or what?"

"You remember that Reese kid who killed himself at the college last year? It's his wife."

Lou sat back in his chair, seemingly exhausted by their conversation. "Man, you sure make things hard to sell, don't you?"

Rino snorted. "Well, at least that's all of it." But then his face grew grim. "I'm gonna have a hell of a time with the kids and Connie. Everybody's gonna think I've lost my mind."

"Rino, you gave those kids everything you could. And Connie—she forgets all those 20s you slipped her when Guy was sick and couldn't work. You don't owe them a thing. And as for everybody else, they might make jokes, but they'll envy you. Bet on it."

"Thanks, kid," said Rino.

"So, tell me. What kind of body does she have?" Lou said, twinkling.

The next day, Rino went to work feeling better. Telling Lou about Lee seemed to take a load off his mind. Somehow, if his brother thought it was okay, then he didn't worry as much about anyone else.

When he saw Sammy at the far end of the cafeteria, he blew him a kiss. Sammy glared at him and gave him a discreet middle finger. Rino sat, having coffee with another worker, a small, slender black man named Barly Davis.

"You sure like to pimp Sammy, don't you, man?" said Barly.

"Yeah," said Rino, "it starts the day off right. How's the union business, Bar?"

"It's been quiet since we settled, Rino. Unless Sammy fires you, I ain't gonna get much action."

"So, where's all the union dues going, Bar? Are the new Cadillacs out yet?"

Barly chuckled. "No, man, it goes into the Rino war chest, in case you piss off another head snake around here."

Just then, Sammy approached without their noticing. "Hey, Rino, you gonna stay here all morning? You act more like a prof every day." He was trying to contain his mock seriousness.

"Sam, that K'bossy must have been bad at breakfast, huh?"

Barly chuckled, shaking his head. He loved to hear Rino torment Sam.

"Come over to my office when you're done, goombah. I got lots of work today—especially for you."

"Damn," Rino said as Sammy walked away, "that means we're painting again."

"Probably those windows in the biology lab," Barly said. "That or the hallways of Crandall."

"Man, I hate to paint," Rino grumbled.

But Sammy had them all painting, a full crew of five men: Rino on the third floor, the most exacting job, and two each on the other floors, all painting the north-south hallways in Crandall Hall. Rino didn't mind being alone. He could work at his own pace, break when he wanted, and didn't have to clean up after anyone but himself.

Carefully, he put the scaffold together to firm it and make it sturdy. Then he began the worst part of the job, the one that would take most of the day, the ceiling. The paint splashed from the roller onto his goggles and dripped down onto his hand through the brush when he painted the soffit. He would curse softly to himself, because his hands were so sticky with paint that he couldn't change the radio station when it lapsed into the wrong kind of music. The morning went by slowly, and lunch seemed too brief a respite of kerosene-smelling coffee and a hamburger. His hands and arms reeked of paint remover.

The afternoon passed slowly, too. He hoped Lee would call tonight. Everything would have to be right. Her mother had to be in bed, and he had to be alone in the family room.

"Hey, janitor!" a familiar, high, reedy voice called to his back.

He had to think for a second to sort the voice and the image. It was Chandler. The hair on Rino's neck bristled as he turned around slowly. "What?"

"I have to get a window in my new office unstuck."

"I'll fix it when I come down," Rino said from the scaffold. "I'll be done in a little while."

"Oh, but you'll have to do it now, I'm afraid," Chandler said.

"I told you; I can't get to it now. I'll be down soon."

"You're here to help, pal. My office is stuffy, and I want that window unstuck," said Chandler.

"Look, I'm all dirty. And I have only one more panel to do. If you can't wait for me, then call Sammy. He'll send someone up to fix it."

As Chandler walked away, Rino cursed him. *Why is he doing this?* he thought. *He's going out of his way to get me, a goddamned janitor. Jesus. He goes after anyone who crosses him. Sammy was right.*

When Rino was done painting, he went to Chandler's office. Chandler had a young female student in there, and he was talking to her. Rino knocked on the half-open door. "Did Sam send anyone up? If not, I can fix it now."

"Just wait outside till we're done," Chandler said coldly.

Rino went outside and stood in the hallway. As Chandler talked in an animated, jovial voice, the girl would laugh often. *It isn't a personal or intimate conversation,* Rino thought. The bastard could easily have let him fix the window instead of making him cool his heels in the hallway.

After 20 minutes of small talk, the girl left. Rino didn't even bother asking; he just walked in and said, "Which window is it?"

Chandler pointed to the large casement window to his left. Rino took a putty knife and a rubber mallet and gave two blows to the edge. Immediately the window opened. Rino closed his eyes in quiet fury. That bastard could have easily opened the window without him.

"Did you try to open this?" Rino asked.

"Of course. Why do you think I called you, pal?"

"It opened pretty damned easily for me."

"Well, that must mean you have a talent. The super window opener."

Rino just walked out of Chandler's office and went down to the locker room. Sammy was there. "How'd it go?"

"The ceiling, the soffit, and about a third of the west wall are done."

"You're all right, Rino. Can you do the rest in a couple of days?"

"Yeah. No problem."

Supper was uncomfortable for everyone. Rino had something to tell Frank and Jean, and they knew it. But he didn't want to discuss it with his grandchildren at the table. They all made small talk until Libby and Larry left the room and went upstairs.

"Uh, I have something to tell both of you," Rino said.

Jean sat down next to Rino, and his son stared anxiously at his father across the table. Rino talked softly and deliberately. "I've been seeing another woman," he said solemnly. Frank shifted uneasily in his seat but said nothing. Jean placed her hand on Rino's. "The only one who knew about it was Uncle Lou, and he's only known about a week. None of you know her. And for a while I want to keep it that way. Okay?"

"Pop, couldn't you have just told us a long time ago and spared us all this?" Frank said.

Jean looked at her husband and rolled her eyes. "I'm happy for you,

Dad. My dumb husband will be, too, if he can just stop and think rationally for two minutes."

"So why all the secrecy, Pop?" Frank asked. "What did you think we would say?"

"Oh, for heaven's sake, Frank. Let it alone," Jean said.

"It's a long story, Frankie, and I'm new to all this, okay? And the fewer people that know right now, the better."

Later that night Rino was sitting, watching television. It was past 11:30. Frank and Jean were the last of the family still awake. "Don't you work tomorrow, Dad?" said Jean.

"Yeah, but I'm gonna stay up a little. I'll see you in the morning."

"Goodnight," they both said.

So far, so good. It was quiet, and everyone was in bed. After a few minutes, the phone rang. Rino picked it up immediately. "Hello," he said quietly.

"Hi," said the soft voice on the other end.

"How've you been?" Rino said.

"Okay. Mother was glad I came here."

"Good, good. Everything okay?"

"No."

"Why not?"

"Because I'm lonely."

Of all the thrilling things she'd say to him, he still felt a rush when she said she wanted to be near him. "I'm glad you remembered to call," he said.

"Remembered? Rino Bellanca, I've been waiting two whole days to talk to you."

"What have you been doing?"

"Oh, we went shopping and then out to supper last night. My sister came over from Akron today. She showed me how to make a new coffee cake."

"Good. I was getting tired of the old ones, anyway."

"You talk like that now when I can't reach over and choke you," she said, laughing softly.

"This is driving me crazy. I miss you," Rino said.

"You're supposed to miss me, aren't you?"

"How have you been sleeping?" he said. Some new chemistry seemed to be evolving between them. He was so confident in her love that he found it easy to play. And of the few people that he could play with, Lee had suddenly moved to the top of the list. Maybe play is best with someone you can touch. And he loved touching her.

"Not too well," she said. "How about you?"

"Like a rock," he said. "I just take a glass of anisette and..."

She didn't respond for a few seconds. "You're teasing me, aren't you?" she said. Rino laughed. "What's gotten into you, Rino? Why are you showing me this evil side of you now?"

"I told Lou about you," he said.

"You did? What did he say?"

"Well, the first thing. He wanted to know your bust size, and–"

"Oh my God!"

"I took a guess," he said. "I told him I wasn't sure, either 42 or 44–"

"That did it, Bellanca, it's been nice talking to you," she said. He could hear the music in her voice. She pouted wonderfully, even over the phone. Finally, she giggled. "Do you wish I were that big, Rino?"

"No, kid. I wouldn't change you one bit. You don't mess with God when he does something perfect."

"You mean that?"

"Yeah, I mean it. I told Lou a little more than I did Frank and Jean. Lou agrees with you; he says I worry too much."

"Rino, do you love me?"

"I'm crazy about you, Lee."

"I'll be home Thursday afternoon, okay?"

"I'll be there after supper. Around seven."

"I've told my mother about you," she said. "We talked about three hours tonight."

"How'd it go? She didn't like it because of my age, right?"

"After we talked a while, she came around. Really."

"Good. That makes me feel better."

"I love you, Rino."

"I love you, too, Lee."

Thursday. The day seemed to last forever. About 3:30, Rino took a break and called Lee. The phone rang twice before she answered. "Hi," he said. "How long have you been home?"

"I've been here a couple hours. I left after lunch."

"How are you, kid?" Rino said.

"I'm better than I've been in four days," she said. She seemed subdued.

"You sound tired," he said. "Why don't you get some rest this afternoon? I don't want you to conk out on me later."

She snorted. "It was nice being with Mother," she said, "but I had too many things on my mind—like what to do when the man you love discusses your bust size with his brother and God knows who else. You'll pay for that, Bellanca."

He chuckled. "I'm glad you're home, kid. It was a long four days. I'll see you later, okay? Then you can get even with me."

"I've never been happier in my whole life. Do you know that, Rino?"

"I usually have that effect on women," he said.

"Goodbye, Bellanca," she said.

After work Rino shaved and showered and then put on navy-blue corduroy slacks and a white shirt under a light blue, crew-neck sweater. The whole outfit was made up of gifts he had never worn. In recent years, soft virgin wool had seemed too luxurious for him, and he just never had the inclination to look that dressed. It was as though he had decided that his life was almost over, and there just wasn't enough music in his heart for him to dress only to look nice.

But then he met Lee. And there he was in cords and sweater, looking for all the world like his grandson going to a basketball game. When he went downstairs, only Jean was in the kitchen. "Where is everybody?" he said to her.

Jean turned toward him, and suddenly something dawned on her. This was not a passing fancy for her father-in-law. She knew it the minute she saw him. The straight, gray hair, the thick, muscular body—for the first time, she realized that he was handsome.

She stared at him, marveling at how youthful he looked. And her surprise gave way to admiration. *He's in love with someone*, she thought. *He looks radiant—not tired as he did before, but bright and alive.*

After a long pause, with Rino's eyes questioning her thoughts, she said, "I hope this woman knows how lucky she is."

"Thanks, kid. Jean?"

"Yeah, Dad?"

"If I tell you something, would you keep it from Frank just for a while?"

"For you I would. You know that." She was bewildered by his request.

"This girl's younger than you," he said weakly.

Her gaze sharpened. He nodded warily. "And you like her a lot?" she said softly. He nodded again. After a few seconds, she stepped back to look at him. "I'll keep your secret, Dad. But I'll die if I don't see her soon. Can I meet her?"

"You'll be the first, kid," he said.

When Lee opened her door, he stood outside for a moment to look at her. She had on black slacks and a white blouse and gold, backless, heeled slippers on her bare feet. Rino's mind was racing, and he felt warm. *No panty hose*, he said to himself. It seemed that he was no longer worried about her age or whether she loved him. Now he could enjoy freely the passion he felt when he looked at her.

Lee had the same kind of reaction to seeing him that Jean had had. He looked younger.

"Can I come in?" he said.

She reached for his arm to tug him inside. After she took his coat, she held it in her arms and stepped back a few paces, eyeing him. "You're beautiful," she said.

"What's gotten into everybody?" he said. "God, I must have looked awful before."

"You try to hide your natural beauty," she said teasingly.

He snorted. "Well, are we going to shake hands or rub noses or what?" he said.

With that, she was in his arms, letting him hold her tight as those magic soft lips were on his again. He had lifted her off the floor in his embrace. When they separated, she gently urged him to sit on the couch. Then her eyes narrowed as she sat on his lap, facing him. "Where have you been, Rino Bellanca?" she said accusingly.

"What do you mean?"

"I smell perfume on you, on this sweater," she said, brushing a sleeve away backhanded.

"Well, Lee, four days is a long time, and I met this old friend..."

She put her hand over his mouth, and her eyes sparkled, and her lips glistened in a wide smile. "If I had known how terrible you are, I'd never have opened that door all those nights ago. See how a trusting girl gets taken advantage of?"

He was trying to kiss her, but she was pushing him away, giggling. "My daughter-in-law," he said, trying to subdue her. She was still laughing and striving against him. Finally, he trapped her. He was close enough to her to feel her heavy breathing from the struggle. Their eyes met. In an instant, his hand went to the buttons of her blouse.

She pushed her chest forward slightly, her eyes never leaving his. When the blouse was unbuttoned, he lowered his lips to kiss one breast above her bra. She cradled his head gently, holding him to her breast. He couldn't help himself. His excitement was blinding him to everything but her. "Let's go to the bedroom, okay?" he said.

She smiled and softly said, "Come on," as she held out her hand to him. In the bedroom, as she turned to remove her opened blouse, he stopped her. "Let me undress you," he said.

She moved toward him until he could touch her. Slowly he took off her blouse, and then he unfastened her slacks. She sat down on the bed with the slacks down below her hips. She kicked off her slippers as he slid the slacks and her small bikini panties down her legs. As his head came near her, she leaned forward to kiss him. His breaths grew deeper and more frequent. *No panty hose*, he reminded himself. Then he reached behind her to take off her bra. She kissed his neck as he leaned around her. His eyes engulfed her as he knelt before her nakedness.

She reached for the covers on the bed and pulled them down so she could roll inside. As she moved, he stood up and began to undo his own clothes. She watched him as he undressed hurriedly. In a few seconds, he was in bed holding her.

This time he was not acting tentatively. This time his hunger for her made him bold and quick. She, too, matched his longing. Her labia were wet and ready for him. Her breasts were firm and tense. They kissed, and then he moved to kiss her nipples.

She parted her legs as he moved his hand to her crotch to feel the warm wetness. He caressed her gently, and she became more and more excited. Quickly he moved on top of her and slid his penis slowly into her. Her hips moved forward to meet his thrusts. She was panting and gasping, throwing her head from side to side, calling his name and saying she loved him. Then, at the right time, their orgasms came together and brought them the crashing fulfillment they both sought.

When he finally moved from her and lay on his back beside her, he felt better than he had in all his life. The first time, he had been filled with awe of what had happened between them, but this time, their act of love was something that he and Lee had made together easily, willingly, and unafraid.

"I'm sorry I didn't talk to you much when I got here," he said.

"I wanted you, too," she said contentedly. "I was hoping you'd be like that when you saw me."

"You know, I just can't get used to thinking that you enjoy this as much as I do."

"I do, but it's only because I love you. Isn't that the way it's supposed to be?"

"That's the way I like it," he said.

"It wasn't like that with Ted, Rino," she said cautiously. He raised his head off the pillow to look at her. She turned to meet his gaze. "Does that surprise you?" she said.

"Maybe… I guess not. It wasn't like this with Mary, either," he said.

"So these feelings are new for you?"

He nodded.

She snuggled near him. "Me too," she said.

They slept for a short while. He awoke when he heard the water running in the bathroom. After several minutes, she came into the bedroom and went over to the dresser. She brushed her hair a few times and took a large powder puff and dabbed it between her legs one time quickly. "I could watch you forever," he said, surprising her.

"I thought you were still sleeping," she said. She smiled and got back into bed. "I had to clean up. I was leaking all over."

It was quiet in the apartment. The small light in the bedroom seemed to create a dim twilight. "Would you like a cup of coffee?" she said.

"That sounds good."

She was quiet for a minute. "You've taken away the stains I had on me," she said.

"Stains? You mean sins? You?"

She closed her eyes and cocked her head, something like a shrug that he had gotten used to. It was her way of saying yes and not talking. Then tears ran out of the corners of her eyes. He was suddenly puzzled and anxious. "Lee?"

"Hold me, Rino. Please hold me."

He held her tightly, kissing her face and her eyes. "Are you okay?" he whispered.

"Yes, I'm okay. You make me okay."

"In that case, I'll give you a dime for a cup of coffee."

He had broken into her melancholy, and she laughed. "Each time I go to bed with you, you get more... more arrogant," she said.

"You know what I thought about tonight when I first saw you?" he said.

"What?" she said, propping her head up on her hand.

"I said to myself, 'Since she's got bare feet, I don't have to bother taking her panty hose off.' How about that?"

"So?"

"So all I could think about was getting your clothes off with the least trouble."

She smiled. "Are all Italians like you?"

"Some longer, some shorter," he said, chuckling softly. "Mostly longer."

She punched his shoulder gently. "That wasn't what I was asking,

Bellanca. What am I going to do with you, Rino? You're terrible."

"You make me terrible."

"Me? What do I do?"

"I don't know. But when I'm around you, I want to do weird things. Like now. I want to rub coffee all over your body and lick it off."

Suddenly she jumped out of bed and ran down the hall. He lay there for a few moments. Out in the kitchen he could hear the water running and the cupboard doors opening and closing. She was making coffee. He slipped his pants on and tucked in his white shirt. When he got to the kitchen, she was calmly slicing coffee cake. *God, how different she is*, he thought. *I love it.*

"What are you looking at?" she said, knowing well that he couldn't take his eyes off her nakedness.

"Will you always make coffee for me like this?"

"Certainly. They can cure pneumonia in just a few weeks now."

She was learning how to play with him. He walked up to her and enfolded her in his arms. She stood on his bare feet and clung to his chest. "I have to put something on," she said.

Back in the bedroom, he sat in a chair and watched her comb her hair. She hadn't yet put any clothes on. She was facing the dresser mirror, able to see him through it. "I want to buy you something," she said to his image.

"Buy what?" he said.

"Well, right now I'm going to put on a robe. But you have to wear your slacks and shirt, so I'm going to buy you a robe."

"I already have a robe I never wear. I'll bring it."

"No, I want to get you one. It will mean you live here, too."

They went back into the kitchen after she put on her robe. When she sat down at the table, she said, "Tell me why you came back all those nights. What were you thinking?"

"You may not like the truth," he said. "It's not so..."

"I'll be the judge of that," she said. "Tell me."

He began carefully. "The first time I saw you, I felt sorry for you, especially when you cried, but there wasn't anything I could do about it. The second time, I don't know—maybe I was just concerned about you, but maybe I was lonely. But that was the night you had this robe on. I kept looking at you and thinking about you, and I kept coming back. But no matter how much I wanted you, I thought you couldn't feel the same. You were a dream that could never happen to me—yet I kept coming back."

She touched his hand as he spoke. "That was just the way I wanted it to happen," she said. "Rino, what color was your hair before?" she was smiling as she spoke. He laughed softly. "Was it like... light as it seems now, or dark as it is down there?" She pointed a silver-tipped index finger through the table toward his pubic hair.

Rino chuckled heartily. "You're a nut, Leila."

Just then she seemed like a little girl, animated and curious, almost reminding him of Libby. "Well, what's wrong with wanting to know more about you?" she said.

"Tell me, Lee. Which is the real shade of your hair? This?" He pointed to her hair. "Or this shade down here?" He reached across the table, trying to untie her robe with his finger. She pushed him away, squealing.

"Okay," he said. She was up now, getting more coffee. "It was dark brown, kind of like it is down there. The gray hair just makes it seem lighter."

She sat down again but kicked off her slippers and sat cross-legged on the chair.

"How did you feel about me coming those times?" he asked seriously.

"The first time you were so nice, but I never thought you would ever come back. People usually don't do that, care that much. But when you came, I liked talking to you." She paused for a moment to grab his hand again, as though she needed to touch him for what she was going to say. "But that second night you came, I knew you were looking at me." Rino groaned. "No, Rino, it wasn't vulgar or obvious. Really. And I wanted you to keep coming back to look at me."

"But didn't you ever think about my age? What a fool I must have seemed, coming around all those times."

"No!" she said firmly, annoyed with him. "At first I thought you were just a nice guy being kind to me. Then I was feeling so good after our visits, thinking about you, falling in love with you. I said to myself, 'I'm in love with a 62-year-old man, someone better than anyone I've ever known. And now things are going to be different.'"

He didn't say anything. Instead, she could see the sense of amazed satisfaction he had. "Let's go into the living room," she said.

They both settled on the couch in their now-familiar postures, him facing forward and her facing him cross-legged and sideways. Suddenly she got up, went over to the étagère, and poured a small glass of B&B. Then she returned to the couch, sitting close enough for his hand to play gently on her legs, stroking the smooth softness of the skin on her thighs.

Once he moved his hand lower beneath the robe until he touched her pubic hair and brushed it with the back of his fingers. She continued talking to him, never flinching, yet imperceptibly thrusting herself forward so that he could touch her as much as he wished. She seemed to know how much he needed to touch her.

"I have to go away for a few days soon," said Rino. "Lou and I and a couple of other guys always go up to Canada around Thanksgiving week."

"Oh, Rino, a whole week," she drawled.

"In past years, I looked forward to it for months, could hardly wait. But now... Lou asked me not to cancel out—warned me, in fact. I don't want to go, but..."

"Oh, I'm selfish. I just don't want you to be away from me at all," she said.

"We've been doing it for years—fish a little, hunt, play cards, drink beer. Mostly I fish and walk around a lot. It's way up in Ontario."

She made a pouting face and then offered him the glass she had been holding. He knowingly took a sip and handed it back to her. Then she put the glass to her lips and drank.

"Why do we always do this?" he asked. "I don't mind; I'm just curious."

"Do what?"

"You never drink by yourself—never pour two glasses."

She lowered her head, avoiding his gaze. "Because I never want to drink anything that you aren't drinking. I never want us to drink separately."

Whatever special reason she had for her answer, it didn't seem she wanted to talk about it. So, he let it pass.

"What color robe do you want?" she said. "And slippers... what size?"

"Do you really want to buy me a robe?"

"Yes, and slippers. Look at us. I'm in a robe, and you're in a shirt and slacks. That's terrible."

"You pick the color. Anything you want."

"What size are you?"

"44... and I have a 10-and-a-half E foot. Don't spend a lot of money on it, okay?"

"I've always had plenty of money," she said.

"And don't get pink, okay?" he said.

She laughed. Then she was quiet, just examining his face. Neither of them spoke for several seconds. He rested his hand on her thigh under her robe. She took a sip of the B&B again. Only this time she moved her head toward him to kiss him. But she hadn't swallowed the B&B, and as she kissed him, she opened her mouth and let her tongue slide onto his while the liqueur flowed from her mouth into his.

All of it inflamed and intoxicated him: the feel of her, the liqueur, her full, soft lips parted on his. He pulled her close into his embrace, cradling her head and shoulders in his hands. When they broke away, he held her so close that their faces almost touched, just far enough so they could see each other. "Come on," he said, taking her hand. She followed him willingly.

But this time he told her to kneel on the bed, facing him. He undressed quickly, his slacks and shirt coming off easily. Then he undid the tie and took her robe off. Slowly he eased her back, her body suspended by her arms around his neck. He lowered his lips to each breast, then her belly, and finally to her vagina, where he stopped. She gasped when he began to lick the whole region—the cavity, the labia, and the clitoris.

The more he kissed, the more excited they both became. Then, suddenly, she closed her thighs on both sides of his head as she reached a climax. She shuddered in one spasm after another, and still he kept on.

After several languorous and wonderful minutes, he moved away from her vagina and up to kiss her lips. She held him tightly, lashing her tongue to his. If the world had ended then, they wouldn't have known it. It was a perfect act of love.

When it was over, after many minutes of savoring the thrills they had both experienced, they moved apart, and she lay face down beside him while he ran the back of his hand over her buttocks gently.

"Ted never did that to me, not once," she said, looking at him sideways but not lifting her head from the pillow. "Why did you?"

He snorted. "You have no idea, huh?"

"Do you like it? Does it feel good? It feels wonderful to me... Rino?"

"Of course I like it. Some men do; some don't."

"Did you do it to Mary?"

"Yes. But not very much. I don't think she liked it," he said. Then he wrinkled his brow and looked at her. "How did we get on this? You like it. I sure do. Count your blessings."

She giggled and rocked her hips back and forth on the bed—the way little girls do, he thought. "Rino?"

"What?"

"I think this is the happiest day of my life," she said.

He patted her buttocks. "Weren't you happy with Ted?"

"Not very. I thought we were at first, but after a while it was... dreary." She thought about what she had said. "He didn't need me, Rino. He didn't want me the way you do."

"Maybe because he was young," he said.

"No. Studying was everything. He loved being a student, and he was always so good at it. Even after he got his doctorate, he started a new study—gathering data, writing books, going to conventions..."

"What kind of books did he write?" Rino said.

"He had started one on educational research, had published some articles. It wasn't because he was young; it was because I really wasn't part of his life... but the data and the computers were."

Rino didn't answer her. "Let's go out Saturday night," he said.

"You aren't coming tomorrow, are you?"

"No," he said.

"You'd rather play poker than play with me," she teased.

"Never. Except that I've been doing it since before you were born."

"I hope you lose. That'll teach you," she said in her smiling, fake pout.

"Hell, besides, I need the rest. You think guys in their 60s can do what we did tonight all the time?"

"You're not old, Rino Bellanca. Here. Let's see if I can get you puffy again," she said, laughing.

He rolled her over on her side. "So, what brings out this evil side in you, Leila?" He had her arms pinned down to the bed. She looked back, defiantly smiling, her eyes sparkling. "Where do you want to go Saturday?" he said.

"Anywhere you want. Italian. Okay? Please kiss me, Rino."

He kissed her and released her hands. Then he said, "I know a nice place. All the dagos go there for good Italian."

"Then that's where I want to go," she said.

"Lee, I think I'd better not stay tonight..."

"Rino Bellanca, would you go home to your cold, empty bed and sleep alone rather than sleep here with me?"

Jesus, Rino thought, *I must be crazy. All my life I've waited for this, and now I'm worrying about what the kids would think.* "You talked me into it," he said and nestled into her arms.

She wrapped her small body around him and held him to her. She could soon feel him breathing heavily and steadily. She touched his head and felt the slight dampness of his shoulder and neck muscles. Then she fell asleep.

Rino had an easy day at work. He waxed and buffed the hallways of Crandall. When he got home from work, Frank was already there. When his father walked into the kitchen, Frank was alone having a cup of coffee. No one else was home. "Hi, Pop," he said.

"Hi, Frank," Rino said. "Where's Jean?"

"She went to get Libby."

The tension that had lately been between them was new to them both. Frank had always been Rino's favorite, and the estrangement between them bothered Frank. "How d'you feel, Pop?"

"Okay, Frank. Why?"

"I don't know," Frank said uncomfortably. "It's just that I don't know what you're doing anymore. I worry if you don't come home at night. Then the kids want to know if you're mad at us."

"Libby and Larry think I'm mad?"

"Can you blame them, Pop? I don't know what I'm supposed to tell them. Sooner or later, all this is gonna come out. Why don't you just level with everybody?"

"Soon, Frank. A little more time... please. I have to settle some things, okay?"

"Yeah. Sure, Pop."

"Tell the kids I'm not mad at all. I've never given them any reason to—"

"You and I don't have much to say to each other; they notice that. And they're not babies anymore. Hell, Pop, Larry's 20 years old. He knows you're staying overnight with a woman."

"Has he said anything?"

"No. But if he knows, so does Libby."

"Sorry, kid, just a little more time... a little."

Later that night at the Tre-Sette, it looked as though they might get only one card game going, and that wasn't a sure thing. Everyone sat around the front barroom talking. Rino and Lou were sitting at the bar alone. "Goddamn, Luigi, this thing is getting out of hand now," Rino said.

"What d'you mean?" said his brother.

"Frankie's leaning on me because I don't come home some nights."

"What's so new about that? You may not go home tonight if you're winning big. How many stags have kept us out all night?"

"He says this is different. Libby and Larry think I have a girlfriend, and he's... embarrassed."

"Well, what did you expect?" Lou said. "You know you have to tell everybody sooner or later. So drop it on them quick."

"Lou, you know damn well it's gonna boggle their minds when they find out how old she is. We haven't talked about the future. What will I say?"

"I'm not talking about the future. The hell with the future. You go in and say it. 'Look, everybody. I'm seeing a woman. She's 33 years old, and I love her. When we make some plans, we'll let you know. Any questions? Thanks. Goodnight.'"

"Well, Jesus Christ," Rino said sarcastically. "Why didn't I think of that?"

"Well, how else do you want to do it, man? Play 20 questions? Get it off your chest and make it easy on yourself. Short and sweet."

Rino snorted. "I'll think about it."

Neither Rino nor Lou did well at the poker table. Both took turns being second best–all night. Rino excused himself about eleven and went into Agee's office to call Lee.

"What are all the phone calls, Lou?" said Marty, who was glowing as only a man could who had filled two inside straights and had rolled a full house over two weaker ones so far that night.

"He's checking on a sick friend," said Lou.

"Sick girlfriend?" Marty chuckled.

"A friend," said Lou.

"Cut the bullshit, Lou. Rino never made two phone calls in a row during these games in 30 years."

"Hey, Marty, deal the fucking cards, okay? I came here to play poker, not answer all your goddamned questions."

While Lou and Marty were sparring, Rino was on the phone with Lee.

"Are you winning?" she asked.

"No," he said.

"Are you thinking about me?"

"Yes. I used to be a pretty good poker player before I met you. You've been costing me."

"Aw," she drawled, mocking him. "What on earth are we going to do, Rino?"

Rino chuckled. "Thanks for all the sympathy, kid."

"Well, I'm worth a few dollars in poker, aren't I?"

"How many dollars did you say?" said Rino.

"God, Rino, you're a devil," she said.

"What are you planning for tomorrow?" he asked.

"Aren't you taking me out?" she said.

"That's tomorrow night. How about during the day?"

"I was just going to do some chores, call Mother. Why?"

"Let's go for a ride during the day, okay?"

"Really? Sure. What time?"

"10 o'clock."

"Okay. I love you, Rino."

"I love you too, kid. See you tomorrow."

Rino returned to the table amid chuckles of smug satisfaction from his opponents. Lou seemed grouchier than usual. *Maybe he's losing more than I am*, Rino thought.

When the game broke up, Rino asked Lou how much he had lost. "About 50 bucks," said Lou. "How about you?"

"I think I dropped about 80," said Rino. "Haven't lost that much in a couple years."

"Jesus. See what happens when you're a playboy? You not only blow your own wad, but you take your brother down the tubes with you."

Rino got up around eight o'clock the next day. Saturdays were always hectic times at the Bellancas'. There was movement in all directions, and no one kept a schedule.

Jean wasn't up yet, but Frank and the grandchildren were. "Where's everybody going?" Rino said to Frank.

"Larry and I are going to the club golf outing—it's the last one of the year—and Libby is going to a cheerleading workshop," said Frank.

"Jean'll be home all alone today, then?" said Rino.

"If you go out, she will be," said Frank matter-of-factly.

"Well, everybody, have a good time," Rino said. Jean had just gotten up. "What're you going to do today?" he asked her.

"Not much, Dad. I'll probably go shopping this afternoon."

"Oh," he said. "How about this morning?"

"Do you want me to do something for you, Dad?"

"No. I'm fine, kid. Look, I'm going out for a while. See you later."

He left the house about nine o'clock. He stopped for a fill-up at a gas station, and then he arrived at Lee's apartment about 20 minutes to 10:00. He rang the doorbell, and she opened the door. She had on jeans, white leather jogging shoes, a white shirt, and a gray corduroy vest.

"Hi," he said, kissing her lightly as he went in.

He seemed preoccupied with something. "Is everything okay, Rino?" she said.

"Sure. There's nothing wrong. You look very nice."

"Thank you. So do you. Where are we going?"

"Let's just ride, okay? We'll see where we end up."

When they got into Rino's Buick, she said, "Rino, have you always had cars like this one?"

"Since I could afford them. I had my share of clunkers when I was young. Now I like nice, comfortable cars."

"You know that a lot of people will think I'm after your money?"

"And some will say I'm after yours, right?"

"I'm glad you have it. The fewer of those battles we have to fight, the better," she said.

As they talked, Rino had been driving deliberately, and she hadn't paid attention to where he was going. But it occurred to her that they didn't seem to be going anywhere worth a ride; they were still in the city. "Where are you going, Rino?" she asked.

"Just riding."

She shrugged. As they drove farther, she realized that they were in a residential neighborhood of large brick houses, old trees, and beautiful, big lawns. A few people were working in their yards, preparing shrubs for winter, and a few kids were playing and riding bicycles. Rino drove slowly through the winding streets. "Where are you going, Rino?" she said suddenly, with a slight edge in her voice.

He didn't answer. Instead, he pulled into a driveway and drove back to a large triple garage with a wide side patio that covered the ground between the garage and the house.

Rino turned the key off and turned to her. Her eyes implored him to spare her what he was going to do. "This is my house," he said quietly.

"Oh, Rino, how could you do this to me?" she said. "Look at me—I'm not dressed right. God, what if they don't like me? Rino!"

He kissed her gently on the cheek and said, "You're fine. Now, come on. There's only one person home."

Reluctantly, she got out of the car and walked behind him the two steps up to the kitchen. Jean wasn't there. Rino called to her, and she answered, coming from the living room. She was startled when she saw Lee standing next to him.

"Switzerland, meet Germany. Lee, this is my daughter-in-law, Jean. Jean, this is Leila Reese," Rino said.

He had never before seen what went on between the two women in that moment. Lee stood quietly, looking at Jean, holding her gloves in front of her with both hands. Lee was wearing a waist-length jacket and blue jeans. Jean noticed the pearl-tipped fingers of her hands, the soft, medium-long brown hair that cradled her face, the wide, full mouth, and the large, glistening eyes with long brown lashes. *God, she looks like a little girl*, Jean thought.

Neither of them spoke for what seemed to Rino like long, agonizing minutes. They just looked at each other. Jean looked sharp and alert, wary of Lee. But Jean didn't see what she had expected. She didn't expect her to be so lovely, so simple and clean. She expected a coquette or a sophisticate with a visible, hard edge, someone false whom Rino was too blind to read, a determined gold-digger, putting on airs and insinuating herself into the family. She expected possessiveness; she expected a smug challenge and coy, smiling condescension.

But instead, she saw what Rino had always seen, and she felt what only another woman could feel when confronting this stranger. She could read the pain in the girl's eyes that Rino had helped to assuage. She saw the capacity to love Rino, and just looking at her, she realized that she did. And she saw the fear in her eyes that the family might reject her.

She saw in this small, gentle, vulnerable creature the reason why Rino glowed now, the reason why, of all the women he had ever known, none had ever captured his whole heart—not Mary or Nancy or Libby or herself. This girl had been waiting all her life to do it.

Jean knew that Lee was Libby as a mature grown-up. She was herself in her best dreams. She was part of the goodness that Rino had within him, the part that, until he met her, was incomplete.

Lee was letting herself be seen and judged. But by the long look between them, Jean's searching eyes, the expectancy, the hesitation, and the fear, Lee knew that Jean was at once the judge and the petitioner. She knew that Jean and the rest of the family dreaded her power over Rino. "I won't hurt him," she said softly to Jean, their eyes never having left contact.

Rino had been helplessly watching this small drama play itself out. But to his great relief, Jean rushed to Lee and threw her arms around her. They both clung to each other silently. Finally, Jean released Lee to hold her out at arm's length and look at her again. Then she touched the soft brown hair on Lee's forehead that she had disheveled. She brushed it back as she so often did for Libby, and then she touched her face. "You're so beautiful," she said, then hugged her again.

Rino sighed a great wail of relief. All the bad things he had feared had been dissipated by these two wonderful strangers. The weight he seemed to carry, despite the joy of knowing Lee, was gone. "I guess this means you're going to like each other, huh?"

After having coffee with Jean, Rino and Lee left. She had talked and laughed with Jean, and all the strangeness she had felt was gone. But when they were in the car, driving away, Lee said very little. Finally, she said, "Rino, please don't ever do that to me again."

"Didn't you like her?" Rino said apprehensively.

"Of course I liked her. She's wonderful," she said. "But I almost died in there. Don't you know that? What if I would have said the wrong thing?" Then she said quietly, "You didn't have to trick me, Rino."

"She didn't know anything about this," he said weakly.

Lee was still annoyed, but she softened a little. "Is that true? She didn't either?"

"No," he said.

She looked away for a few minutes. Then she touched his hand as it rested on the steering wheel. Her anger was gone. "But what if she didn't like me, Rino? You know how important first impressions are. I might have ruined it. I didn't know what to say."

"You couldn't have said it better, kid. I wanted you to see her first. I figured that if you two hit it off—and I knew you would—then you'd have a friend when you saw everybody together."

"And some others in the family won't be like Jean, will they?"

"Maybe not at first. But you can't lose now."

Rino and Lee took a long ride through Amish country. She loved seeing the farms and the horse-drawn buggies in the town squares and the bearded, black-garbed men and the bonneted women in cotton and wool long dresses. The warm sun was shining against the cooler, darker sky that ringed the horizons, promising rain that night. In a small valley town, they stopped at a tavern known for its sandwiches, soups, and fruit cobblers. They drove back after a light but filling meal. Rino told Lee more about his past. She had question after question about his family. How many children did each have? Who had married whom? Who were his favorites? He walked her into the apartment, kissed her, and went home to change.

When he got home, Frank and Jean were getting ready to go to a school board dinner. As Rino went upstairs to his room, he could hear that Frank was taking a shower. Jean was in their bedroom. He had no sooner shut his door when there was a knock. It was Jean. When Rino opened the door, she walked in without speaking. She had a long robe on, and her hair was still pinned up. "I'm mad at you," she said.

"Well, that's two out of two," he said wearily.

"How could you do that to her? To me?" she said.

"I wanted you to see her right away, and I didn't know if she would come."

"Didn't know? Dad, that little creature will do anything you ever want her to do. You should know that."

"Yeah, I guess so," he said. "I just didn't think it'd be such a big deal. Do you like her... really?"

"You knew I would."

"I'm glad."

"I believe she loves you, too. How about that?"

"That means a lot to me, kid, especially from you."

"She's beautiful and gentle and good, but she's going to need a lot more than that to handle you," she said, smiling. "By the way, are you coming home tonight?"

He reddened a little. "I don't know," he said. "You really like her, huh?"

"She's going to be my little sister, Dad," she said, kissing him on the cheek before she left.

It took Rino a while to motivate himself. He lay across the bed, thinking about the day. What was going to happen? Should he ask her to marry him? Would she? He couldn't keep staying overnight, not without his friends gossiping. Frank and the kids were thinking crazy things as it was—that he was a dirty, old skirt chaser, probably. God, life was complicated.

When he picked Lee up, she was in a navy-blue dress with shoes to match and a floppy white tam that was pinned on one side of her head. He enjoyed having the door open and being stunned by how she looked. He helped her on with her coat, and they left.

In the car, as they drove, he said, "You never talk much in the car."

"I'm always thinking things whenever I'm with you. Thinking about what our lives—life—is going to be like." It started to rain steadily as they rode.

"You know we'll probably see someone I know at this place?"

"I know."

"Can you handle it?"

"I think so. This isn't another setup, is it?"

"I told you I wouldn't do that to you again," he said curtly with some irritation. Then he caught himself quickly. "I'm sorry, kid."

"Rino, what will it be like when we have our first argument?" Her tone was less serious, but she meant what she said.

"I'll yell, you'll cry, and then we'll forget it," he said.

She laughed softly. "Never go to bed mad at me, will you?"

"Okay. How about you?"

"Me too. Rino, do you mind being seen with me?"

"No, I'm proud of you. It's just that people will wonder why someone like you would take up with a guy like me. When they laugh at me, some of it will rub off on you."

"I know you've had that on your mind. But just remember, no matter what they say..." She stopped to touch his hand. "They won't be able to come into our lives unless we let them... ever. Okay?"

He nodded.

Castorina's was Rino's favorite, one of the few Italian restaurants good enough for the Italians in town to patronize. It was a long, plain, single-story building of beige brick. There was a canopy leading to the main entrance, which was in the middle of the broad side of the building. A large entry lobby branched into two rooms, each entered through archways from the lobby. The smaller of the two rooms had booths, lower light, and a quiet bistro atmosphere. The other, larger room had open tables, more light, and more noise.

As they drove into the parking lot, the rain was falling steadily. The lot was crowded with cars, each as close to the entrance as possible. Quickly Rino opened his door, but before he could go around the car to open Lee's, she was out. They ran to the building. It was now starting to get windy and cold. When they reached the shelter of the canopy and started for the entrance, Lee hesitated.

"What's wrong, kid?" said Rino.

"Oh, Rino, I must have dropped my clutch purse," she said.

"Could you have left it in the car?"

"I don't know. I'll go see."

"No, Lee. It's raining too much. I'll go and be right back. Here, wait inside." Rino opened the door and ushered her into the small vestibule just outside the main door. There were two wooden doors with small four-by-four translucent glass panes arranged in a square on the upper half of each door. Lee waited while Rino went back outside to look for the purse.

As Lee waited, a tall, distinguished-looking woman entered the vestibule from the lobby and waited also. She noticed the girl standing on the opposite side of the room. *What extraordinary beauty*, the woman thought. She had never seen her before. They looked at each other and nodded greetings. Lee smiled and said, "It's really pouring out there... and windy."

The woman nodded again and spoke a soft, "Yes."

Lee admired the slender grace of the other woman, her gray hair swept up fully on the crown of her head. She always envied tall, attractive women who carried themselves so regally. She noticed her large eyes, the dark elegant coat, the long, slender fingers of her hands.

Both women stood silently for a few minutes. The vestibule was well lit, lined with light-stained wainscoting and pastel beige paintings of scenes from Italy. Just then, Rino entered.

"Did you find it, Rino?" Lee asked anxiously.

He smiled and nodded. "It was outside the car by your door. It must have dropped when you got out."

She touched his hand with hers and smiled. "Thank you. It was a gift from my mother. Are you soaked, Rino? I'm sorry I—"

"No, I'm fine. Let's go." He turned toward the lobby door, guiding Lee ahead of him with his hand. It was only then that he noticed the other figure in the vestibule, who was staring at him with amazed and questioning dark eyes. It was Andrea Manasseri.

Rino suddenly became flustered. *God! Of all the people to see first with Lee*, he thought. *Damn Lou for ever making me get involved with her.* "Uh, just a minute, Lee," he said softly, restraining her by touching her arm. Lee turned to him with a quizzical look on her face. "Hello, Andrea," he said.

"Hello, Rino." She looked at Lee again as they approached her. This was not a relative of Rino's, Andrea thought. No. The look that passed between them, the way she brightened when she saw him enter, the touch, the look of enchantment in his eyes—this girl was Rino's inamorata. It had to be. She couldn't have mistaken those few seconds of soft words and gestures. And, looking at Rino, one could see, as uneasy as he seemed now, that this girl was special to him.

She watched the girl look toward Rino for guidance in what they were about to do. She studied the lovely dark eyes, the small nose, and the flawless tan complexion. The look was unmistakable; she had seen it all her life—the look of magic, the look of belonging that glows from within.

"Andrea, may I present Lee Reese? Lee, this is Andrea Manasseri, whose family has known ours for many years."

Lee was surprised at the formality and courtliness of his manners.

"I'm pleased to meet you, Mrs. Manasseri," said Lee, assuming she bore the married title.

"And I, you, my dear," said Andrea.

"I'm afraid it's raining pretty hard out there, Andrea. Are you waiting for someone?" said Rino.

"Yes, my son is borrowing an umbrella from John. He must have seen someone else to talk to in there."

"How is your family, Andrea?" said Rino uncomfortably.

"They're fine. And yours?"

"Fine," said Rino.

Just then, her son entered from the lobby. Rino at once turned and began to urge Lee toward the door. He nodded to her son, who nodded back gravely, studying Lee intently. "It was nice seeing you again," Rino said to Andrea.

"Enjoy your meal," she said, more to Lee than to Rino. She gave a slight bow with a nod of her head, smiling weakly.

When they stepped into the lobby, Rino said, "Jesus, I didn't expect to see someone so soon."

"She's very nice," said Lee, "and so... beautiful."

"Yeah, very nice," he said indifferently.

The lobby was crowded. Rino nodded to John Castorina, who was behind the reception desk along with two of his hostesses, and pointed to the smaller room. John, who often played golf with Rino and Lou, beckoned to them to follow him into the room. When Rino and Lee drew near him, he held Rino's hand after their handshake. But his eyes were on Lee. "You haven't been here in ages, Rino," he said.

"A month... and if you wouldn't win my poker money all the time, I might be able to afford this place more often," said Rino jovially.

But John squeezed his hand, not letting him go. In that wordless Italian eye movement that so often communicated for them, Rino understood; John wanted to know about Lee.

"Johnny, I'd like you to meet Lee Reese. Lee, this is John Castorina, the owner of this place and a well-known millionaire friend of mine."

John laughed heartily at Rino. But Lee seemed shy all of a sudden. All she said was, "Hello, Mr. Castorina."

"She's lovely, Rino," said John. He was obviously trying to figure out their relationship. Could she be Rino's niece... or cousin... or daughter-in-law? The thought that she might be Rino's inamorata occurred to him, but then he doubted it. "Well, there's a booth. Is that one okay, Rino?"

Rino nodded, and John led them to the booth. "Enjoy your meal, my friends." Then he turned to Lee. "Signorina, my pleasure."

Lee nodded and smiled. When John left, she said, "Are all your friends like this, Rino? That woman was so lovely, and he's so... so..."

"Oily?" said Rino mockingly.

"Rino! He's charming."

When Rino took their coats to the closet, John caught up with him again. "Rino, who is that?" he said. John was a generous, gregarious busybody, the perfect restaurateur.

"Who?" Rino said coyly, hanging up the coats and avoiding John's gaze.

"Who do you think, for Christ's sake? That angel over there."

"She's a friend of mine," Rino said.

"A friend of yours?"

"Yes. And we came here for some good food and quiet, okay?"

John was too surprised to make any funny comments. "Rino?" he said, still trying to verify what he was beginning to believe. "She's yours... your friend?"

Rino nodded, and John grew more serious. "Rino, she's absolutely stunning. Congratulations."

"Thanks, Johnny."

When he returned to the booth, he said to Lee, "I think it's going to be like this for a while. At first, they can't believe their eyes, and then, when they realize it's true, they can't stop asking questions." He stopped to look at her for a moment. "You look great. How do you feel?"

"I feel like you think I look," she said.

He arched his eyebrows in response. The waitress came to them with two wine glasses and a bottle of Chianti Classico. "Mr. Castorina asks that you accept this bottle with his compliments," she said.

But as she began to pour wine in Lee's glass, Lee said, "No... I..." She looked to Rino for help.

The waitress turned questioningly to Rino. He nodded and said, "It's all right. Just leave the glasses and express our thanks to Mr. Castorina."

When the waitress left, Rino didn't say anything; he just poured the wine. "You must think I'm crazy, don't you?" she said.

"No," he answered. Then he took a sip of wine from the glass. Without removing his eyes from her, he slid the glass across the table. She took a sip of wine as she usually did in their little ritual. "Thank you," she said.

"I wonder if this rain will spoil the golf outing tomorrow?" he said.

"Tomorrow early, Rino?"

He nodded again, and her visage grew grim.

"It'll be over about three o'clock, and I'm off all day Monday," he said, trying to appease her.

She snorted and smiled, looking away from him. *That was fine*, she thought. She just wished he didn't know it would always be so easy.

"Lee, we have to do something–"

"Something new?" she interrupted, teasing him.

"I'm serious, kid."

"Other than marrying me, what else did you have in mind?"

Rino sat back in his seat dumbfounded. "Jesus! What am I going to do with you?"

"A lot, I hope," she said, enjoying the easy play with him.

The waitress returned. "You order for us, Rino," said Lee. "I don't know much about Italian food."

Rino looked at the waitress and began. "Antipasto... and tell the cook we want baby pastina, cheese ravioli... and braciole."

Lee was mystified. Her eyes sparkled as she watched him order. He had self-assurance that comes from knowing himself and from not ever taking himself too seriously. He never seemed aggressive or hostile, yet he seemed quietly in control of his small world. "What did you do?" she asked. "Baby what?"

"Tiny little pasta stars they serve to babies in chicken soup. I've always liked it, and Johnny carries it for the few of us that ask. Braciole is steak rolled around hard-boiled eggs and seasoned breadcrumbs and cheese and cooked in sauce."

"I didn't know what a gourmet you are," she teased.

"It's peasant food, but you'll like it," he said, ignoring her taunts. "You think we should get married, huh?"

She was now enchanted. She was talking of marriage with the man she was growing more in love with every day. She was teasing and playful, her face glowed, and her eyes sparkled. She took a sip of his wine.

"May I take your order?" a voice said.

Rino's heart sank. It was Lou standing at their table.

"What the hell are you doing here, Luigi?"

"Having dinner. How about you?" he said as he slid into the seat, forcing Rino to move over. Lee couldn't quite understand what was happening in those few seconds. But when the man sat down, she could see the resemblance to Rino.

"Lou, this is Lee Reese. Lee, this is my brother, Lou."

"Hi," she said.

Lou looked at her approvingly. "So this is the dumpy, plain-looking woman you've been lying to me about," he said to Rino.

Lee, for a second, looked at Rino, wondering if it was true. Lou and Rino both caught her reaction, and both were beaming as she realized that Lou was playing with her. "God," she said, shaking her head, "how will I ever handle two of you?"

Both men chuckled. "Hell," Lou said, "Connie's been trying all her life, and she still can't do it."

"How do you happen to be here, cowboy?" Rino said.

"Annie and I and Marty and Peggy are out in the big room. I didn't see you come in, but Peg did."

"Listen, Lou, don't keep yourself from them on our account. We'll be fine here," said Rino with false earnestness.

"Rino!" Lee said, scolding him yet smiling. "Shame on you."

"Did he order yet, Lee?" Lou asked.

"Yes, a few minutes ago," she said.

He looked at his brother, who was slowly reddening.

"Don't start, Lou," Rino muttered. Lou was twinkling.

Lee delighted in their byplay. It was strange seeing so much of Rino in the two of them. Lou was more slender and had curly hair. He had probably been handsomer than Rino when they were young. But now Rino's rugged face and thick white hair were equal to Lou's finer features. The obvious affection between them and the lightness of their spirits delighted her.

She looked at Rino, who was waiting patiently for Lou to play his game. He didn't help. He was just suddenly thrilled for Lou to see her. He knew now that Lou would fall under her spell. He knew also that Lou would love her and charm her, and that she would be a wonderful new thing in all their lives.

"All right, then," Lou said. "Let me tell you what my brother ordered." He looked at Rino, who was trying to hide his reluctant smile, and then he continued. "Antipasto..." Lou dramatically numbered each item on his fingers, starting with his thumb as Italians usually do. "Baby pastina... cheese ravioli... and veal..." Lou looked at Rino for a cue. "Oh no," he said after seeing Rino smile at a mistake, "that must have been the blonde you ordered that one for. It was... Let's see... Braciole, right?"

"Oh my God, Rino!" Lee said in smiling, wide-eyed horror over Lou's fantasy. "How does he know all this?"

"Because he's a goddamned malandrine, that's why," said Rino.

"A mal..."

"A wisher of evil," said Lou. "But don't you believe it, Lee. Was I right or wrong, Rino?"

"All wrong," said Rino.

"Lee! Answer me. Was I right?"

"Rino," she said in mock sincerity, "you don't expect me to lie for you, do you?"

"Hell yes, Lee!" Rino said.

"Lee?" said Lou.

"You're right, Lou. I hate to admit it, but that's what he ordered."

Lou settled back, grinning in smug satisfaction.

"Does he do that with all the girls, Lou? I should know that about him."

"Lou, you bastard, tell her."

Lou chuckled and drew the moment out a little longer. "Well," he said, "whenever he feels really good, he always orders his favorite things, especially in this place. Always the same meal, since he was a baby. So, looking at you, I just knew what he would order."

"Who's the blonde, Rino?" she teased.

"The 'blonde' is in the twisted mind of this malandrine who calls himself my brother," said Rino.

"Is that true, Lou? I'm just one of a long line of girls?"

"You're the youngest and the prettiest. God, some of them were ugly."

"Lou, Annie must be wondering where you've been. You don't want her to be lonely. Why don't you go join her?" said Rino.

Lou winked at Lee. Finally, he said, "All right, I'm going. But if he ever gives you any trouble, he'll answer to his older brother, okay?"

She nodded. Lou patted his brother's forearm and then stood up. Suddenly he was serious. "You've worked magic on him, angel," he said to Lee. "And after seeing you, I understand." He reached for her hand and kissed it. "God bless you both," he said.

When Lou left, the waitress came with their soup and antipasto. "Rino, he's fabulous," said Lee. "Is he always so crazy?"

"Sometimes worse."

They ate slowly. Rino answered her questions about the foods and told her stories about his mother making them. From time to time, they would both sip wine from the glass. When they left, Lou and his party had long since gone.

On the way home, she said, "We're going to be so happy, Rino." He turned toward her. The light of oncoming cars highlighted her hair and her face and made her eyes shine. "Let's not go out for supper tomorrow, okay? I want to make it for you," she said.

"What time?"

"Whenever you're done."

"I'll go home and change. I'll be there about six."

"Are you staying overnight tomorrow?"

"Is the invitation still open?"

She pushed his arm in response.

When they were back in her apartment, she clung to him as he kissed her. "Tonight was wonderful. I've only seen two members of your family, and I love them both," she said. "Are you sure you'd like to get up 'early' and go golfing?" she said impishly.

"You're bad. You know that?" he said. He sat on the couch, and she curled up next to him. He draped his arm over her shoulder. "Would you really like to marry me, Lee? God, it'll drive everybody crazy."

"I want that more than anything else in the world," she said.

The next day Rino went golfing early with his brother. The ground was wet, and the sky was gray and threatening, but the foursomes all played their rounds without getting rained on. After the games, there was an outdoor picnic supper at the pavilion. Rino only had one beer and left early, much to Lou's chagrin.

He went home, showered, and dressed in comfortable slacks and a turtleneck jersey. He also managed to tell Jean that he probably would not be back that night. It was still embarrassing to have to tell her; he felt like a small boy doing something sneaky.

When Lee opened the door of her apartment, she had on dark blue wool slacks and a light blue boatneck sweater of soft angora. Rino also noticed to his great satisfaction that she had the gold slippers on. No panty hose again.

It seemed that he hadn't spent much time with her that week. As he watched her, he wondered how he would be able to keep his hands off her through dinner. There was something about her when she was doing things—making coffee, setting the table, cooking—that made him want to touch her.

She knew he wanted to make love to her; the chemistry was there between them. She also knew that she had dressed to make him want it, and nothing he did that night—help her clear the table, pour a drink—nothing would let the thought of her body escape him.

Rino sat quietly in the kitchen drinking wine while she prepared their meal. They talked occasionally but were mostly quiet. Finally, she said, "Rino?"

"Yeah?"

"You never asked me about... whether I use birth control."

"I never gave it much thought," he said uneasily. "You think I should have?"

"No, I didn't say that," she said without looking at him. "But what if I told you that I haven't taken anything for it?"

He didn't answer. Instead, he made a wry grimace and a shrug that meant he didn't know "what if."

"Rino?" She stared at him as he looked away from her.

"Kid, I'm too old to think about this stuff," he said.

"Picasso wasn't," she teased.

"I'm not Picasso. He was a little strange, anyway."

"You really think you can't get me pregnant?" she asked.

He glanced up at her, and she was smiling. Suddenly she came over to him and knelt before him.

"Lee, you're trying to mess with my mind now," he said, pointing at her. "I can't..."

"You can," she said emphatically. "I know you can."

"You're crazy, Leila, you know that? Do you know that my youngest child is older than you?"

"You can, Rino," she said.

"You're talking about you and me having a baby? Jesus Christ."

"I'm not saying we will, but we might," she said. "And the more we make love, the more chances we have of making a baby, right?"

"Why are you smiling, Leila? We're talking serious stuff here."

"We can stop making love?"

"Right. Hell of an idea. Why didn't I think of that?"

"Or... we can be really careful when we do."

"You don't take pills or anything now, huh?"

"No. I stopped taking them after Ted died."

He talked to himself in amazement. "A 62-year-old man having a baby with a 33-year-old kid? Jesus."

"I'll have it. You just have to give it to me," she said smugly. "Rino, I can go on the pill or wear a diaphragm or do nothing... like now."

"So what do you want me to say?"

"I want you to tell me what to do," she said. Then she said deliberately, "Should I do something about birth control or not?"

"Why are you doing this to me, Leila?" he said.

"I'm not doing anything, Rino. Should I?"

He brought the fingers of both hands up to cover and massage his eyes. "You don't do anything now?" he said, looking at her again.

"No." He mouthed the word as she spoke it.

"And if you don't do anything, you might get pregnant... from me?"

She laughed. "Of course from you, you nut. Who else do you think?"

"Me, the father of a baby," he said thoughtfully. Then he stood up and walked away. She stayed kneeling, but her eyes followed him. "A baby whose father could be dead before he's old enough to drive," he said, turning back to look at her.

"Maybe," she said. "You could be dead. But so could I, Rino."

"Bet on me for that one, kid," he said. Then he walked into the living room. She wanted to follow him, but she didn't.

She made the rest of the meal, worried now about what he was thinking. When the meal was ready, she went out to the living room and sat beside him on the couch. He looked at her and said, "How would any kid feel, having a father older than some of his friends' grandfathers?" he said sadly.

She had tears in her eyes as he looked at her. "It's happened before, Rino," she said. "And if she were part of you and part of me, it wouldn't matter. Rino, I'm sorry I did this. I didn't mean to hurt you."

He snorted and shook his head. "No, kid, it's just in the cards that way," he said.

"I could be pregnant now, Rino," she said. "And you know something? I could have done something to prevent it, and I didn't."

"You think you could be... really? And you wouldn't mind?"

"Mind? Rino, what do you think I've been saying tonight? What do you think I'm asking?"

"What if I die before he's in high school? What would you do?"

"Well, certainly money would be no problem. Besides, I'd have you yet, wouldn't I?" He looked at her and sighed assent. "But if that's what's in our cards, don't we have to play them? Don't we deserve to try to live and be happy? All we want is what all kinds of other people take for granted. And, Rino, all I want is to live this dream we've started."

He didn't respond. After a few minutes, she said, "Come on. Supper will get cold." *How easily something wonderful could be hurtful*, she thought.

Rino barely touched his food. Most of the time he talked about the golf outing. But he and Lee both knew that they were talking around what bothered them. Then he said, "Why couldn't this be different? Why didn't I meet you 25 years ago?"

"Because I was eight years old then," she said, trying to make him smile.

He did, slightly. "You know what I mean, Leila."

"What would you have done with Mary? What if it was 25 years ago, and we felt about each other as we do now? You know what, Rino?" she said, raising her voice slightly. "You would have had to choose... and you would have chosen Mary."

"How do you know? What if I loved you more than I loved her?"

She sighed. "You would have chosen her anyway, because she was your wife, and you wouldn't hurt her." He cocked his head and shrugged. *Maybe*, he thought. "So isn't it better now that you can love me as much as you want and it doesn't hurt anyone, especially Mary?"

"You know, Lee, I think you've done something to my brain."

"Really?" she said, smiling. "And all this time I was working on your body."

"You're crazy. In just two minutes you can turn my whole life upside down... any time you want."

"Rino?"

"What?"

"Please answer this question honestly."

"Right. I'll try anything once," he said.

"Rino Bellanca, I didn't say you've ever lied to me. All I'm asking is that you answer me. Would you like me to have our baby?"

He began to say something. "Wait," she said, touching his lips. "Would you like it just for you?" She pointed at him. "Not because you think I'd like it... just for you."

He stared at one of the gold slippers she had kicked onto the floor beside them. "Leila, it's hard to imagine being happier than I am now, but a baby girl might do it. Yet I never paid dues enough to get you, let alone you and a baby."

"I don't care about your dues, Rino. Other people don't pay dues just to be happily married and have kids. Correct me if I'm wrong, but I have the feeling that we're going into that bedroom there and making love later." She pointed a graceful finger back behind him. "And I just want to know, if you could make me pregnant tonight, would you do it? Or would you want me to do something to prevent it?"

"You know I'd do it," he said.

"Say it again, Rino," she said.

He snorted. "Yes, I want the baby, and no, I don't want you taking any pills or putting anything inside yourself… except me."

She suddenly got up off the couch and looked down at him, smiling. "I'll think about it," she said nonchalantly as she walked into the kitchen, knowing he would follow her. He just shook his head in amazed happiness.

By then, their supper was cold. "What should we do tomorrow?" Rino said as he helped her clear the table.

"Oh, are you sure you have time to stay tonight? To fit me into your busy schedule?"

His response was to shove her gently. But when he reached to do it, he touched her side and part of one of her breasts, and she flinched. She giggled and moved away, almost dropping a cup in doing it.

"Hey, wait a minute," he said seriously.

She looked at him questioningly. "What's wrong?" she said.

"Come here, let me see something."

She came toward him warily, but only because he seemed so serious.

"What is it, Rino?" she said as he put his hand on her shoulder and guided her into a turn so that she faced away from him. For a moment, he didn't say anything. Finally, he reached around front of her and cupped each of her breasts in his hands.

"Isn't this strange?" he said in false sincerity, hefting each small, pliant orb in his hands. "This must be some new kind of bra, huh, Lee?"

She shrieked and sprang away from him. But he caught her by one wrist and forced her backward, step by step, into a corner of the kitchen. "Rino, what are you doing?" she said. "Let me pass."

"It must be one of those kinds they show on TV, huh? The kind that doesn't look like a bra? Here, let me have a look."

She held him off as best she could for a few seconds, giggling as he pressed forward toward her. "Maybe one of those fishnet ones," he crooned.

"Get away from me, Bellanca," she said.

"Fishnet or nylon maybe..." He kept struggling to unbutton her sweater. "Nice buttons here, Lee," he said as she screamed in playful anguish.

"Rino! What are you doing? Rino!"

But to no avail. He had gotten enough buttons loosened against her protestations that he could pull back part of the sweater to expose the small, wonderfully full, upright breasts. "Hell, Lee, that's a new material to me," he said, laughing to himself.

"You're a devil, Rino. A mal... malan..." She was pouting and at the same time guiding him, with her hands on his shoulders, to be near her.

"You can't even see this bra," he said. "Where's the clasp?"

"You think you're so smart, don't you?" she said as she began to blush. "I just did it so it would be easier for you."

He kissed her neck and slid his hands beneath her sweater and up her back, holding her to him. She hugged him tight when the kiss was done, seeming not to want to let him get away from her. "Rino, we may not have a long life together, but every bit of it will be happy. And every bit of it will be an answer to my prayers."

Later they sat on the couch, listened to music, and talked. "That was a terrible meal. I'm sorry," she said.

"I'm over it," he said.

"Are you?"

"Yeah. You know, when I'm with you, things that should usually scare the hell out of me seem ordinary... like being a father again."

"That's the way it should be, shouldn't it?"

"Yeah. I just never expected it to happen at this time of my life. Are we gonna get married?"

"My God!" she said. "That's the worst marriage proposal I ever heard."

He laughed. "Okay, okay... Lee, will you marry me?"

"I'll think about it," she said, putting her arms around his neck and drawing him toward her on the couch for a kiss.

"After I get back from Canada," he said. "It's only a few weeks, and we can straighten out some things, okay?"

"What if the baby's born six months after we get married? People will talk."

"Hell, people are gonna talk no matter what. Lee, do you think you're pregnant?"

"Maybe. My period's late, and I always work like a clock."

"Late or missing?"

"Kind of missing."

He was thoughtful for a minute. "Not bad for an old guy, huh?"

She laughed and clung to him. "What baby names do you like?"

"Lee for a girl, and..." He paused for a moment. "James for a boy?"

"James?"

"For my son that was killed."

"I like Suzanne," she said.

"How about for a boy?" he said.

"James."

He beamed when she said that. "Aren't you tired, Lee?" he said. "That fantastic meal must have made you sleepy."

"Oh no, I'm wide awake. In fact, I think I'll be up for quite a while, planning another great meal for tomorrow." Rino groaned. "Oh," she said, "a wave of sleepiness just came over me."

Without talking, they walked down the hall to the bedroom, Lee leading the way. Inside the room, Lee turned to him and asked him to sit down on the bed. She walked over to the closet and took out two boxes wrapped in red, white, and green stripes. She returned to him and stood before him. "These are for you," she said.

He seemed flustered. He tried not to tear the wrapping paper. But he was fumbling and awkward in his nervousness. He looked up at her for help, and she gently assisted him. She held the paper, helping him to unwrap each box. Inside the large one was a robe of light blue wool, thin and soft and floor length, with a tie at the waist. It seemed more of a dressing gown than a bathrobe. In the smaller box were black leather slippers with open backs.

Instead of speaking, he reached for her, buried his face in the warmth of her belly, and held his arms around her hips. She cradled his head in both her arms and held him. For several minutes, they stayed in that embrace. Then, as he looked up to her, she sat beside him on the bed. "I like them a lot," he said. "Thank you."

She nodded to him and brushed his hair off his forehead. "You have no idea how hard it was to find the Italian colors in this paper," she said. "It took me an hour for the robe and slippers and three hours for the paper."

They made love slowly and languorously that night. He fell asleep easily, and she, content to hear his heavy breathing during sleep, fell asleep beside him, nestled in his arms and trying to touch him with every part of her body.

The next day, Sammy grinned broadly when he saw Rino. "Hey, goombah," he said. "I have a ballbuster for you today."

"What you mean is that you, Polski, can't do something. Right?"

"Okay, okay. We have to run a conduit and wire down to Chandler's office. He's getting a computer terminal."

"We have to go through any walls?"

"Yeah. But that shouldn't be much trouble. I'll help you."

"Jesus Christ. You? You remember how to work, Sam? Or do I just have to worry about being electrocuted?"

"I want to learn from the master," said Sammy half-seriously.

"You got that right, stash," said Rino.

The work was dirty and difficult. They ran conduit in the dark through walls and ceilings, above recessed ceiling tiles, and across great lengths of space. The sawing and drilling they had to do was the most time-consuming and difficult part of the job. But finally, with the extra help of Barly and Joe, they got it done by the time the day was over.

Chandler wasn't in his office when Rino pulled the lead wire through the conduit and wired up the junction box. He had it all set for the computer installers to use immediately. It was, as usual, a good job, neat and professional looking.

They were both grimy and sweaty when they sat in Sammy's office, talking about the day's work. "I'm going to be gone a few weeks soon, Sam."

"When?"

"Well, you know I'm off next week. Then I might have to be off for a couple weeks after that."

"Three goddamned weeks! What if they need some more wiring? What am I gonna do?"

"That Puerto Rican kid in the science building used to be an electrician's mate in the navy. I'm sure he can do it. You know, Sam, one of these days I'm going to quit this bullshit."

Sammy nodded knowingly. "Well," he sighed, "let me know about those other two weeks." He paused for a few seconds. "That'll be November. Where the hell you going in November?"

"Honeymoon," said Rino casually.

"Right. Honeymoon... you and your high button shoes," said Sammy, not believing him.

"I'll let you know, Sam." *Hell,* Rino thought, *that's what everybody's going to do when they hear it.* He fretted at the traffic going home. By the time he showered and ate supper, he'd be late to Lee's apartment.

But when he drove down the street to his house, the driveway was full of cars. Frankie's and Nancy's, Jerry's Cadillac... *Wonder what the hell's going on?* he said to himself.

He parked in front of the house, on the street. It bothered him for his kids to see him so dirty and foul smelling, especially Jerry, who never felt that Rino lived up to expectations, anyway. They had become so middle class that his being a janitor-maintenance man was an embarrassment to them. They had grudgingly accepted his job as a millwright. That would at least make him a skilled craftsman, someone elite among the millworkers. But there was no glossing over the maintenance job. And he didn't even have to work, Jerry would say repeatedly.

But, of course, he did need work. When they were young, they never understood his judgment and maturity, and when they were adults, they never understood his accommodations to life, the fear of age, the fear of dying. So the distance between them, parent and children, especially when the parent was suddenly growing again, changing and evolving, still meant trouble.

As he entered the kitchen from the back door, he realized that neither Jerry nor Nancy had been there for several months. Rino took off his shoes on the landing of the steps, hung his coat in the small closet there, and came upstairs. Jean met him in the kitchen with a strange look on her face. It wasn't fright, but anxiety at least.

"Everything okay?" Rino said.

"Dad, they're waiting for you in there."

That was strange in itself. Usually if one of them was visiting, they would greet him in the kitchen and begin to talk to him, especially if he or she had not been there in a while to see him.

Rino entered the living room and greeted each of them by name. "Frank, Jerry, Nancy. How are things? The kids okay?"

"Yeah, Pop," said Jerry, "the kids are fine. Rita's fine."

"Mine too, Daddy," said Nancy. "We're all fine."

"Good. Can I get any of you a drink or something?" said Rino. They declined.

Jerry was standing in front of the fireplace, and Nancy and Frank sat in separate chairs on either side of him. Jean handed Rino a cup of coffee royal and a saucer, his customary drink when he got home on cold days. Then she went to sit on the arm of Frank's chair.

This was not a spontaneous gathering. *This has the look of family business*, thought Rino. He opened the conversation, but in a little less fawning and jovial tone than he would normally use. "So? What's up?" he said.

"I think it's time we had a talk, Pop," said Jerry, who was obviously the spokesman for the group. Frank looked very uncomfortable. Nancy kept avoiding her father's gaze. "We've been hearing some disturbing stories," Jerry said.

If there had been any doubt in Rino's mind about the purpose of the gathering, it was gone now. He was about to be upbraided by his children for living in a forbidden, secret fantasy world and for doing something that was probably immoral, and worst of all—he could see it in their eyes—embarrassing. But his blood began to flow faster, impelled not by contrition but by resentment. "What stories?" he said wearily.

"Daddy," Nancy said, fearful of what Jerry might say in his obstreperous way. "Are you going out with someone?"

Rino panned the room in an instant, looking into the eyes of each of them. "Yes," he said. "Is there anything wrong with that?"

"Well, not that," said Nancy uneasily.

"Frank said you often stay out overnight, and half the time you don't even let them know what you're doing," said Jerry.

"Frank knows—or he should know—that I can take care of myself. I've been doing it since before he was born," said Rino. "And I'm not senile yet."

"Doesn't he have a right to an explanation? After all, he lives here, too," Jerry insisted.

"I promised him one," said Rino softly, still standing, poised against the rest of them arrayed around the other half of the room.

"Pop," Jerry said, "we've heard that this person you've been seeing is just a young girl."

Rino flashed a look at Jean, who was sitting in helpless despair opposite him. She had moved away from the arm of Frank's chair to neutral ground. "Did you say anything?" he muttered barely audibly to her.

"No," she said softly, hurt by the tone, which he had never used on her.

Frank vaulted to the edge of his seat. "What do you mean, say anything? What could she have said? What did you tell her?"

"I've talked to her." Jean sighed. "We met right here in the kitchen last Saturday. Dad brought her."

"And you didn't tell me, for God's sake!" Frank said angrily.

"I asked her not to say anything for a few days, Frankie," said Rino. "I wanted to find the right time, the right way to tell all of you. I was going to bring her here—probably this weekend."

Frank snorted and shook his head in disbelief, still glaring at Jean.

"How old is this girl, Daddy?" asked Nancy.

Rino could see that they already had some idea of what he would answer. "33," he said quietly.

"Jesus Christ!" said Jerry, turning to his brother. "Can you believe it now, Frank?"

Frank didn't answer.

Rino made one last try to settle it. "Look. Why don't you all go home? The way we're doing this now isn't right. We can talk later. I want you all to meet her soon. I swear you'll be crazy about her."

"Go home?" Jerry said. "Pop, I canceled my patients, and Nancy was supposed to be helping Phil in the shop today. All that just to come down here before this thing got out of hand. Don't you owe us a better answer than 'go home'?"

"Owe you, Jerry?" Rino said coldly. "Did you come all the way from Akron just to tell me that I owe you?"

"Pop, for God's sake, she's 33 years old! My own daughter's almost 22. Don't you see what all this looks like?" Jerry said. "There has to be something wrong with a girl who—"

"Who are you all so damned worried about?" Rino said. "Your kids? Me? Or your own reputations? I told you—all of you..." He looked around the room at them, suddenly softening his tone. "That you're jumping to conclusions. You don't even know her."

"It's embarrassing, Pop," said Frank. "People see you out with her, and they ask me about it. Half the time they're just grinning."

"Look, kids, I know it's hard—"

"We're not kids; that's the trouble," Jerry snapped. "And we can see things about this that you're too infatuated to see."

Rino summoned the last bit of patience and calm that he had in him. He began to speak slowly. "Look, there's nothing wrong. We don't bother anybody; we keep to ourselves. Now, I just can't believe that my taking that girl to a restaurant can cause you all such shame. My God, no one gives a damn about what people do anymore. It's just you."

"Daddy, it wouldn't be the first time that a young girl went after a man for his money. She must know what you've got," said Nancy.

"Nancy, look, I've set you all up just fine. Leave it alone. She doesn't want my money. She's got her own—maybe more than I have. But even if she did, you're all in good shape now. Don't I have the right to spend some of my money the way I want?"

"But, Pop, this is crazy," Jerry cried, his voice growing shriller. "It's an embarrassment to all of us. It's the shame of it. How do you think Libby and Larry feel when they see their own grandfather catting around town and shacking up with a chippy young enough—"

Jean gasped at Jerry's words at the same time that Rino threw his cup and saucer down on an end table with a crash. The saucer cracked apart, and the coffee spilled all over the table. But no one paid any heed to anything but Rino's voice, because it was a prelude to something they had never seen before.

Rino's face contorted into a snarl, and his eyes narrowed. He spoke in a quietly menacing voice, "Did you say 'shacking up,' Jerry? You know, in this whole thing, aside from my love for that girl, all I've ever thought about was whether all of you would accept her. But you know something? Right now, I don't give a goddamn whether you accept her or not. And this is as good a time as any to tell you: I'm going to marry her, whether you like it or not, whether you want it or not... without your blessing that I gave each of you when you got married—and, so help me God, without any of you being there."

He paused to catch his breath as he realized all his muscles were tensed, and his forefinger was gesturing at them in his anger. "Now, Jerry and Nancy, you get the hell out of this house." Then he turned to Frank. "And you. You couldn't just give me the benefit of the doubt, could you? That I could be doing something clean and right rather than dirty and wrong?" With a glance at Jean, who called to him, begging him not to be angry with them, he left the room and went upstairs.

He showered and shaved quickly, still fuming at the words that had passed between him and his children. He thought about their presumption—the audacity of them to think that he could be an old fool and that they could not be young fools.

He dressed and went downstairs hurriedly, still preoccupied with his children, wishing he had said so many things or said them better. Everyone had gone, even Frank. Libby and Larry had come home, but for the first time in their lives, they had witnessed their father and mother and grandfather all estranged. They were in their rooms, and in the house there was an awful quiet.

As he entered the kitchen to go out the side door, Jean was standing there alone, cleaning up after a ruined supper. They looked at each other; her eyes were red from crying, her hair uncombed and matted. Her voice was barely a whisper. "I'm so sorry, Dad." Then she covered her face with her hands, and new tears flowed down her cheeks.

Rino took her in his arms and kissed her. "I put myself between you and your husband, kid. I was a damned fool. I had no right to do that."

"If only he would listen," she said. Rino wiped her eyes and nose with his handkerchief. "He makes me so mad sometimes!" she said in frustration.

He held her at arm's length to look at her. "I was just angry with them. I'll get over it. But I wasn't mad at you, okay?"

She smiled, looking still unconvinced. "I might have been just like them unless I'd seen her," she said.

"Well, you're going to see her more often," he said gently. "Listen, I'm not coming back tonight. Let Frankie know, okay?"

She nodded. "You deserve all the happiness you can get, Dad."

When he arrived at Lee's apartment, she was waiting for him in gray slacks and a white turtleneck sweater. It was already dark outside. "Hi," she said, kissing him.

"You look wonderful," he said.

"What's in here?" she said, pointing to the duffel bag he was carrying.

"Work clothes for tomorrow," he said.

She beamed at his words. "You're finally catching on, aren't you?"

They talked a little about what they had done that day, she about the library and he about work.

"Rino, is something wrong?" she said, finally.

"No," he said, angry with himself for not being able to hide his troubles from her.

She looked at him again. "There is, isn't there?"

"Yeah, a little. We had a big blowout at my house tonight."

"Who? You and Frank?"

"No... the whole crew. Nancy and Jerry and Frank were waiting there when I got home from work." He shrugged to somehow sort out what troubled him. "We had an argument... and," he sighed, "I threw them all out."

"Oh, Rino, was it that bad?"

"When I told them you were 33 years old, it was bad. It was just the way they did it, you know? They had all talked it over, decided it was wrong. And that was it."

"Did Jean tell them?"

"No. And that was another problem. I asked her not to say anything about you, not even to Frank, at least for a few days. So when Frankie found out that she had met you in our house, he blew a fuse."

"Well, what happened? Did they just go?"

"I guess so. I told them to get out and then went upstairs to take a shower. When I came back down, they were all gone—except Jean."

"God, she must have felt awful," Lee said.

"Yeah. But we talked a little before I came here. She'll be okay. I feel bad because I put her in that position against Frank. What the hell was I thinking, to do that?"

"Maybe you're in love. They say it makes you act funny sometimes... clouds your judgment," said Lee.

"Yeah, but they didn't want to hear any explanations. They just wanted to believe the worst."

"How do you feel now?" she said, trying to lighten up his mood.

"Better," he said.

"Well, good. Let's watch television like an old married couple, okay?" she said.

"Sure. What do you want to see?" he said.

"There's an old movie. A mystery with Van Johnson."

She put the television on and sat back on the couch. In a few minutes, the movie started, and she curled up next to him. A feeling of contentment came over Rino—the warmth of her body against his, the peace and stillness of the apartment, the soft light, the sound of her regular breathing, the scent of her hair and skin. Out of the corners of his eyes, he watched her as she looked intently at the screen. He felt a warm rush as he studied her profile, her hair, her eyes. *How beautiful she is*, he thought, *especially when she's concentrating on something and thinks no one is looking. Could she really be in love with me?*

It was a mystery to him. He could understand any man falling in love with her, but he couldn't imagine her falling in love with him. *Jesus, what the hell could she see in me that some younger, handsomer, richer guy in much better shape doesn't have? And yet, with all those guys out there who would give their eyeteeth just to touch her, she waits in this place for me to visit her every night... waits to have our baby.* He took a deep breath. Mystery.

He paid just enough attention to the movie to follow the course of events. And grew more restless as the movie went on. She sensed it, but she stayed close to him, stopping only once at intermission to put a drink in one glass for them to share. When the movie was over, she turned to him and said, "Now. What's the trouble?"

"No trouble. What d'you mean?"

"You didn't enjoy the movie. Why not?"

"I've seen it," he said.

"Don't lie to me," she said playfully, shaking his arm.

"About 10 years before you were born," he said.

"You couldn't have. The movie's not that old."

"Well, maybe five years," he said.

"Why didn't you watch that movie, Bellanca?" she said.

"I sat right here beside you and watched it, didn't I?"

"What were you thinking about?" she asked.

He shrugged. "You."

"Me, what?"

"Your... body," he said, chuckling.

She pushed him again. "Is that true?"

"I told you, dirty old men can't stand to have young girls near them and not want to touch."

"What did you have in mind?" she said.

"I can't explain it. I have to show you."

"Here?"

"No. Down the hall, to the right," he said as straight-faced as he could.

When they walked to the bedroom, she wanted him to be in bed before her. She helped him undress, and he got into bed. Then she slowly took off her clothes: slacks, panties, sweater, and bra. As he lay there, he was fascinated by her—not just her beauty, but by the ease and grace with which she moved and the natural, unselfconscious way she could stand naked before him.

As she put her knee on the bed to swing her hips onto it, she said, "Now, what were you going to show me?"

"I better be careful here. I don't want to promise more than I can deliver."

"Too late now, Bellanca," she said.

This was something new to them: making love for the sheer joy of it, playing and experiencing pleasure. Lee had never felt the release she was able to feel with Rino. It was as though, in the face of the outside world that had wearied and punished her, she was able to work her own magic with a good, loving man whose thoughts were undistorted by guilt or pride. She was able to be her best self, to be guiltless and happy and gentle and caring. Modesty and decorum were secondary to the natural instinct to make Rino happy.

As they kissed, he explored her body, the body that always looked better than he could ever imagine it. It was as though whenever he had fully appreciated her softness and lean musculature, the curve of her calves, the soft flow of her thighs, she always changed, and he saw new muscles, new dimples, and new curves to excite him. Her breasts would seem fuller than he remembered, yet... as she stretched on her back, they'd flatten out into small, graceful mounds that rose above the low, flat plane of her belly. Her ribs were not lean and countable; she was compact enough to be smooth and glossy.

He liked to be on the bottom sometimes, having her atop him so that he could nurse on the firm, small, brown nipples and smother his face in the fabulous softness of her breasts. This night, she crooned words of love and encouragement to him as she rubbed her pelvis against his.

Then, to her surprise, he began to urge her upward, seemingly over his head. At first, she didn't understand what he wanted, but at his urging she moved upward until his two hands stopped her by grasping her upper thighs. She sat astride his head, with her knees on either side of his neck. Then his mouth went to her vagina, his lips and tongue exploring her labia and her clitoris. She gasped and made little squeaking noises deep in her throat. As he continued, she began to lose control of herself and churned her hips against his mouth as he held her fast to his lips. Finally, she was engulfed in an orgasm that made her shudder and stretch herself upward on her knees. She felt faint. Her breath came in gasps, her mouth seemed dry, and her skin tingled. She was always conscious of his lips upon her, and she climaxed again and then again.

Finally, she moved away from him to the position she had been in before, lying with her body on top of his. She kissed him, looking into his eyes, and said, "I love you so much, Rino."

"Heaven can't be better than this," he said. They lay still a few minutes without talking. "Lee, don't you ever wonder, why us? Why you and me?"

"I did at first, because you were something I never expected. My life was so miserable. Ted's death, and the way he did it... I had given up hope of ever being happy."

He ran his hand over her leg that she had draped across his body. It felt so smooth and soft to his touch that he shook his head in wonderment. She would often rub her feet against his legs or move her breasts near his face or her lips near his. She liked to be in the air he breathed; she liked him to feel her and sense her whenever they were close. She knew what touching meant. She knew that it was a way of offering herself to him, to be close to his hands and mouth and body, every fiber of him.

"You drive me crazy when we make love, Rino. I lose control and forget where I am." She swung her leg across him, and one foot slipped out of the covers. He looked at the slender, still-tanned foot peeking out.

"You changed your nail color," he said.

"Uh-huh... something different. Do you like it? I'll change it if you don't."

"I like it," he said.

"Rino?"

"What?"

"Did you and Mary make love the way we do... all the things we do? Did Mary do what I just did to you?"

He sighed. "No." Then he reflected for a moment. "We never had this. So I guess I never expected it. We were different—not like you and I are. But it was still good enough to be happy with her."

The next morning, Lee was merrily making breakfast as Rino came into the kitchen dressed in his new robe. "See?" she said. "I can always make breakfast for us when we're married." She had the short, powder-blue robe on that he liked so much, the one that showed her legs.

"Aren't you cold in that?" he said.

"Sometimes. But I like it when you look at me in it."

"That was when I looked but couldn't touch. I'm way beyond that now," he said. "Hell, I undress you in my mind anyway, no matter what you wear."

She came to him as he sat down, poured him coffee, and kissed him. "I'm not going to see you much this week," he said thoughtfully.

"Aren't you coming Thursday?" she asked.

"Yeah. But first I have to go see Connie, tell her about you, and get ready for the trip. Let's go out Saturday night, okay?"

"Sure. Where to?"

"Someplace for dinner."

When he arrived at the college, he met Joe Potokar and Barly. Today they would change the fluorescent lights, and Rino would put new ballasts in some of the fixtures. "How you been, Rino?" said Joe. "I ain't talked to you much since I got back."

"I'm okay, Joe. How's the wife?"

"Fine. She says for me to bring you home for some pig in the blankets someday."

"Tell her I'd be honored," Rino said sincerely. "They're the best I've ever had." Despite his sometimes-gruff manner, he was also very cordial and polite to people he liked.

"Wonder where Sammy is?" said Joe as they worked. Rino did the wiring, and Joe helped him with the tools and ladders. "I ain't seen him all morning."

"His car was in the lot when I came in," Rino said. "I'm sure he's here."

Just then Barly came off the elevator onto the floor where Rino and Joe were working. When he found them, he said, "Hey, Rino, Sammy just called me. Said he wants you and me to come right down to his office." He seemed puzzled.

"What's he got, Bar? Another scaffold job?"

When they got to Sammy's office, he had a strange look on his face. "What's up, Sam?" said Rino pleasantly.

"Close the door," he said.

Rino and Barly looked at each other. "Sit down," Sammy said. "This is a union conference."

Rino laughed. "Cut the bullshit, Sam. How high's the scaffold?"

"I'm not kidding," Sammy said somberly. "Barly, you have to be here because you're the union rep."

"What the fuck's going on, Sam?" said Barly.

"Look. Let me go through the motions on this one, okay? Then I can tell the bastard that I did it. Here it is: Chandler has accused Rino of stealing money from his office—and for damaging his new computer."

"When?" said Rino angrily, trying hard to control his temper.

"The day we ran the cable to his office," Sam said.

"And how much was I supposed to steal?" Rino said.

"52 dollars... and he says you cracked the stand of his new TV monitor."

"52 fucking dollars and a piece of cracked plastic!" Rino screamed, his face red with rage. "I lose 52 dollars in poker before midnight." He was trembling. Of all the people in the world who could make him lose control, it was the new enemy who haunted him at the college.

"Now, come on, Rino. Calm down so I can finish this. I've been up in the dean's office all morning. I finally told him that unless that fucking Chandler can come up with something better than an accusation, he'd better shut his goddamned mouth."

"Where was this money?" said Barly to Sammy. Then he turned to Rino. "Did you see 52 dollars up there?"

"No! I was doing my job. I didn't see any goddamned money. You need 52 dollars, Barly? Here it is in my wallet. Why would I have to rifle someone's office to get it?"

"Okay, man, okay. I'm with you."

"What's his program, Sam? Why is he trying all this chickenshit stuff?" said Rino.

"I told you, Rino. He's a prick. And once he has a hard-on for someone, he goes after them, janitor or president."

"So what now?"

"So, nothing. See, he likes to throw out a lot of accusations he can't prove. Then he drags you into it, tries to fuck your name over, then walks away. He's an asshole, but he doesn't have the balls for a big fight."

"So what's he gonna do now?" said Barly.

"Nothing. I told the dean that this is stupid. I also told him that I'd formally notify you of the accusation, but that's it. Unless Chandler wants to keep it going—which he won't—then this meeting is the end."

For a moment, all three were silent in their thoughts. Then Barly said to Rino, "We could grieve this one, man."

"But why keep it going now?" said Sammy fretfully. "You know Chandler isn't going anywhere with this. Let it die, Rino."

Rino shook his head. "No, Sam, Barly's right on this one. The only way he's gonna get off my back is if I shove this one up his ass." Then he turned to Barly. "Here's what I want out of it: I want a letter to the dean—and to me—saying that Chandler had no goddamned reason in the world to smear my name and," Rino's features hardened, "that he's fucking sorry."

"Jesus Christ, guys," said Sammy. "Why back him to the wall over this little thing? No one knows now but Chandler and the dean. If you grieve it, you get me, the vice president, the union involved, and then the whole goddamned world will know it."

"Maybe it's time they should," said Rino. "Maybe everybody should think about what a no-good bastard he really is."

"This is crazy, Barly. Talk to him. It doesn't make sense," Sammy said.

"Sam," said Rino, "you know he's a prick who never gives up. So if I let this one ride, he'll be back at me again, right? No. You tell the dean this grievance is coming. I want my letter."

When they left Sammy's office, Barly was shaking his head. "Man, I hate grievances."

"Hey, Barly, that's why you drive the big car. It's your business."

"Yeah, I know. But you're gonna push this one all the way to arbitration, ain't you? Chandler won't give in because he's one of them nobles, and you won't give in because he's a prick. So here's Barly in a goddamn hornet's nest with a pissed-off rich man and a pissed-off dago."

"Barly, you know this is the right way, don't you?"

Barly reluctantly agreed. "Yeah, I know," he said. "But I also knew this was coming."

"How?" said Rino.

"Because when you don't like someone, they can see it in your face. Understand? You don't have to do nothing or say nothing. In your face, they see you hate them. And Chandler sees it all the time."

That night at the Tucker Café, Rino was telling Lou about Chandler. "He's a goddamned malandrine, Lou. Every time I think I'm done with him, he tries to start something."

"But what'd you ever do to him?"

"Barly says he can see I don't like him in my face. Can you believe that? A prof who's just been elected department chairman worried about nailing a janitor? I think he has a screw loose."

"So how's the family?" said Lou, changing the subject.

Rino raised his eyebrows in a gesture of resignation and dismay. "I have to go see Connie tomorrow... and tell her. That'll be fun," he said sardonically.

"Frankie called me today. Says he feels bad about what happened."

"They all should feel bad, goddamn it."

"Rino, you know how this looks to them. They think you've lost your mind. They think she's some conniving little bitch who's after your money."

"Hey, Lou, did your kids ever call it 'shacking up' with Annie? Well, my kids did. And they don't know a goddamned thing about Lee."

"Look, kid, I've seen her, and I've seen you, and I have to tell you, it would look strange to me, too, from a long way off. I believe it only because you're my brother and I know you."

"Luigi, I never felt like this before. Never," said Rino.

Lou stared at Rino for a long moment. "You see what I mean, cowboy? That's what scares everybody. You've known this kid for only a few months, and you're telling me you've got more with her than you did with Mary in 40 years, right? How in the hell can you expect people like your kids to understand it? Or like it? Mary was their mother."

"I never dishonored Mary, Lou. I loved her and treated her right. But it's over. And I don't know why, but this kid means more."

"Hey, look, maybe it's—don't get this wrong now—but maybe it's because... because you're closer to the end of your life than you were. It's easy to see how you could feel this way about a girl so young and beautiful. It must seem like heaven just to touch her. But what happens when you can't get it up for her in 10, 12 years? Are you just gonna look at her? She's gonna want you to do what you do now. Jesus, Rino, someday our kids are gonna have to take care of us—if we live that long. Do you want her to have to take care of you when she's 45 and still looks like a million bucks?"

Rino didn't answer. Could Lou, who never seemed to be wrong about life, be seeing it the only way it could be? As they talked, Marty and Pete came to sit at their table, and that ended the serious conversation.

But through the evening, Lou began to worry about his brother again. Maybe he had hurt him. *Maybe he thinks that by talking that way, I'm wishing it away*, he thought. *Maybe he thinks I envy him, so I'm always looking at the wrong side of this. Hell, maybe I am. Yet why shouldn't he, of all people, have that magic chance to have it all work out? There is something different about that girl.*

Look at him, Lou thought. *He dreams of her when he's not with her. And he's the same guy who has fought for me and cried with me and been by my side through so many dark nights. How could he ever be a fool? Jesus. This thing is for real.*

After supper, it was about 9:30. Rino and Lou stood in the Tucker parking lot near their cars. "Look, I'm sorry," Lou said. "I just let my own doubts get in the way. You want to know the God's truth? You're thinking young, and I'm thinking old.

"Listen: take this girl and make a life with her. She deserves you, and you sure as hell deserve her. And when your kids call me from now on, I'm gonna tell them to mind their own goddamned business. That's not a bad idea for me, either."

When Rino knocked on Lee's door, she greeted him with a smile. But as he entered, she could sense that he was pensive and dispirited. She kissed him lightly and took his coat. "How was your day?" she said, hoping he had not been hurt again by his family.

"Not bad. How was yours?" he said. She followed him to the couch and sat next to him.

"What's the trouble?" she said as she straightened his collar and smoothed his windblown hair.

"I just had a long talk with Lou." Rino shifted his weight on the couch. "I think he feels just like everybody else. He can't see how a young girl like you can decide to live with an old man. It always means trouble."

"Trouble?"

"Trouble because I won't be able to satisfy you... because I might get sick or senile..."

"Rino, why do you always insist you won't be able to 'satisfy' me? Other men are happily married to younger girls. Do you really think we're unique? Rino, we could live another 20 years just like we are now... maybe longer." He raised his eyebrows in a silent gesture of doubt. "Am I that easy, Rino?" she said with an edge in her voice. "God, I don't know what to say to you about it anymore. If you think I could just transfer my feelings to someone else..." As she listened to the words she was saying, she grew more hurt and more resentful. She stood up and moved away from him.

He had never seen her upset at him or angry with anyone. "You must not think too much of what I say and do, Rino. Could I respond the same no matter who touches me? Isn't there anything special there because of you?"

She walked around the side of the couch to get a tissue for her eyes. But he grabbed her wrist as she walked past him. She stopped but tugged her hand to free it. He held it firmly, looking up and imploring her not to be hurt. Finally, she relaxed and stopped straining against him. He pulled her over the side of the couch into his arms and then buried his face in her neck and held her tightly. She was surprised at the force with which he clung to her.

"I never want to lose you, Lee," he said. "I'm so afraid that this is a dream, and I'm going to wake up someday and it'll all be gone."

She cradled his head in her arms as she sat astride him on his lap. "You'll never lose me, Rino," she said as she kissed his hair and his forehead. "You'll have me forever, just as I'll always have you... forever, Rino." He held her, gathering his thoughts about what she had said. Her soothing voice had worked its magic one more time. Then he held her away to look into her eyes. "Forever," she said again.

She sat back on his thighs, her hands clasped behind his neck. "I'm a damned fool," he said disgustedly. "I let other people convince me that you're somehow different than I know you are. I begin to doubt you when..."

"It's you, isn't it, Rino? You're afraid of me."

He nodded. "I know so many guys who've been looking all their lives for somebody like you but then settle for something less... and end up bored and sour. So why me, huh? That's what I think all the time."

"Rino, what you see in me is you. With anyone else I'm not the same Leila that you know. Don't you realize that?" She stopped and lowered her eyes away from his. Then she looked back at him. "There were times with Ted that we didn't have sex for weeks—sometimes months. And I never needed it, never missed it. Did you hear what I said? 'Have sex,' not make love. Make love is what you and I do, Rino. And you don't have to worry when you're too old or sick to make love with me. I'll have you near me, and these memories will be enough. I'll have someone else near me, too."

He suddenly thought of her last words. "No period, huh?" he said.

"No period, Daddy," she said as she kissed him. She moved away to look at his face, her eyes sparkling again and her wide mouth glistening in a broad smile.

"I'm not playing poker tomorrow night," he said.

"Why not?"

"Because I'm leaving Sunday, and I want to be with you."

"You're giving up poker just to be with me?" she said, smiling.

"Yeah. Amazing, isn't it? But it's only for this special occasion."

"You mean you're not going to give up Friday-night poker after we're married?" she said, taunting him.

"I don't give up anything I've been doing since before you were born. That has to be part of the deal."

"That isn't fair, Rino!" she said with a squeal, shaking his head by the ears.

He wrestled with her and caught her wrists together in front of her. She reached forward and gave him a long, open-mouthed kiss, and her tongue played in his mouth, reaching for his. He was breathing heavily after she moved away. "Now who isn't playing fair?" he said. He had lost control of her wrists.

She was delighted with the power she had over him. But she used it only in play, never for something serious. She wouldn't manipulate someone she loved.

"What are we going to do tomorrow night?" she said.

"Let's go somewhere where we can have a drink."

"Will you take me to a movie?" she said.

"Sure. Which one?"

"I'll pick one out... something old."

She got up off his lap and sat beside him on the couch. "I'm sorry I hurt you," he said. "I never want to do that."

"I'm sorry I talked to you that way, too," she said. "I can't believe I could ever get mad at you."

"After we're married, I'll make you mad enough to strangle me. Once I've got you, I can show my true colors—being an old-fashioned dago husband."

"Then I'll show my true colors, too. I'll be an evil witch, and I can stop being so nice to you."

"You couldn't do anything evil if you tried," he said, patting her thigh with his hand.

She snorted. "I'm capable of it, Rino. I've done it."

"I don't believe that. What seems bad to you is probably normal for everybody else," he said.

"Do you really feel that way about me?" she said.

He nodded.

Until almost midnight, they lay in bed together talking about their wedding and the baby. He lay on his back, and she lay on her belly, looking at him as they talked. Later she rolled on her back and rested part of her body against him. Finally, he put his arm around her, pulling her close to him backward, and they both fell asleep.

Lou had been fixing shoes for most of his life. It was his sideline. All the children of immigrants seemed to have sidelines in Youngstown. When he retired from the mill in 1978, shoemaking became his hobby and his work. But, lately, it barely paid the overhead. The shop was a 15-by-30 room that had a small sun porch jutting from the side of it. There was a vacant corner lot next to the shop that Lou owned and kept green and mowed.

As customers would enter the shop, they'd meet the short part of an L-shaped counter. At each side of the entrance there were chairs where people could wait to have their shoes repaired, though almost no one did that anymore. In front of the sun porch was a gas heater that made the small shop warm even on the coldest days of winter. The sun porch was lined with a bench covered with leather pads. In the middle of the small porch was a large, low coffee table strewn with magazines and ashtrays.

The long part of the counter, hinged at the back end, faced the sun porch. Awls, knives, hammers, and other exotic tools were lined up neatly in racks along the long side where Lou worked. Behind the counter, against the wall, was a massive lathe that turned grinders, buffers, and sanders by means of a series of straps that ran from one axle to another. The Machine was what Lou called it. It always groaned to a start and vibrated more than it once did and ran too noisily, but he was satisfied that it would last long enough for all the shoes he would ever fix in his lifetime.

Rino had taken Lee's car to be tuned up at a garage near Lou's shop. The owner, Hugo, was a good friend and offered him a ride to Lou's place while the car was being serviced.

Lou was standing, reading the newspaper that he had spread on the counter. "How're you doing, cowboy?" said Rino.

Lou looked surprised. "I'll be damned," he said. "You haven't been here in weeks."

"Last time I came, the coffee was stale and you were out of anisette," Rino said brightly.

"What are you up to?" his brother asked.

"I'm getting Lee's car tuned up down at Hugo's. She's going to spend the week in Canton while we're gone."

"That where she's from?"

"Yeah. Her mother lives there—a widow. And she's got a married older sister in Akron."

"What nationality is she?" Lou asked.

"Swiss and French... Alsatian, I think. Gallatin was her maiden name."

"You can't get those French girls out of your mind, can you, Rino?"

"Does she look French to you?" Rino asked, suddenly curious.

"Of course," said Lou. "She has that look we used to talk about during the war, when I'd come down to see you in Paris."

"Well? Like what?"

"I don't know. But French girls look different somehow. Some are sexy but not beautiful, some are beautiful but not sexy... and like your Lee, some are both sexy and beautiful."

"Does she really look like that, Lou?" said Rino, almost as a revelation to himself.

"She sure as hell does," Lou said, smiling smugly as he poured his brother a cup of coffee and a side glass of anisette.

"So what if she does?" said Rino, chuckling to himself. "Anyway, it's not her body; it's her mind that I'm interested in."

Lou groaned. "Right. But her mind is somewhere inside that body, kid. And that's the biggest line of bullshit I've heard in years." Lou poured himself more coffee. "Did you ever find out why her husband killed himself?"

"She doesn't like to talk about it much. And I don't try to pry it out of her. I know they weren't very happy."

"That right? What was he like?" Lou said.

"I don't know... kind of standoffish, I guess... a scholar... more interested in a career than he was in her. She was just window dressing."

"But some guys just get a divorce and move on," said Lou. "This one did a job on himself."

"Yeah. Crazy, huh? If Lee can't make someone happy, he's really in bad shape."

"She didn't make him happy, Rino. He put a noose around his neck."

"Yeah," said Rino thoughtfully. "There has to be something else to it, but I don't know what it is. She cared enough for him. It just about blew her away when he died."

Lou shrugged. It was something not to be pursued. "Have you heard from any of your kids?" he said.

"No," said Rino.

"They're probably afraid to call you... or ashamed," he said matter-of-factly.

"They'll get over it," said Rino. He was in no mood to hear a lecture about his kids.

"What are you going to do with this girl, Rino? Frankie—"

"Frankie?" said Rino, his voice rising.

"Yeah, Frankie. What'd you expect? He called me again last night. He says you're getting married."

"What's wrong with that, Lou, goddammit?"

"Nothing's wrong, kid. Take it easy. All I'm asking is if there's anything I can do."

"You can be best man if you want," Rino said.

"What d'you mean 'if I want'? Of course I want to," said Lou.

"Maybe if you think it's a bad idea; you don't want to be part of it."

"Shut up, Rino. Before you make me mad."

Just then, a horn blew in front of the shop. Hugo had brought the car. Rino turned to his brother. "I'll see you Saturday. I'm not playing poker tomorrow night."

"Not playing poker?" Lou said in wonderment.

"I can't, Lou. I'm gonna be gone all next week. I... well, I have to see her the next two nights."

Lou nodded. "Are you all packed?" he said.

"All but a few things. I'll do the rest tomorrow. See you later, huh?" It was a conciliatory tone, a question almost, to see if Lou was feeling bad about all the changes in their once-placid lives.

Lou understood Rino's intent. "Take it easy, cowboy. Maybe if you're not there, I'll win a few hands tomorrow night."

Rino nodded and walked out to the car to drive Hugo back to the gas station.

After he paid Hugo, Rino checked his watch. It was 11:30. He drove faster than he usually did; the Rogers Library was on the other side of town. The car seemed to drive better now that it had been tuned up. Everything was ready for Lee's trip to Canton. The tires were in good shape. It was a nice little Pontiac.

When he arrived at the library, he could see his own car, which Lee had driven, parked in a small employee's lot opposite the side entrance. In a few minutes, when she got into Rino's car, Lee said, "Is my car fixed already?"

"Yeah, it's all set. It's a nice little car."

"How much was it?"

"71 dollars. But Hugo does a good job."

"I'll give it to you tonight."

"Give me what?" he said.

"The money," she said.

He frowned. "Leila, you're carrying our baby, and you're going to marry me in two weeks, and you want to pay me for having your car fixed? Isn't that a little weird?"

She sighed. "All I wanted to do was make sure you weren't short of money because of me."

He grinned. "I'm never short of money, kid."

She punched him gently in the arm. "Well, you don't have to be so... so smug about it." Then she thought about what he had done. "Thank you for doing that for me. I hate getting my car serviced."

They ate at a small restaurant near the library. "How is it you have so much money?" she said.

"Millwrights make pretty good money and almost never get laid off, so Lou and I always did okay at the mill. And years ago, I used to do other side jobs: tend bar, put in storm windows. Once I bought into a bowling alley and made some money there. Then when I sold my share, Lou sold his, too, and we kept buying property whenever we could. We'd sell it off to builders. The best deals we made were when we sold some land to the developers of two shopping centers. That's what did the trick for us."

"I'm impressed, Mr. Bellanca," she said. "Your baby's going to be rich."

"Any baby that has you as a mother is gonna be rich, kid," he said.

She beamed at him. "But only with you as the father," she said.

When they were done eating, he drove her back to the library. "I'll see you after supper. I guess I'll go see Connie and then try to patch things up a bit at home," he said.

Rino spent the rest of the early afternoon with Connie. It wasn't easy, but it wasn't as hard as he had feared. At first, she was still troubled by Lee's age. But since Rino had come to her alone, without Lou, and talked to her earnestly, she softened after a short while.

"Is she as good as you say? You're not just being a damned old fool?"

"No. She's all heart, Con. You'll know it in a minute when you see her. And Jean likes her."

"Well... she's got more sense than any of your own kids, anyway."

"So what d'you think, kid?" Rino said.

She sighed. "I think I want you to be happy, Rino."

"Well... I want you to like her, Con. It's important."

"I'll like her, Guarino. But she better be good to you, or I'll hate her." He laughed. "You know, Rino," she said thoughtfully, "I know your kids gave you a hard time. But none of our kids know what it's like being lonely... and we do... so I want you to bring this girl to me before you get married. And she'll get my blessing. And I have some things upstairs I want to give her... some of Mom's... and some of mine."

Rino kissed her on the forehead. "You know, Con, I don't give you enough credit. You're just like Mom, you know that?"

Her eyes filled with tears, both at the invocation of her mother's name and because her brother had said the words. "Damn you, Rino," she blustered. Rino hugged her again. "Stay for supper," she said, wiping her eyes with her handkerchief.

"No, kid. Thanks. I have to go home and mend some fences."

"Bring her to me, Rino. Don't forget."

"As soon as I get back," he said.

Later, before everyone else got home, Rino was in the kitchen having coffee with Jean as she prepared supper. "How's your husband?" he said quietly.

"He's okay," Jean said. "He wants to... he wants to tell you he's sorry, but he's afraid you're still mad at him."

"I'm not mad at him." Rino sighed.

"Are you staying for supper tonight?" she said.

"Yeah."

Later, when Rino was alone reading in the family room, Frank walked in. "Hi, Pop," he said.

"How are you, Frankie?"

"Oh, okay, Pop. Look, I'm sorry about that whole damned thing the other night. We shouldn't have ganged up on you."

"It's okay, kid. I know you're sorry."

"You know Jerry felt bad about what he said, don't you? I don't know why he said it, but... well, he was frustrated, too."

"Being frustrated doesn't mean you can say anything you damned well please, does it? Especially when you don't know what you're talking about."

"No, Pop, it doesn't." Frank looked tired. "Pop, Jean says that your girl… that Lee is beautiful, and more than that, she's good."

"Do you believe her?"

"She's never wrong about people, Pop, especially other women. She says she believes this girl loves you, too—as young as she is."

"And as old as I am, right?"

Frank's face grew red. "It's just something I never thought would happen," he said.

"Neither did I, Frank," said Rino. "But I never thought your mother's death would happen, either."

"I should have listened to Jean—and to you. You have every right to be happy, too, Pop."

"Thanks, Frank. You know… we won't bother anybody. We'll live in her apartment. You can come to see us there anytime."

"You mean you're not going to live here?"

Rino shook his head. "This is your house, kid."

"You don't have to go, Pop."

"I want to. This is another life for me now, and I want a fresh start."

Frank's eyes were glistening. "Is it too late to give you my blessing, Pop?"

Rino shook his head. "No," he said softly.

Frank stood up, and so did Rino. Frank hugged his father and kissed him. "Every happiness and long life, Pop… for all you've been to us. Lee can call this her house for as long as she lives. And always remember that the first bedroom upstairs will always have a bed for both of you."

Rino was beginning to get misty. He patted his son's cheek in an Italian gesture of affection. "I'm sorry about Jean, Frank. I didn't mean to come between you. You know she wouldn't hurt you for the world."

Frank nodded. Rino went upstairs to change before supper.

That night, when Lee opened the door to let Rino in, she had on the short blue robe and was barefoot. "Jesus," said Rino when he first set eyes on her.

"No, Lee," she said, mocking him.

"Aren't you gonna be cold?" he said.

"Well, I thought you'd keep me warm. There's an afghan I can put over my legs... but if you think I should put slacks on..." She turned to walk toward the bedroom.

"No... no," he said frantically, grabbing her by the hand. She laughed at the way his voice sounded as he pulled her to him. "Damn," he said. "I can't believe you do this to me so easily. Who's being smug and arrogant now, huh?"

Her response was a warm, wet kiss that took his breath away.

"I take it we're not going out tonight," he said.

"I take it you're sleeping here tonight," she said, eyeing his duffel bag.

He snorted. "See what I mean?"

"When are we getting married, Daddy?" she said merrily as she led him to the couch. He sat down, and she sat beside him cross-legged. She put the afghan over her legs.

"How about the week after I get back?" he said.

"I know that, Bellanca. But what day?"

"I don't know. You pick the day. Girls are supposed to do that stuff, right?"

"Okay. Wednesday. Monday we'll get the license, and Tuesday we get everything arranged, and Wednesday—"

"And Wednesday I marry a 33-year-old 'chippy'—as my son says—who has a fantastic body."

She reached for his throat to choke him. He pulled her onto his lap and kissed her. She giggled through the kiss as she tried to keep the afghan over her legs. She pulled away. "In case you haven't noticed, I don't have much on, and it gets drafty this way."

He chuckled. "I really didn't notice," he said.

"Did you make peace with Frank?" she said, changing to a more serious mood.

"Yeah," he said. "I also told Connie about you. Frank gave us his blessing, and Connie wants to see you before we get married. She has some things of my mother's she wants to give you... and some of hers."

"Oh God, that's wonderful, Rino." She sighed.

"Frank seemed surprised when I said we'd live here. I guess he thought we'd live at the house."

"Do you want to live there?" said Lee.

"No. I want a fresh start."

She smiled to herself. As he was talking, his hand had infiltrated first under the afghan, and then under her robe, and then he began to gently touch her pubic hair. She kept talking. "I called Mother tonight... told her I was coming next week... and told her we were getting married the week after."

"What did she say?" he asked.

"She seemed relieved that you're making an honest woman of me... and glad. I think she was like your children. At first, she couldn't believe it and tried to talk me out of it, then she became resigned to it... now she wishes us happiness."

"Are we going to invite anyone to the ceremony?" he said.

"I don't know. We've been so private up to now. Only two people in your family have seen me, and no one in my family has seen you."

"I'll do whatever you want," said Rino. "Think about it next week."

"Mother did ask me to be married in church. Is that okay, Rino?"

"Sure."

"There's a Lutheran church that I go to occasionally. The pastor's very nice. He helped me a lot when Ted died. I'm sure he'd marry us."

"Call him tomorrow and set it up," said Rino.

She smiled, seemingly as delighted as a little girl. Yet all the time they were talking, his hand had been moving. His fingers caressed her labia, her clitoris, and the insides of her vagina. She was becoming wet, and his fingers were growing slippery.

It was becoming harder and harder for her to ignore what he was doing. Her breathing increased, and she shook her head, distracted. "What are you doing, Bellanca?" she said huskily, their faces now just a few inches apart.

Suddenly Rino, without taking his eyes from her, moved his wet, slippery hand from under her robe and the afghan and brought it to his lips. He licked the wetness from two of his fingers.

This released the tension that had been building since they first saw each other that night. She made a little cry in her throat and kissed him hungrily. They were both so aroused that they didn't bother going into the bedroom. They couldn't even get all their clothes off. He loosened the tie of her robe and unbuckled his trousers without taking them off. He led his penis easily into her. They made love wildly as he kissed her lips, her neck, and her breasts. They climaxed easily and quickly, then lay together in a mass of rumpled clothing, partly on and partly off. She kissed him again and again and whispered softly to him how much she loved him.

The next morning, Rino drove happily to the college. The weather was foggy and dreary, but the scent of Lee was still in his nostrils, the warmth of her still radiating from his body.

When he entered the utility room near Sammy's office, he went to the small locker room at the far end. Barly came up to talk to him. "Hey, Rino, we did the third stage of your grievance yesterday," he said.

"Third stage?" Rino said.

"Well, the first stage was the meeting with Sammy, right? Then the second's supposed to be with the chairman, but Chandler's the chairman. So we went to the dean—third step. Well, the dean, being a wimpy asshole, said that he had no right to tell a faculty member to apologize to anyone."

"Hell, you know he wasn't going to do anything, Barly. He can't embarrass one of his fair-haired boys."

"We tried to tell him it was only a letter, but he got pissed off. Like, who the hell are you to demand that a professor apologize to a custodian? Sammy tried to tell him that arbitration would cost them—and they'd sure as hell lose it anyway. But..."

"So now we go to step four, right?"

"The College Affairs Committee meets Friday. Since that's an all-college thing, maybe they'll have more sense than those guys in education."

"I'm on vacation next week, Bar. When the committee decides, how long does the president have before he does something?"

"One week."

"Good. Maybe in a couple weeks we'll know, huh?"

"You know, man, the union board might not want to go to arbitration on this. You realize that, don't you?" said Barly.

"Yeah, I know," Rino huffed. "But you know the reason for this, Barly. That son of a bitch keeps coming after me. I never even go near him if I don't have to."

"Yeah, yeah. Just keep my ass out of hearings from now on, y'hear?" Barly sighed.

That night, Rino felt lighthearted and relaxed. He would not work for three weeks. Chandler would be off his mind, the Canada trip would be over in a week, and he would marry Lee. Things were working out. Even Frankie had come around.

He sang as he shaved and showered. How long had he lived without feeling like this? Does everyone feel this good? Does every guy who's going to marry one of those young brides in the Sunday paper sing in the shower?

He put on new clothes again. The last few years he had gotten gifts for Christmas and Father's Day that he had never worn. The kids always wondered why. It was as though the newness bothered him; the quality of the gifts bothered him. His children always bought the best, season after season. Yet new, fine things never seemed to fit into his life then. They were the things a young man needed, someone who could look into the future and see time, years of life and dreams. But he had been afraid to imagine the future. So gifts were left in drawers or in boxes on the closet shelf. Old things suited him better.

But lately he had been dressing in new things. And he dressed for show in outfits that made him look good. And he dreamed of the future now, just like younger men: Lee, the baby, all the plans they had. It was good enough; he'd settle for a short future. What he couldn't face before was a future with no dreams left to fill it.

Downstairs, he said to Jean, "I won't be home tonight. I'll see you during the day tomorrow."

Just then the telephone rang. "A man whose voice I don't know," Jean said, handing him the phone.

When Rino said hello, Barly answered. "Hey, Rino, I got good news. The College Affairs Committee voted five to one in your favor. It looks like you might get your letter."

"How about the president, Bar? What do you think?"

"No way he's going to arbitration after that vote, especially if all it's gonna cost is an apology."

"Thanks, Bar."

"Okay, man. Have a good vacation. Y'know, I'm surprised at that vote. That bastard must have more enemies than we thought."

Rino was thrilled by the news. Now going back to work wouldn't be so bad, even after a three-week vacation. Chandler would stay off his back.

On the way over to Lee's apartment, he stopped to buy a bouquet of flowers. Anything pretty and bright that reminded him of spring. When Lee opened the door, she smiled brightly at the flowers. She was dressed in a white blouse, black slacks, and black pumps—a beautiful librarian.

They talked softly as she put the flowers in a milk glass vase. As usual, he studied her. As she talked to him, she would find him looking at her, noticing how she moved or how she looked. She loved knowing he couldn't keep his eyes off her, knowing that he never seemed to get used to the way she looked.

"Where are we going?" Rino asked.

"The Cambridge, up by the college, shows old films on Fridays. *Dark Victory* is on tonight."

"I remember that," he said, smiling to himself.

"When did you see it?"

"1946," he said, arching his eyebrows at her.

"Rino," she drawled. "Don't start having all those doubts again... okay?"

"Okay," he said.

"Anyway, we both like old movies," she said. "We just saw them at different times, right?"

"Right."

During the movie, she had the same childlike concentration as when she watched one on TV. She held his hand all the while, clutching it tighter from time to time as exciting or tense things happened.

What's she thinking? he thought. But then he realized that she was completely absorbed in the story, conscious only of the warmth of him and the touch of his hand. Maybe now that the world was so right for her, now that she had Rino and their baby, she could enjoy these movies without the outside world impinging on her concentration.

After the movie, they went to the Seidler, a German bar and restaurant not far from the college. When they went in, the booths were all taken. Instead, they sat at a table at the far end of the dining room in a quiet corner.

When the waiter came, Rino ordered a glass of white wine. Lee, as usual, ordered nothing to drink. When the wine came, she ordered sauerbraten for two.

"You really aren't too daring about trying other kinds of foods, are you?" Lee said.

"No. I don't eat too many things. I remember, when I was a kid, we had to eat things like tripe and pigs' ears. All these other foods remind me of tripe. I never had the nerve to try them."

"Did your family have a hard time during the Depression, Rino?"

He raised his eyebrows in assent. "We lost our house... My baby brother died from flu, and my little sister died from pneumonia."

"Were you really poor?"

"I remember a few days when there wasn't anything but bread in the house. We had meals of bread dipped in bacon grease... and coffee." He shook his head in wonder. "My mother and father were tough people. We ended up buying another house and paying for it. It took them 20 years to pay off three thousand dollars."

She marveled at what he said. "Was your childhood unhappy?"

"No. But we didn't have much of a childhood: for Christmas, we got cookies, some oranges maybe. The worst part I remember was the way people died. It was so easy to die in those days, especially for kids."

She shuddered slightly. "You're really something, Rino," she said, touching his hand as it rested on the table.

"No, kid. Everybody was in the same boat in those days. Nobody had anything. If you had food, you were damned lucky. If you had a job two days a week, you felt like a king."

"Hello, Lee," said a voice, intruding upon their conversation.

Rino was looking at her. She froze as she heard the voice, almost as if her heart had stopped beating. In an instant, her face blanched pallid white. Rino, too, was vaguely troubled by the voice. Then he realized whom he had heard; it was the voice of Chandler.

"Hello, Dale," she said, glancing up at his tall frame standing beside their table. Her voice was thin and weak as she spoke. Rino could see the strange anguish and disorientation in her face.

Chandler looked at Rino for a moment but then ignored him. He was his usual cool and haughty self, confident and smooth, a handsome man from a distance. But, up close, his eyes betrayed a coldness and meanness of spirit that he couldn't hide from anyone who searched for it.

"I didn't know you liked German food, Lee. Do you come here often?" Chandler said.

Lee was trembling; suddenly the sparkle had deserted her. "Uh... no, we don't..." She stopped for a moment to collect her thoughts. "Dale, this is—"

"We've met, Lee. He's a janitor at the college. He cleans my office once in a while," Chandler said, still looking down over her.

Rino hated him for his pride and presumption. And he was angered by the intrusion on this night. But, looking at Lee and seeing the chilling of her spirit, Rino began to feel something new about Chandler: fear. He was the dark shadow from Lee and Ted's past that Rino had always thought was there. Chandler and Lee knew each other. And he was talking to her with a triumphant look on his face, the easy smile that meant Lee had been a victim.

Chandler stood there, savoring the way he had set them both off balance, smug in the knowledge that he could bother them from a distance, just by a few softly spoken words. "You know, Lee, you never seem to learn, do you?" he said in his soft, taunting voice that he had practiced so well. "A janitor, for God's sake? And a granddad at that. You go from one loser to another."

Rino collected himself, no longer learning or wondering about the figures and voices before him. His hatred and anger had brought him back to reality. "That's enough, Chandler," he said in a quiet, menacing tone.

Chandler smiled patronizingly at Rino. "Are we on a date tonight, Lee? You and your blue-collar friend... old friend?"

"Go back to your table, Chandler," said Rino, louder this time as he stood up.

"Rino, it's all right," Lee said weakly. "Please, Dale, we never did anything to you. Leave us alone."

Chandler laughed softly, still in control of himself. "You hear that, janitor?" he hissed. "You've never done anything to me, have you? Except steal and then lie about it."

"Please, Dale," Lee begged, "there's no reason. Please. You won. You won."

"Oh, I always win, Lee," he snapped. "Do you hear me, janitor? I always win. Lee knows it from way back. I get what I want... and I can even make them like it. Didn't you, Lee? She even came back for more, janitor. She couldn't get enough... She was as hot—"

Rino hit him backhanded as he spoke. The blow grazed Chandler's face but caught him squarely on the neck near his throat as he flinched. Chandler showed embarrassment at first, then fear as he tasted blood and felt the pain of the heavy blow. He coughed and staggered backward about three steps, bumping into another man seated at a table. He had looked clumsy and awkward, but he didn't fall. He turned from side to side, surveying the faces of the other diners who returned his gaze, looking amused and fascinated. He had lost the crowd to Rino.

He stood still and erect, trying to clear his head and keep his balance, looking at Rino, who was standing at his table. "You'll never get that letter from me," Chandler croaked. "Never!"

"I'll get it, cowboy. That's one game you're gonna lose," said Rino coldly, glaring at him.

Chandler looked back at Lee and smiled. "Tell him, Lee," he said. "He's curious now. Maybe he'll learn something." Then he turned and walked stiffly to the other side of the room to an anxious young blonde woman seated in a booth.

Rino took a deep breath and sat back down. Lee looked confused and tormented. "What did he mean about the letter, Rino? What letter?"

"I filed a grievance against him and demanded a letter of apology. He accused me of stealing."

"He was the one you told me about the other night?"

Rino nodded. Suddenly she began to tremble. Her fist went to her mouth to stifle a cry. "Oh no!" she groaned. "Oh my God!"

"Let's go, Lee," said Rino, standing and helping her up by putting a hand on her upper arm and almost lifting her out of her seat. When he got her coat, he held it for her as she put it on. She had become a zombie, doing what she was told, standing before him with dull, glazed eyes. She tried to button her coat but couldn't do it. Rino carefully fastened the top few buttons and urged her toward the door. As he did, the manager came up to him to apologize, and Rino nodded acceptance.

Lee walked unsteadily as he held her elbow and guided her toward the car. When he opened the door, she sat on the seat heavily, leaning her head back against the headrest. Rino closed the door and opened his on the other side.

"Lee?" he said, frightened by her almost catatonic silence. Suddenly his mind recalled the afternoon when he had first seen her so many months ago. She had been crying then and looked tired and helpless. Now, tonight, she seemed worse—trembling and morbidly quiet. How quickly the brightness, the joy of her, the warm, soft beauty had changed.

"I'm okay, Rino," she said. "Please take me home."

In the car, he didn't talk to her. Occasionally, he would look over at her, and she'd be unchanged, her head propped against the headrest and her eyes closed. When they got to the apartment, he took the key from her and opened the door. She walked in and hung her coat in the closet and made no move to take his. "Please go, Rino. I'm tired. I have to sleep."

"What?" he said.

"I'm tired, Rino, and I have to lie down," she pleaded.

"I don't care about the sleep," he snapped. "Why do you want me to go?"

She didn't answer for a moment. Instead, she walked toward the kitchen and paused in the entry, her hands on either side of the doorway. She had her back to him. "Because I don't want you to see me like this," she said, half turning her head back in his direction.

His fear had also made him angry. The evening he had waited so long to have, and to cherish, had been shattered. He grabbed her and spun her around, holding her up to his face. "Listen to me," he said. Her eyes were closed, shutting out his plea. "It's over. Chandler can't hurt us. He tried tonight, and it didn't work. Understand? It's the last shot he can take."

She shook her head, still firmly in his grasp. He realized that the way he was holding her, almost suspended, was hurting her arms. She said nothing about it, but he could see the pain in her face. He let her loose.

"You don't understand, Rino," she whispered.

"What am I supposed to understand? That some loony who walks across a crowded restaurant to hurt you and embarrass me is going to come between us?"

"He already has." She sighed.

"The hell he has," Rino said. "Look. Forget him, he can't hurt us."

"He already has," she said.

"Jesus, Lee, will you stop this? He hasn't done anything but spoil one goddamned meal. That's all."

"He spoiled me, Rino... two times."

Rino had been right all along. Chandler was the one between Ted and Lee—the malandrine. "What?" he said.

She was crying now. "You heard him, Rino. You know what he meant." She screamed the words at him through her tears. "He meant—"

"Stop it! I don't have to hear this, Lee. It doesn't make any difference."

"That's what Ted said. 'It wouldn't make any difference.' But it did. It made a difference to me," she cried. "He's going to get you... us. He got Ted. He got me. And now he's after you. Oh God!"

"Nobody's going to get me. And nobody's going to get you... unless you want him to," said Rino.

Her laugh seemed to come from a demented stranger. "That's something else you don't know," she said. "The first time it was so Ted could get tenure. The second time I just let him... I wanted him to.'" She walked away as she talked. "I'm tired, Rino. Please let me sleep."

"I'm not leaving," said Rino.

"Rino, you don't know what he's like. He'll hurt you."

"I told you, no one..." Rino stopped in midsentence and walked over to her and took her in his arms. He bent to kiss her gently, but she moved her chin away. It angered him, and he shook her. "What the hell do you think you're doing? Do you enjoy hurting me like this? Don't you see that this is what that bastard wants? He's back in that restaurant just hoping you and I are up here screaming at each other." He released her and went to the arm of a chair and seated himself against it. He waited several seconds. "I don't have anywhere to go, Lee. There's no home out there. I thought this was my home."

She folded her hands behind her neck as she began crying loudly. She fell heavily to her knees and then lowered her forehead to the floor and sobbed. "Oh God, I'm sorry, Rino. I'm so sorry!"

He went to her and helped her stand. Then he led her to the couch and sat her down. As he did, he knelt in front of her. Her head was lowered, and she didn't look at him. She brushed the hair from her face with one hand and then put her hands together in her lap. Her nose ran from tears.

"I put all my eggs in one basket here, kid," Rino said softly. He clutched her hands with one of his own. "That house out there isn't mine anymore; it's Frankie's. All I've got is this place… and you."

She shook her head. "You don't know him, Rino. He'll do anything to get what he wants. He's possessed. He ruined Ted by contaminating me. He manipulated him until he couldn't stand it anymore. That was when he killed himself. Oh, Rino, I don't want him to destroy you, too."

"Why did you turn away from me?" Rino said.

"Because the closer you are to me, the more harm will come to you. I've contaminated you, too, Rino."

"Jesus, Lee," he said, "look at me." She looked up at him. "I'm not Ted, and I don't want anything from Chandler the way Ted did. I don't have a career to worry about. All I have, all I want, is you. And I won't let some crazy malandrine drive us apart, Lee. I won't run from him. I'll fight… and he'll lose."

She was quiet for a few moments. Then she spoke softly, "Please kiss me, Rino."

Rino reached toward her. But then he hesitated, waiting for her to move toward him. She did. She put her hand to his cheek and drew his lips to hers in a gentle kiss.

"Can I stay?" he said, smiling wanly.

She threw her arms around his neck and held him tightly. "God, how could I say those things to you?" she said. "Forgive me… and stay always."

In the bedroom, he undressed her carefully. "You look tired," he said.

"I've never been so tired in my whole life."

He took off her panty hose slowly. Though they weren't going to make love, the feel of her bare legs was erotic as he slid the hose down. His heart beat faster and faster, and his penis thickened. But he hesitated after the hose. She still had a bra and panties on.

"Take them off, Rino," she said.

He slid the panties off and undid her bra. He took a deep breath and looked at her. "I love you, Leila," he said.

He undressed and got into bed beside her. She fell asleep in his arms, and he held her for almost an hour before falling asleep himself.

He slept soundly; the evening had drained the energy from him, too. Often, he would stir or roll over and awaken for a minute, but always he would fall back to sleep again.

But during the night, as he slept his soundest, he awoke to Lee calling him. He was startled. Somewhere, in his mind, fear had lingered, and when he awoke, it intruded upon his first thoughts. It was fear without a face or name, fear of Chandler's hatred, of losing Lee, of something not yet imagined.

"Rino," she called softly to him. She was sitting cross-legged in bed with tears running down her cheeks.

"What is it?" he said.

"I'm sorry about not letting you kiss me. I was afraid. It wasn't because I didn't love you. I was afraid..."

He could see in her eyes that she was serious. "I know, kid," he said.

"I never wanted there to be a time when I didn't want you to touch me... like there was with Ted. God, how could I do it? And how could I ever tell you to go?" She propped her forehead on her hand forcefully, her elbow resting on her leg. "I'm so sorry, Rino."

Rino stared at her for a minute. *She really didn't know how much her simple, magical love mattered to him*, he thought. Suddenly he chuckled and then laughed softly, turning his head away from her, trying not to let her see his face.

"Why are you laughing at me, Rino Bellanca?" she said, both frowning and holding back a smile.

He tried to be serious. "Lee," he said, "you realize you're sitting here in bed like a naked Indian, and you woke me up in the middle of the night to tell me you were sorry?"

"I'm always naked in bed with you, Bellanca," she said, punching his arm, annoyed with him. "And I'm trying to say I never meant to hurt you."

"No offense, Leila. I still love you. Now let's go to sleep, okay?"

Once again, they both fell asleep. But later, when the pale, early light of morning made dim forms and shadows in the room, Rino stirred and sensed that she wasn't in bed. He called her name softly. He got up, put on his robe, and looked into the bathroom. She wasn't there. Then he walked down the hall and found her sitting in her blue robe on the couch, crying.

"Lee?" he said. "What the hell are you doing out here?" He sat down beside her. She didn't answer him; instead, she turned away, still crying. He reached for a tissue and turned her face toward him. He wiped her eyes and her face as he would for Libby. She didn't talk to him. "Jesus, you're freezing, Lee. Why didn't you put something over your legs?" he said.

She watched him as he gathered the afghan and draped it over her legs and tucked it under her feet. She kept staring into his eyes with the childlike earnestness that he had seen so many times without the pain. "Rino, I can't believe I did those things. I never want to hurt you... ever."

He hugged her to him, cradling her head in his hand, kissing her hair as she continued to cry. "Lee... it wasn't the kiss, or telling me to go... I know you didn't mean it. But that's just it: you were doing what he wanted you to do. What bothered me was what was happening to us... understand? I can't stand it when something hurts you... or makes you like this."

"Doesn't it bother you? What I did?" she said.

"Look, Leila, I was upset because you were falling apart, okay? But now it's over." He reached over to kiss her. She kissed him back gently. "There," he said. "I know you like to kiss me, okay?" Then he smiled. "Now, refresh my memory. Where did I sleep last night?" She looked at him curiously. "Where did I sleep, Leila?"

"You slept in there with me," she said, still puzzled.

"Okay. Then you changed your mind about both things, right? So you're off the hook. I'm fine, you're fine. And I don't hold any grudges. Got that?" She nodded. "Now are you gonna be like Saint Peter and do this thrice? Where am I gonna wake up next and find you crying? In the shower?"

She laughed softly. And it felt good to hear her laugh. "Is it really over, Rino?"

"It's over, kid. Chandler's an old story. Besides, a prick like that will soon have plenty of new enemies to keep him occupied. We just caught him when he needed something to do."

"I've never heard you swear before, Rino," she said, smiling at him.

"If you keep waking me up like this, you're going to hear a lot more of it, Leila," he said.

She was feeling better now. Some of the life and sparkle was coming back into her red eyes as he made her laugh. "There is one thing that's bothering me," he said.

"What is it?" she said apprehensively. "Did I say something else?"

"I don't know if it's crossed your mind, Leila, as you've kept me up half the damned night, and that crackpot spoiled our supper at the restaurant, and I haven't had a cup of coffee since I can't remember. I'm hungry, okay? I work for a living."

She laughed softly. "God. I never thought about that, Rino. I'm sorry."

"And quit apologizing to me! Apologies are cheap, kid. Breakfast… now that takes some doing."

She stared at him silently for a moment. She was going to say she loved him, but her eyes clouded as she began to talk.

"Don't you dare cry, Lee."

She snorted. "Okay, okay. Bacon and eggs, Bellanca."

"I'll help," he said. "Unless I faint from weakness before I get some food."

She punched him. "Rino, it'll always be like this, won't it?"

"I hope not," he said.

"I meant the good things, Bellanca... like now."

Rino went home and finished packing for the trip. As he went back and forth from the basement and garage to the station wagon, stashing his gear, he mulled over the last 24 hours in his mind. Chandler. How could he go so far? Crazy how it all intertwined, one man able to hurt so many people. But now he hadn't just tried to hurt Rino; he had hurt Lee.

Maybe it would be better if he quit his job at the college. But then what would he do? He couldn't just sit around the apartment all the time. And he liked the college. Sammy was good to him; Joe and Barly were good friends. Only Chandler. Only a malandrine.

Rino said goodbye to Libby and Larry. He wouldn't see them before he left in the morning. Then, at supper, he told Frank and Jean, "We'll be back late Sunday afternoon. We'll leave Saturday and take turns driving all night."

"Okay, Pop. You be careful driving," said Frank.

"And be careful in the woods. We don't want one of your 'hunting' buddies mistaking you for a deer," Jean said.

"Look, I'm not coming back tonight. You both know that I'll leave straight from Lee's apartment tomorrow. By the way, next week we're getting married, so that should save you some embarrassment... or maybe cause you some, too."

"We won't be embarrassed, Dad. You just be happy," said Jean.

"Pop, can I meet her next week? Before the wedding?" said Frank.

"Yeah, Frankie, I'll bring her here," said Rino.

"Jean says she's so beautiful that none of the guys in the family are gonna leave her alone, Pop. Does she know about my crazy cousins?" Frank said, smiling at his father for the first time in a long while.

Rino chuckled. It felt good to be joking with his son again. "If Uncle Lou calls, tell him I'll pick him up at 6:30."

When Rino arrived at Lee's apartment, he put the station wagon in the garage, in the spot that she had arranged for him. When she opened the door, she was dressed in her robe as she had been when he'd left her that morning. "Jesus," he said. "Didn't you change all day?"

She kissed him. "Of course, Bellanca. Do you think I just lounge around here eating bon-bons and never doing any work?"

"Right. You worked like a dog all day. That's why you look so beautiful."

"Rino Bellanca, I did work all day," she drawled.

"Okay, okay," he said, suddenly loosening the tie of her robe as he walked past her, "just checking." She had nothing on under the robe.

She pushed his arm away, her eyes narrowing in mock anger. "You're pure evil, Rino." She was blushing.

He sat down on the couch, and as soon as he did, she sat down on his lap, facing him. She straddled his legs and locked her hands behind his neck. "So what are you going to do in Canada?" she said.

"Fish, mostly. I don't hunt much. Lou and the guys want an elk or a deer. Hell, they're lucky if they can bag a few squirrels and a rabbit. We almost never get much."

"Bring me a nice fish, will you?" she said.

"You want to have it stuffed?"

She giggled. "No, silly. I want to cook it for you."

"What do Swiss know about fish? I hate to waste a good fish."

She tried to choke him as they both wrestled and laughed. He managed to untie her robe again, and she pushed his hands away. He fought her so that he could kiss one of her nipples. She pushed his head away, giggling. "I'm part French, Rino," she said. "They know how to cook fish."

"French women are supposed to be hot stuff, Lou tells me," he said.

"Oh, really? Lou tells you? You didn't learn that firsthand in France?"

"Not me." He chuckled.

"Well, I'm not 'hot stuff.' I'm going to start being cool and aloof. And I resent being told that I'm not a good cook. The Swiss are all good cooks."

He reached for the tie of her robe, but she pushed his hand away. "You leave this tie alone, Rino. I have to talk to you."

"You think if I loosen the tie, I'll go deaf, right?"

She giggled. "No. But I don't want to be distracted."

"Hell, it'll be easy. You just talk and leave me alone. Everything'll work out fine. You'll see." He reached for the tie and undid it. His hands reached behind her buttocks and moved her forward on his lap until his lips could get to one of her nipples. After a few glorious seconds, he said, "Okay. So talk."

"I'm distracted," she said. "Look, this isn't working out the way I planned. Now, I'm going to give you one kiss, and then I want you to let me move away."

"Where do you want to go?" he asked.

"Over there." She pointed to the chair opposite the couch.

"That's too far. Sorry," he said as he kissed her neck and ran his hands over her belly, stroking her pubic hair.

"Rino, please. If you start this, I won't be able to stop... and I have to tell you."

"One kiss," said Rino.

Her lips met his, and she slid her tongue into his mouth. She kissed him fully, moving her body on his against the back of the couch. Gently she pushed herself away from him, but he held her, moving his hands over the magical smoothness of her back.

"Rino, you promised," she scolded gently.

"I lie about things like that, Leila. Come here."

She put both her hands on his shoulders, holding him away halfheartedly. "Don't you want to hear what I have to say? I have something horrible to tell you."

"It doesn't matter, kid. Don't you understand? Horrible or not."

"I have to, Rino. Please?" She seemed so childlike as she sat on his lap with her robe open. He would do anything she wanted, and they both knew it.

"Okay," he said. "But tell me right here, not over on the chair."

"I can't tell you while I'm sitting here like this. I have to sit beside you." She moved beside him, sat cross-legged on the couch, and tied her robe. Then she paused for a few moments to collect her thoughts. "This is hard for me, Rino," she said.

"Okay. Say it and get it over with, Lee. Before you start, I want you to know that you're the best thing that's ever happened to me... understand?"

She nodded. Her face was pale and grim. "Ted... you know I've been unfair to him, Rino. It wasn't all his fault. I wasn't the kind of wife he needed. He wasn't a bad man. He would never deliberately hurt anyone. All he ever wanted was to be an important scholar."

She paused a little. It was harder than she had thought it would be. Her mouth was dry, and her hands were sweating. "When he was up for tenure two years ago, there were five people on the tenure committee. Dale Chandler was one.

"Ted and Chandler had been friends; they played racquetball, golf, tennis—everything together. Before Dale's divorce, we used to go places together, the two couples. But Dale was a better politician at school. The administration liked him: he was young, rich, and good-looking. Ted wasn't as sure of himself—or as glamorous.

"So, Dale and Paul Bergland from psychology started writing a book. They could have used Ted to write the chapters on statistics, but instead they used a friend of Paul's from Wisconsin. Ted was crushed, but he didn't say anything to them. Instead, he started writing a book on his own. When Dale found out about it, suddenly he and Ted weren't playing ball together anymore. I know he was worried that maybe Ted's book would be more successful than his.

"Dale got tenure two years before Ted, and he also got promoted sooner. And finally, he got elected to the tenure committee."

Rino snorted. He had a good idea of what she was going to tell him.

"The committee had two men who didn't like young, non-Ivy League professors and wanted to keep the profession pure—the old guard. Two were in favor of Ted because they liked his research. And Dale Chandler was the deciding vote."

She stopped for a few seconds and turned her head away from Rino. He reached for her chin and turned it back toward him. "I know what you're going to tell me, kid. And I know why you did it. You've said enough. Give yourself a break."

She shook her head and lowered her eyes away from his. Her hands were twisting the tie of her robe nervously. "So... uh... He told Ted that he thought... I was attractive... and he just made a proposition—his tenure vote for me."

This time she couldn't continue. Tears dropped onto her robe and his trousers. "That's it. I don't want to hear any more of this," Rino said.

"No. It's almost done, Rino. Please let me do it just this one time. So Ted asked me if I would..." Her voice cracked again, but she continued, "It spoiled whatever we had left of our marriage, Rino. I thought, if he thinks so little of me that he can ask me to be a whore, then what am I preserving?

"I cried all night, walking around the apartment. Then, the next morning, I told Ted that I would. A week later, the dean's party was on a Saturday night. So, Ted and I went... and I had several drinks, enough to get almost drunk. And then I left the party with Chandler.

"After we had sex in the dark at his apartment, I was supposed to leave. But I didn't..." She stopped suddenly and sobbed against Rino's shoulder, her breath gushing in great loud spasms. He hugged her to him and kissed her hair. And from her throat, she made a full, low wail. "I didn't have to stay that night, Rino," she continued a few seconds later, determined to maintain her composure. "I felt so used and contaminated that I didn't care about anything. I hated Ted for asking me to do it, and I hated myself for staying that night. But I didn't have anyone to go home to. Going home to Ted seemed worse than staying.

"The next morning, I heard him in the bathroom. When he came back into the bedroom, he was smiling. He knew I was waiting for him to do it again. And when he got into bed... and kissed me... We screwed again."

Rino winced. The word "screw" seemed so vulgar and unnatural coming from her. She continued resolutely. "The night before... it was as though, if I couldn't see him, I could pretend later that it never happened. But I wasn't drunk that morning, Rino," she said, still looking down at the tie of her robe, which she was nervously twisting, "and it wasn't dark. As we did it, I could see him... and see myself. Oh God, I don't know why I stayed, Rino. I think I wanted to be needed... or maybe even just wanted. I hoped that the second time it would mean more, be exciting or warm, different than it was with Ted. But it wasn't. It just made me feel dirty.

"I knew when I looked into his eyes. It was the same look he had when he played tennis or racquetball: aggressive and unfeeling. He could never care about me, much less need me. So then I left... and went home... and cried for three days. Chandler called me several times, wanting to meet me again. But no one ever touched me after that night—not Ted, not Chandler.

"A few days later, Chandler told Ted that in spite of what I had done, he couldn't vote tenure for him. He said the dean was against it. So, the committee voted Ted down.

"Ted almost fell apart. He knew he had lost me, and he was about to lose tenure. So he went to the dean and told him that Chandler had tried to sell his tenure vote. But the dean wouldn't believe him. He told Ted that tenured jobs were very hard to get nowadays, and if he made those charges, it would ruin his chances of ever landing a tenured position again. A month later, Ted killed himself."

Rino was silent. Lee searched his face for sympathy and understanding. He reached out and wiped her tears away with his fingers. "How about a cup of coffee?"

"What?" she said with a grimace of hurt on her face.

"I need a cup of coffee."

"Didn't you hear what I just told you?" she said desperately.

"Yeah, I heard it. Now what do you want me to say? That it was nice? Well, it stinks, okay? Ted should have..." Rino stopped and calmed himself. "You degraded yourself for a man who could take you or leave you. And then you went to bed with a man who hates women, who used you because you were another man's wife. That's what the smile on his face was about, Leila."

He stopped again for a minute, trying to contain his anger. He spoke quietly and deliberately; his tone had changed. "Lee, when I think of someone touching you, I feel like killing them. Even thinking about it makes me crazy."

They both sat in the same positions for several minutes, not talking or looking at each other. Finally, Rino sat forward and put his face in his hands for a few seconds. He couldn't get the images out of his mind. He thought of Chandler kissing her breasts, those small, perfect breasts he loved to kiss so much. He thought of her spreading her legs and him putting himself into her. Could she have enjoyed it? God, how he hated Chandler.

He suddenly stood up and walked, stopping near the fireplace to rest his forearm against the mantel.

"What are you thinking?" she asked.

"I'm thinking I wish you would never have told me this," he said, still looking away from her.

"I didn't want any secrets between us," she said plaintively.

"I knew what you did," he said gruffly. "How you did it is what bothers me."

She was quiet for a few seconds. "Rino, I wanted to belong to you. But I couldn't as long as you didn't know what I'd done. There'd always be something in my heart that I'd be afraid to tell you." She watched Rino's reaction to her words. He made no move toward her. "I had sex, but I never made love to anyone until I met you, Rino. Do you believe that?"

He sighed, went over to her, and knelt on the floor in front of her. She welcomed him to her as he laid his head on her shoulder and rested it there. "You made me jealous tonight, kid," he said. "I've never been like that before. I can't stand it."

Somehow she derived pleasure from what he said. As guilty and shabby as she felt, she exulted in his possessiveness. "Rino? Do you remember when you said I was the best thing that's ever happened to you? Can you ever feel that way about me again?"

He snorted and looked away. "I'm too old for this," he said aloud to himself.

She smiled grimly. "Rino, if you don't love me with your whole heart and soul, I think I'll die."

"Well, I don't want you to die," he said with a smirk.

"What does that mean, Rino? Do you still love me… even after all I've done?"

He lifted his head to face her. "Did you really think this story was going to make me not love you?"

"Rino, please say it!" she pleaded.

"You're my whole life, Leila. I love you more every day—so much it scares me."

"Rino?"

"What?" he said, settling beside her on the couch.

"Did you ever cheat on Mary?" she said.

"No…"

"Can you imagine ever cheating on her?"

He shrugged. "With you, I might," he said honestly.

"Really?" She was smiling again. "Do you mean that? Only with me?"

"You've got something over me, kid," he said.

"That's called love, Rino."

"But I did love Mary, Lee," he said. "It was nice being married to her."

"I'm jealous of Mary. Do you know that? I don't even like you to think about her."

Rino snorted. "I don't much anymore," he said. "I can't think about the two of you at the same time."

"Why not?"

"Because I lived with her almost 40 years, and I loved her. And yet you're the one I want… and always would. Where's the coffee, for God's sake? I thought the Swiss liked to show hospitality."

"The coffee is coming… after I choke you." She reached for his throat. But as soon as she put her arms up, he untied her robe.

"Jesus. I love Switzerland," he said as he kissed one of her breasts. "You know, I really don't want coffee."

"What do you want?" she said knowingly.

"You know what I've wanted since I walked in that door tonight."

"Come on," she said, grabbing his hand.

In bed, they kissed each other hungrily, and their lovemaking was joyful and thrilling. He guided her onto her side and then straddled her lower leg and entered her sideways. She gasped and twisted her hips against him. From his position, he could touch every part of her: her breasts and belly, her legs and back. After only a few thrusts, they both exploded into a violent orgasm. As they grew calm, they talked and kissed and then fell asleep.

Rino was awakened by her voice calling him. "Rino, wake up! I want to talk."

"Jesus," he muttered, "are you always gonna keep waking me like this?"

"What are you going to do in Canada when you're bored?"

He smirked as he yawned. "God, I hope that camper of hookers doesn't show up at the same time again this year."

"Hookers… again?" She was smiling and decided to take his bait.

"You know, I never realized how nice young girls felt…"

"Until what, Bellanca?" she said.

"Lee, I want you to know that I'll fight the temptation as hard as I can."

She was still smiling. "And if you can't resist temptation?"

"Like I said, I never knew how nice young girls…"

"How old are these hookers, Bellanca?" she said, still playing along with him.

"Some are getting old—one's almost 33."

Finally, she screamed and pounded his shoulders with both fists, careful not to hurt him. She was laughing as he grabbed her around the waist and pulled her toward him. "I'm going to have to keep this sick and evil side of you from my mother," she said.

He raised his eyebrows up and down a few times. "By the way, is your mother good-looking?"

She went for his throat again, laughing. Then she stopped suddenly with a look of amazement. "Rino, I'm so happy now, I can't believe it," she said seriously.

"So am I, kid. Sometimes this all seems like a dream."

She took his hand and put it on her breast. "I'm here," she said. "See? What you're feeling is real." He pinched the nipple gently, and she made a little squeak. "Rino, do you know that I think of ways to seduce you all day long?" she mused aloud, amazed at her new personality. "I almost never have anything on when you're here, you know that?" She shrugged and shook her head. "The horny librarian," she said to herself.

It struck him funny, and he let out a throaty laugh. She was surprised, but she loved the sound of joy that enveloped the two of them. "You don't hear me complaining, do you? Just keep that horniness coming in my direction," he said.

"I'm not kidding," she said. "You've done something to me, too. Look at me now: sitting here naked and talking to you. And I don't even feel naked—most times I forget that I am. I've never been like that before. I never sat and talked like this with Ted. I used to be... modest."

"Now that's hard to believe," he huffed.

But she remained serious. "You know what it is, Rino? Really? It's that I've waited all my life for you. You're the only one in the whole world who could have done this to me."

"You said that's called love," he said.

"I loved Ted once; you loved Mary. But it wasn't like this, was it?"

"No," he said, "but I don't ask myself why anymore. As long as you're right here, I don't care."

"Rino?"

"What?"

"Let's make love again?"

He snorted. "I don't know if I can this quick, kid. I'm not some young stud–it might take a while."

She giggled. "Come on. I'll help you. I can get you real puffy." She took his penis into her mouth and made him get hard again. Then she moved away to kiss him and to let him kiss her breasts. After a few minutes, she mounted herself on top of him and lowered herself onto the shaft of his penis. She moved sensuously, thrusting and twisting in slow, rhythmical turns until she could feel her heart beat faster and his breathing grow deeper and more frequent. Then, when she was ready, she made a few strong bucking movements, and he spurted his semen into her in a few quick, pleasurable pumps.

She smiled to herself. She loved what she could do to him. She loved the kind of person she became when he was near her.

As they lay in bed quietly, Rino chuckled to himself. Jesus. He couldn't do it when he was 40, and now he had come twice in two hours when he was 62.

"Rino?"

"What? Not a third time?"

She giggled. "Let's take a shower."

She got out of bed, holding a towel between her legs, and went into the bathroom. A few minutes later, she came back into the bedroom, holding folded towels and washcloths. He was still lying in bed, savoring the loose, warm feeling in his body. She held her hand out to lead him into the bathroom. She stepped into the tub, but he hesitated. "Come on," she said. "Are you afraid?"

He stepped in. "You know, I've never done this before."

"You never took a shower with Mary?"

"No. Did you with Ted?"

"Only on our honeymoon."

He shook his head. "You know, as good as she was, we never had this. We never played the way you and I do. Isn't that something?"

"I always want to honor her memory, Rino. Because she meant so much to you."

"And Ted?"

"Ted, too. I want to remember only good things and put them away in some corner of my mind. Now I only have dreams to fulfill, with you and the baby."

She stood under the shower and soaked herself as he watched. Then she soaked a washcloth and washed his face. When she was done, she handed him the cloth. "Wash me," she said.

He washed her face and her neck. Then he turned her to wash her back and buttocks. Then he turned her toward him again. "Do you mind doing this?" she asked.

"Jesus, how could you say that? I'll do it twice a day if you want."

He washed her arms and her breasts. She bent forward to kiss him as he concentrated on the washing. He slowly washed her belly. "That's going to be round and tubby soon," she said.

"Hell, it's kind of chubby now," he said, laughing softly.

"No it isn't, Rino! How could you say such a horrible thing? It's flat, see?" She ran her hands down the front of her.

"When you suck it in that much, your face turns blue, you know that?"

She punched him. "You're evil, Bellanca."

He slowly washed her legs and feet. Then he looked up at her from where he knelt on one knee and said, "Can I wash you there?" He pointed to her vagina.

"Wash me everywhere, Rino," she said softly.

He washed gently between her legs and her buttocks. And then he kissed her navel. "I'm gonna love watching this grow," he said.

"Let me do you now," she said.

She soaked the other washcloth and began to wash him. When he was turned away from her, and she was washing his back, he said, "Is that why we always drink out of the same glass?"

"What made you think of that?" she said.

"Your story," he said.

She stopped washing and turned his shoulder toward her. "Once I was with a man, and I drank to get drunk. I promised myself then that if I ever found you—I didn't know who you would be—that we'd both drink together always and never use drinks to hide our feelings."

They both rinsed off and stepped out of the shower to dry. She studied him while he dried his hair with the towel. "You've cleansed me, Rino. You've washed away all the stains and bad memories tonight."

"You're sure, now? No more guilt or hating yourself?"

"No more. Now it's you and Baby forever."

They slept a few more hours, and then the alarm woke them. Lee made breakfast for him. Then she cried as he put on his coat. "I'll be waiting for you when you get back Sunday." Then she kissed him. "Be careful, my darling. I love you."

They drove all day, finally arriving at their outpost late in the evening. The owner of the small airstrip greeted them and set them up in bunks for the night. The next morning, the pilot showed up early to take them farther north to their cabin. He remembered them from the years before. "You guys always come in November, right?"

"Yeah, just before the real bad weather," said Lou.

"Old Jim has his son and son-in-law working for him now," said the pilot.

"I'm glad we got Jim again this year," said Rino. "I'll catch a few more fish now."

Jim was an Anishinaabe tribe guide to the hunters who were flown up to the camp. He worked out an arrangement with the airport owner, who also owned the camp. Jim looked after the place and kept it clean. The paved road stopped at the airport, and then the pilots would fly the clients farther north about a hundred miles. Then Jim and his crew would take them hunting and fishing, help them filet fish, skin and butcher game, and even cook for them.

The only people in the camp were Rino's party. They had always chosen November because no one came to the camp that late in the year, and it was the off-season, with off-season rates that had been so crucial to them when they were younger and less affluent. And after so many years, it became a habit. With no one else there, the four Youngstowners had the rivers and forests to themselves.

"Did they ever get a telephone hookup at the camp?" asked Rino.

"No," said the pilot. "Jim didn't want one. He said it would spoil the camp, ringing all the time. He has a bad enough time tolerating the shortwave."

When they arrived at the camp, Jim and his son and son-in-law greeted them in the same friendly but not-too-familiar way they had always done. They all helped carry the gear into the cabin. It was a windy day, and the damp mist blowing on the cheeks of the men gave a hint of how cold the night would be.

The fireplace already had logs blazing. The pilot unloaded beer and whiskey to tide the men over. It was a protocol most campers observed. The cold north woods were made as much for drinking as for hunting and fishing.

The pattern was the same: They'd be up early, overeat a big breakfast prepared by Jim and his sons, and then go out. Every night was spent playing pinochle, reading, or talking. Their only tie to the outside world was a shortwave radio tuned to the clearest station that had music.

The lake upon which the camp was fronted held sturgeons and lake trout. Rino caught lake trout both days, and Jim cooked part of Rino's catch for supper on Wednesday night. Everyone liked the meal. The outdoors seemed to do something to food that made it taste different than it would in the city.

Rino enjoyed himself. But at night he seemed quiet and detached. He went to bed early the first two nights. The next day, while the others went hunting with Jim and his boys, Rino fished alone in a trout stream near the camp. Suddenly, he could hear Lou's voice in the distance. Lou called his name, and Rino answered. In a moment, Rino could see Lou emerge from a stand of pine trees.

"Hi, kid, catch anything?" Lou said.

"Not so much in this weather."

Lou sat down beside Rino and smoked a cigarette as Rino trolled. When Rino caught a trout, he returned to the bank, and Lou helped him unhook the fish and set it in Rino's cooler.

"Where are the others?" Rino asked.

"Out there trying to bag an elk. Hell, I don't know what we'd do with one if we caught him. Nobody in Youngstown cooks stew like Jim."

Rino snorted. Both men sat silently, staring at the lazily rushing water of the stream. "You miss Lee, cowboy?" Lou asked. Rino shrugged assent.

He was sorry that it was so obvious. "This is the last trip for you, huh?" Lou continued.

"I guess so. A week's just too long a time."

Lou marveled at his brother but also felt a pang of envy. Old men often marry young girls, but not many old men looked like Rino; not many had the look of love that you see on the faces of 20-year-olds. No wonder a week away from her was too much. He'd feel the same, if only he had someone like Lee. "I'm sorry I forced you into this, kid," Lou said. "It's getting so I don't make the right moves at all with you anymore."

"We've been doing it for 26 years. You didn't force me," said Rino, still not looking at Lou but trying to salve his brother's guilt.

"Rino, I know things are gonna change from now on. I have to get used to that. But I've known you all my life. Is this girl gonna change it for us, too—you and me?"

Rino looked at his brother and saw for the first time that Lou was feeling just what had troubled his kids so much. They knew that things would never be the same again, and it bothered them. Rino had been so stable, his presence so constant in their lives, that they couldn't adjust to him suddenly departing and living a life they themselves had never experienced.

"She's not like that, Lou—I swear."

"Will she go out with us once in a while? With Annie and me?"

"Lou, she'll be crazy about you and Annie. Don't worry about it. Of course we'll go out with you."

"What about her own friends her age?"

"She doesn't have anyone close. Everybody faded away after her husband died. All she has is a sister and her mother." He turned to Lou. "And us."

Lou didn't respond. He took a last drag of his cigarette and then crushed it out with his heel. He spoke without looking at his brother,

"Rino, if she's like that, why didn't you bring her to see me? Why did you take her to Jean... and I had to bump into you at a restaurant?"

The quaver in Lou's voice made Rino turn to face him. "I don't know, man." Rino sighed. "Maybe, at first, I was afraid you'd see something I couldn't. Then... I thought Jean might not scare her as much..."

"Jesus," Lou muttered, shaking his head.

"It seems so stupid now, Lou. I know you'd never hurt her. But I was afraid of your common sense. I'm sorry, Luigi. After all these years, I was afraid of you."

Rino put out his left hand to his brother, who could see the gesture out of the corner of his eye. After a second's pause, Lou grabbed the hand and held it. "So what do you think, Luigi? Should we get drunk tonight?"

"Sounds good, kid."

For the next two days, the men were not as energetic. Some were feeling the effects of too many beer chasers after too many Canadian Clubs. Some were tired and discouraged by the hunt—once again they'd go home to the knowing smugness of friends and relatives to whom they had promised that this would be the year of the buck deer or the moose. And some were thoughtful, sensing that an era was over. Rino would not make this trip again.

On Saturday, they stood outside the cabin at noon, hoping to hear the distant droning sound of the plane as it made its way across the treetops. The plane came about 12:15. They loaded it quickly and were gone. As the plane banked to head south, Rino took one last look back at the lake and the camp retreating into the mist, the place of so many pleasant memories. "It's not the same up here without Polly, anyway," he murmured.

Instead of sleeping all night at the airport, they rested a few hours and left in the car around four o'clock in the morning. Rino drove the first leg of the return journey; when they stopped for breakfast at eight o'clock, Lou took over. The day was a nice one. The sun was shining, and the skies were clear. The forecast, at least in Canada, was for weather around 40 degrees.

Lou drove till noon, and then they got out to stretch their legs and have lunch. As everyone was finishing his last cup of coffee, Rino left their booth and went down a short, dim hallway to a pay phone. He called Lee's number collect, but there was no answer. Finally, he thanked the operator and returned to the dining room, where Lou and the others were waiting for him. On the way to the car, Lou said, "What'd you do?"

"I called Lee, but there was no answer," Rino said.

Pete took his turn at the wheel and drove until three o'clock, when Marty had to stop to use a restroom. Lou filled the car up with gas, and Rino went inside the station to call Lee. Again, there was no answer.

When he came back to the car, Pete and Marty hadn't come back yet. "You get through?" asked Lou.

"No," Rino said with a puzzled look on his face. "She must have left her mother's place late. I thought she'd be home by now."

"How much longer do we have?" asked Lou.

"We should be home about six or seven," said Rino. "Look, you know Jean's gonna have a meal waiting for us, so you have to stay, okay?"

"Yeah. I'm in no hurry," said Lou.

"I'm gonna leave as soon as supper's over, Luigi."

"No problem. You hear they had some bad weather around Youngstown last night, lot of wet snow? The attendant said it was foggy, too."

"It's starting to be cloudy again," Rino said. "We might run into it."

As they drove down Pete's street, the weather had held up better than they had thought. It was cooling now as darkness approached but not yet freezing. They quickly unloaded Pete's gear and said goodbye. Then they drove to Marty's and unloaded his gear.

They were all tired, and it felt good to be home. As they turned down Rino's street, he breathed a big sigh. *God, it would be good to see Lee again,* he thought.

"Looks like a party at your place," said Lou.

"Jean probably invited them all over for supper," said Rino.

"Danny's here, too," said Lou. "Are you up to a big blowout?"

"We don't have much choice, cowboy," Rino sighed.

The driveway was full of cars, and some others were parked in front of the house. "Let's just park in the street and then come out and get this stuff later," said Rino.

"Yeah. If we work it out right, they'll do all the hauling for us," said Lou, chuckling.

They walked up the stairs of the front porch. The lights were on inside the house because it was now very dark outside. The door was unlocked, so Rino just opened it and walked in. Lou followed. They both were smiling and shouting loud greetings that rang through the house. But in an instant both men knew that something had changed.

"What's wrong?" said Rino. "Danny, is your mother okay?"

"She's fine, Uncle Rino."

Rino had a fearful grimace as he spoke. "What is it? Are all the kids all right? Why are you all here like this?"

None of them spoke for a second. Now Rino realized that Jean was crying, and Nancy's eyes were red. "Uncle Rino," Danny said softly, his voice quavering and weak, "Leila Reese was killed last night in an automobile accident."

Lou gasped behind Rino, but Rino said nothing. He just stared dumbly at Danny. "Are you sure? My Lee?" said Rino.

Danny nodded tearfully. "Could there have been some mistake? Some mix-up?" said Lou.

"No mistake, Uncle Lou. It's Lee," said Frank, answering for Danny.

Rino heard the words, but the icy feeling in the back of his neck, the numbness he felt in his hands and feet made him unable to move or show any emotion. For an awful minute, no one talked. Then, slowly, as if he were lifting a great weight, Rino clasped his hands in front of him and raised them to his forehead as if trying to drive something into his brain. He held them there for an instant, and then through his clenched teeth he uttered a low wail. Lou's hands were under Rino's arm, just supporting him at first, and then guiding him to a chair, where he sat down heavily.

Finally, without looking up, Rino said, "How'd it happen, Danny?"

"It rained here yesterday, Uncle Rino—sleet and drizzle. She was coming home from Canton about 5:30. The Canton police said that she must have hit a patch of black ice on Route 62, because the car rolled over and down a bank after it slid off the curve."

"Her mother told the police to call here, Pop," said Frank. "Danny was on duty, but none of the police realized who she was when the call first came in."

Rino struggled to control himself. Seemingly in a daze, hoping it was some kind of frightening dream, he looked around at them: Danny, Frank, Jean, Lou... all the kids. "What'd she look like?" Rino said. "Was she all messed up?"

"No, Uncle Rino, not at all. She even had her seat belt on. But her neck was broken. She died instantly," Danny said.

Rino stood up and walked slowly away from them. He climbed wearily up the stairs and went into his room, closing the door behind him.

Downstairs, Jerry asked, "Will he be all right, Uncle Lou? I mean, we don't have to worry about him... doing something, do we?"

"No!" said Lou gruffly, although he really wasn't sure. "Where is she now?"

"Back in Canton. The funeral is Tuesday."

They were still worried about Rino. But Lou kept them occupied with questions about what had happened and what the burial arrangements were. After a half hour, Lou went upstairs alone. He didn't bother to knock on Rino's door; he just walked in. His brother was standing in the dark, looking out a window at what could be seen under the streetlight.

"Rino, I've come up to help you dress," he said.

"Why did this happen, Lou?" Rino said softly, without looking at him. "Why now?"

"Hell, I don't know, kid. You're never ready for it; you never deserve it... and still it happens."

"I'm so sick of people dying, Lou. First Jimmy, then Terry, then Mary, then Polly... now Lee. Jesus Christ."

Lou sighed. There was no answer; there was no consolation. "Rino, the wake's tonight and tomorrow in Canton. We have to hurry and get dressed."

"I'm not going there," said Rino calmly.

"What?"

"I'm not going. I don't want to see her," said Rino.

"Rino, for God's sake, you have to go. What will people think?"

Rino turned toward him. Lou had turned on a small dresser lamp that gave off just enough light to let them see each other. "If I close my eyes now, I can see her just the way I left her. I don't want the other picture in my mind."

"Her family's gonna wonder where you're at, Rino. It'll look bad."

"I can't go, Lou," said Rino resolutely.

"Okay, okay." Lou sighed. "The funeral's Tuesday in Canton. You have to go to that one, Guarino."

Lou left Rino in the room and closed the door behind him. As he came to the bottom of the stairs, all of Rino's children were waiting for him. "Is he okay, Uncle Lou?" asked Nancy. "Is he going to be all right?"

"I don't know if he's going to be all right," muttered Lou. "He's okay now. Later, I don't know."

"Maybe we should go talk to him," said Nancy.

"Honey, there's not a damned thing that anyone can do for him now. You'll know when he needs something. Right now, leave him alone... but take care of him. By the way, he's not going tonight."

"What d'you mean he's not going tonight?" said Frank.

"I'm telling you," said Lou sternly, "that he's not going. He has his reasons."

"But how will that look? All of us there and him not? Jesus!" said Jerry.

"Look, all of you, let's just worry about our own obligations, okay? Something's happened to your dad that's never happened to any of us. So we have to give him some slack on this. Now, I'm going home to change. Danny, I think you should stay here while we're gone. If the rest of you are going, come to get me in a half hour. If not, I'll go alone."

Rino sat in the large stuffed chair in his room. Everyone had gone, and the house was quiet. *What was he going to do?* he thought. All the dreams he had, all the hopes for the future, all of them were lost in just the few words spoken by Danny. Lee was dead. God, how could she be?

In his mind, he could see her so vividly: her eyes, her mouth, her breasts, the smell of her hair, the softness of her skin. How could God do this? How could he deny them that happiness that they alone could give each other? Two lonely people who, quietly and by themselves, had forged a love better than anything in the world. They had made a baby together; they had never hurt anyone. All they ever wanted was what everyone else takes for granted. All they ever wanted was not to be too late.

She had been born too late to give him a lifetime of happiness. But he settled for what he could have. It would have been wonderful enough to be with her in those few countable years before he died. Yet now... when all the while he had been worried about leaving life and her behind, she was the one who was snatched away. Oh God! How could he live without her?

Later that night he heard noises in the driveway. It seemed strange being alone in his room. Had he slept? Didn't they all just leave? There was no time in his room; the minutes and the hours were the same. He didn't feel them pass. He didn't feel anything.

Then Lou walked in and closed the door behind him. "How're you doing, Rino?" he said.

"Okay," Rino said quietly. Lou sat on Rino's bed and kept an awkward silence. "Who was there?" said Rino finally.

"All our kids, most of the grandchildren, Connie, Danny's family."

Rino turned toward him. "Danny's family?"

"Danny was downstairs here all evening," Lou said.

Rino nodded to himself, then shook his head, understanding the reason for Danny's presence. "How about her family?"

"Just her mother and sister and her sister's husband and kids. A few friends. It was quiet."

Rino ached to ask the question, but he didn't want to see the image in his mind. Finally, he asked, "What did she look like, Lou?"

"She looked... okay, kid."

Rino shook his head and let out a long sigh, his hand clutching at his neck. He didn't want to hear that she looked beautiful, and Lou could sense that. She was beautiful only when she was alive and her lips glistened and her eyes sparkled. Now she looked as good as a dead image of her real self could look. She looked "okay."

"Are you going tomorrow, Rino?" said Lou, trying one more time.

"I can't see her dead, Lou..."

"Rino," Lou said uncomfortably, "the kids are worried about you. They're worried that..."

"That what?"

"That you might do something drastic," Lou said. "You weren't like this when their mother died."

"It's crossed my mind," Rino said, not looking at Lou. Then he turned toward his brother. "She was pregnant, Lou... with my baby." Rino put his head in his hands and, for the first time, broke down in grief, his throat emitting the same low wail that Lou had heard earlier in the night when they returned to the awful news.

Lou reached for his brother's head and held it in his arms until Rino stopped crying. When he did, Lou went back to the bed after handing Rino his handkerchief.

"Rino, if you believe in anything at all, if God has any meaning for you, then somewhere Lee and that baby are waiting for you. But she's waiting for the man she fell in love with, for the Rino she was driving through the rain and sleet to meet Sunday night. Don't spoil it. Don't keep your story from happening the way it should because you killed yourself." Rino reached his right hand toward his brother. Lou grabbed it and held it. "Are you gonna be okay?"

Rino thought for a moment. "That was one of the things I asked her when we first met," he said.

"What did she say?" Lou asked.

"Yes."

"How about you, kid?"

Rino nodded. "I'll be okay, Lou."

Lou breathed a sigh of relief. "Rino, I need you, too. Remember that." Rino nodded again. Lou continued, "I'm going home now. If you need anything, or just want to talk, there's the phone. Call me any time. Don't let yourself fall apart. I'll be here."

"Thank the kids for me, Lou," said Rino.

"I'll take care of it," Lou said.

The next morning, Rino was up early, but he stayed in his room. Everything outside—places he had taken Lee and places he had dreamed of taking her—all of it caused him pain. In his room, her presence was in his imagination, and he could hide from the world. Suddenly, this was the only place where he wasn't afraid.

Later, Lou came upstairs with a small tray—a pot of coffee and a few biscotti, the hard, bland Italian crullers usually dunked in coffee to make them palatable. But Lou knew that Rino liked them, and Annie had sent a batch of them to be served to the guests who would assemble at the house after the funeral tomorrow.

"Eat something, Rino," Lou said. "You can't get sick now."

Rino snorted. Lou poured two cups of coffee and handed a cup and a biscotto to Rino. He took them both.

"Rino, when she died, they took blood tests."

"What for? What did they find out? They didn't do an autopsy, did they?"

"No. Only blood tests. There was a bottle of Valium in her purse. But there was no trace of it in her. I guess they thought there might be."

Rino looked surprised. "Really? Valium?"

"Was she having some problem?"

Rino turned toward his brother. "Chandler," he said.

"Chandler? The one that's gunning for you?"

"Yeah. Before he died, Ted Reese talked Lee into getting into bed with Chandler. He told her it was the only way he could get tenure at Spring Common. Chandler just cut him a deal. He was the swing vote on the tenure committee. So... Lee did it. But Chandler shafted Reese anyway. A few weeks later, Reese cashed it in."

"When did all this happen?"

"A couple of years ago," said Rino.

"And she was still taking Valium now?"

"I don't know about that. But the Friday night I didn't play cards, Lee and I were at the Seidler after the show. Chandler was there. He came over to us and made a scene—tried to degrade Lee and embarrass me." He paused to take some coffee. "Maybe she never got over it, Lou. She was ashamed... and afraid. When she found out he was after me, she thought he'd do me in like he did Ted Reese. Funny, huh? She was worried about me."

Once again, the whole family drove by night to Canton, five cars of mourners for a girl only two of them had ever seen. At the funeral home, Lou sat wearily, looking at Lee's mother and sister. They, too, looked pale and tired. With such a small family, who did they rely on for support? Who did they talk to? Her sister sat quietly and cried from time to time. Her mother sat as if in a trance, glazed eyes staring at the carpeting or through the walls into some illusion outside.

In the outer room, the younger people were talking softly. Occasionally, he'd hear a subdued laugh. Yet it was quieter than most wakes. There was enough of a sense of tragedy here, at least among those who knew Rino, to realize that the lovely young girl, seemingly asleep in the casket, was a promise unfulfilled, taken from them by a cruel turn of fate.

Lou noticed that Libby never left her mother's side. Larry was in the other room socializing with his cousins, but Libby sat there, as she had last night, looking as dazed and hurt as her mother. He watched her. From time to time, she would gaze at Lee's body lying in the casket, then avert her eyes. Strange that this young girl would sit in here with the adults, her eyes red from crying, while her brother and all her cousins were in the other room. *She's really like her mother,* he thought. *She feels things more.*

Marty and Pete and their wives came with Annie, and Lou talked to them briefly. They all were stunned by Rino's loss. Annie was worried about Lou. He hadn't rested from his trip, yet he was the one the whole family was turning to for guidance. There were a few others from the church and a few neighbors, just those who had found out by word of mouth how important Lee was to the family. Some came, knowing only that Rino's family was here and that they should be, too.

When visiting hours were over, everyone began to move toward the outer rooms. "Uncle Lou, you're coming back to our house, aren't you?" said Frank.

"Yeah, I'll be with you in a minute. Wait for me in the car."

Almost no one had any link between the two families. The only links were Lee and Rino. So when the families came together at the funeral home, they greeted one another formally and from a distance. Lou was troubled by the sight of the two sad women who sat quietly, while the large family of someone they had never seen descended upon the place to intrude upon their grief.

Lou slowly made his way to Lee's mother, who was still sitting in a large Queen Anne chair, not far from the casket. When he was in front of her, he knelt down on one knee to talk. Without any greeting, he said, "I'm Lou, Rino Bellanca's brother."

She seemed uncomfortable, but she turned to him and said softly, "Hello, Mr. Bellanca." She extended her hand to shake with him. Instead, Lou held it and bent forward to kiss it.

"If there's anything I can do—anything—I'd like to help you... for Lee and for my brother."

She studied his face. She could see the goodness and compassion in it that Lee must have seen in Rino. His eyes were tired and full of grief, yet full of desire to be kind to her.

"Anything I can do..." Lou repeated.

"We'll be all right. I'm staying with my daughter a few days. Will your brother come to the funeral tomorrow?" she said.

"Yes, I think so," said Lou.

She nodded slightly in approval. "Thank you for coming. And would you thank your family for me, too?"

Lou nodded. "We won't be here tomorrow, but we'll be at the chapel for the service. I think you'd like to be here alone."

"That's thoughtful of you. But I won't mind if anyone—your brother—wants to come."

"He won't come here," said Lou with certainty.

She nodded, resigned.

Later, at Rino's house, Frank and Jean and Larry quietly had coffee and sweet rolls at the kitchen table. Libby sat alone in the small sunroom at the front of the house, looking out the window at the dark sky. She held a handkerchief bunched in one hand and used it once in a while to wipe the tears from her eyes.

Lou noticed her but didn't go into the sunroom. Instead, he went upstairs to see Rino. "How are you, kid?" he said. "Did you eat anything?"

"I'm not hungry. Jean brought some stuff up before, and I had some of it."

"Have you slept at all?"

"A little."

"Tomorrow I'll be here at 6:30 to pick you up," Lou said affirmatively. Rino didn't answer. "Did you hear me, Rino? You put that black suit on and be ready for me. I'll drive. We'll go alone in my car. The kids and Connie can follow us."

"Were there many people there?" Rino said.

"Our family. Marty and Pete, their wives, Annie, Agee, Hugo, Johnny

Castorina, a few others, and families from the club."

"How many from her family?"

"Not many—a handful of her mother's and sister's friends. It must be a small family."

"It's good of you to do this, kid," said Rino softly. Lately, he had begun to speak in a vague, detached way, almost always looking away from the person he talked to.

"It was good of you to help me when Terry died, Rino," Lou said.

Rino looked at Lou. "I don't want to go to the funeral home," he said.

"I know. We'll go straight to the chapel. By the way, Annie and Pete and Marty's wives are going to serve back here after the funeral."

Rino frowned.

"Rino, you know damn well everyone expects that," said Lou. "You want people to go to a funeral in Canton and not come back here to pay their last respects?"

"All right." Rino sighed.

"Get some sleep. I'll see you tomorrow."

That night, Rino slept only a few hours. Most of the time he sat in the chair awake. Around four o'clock, he began to shave and shower. Then he dressed slowly. His joints seemed stiff, probably because his muscles were tensed most of the time.

He dressed in his black suit. *Jean must have pressed it*, he thought. She also had several ironed shirts in his closet. Finally, when he was dressed, he started downstairs. By then, everyone in the house was up.

When Rino stepped into the large upstairs hallway, Jean was out getting towels from the linen closet. She turned toward him but didn't speak. She looked pale and drawn, almost haggard. He felt sorry for her. *She must feel this more than all the rest*, he thought. She had seen Lee, had talked to her and embraced her.

Without a word, Rino walked over to Jean and kissed her on the cheek. She smiled wanly. "I'll see you downstairs," Rino said. She nodded.

Suddenly, for all of them, it seemed strange to see Rino downstairs. He sat in his favorite easy chair in the living room, waiting for Lou. Frank, Larry, and Libby all came downstairs and greeted him uneasily. Libby, though, seemed to have more difficulty facing him. She came to him wordlessly, kissed him, and left the room quickly.

Jean finally came downstairs. "Would you like some breakfast, Dad? You haven't eaten anything."

"No. Thank you, kid," said Rino.

Frank sat with his father in the living room, but neither of them spoke. Jean quietly made breakfast for her children. Rino finally spoke to Frank: "Go eat breakfast with Jean, Frankie. Or else she won't have anything herself. I'll be all right."

Frank reluctantly went out into the kitchen and left Rino alone. They all stayed in the kitchen until they heard Lou's car in the driveway. When he came inside, Lou greeted all of them. "Where's your dad?" he said to Frank. Frank motioned to the living room.

Lou walked into the living room, surprised to see his brother fully dressed and ready. "How're you doing, kid?" said Lou.

Rino raised his right hand, held it level, and rocked it back and forth in the old Italian version of a silent "so-so."

"All right. Let's go," said Lou.

"Don't you want some breakfast?" said Rino.

"No."

Rino and Lou left the family and promised to wait for them at the chapel. They said very little in the car as Lou drove. Rino kept looking out the window, avoiding his brother.

"I talked to her mother last night," said Lou.

"What's she like?"

"She's nice. I think her voice is just like Lee's. She looks a lot like her."

"Did she ask about me?" said Rino.

"She asked if you were coming to the funeral."

"What kind of church is this?"

"Lutheran, I think. It's at a chapel right near the cemetery," said Lou.

They were early, so Rino and Lou sat in the front on one side of the visitors' aisle. A few people came in, people Rino didn't know. Friends of Lee's family, he thought. Then his own family began to file into pews behind Rino and Lou. One woman came in alone and sat in one of the front pews.

"That isn't her mother, is it, Lou?" Rino asked.

"No. You'll know her when she comes in."

And he did know them both, the mother and the sister. As the minister intoned prayers, Rino watched Lee's sister. She had black hair and wore it medium length, just as Lee and her mother did. But her skin was paler than Lee's, and she looked more American, less French. She had dark eyes, as they all did, but her features were more elongated. Her mother had Lee's soft brown hair but the sister's paler skin. But her mouth was the same full mouth. She seemed a bit taller and less slender than Lee.

Rino didn't hear the service. Seeing the two women only made him think more of Lee. What if Lee had lived? Wouldn't she be a beautiful woman at her mother's age? In her 50s? He tried to pray but couldn't. All he could ask was, *Why? By what twisted universal plan could Lee's death be made meaningful? Why did you take her from me, God? I needed her as I needed life. Why?*

The minister gave his final benediction and dismissed them. There would be no graveside ceremony; the burial would occur after everyone was gone. Rino sat, watching people file slowly out of the chapel. Then he stood and walked up to the casket, which was shrouded in a black drape with a large silver cross embroidered into it. *Lee wasn't there*, he thought. What she was to him: the magic of her laugh, the playful touch, the sparkle in her eyes—all were somewhere other than this box. Of all the things he had ever done, he was glad that he hadn't seen her dead.

Everyone was gone except Rino and Lou, even Lee's mother. After a few minutes, Lou said, "Rino, take as long as you want; I'll wait for you outside." He patted Rino's shoulder and walked away.

After a few minutes, someone called softly, "Mr. Bellanca?" Rino froze. The voice. The inflection of soft, full sounds he had heard so many times. He turned around to face what was behind him. "I'm Toni Gallatin, Lee's mother." God, he wished this were all a nightmare. He wished his own best love would somehow appear to utter words in that voice that had just called his name. "Tomorrow I'll be at Lee's apartment all day," she said. "Would you come there? I'd like to talk to you."

"Yes," he said softly. "I'll be there."

He took one last look at the casket and stayed his gaze a long moment. When he turned, Lee's mother was heading out the door. He walked wearily down the aisle. Outside in the brightness of the day that made him furrow his brow against the strong light, he met two of his children.

Nancy came up to him and put her arms around him and held him tight. He looked at her without talking. "I'm so sorry, Daddy," she said.

Rino kissed her forehead. "I know, baby. I know."

Finally, Jerry confronted him; he stood crookedly before his father, forlorn and tearful. "Pop, I was the troublemaker. I was the one who got the others together. I was the one who hurt you. But so help me God, I'd give anything I have to take those words back. I didn't want this, Pop."

Rino cupped his hand against his son's cheek gently. "It's okay, Jerry. No one wanted this. It just happened."

Jerry cried, still not touching his father. Rino hugged him. "Someday, remember not to do that again to someone else... and remember that I forgave you. Okay?" Jerry nodded. "I'll see you at the house," said Rino.

On the way back, Lou was quiet and thoughtful. What could he say to a man whose dreams had been so shattered? "Rino, I know it's going to be tough at the house. But you hang in there, huh? I'll be there. Anything you need, just let me know. It won't take long; then they'll all go."

"I'll get through it, Lou."

When they got home, cars were parked all along the curb near Rino's house. Lou drove into the driveway, and Rino got out of the car slowly. Inside, Annie and her two friends were already serving coffee to all who had come to pay respect. They had already set up the buffet. All they were waiting for was the return of Rino.

One by one, his family and close friends sought him out to express condolences. They knew little of the story. All they knew was that Rino seemed dazed and tired and that the loss of this girl, the grief of her passing, and the exhaustion of the trip weighed heavily upon him and made him look old.

Andrea Manasseri approached him. "Rino, I'm so sorry about what happened. She was a lovely girl." She seemed, for the first time, to be speaking from her heart, for the first time without the facade between herself and the outside world.

"It was kind of you to come, Andrea. Please, you and your children make sure you have something at the buffet," Rino said, glad to dismiss her.

Lou was watching him as he talked to Andrea. And after she walked away, Rino caught Lou staring at him. The look in his eyes told Lou all he could want to know. Lee had changed Rino, had taken him far beyond what his brother's machinations or Andrea's mystery could ever have done. He would never be the same again.

In little more than two hours, everyone had gone. Lou came over to Rino. "I'm going home, kid. I'll call you later. Get some rest."

Rino went to his room and collapsed, exhausted, on the bed. He would have to live his life without her. But how? Every breath he breathed, every word he said, she was with him. How could he work and visit and play without her? To have her in his heart and in his dreams, yet never see her again? How?

He slept until evening. When he awoke, he could feel damp sweat on his body. He could also hear a few noises downstairs. But he wanted to see no one; he wanted to be alone in the small space of his room. He took a shower and returned to the room. In bed again, he touched the space beside him. How many nights had he done this and found Lee? How many times had he awoken during the night wondering if Lee was just a dream, only to reach out his hand and touch her breasts or her belly? He fell asleep again.

The next morning, he awoke early. He shaved and showered and then returned to his room. The chair, so familiar for so many years, had now become his refuge within the bedroom. He stayed there until past noon. Then he dressed and went downstairs.

"I'm going out for a while," he said to Jean. "I'll be back later."

How many times had he done this? he thought as he got into his car and headed for Lee's apartment. It seemed strange now, walking up the steps to the second floor. He knew she wouldn't be there to greet him. It was as though he were climbing a mountain. His heart pounded; the steps never seemed to end.

Finally, before the door, he hesitated. For the first time in memory, he said a prayer. He didn't remember praying when Mary died, or Jimmy. But he prayed for Lee. *If only this were a dream; if only the last four nights had never happened; if only it were Sunday and she was waiting inside, behind this door. God, of all the millions of people on earth, this little girl is all I ask. Take everything I have, only take away the last four days and give Lee back to me.*

He rang the bell, and the terrible reality of it all met him face to face;

Lee's mother opened the door. She said nothing but stood aside as he entered. He stood in the middle of the room as if she weren't there. She sat down in a chair, the two of them seeming actors in a mute pantomime.

He walked into the kitchen and turned on the light. Then he walked down the hall and looked in the bathroom, the spare bedroom, and, finally, in their room. The whole apartment was as she had left it: neat and orderly, spotlessly clean. *That was Lee*, he thought. It had never looked any different any time he came. She liked everything in it and had a place for it all.

He looked at the bed they had slept in so many nights. The spread seemed to be a cover now, closing out memories to be held in his heart but not to be made in this bed... ever again.

As he looked around the bedroom one last time and was turning to leave, he saw a small bottle on the dresser. He picked it up. Valium. Dated in March, a year before he ever knew her.

He went back into the living room, took off his coat, and draped it over an arm of the couch. Then he sat in the chair he usually sat in. Toni was a beautiful woman, less slender and athletic than Lee, yet so much of Lee was in her.

"Why didn't you come to the funeral home?" she said finally, her voice betraying the hurt his absence had caused her.

"I didn't want to see her that way." He sighed.

"I had to see her that way," she said with an edge in her soft voice.

"And I had to see my wife and my son that way when they died," Rino said pointedly. "But not her... not Lee."

They were both hurt and tired—and very uncomfortable.

"Did you really love her, Mr. Bellanca?" she said hesitantly.

"More than I could ever love anybody," he said.

"She told me that about you, too," she said. "You know that when I found out how old you were, I was against it and tried to talk her out of it?"

"I knew you would be," he said. "I would have been for my daughter, too. But you changed, didn't you?"

"I changed because of what I saw in her. When she was married to Ted, she was depressed and unhappy all the time; their marriage—their lives—were unraveling. Then, when Ted killed himself, she came apart. She was in the hospital for a week. When she got out, she moved in here. But this fall, I noticed a change in her. She was smiling more, and her eyes seemed to sparkle. Then she told me about you.

"Each time we were together, I could see what was happening to her. She had never looked more beautiful in her life. She had never been so happy in her life. Everything about her: her voice, her personality… She glowed.

"And I realized it was all because she was in love with you. So I made up my mind that after all the awful times she had had in her young life, her 20s… Anything that could change her so, and make her happy, was right and good."

"Thank you," he said. "You were better about it than my own children."

It was such an eerie feeling, hearing her voice… almost like hearing Lee again. "Mr. Bellanca—"

"Rino," he said, interrupting her.

Her eyes clouded. "I can't," she said, shaking her head. "Lee called you that so many times. That was her name for you." He nodded. "You can have anything in this apartment you want. I'm going to get rid of the furniture and just keep her personal things."

"I don't think I want anything," he said.

"Why? Surely there are memories here for you…"

"I'm not sure I can even live without her, Mrs. Gallatin," he said. "I…" He thought for a moment about Lou and what he had said about spoiling Lee's story. "There is something," he said finally.

"Anything," she said, leaning forward with interest.

"I'd like that little blue robe of hers, and those gold slippers. That's all I need."

"Is that all? You can have anything here."

"No. Just those two."

"Mr. Bellanca, I've brought you some pictures of her. When she was home last week, I took her to a friend, who's a photographer, and he took them." She grimaced ironically. "I wanted something of her while she was still mine."

Rino looked at the pictures. His heart ached as he went through them one by one. There was the sparkle, the smile, the big eyes. "May I have this one?" he said.

"Yes. You may have them all. There were negatives, and... after the accident, I had another set printed." Then she stopped, holding her face in her hands. Rino made no move to help her. He couldn't be that close to that voice, that hair, again. In a few moments, she regained her composure. "I was going to give you a wedding present someday, but... well, please accept these from me now."

"Thank you," he said. He hesitated for a few seconds. "There is something I'd like to know. How long was she taking Valium?"

She grimaced and raised her eyebrows, just the way Lee did when she was troubled. "She took it for about two years, before Ted's death, then after. But–and this is why I know how happy she was–she stopped taking them when she met you. That was when I knew what your love meant to her."

"Could she have taken it last weekend, before the accident? They found some in her purse."

"I know," she said. "And I don't know why they were in her purse, but I know she wasn't taking them anymore. She was just too happy."

Rino didn't answer her. He looked around the apartment that he would never see again. He looked at the couch where she had sat cross-legged next to him so many nights.

"I put something in that box," Toni said. "It's the robe and slippers that she bought for you. I'll put her things in the box, too."

Rino nodded. She got up, went into the bedroom, and returned with Lee's robe. "Is this the one?" she said, holding it out in front of her.

"Yes," he said. "That's it."

She folded it and put it and the slippers in the box, atop his robe. Then she went over to her purse on the end table near the couch and returned to the chair across from him again.

"There's something else," she said. "This was also in the car the night she died. Lieutenant Bellino, your nephew, brought this purse to me this morning." She reached into the purse, took out an envelope, and handed it to Rino. It was sealed. On the front of it was "Rino" in Lee's handwriting. Rino opened it and started to read it. Suddenly, as she watched him, he stopped, shook his head to himself, and put it back into the envelope.

"Was there something wrong?" Toni said.

"No. I just can't read it now," he said. Then he shook his head as if to shrug off the pain he felt in reading it. She didn't ask to see it; she must have known it was only a note of love between a man and a woman.

"Mr. Bellanca, I'd like to ask you something personal, but it's something I have to know."

"I'll tell you," he said matter-of-factly.

"Was Lee pregnant? She never said anything to me, but... well, I'm her mother, and I'm a nurse, and..." She looked directly at him.

"We were sure she was," said Rino.

"Oh God," she whispered, lowering her head and clutching her hands in her lap.

Suddenly he was filled with compassion for her. It was as though he were seeing Lee for the first time, suffering and pathetic. He walked over to her, knelt down in front of her, and reached out. She threw herself into his arms and sobbed. He felt the soft brown hair against his cheek and the sweet feel and odor of someone small within his arms. Then he just held her until she stopped crying. When she was done, she moved back to look at him. Then she reached forward and kissed him on the cheek. "Mr. Bellanca..."

"Please call me Rino," he said. "She would want that."

"Rino, I have never known of another woman who did what Lee did with you. The two of you made magic. And do you know what she told me? She said she had waited all her life to be in love with you... only with you."

When he got home, Rino went back to his room. He took everything out of one of his dresser drawers. Then he took both robes, as Toni Gallatin had folded them, and put them into the drawer with the slippers. He picked Lee's robe back up and buried his face in it. The faint scent of her was still there. Then he closed the drawer and sat in his chair.

The rightness of their love, the purity of it—that was what caused him all the pain. If it were hard to come by, if it were easily strained, if they were the same age, if she were not pregnant, if it were an ordinary love, if she were not Lee... if she were not Lee...

He turned on a table lamp on his nightstand and took out the pictures of Lee. He looked at all of them and then put them away in the drawer with the robes in it. Then he went over to a small chest where he had his personal mementos. He took out the letter and read it:

Dear Rino,

It's very late here and very quiet. I'm sure Mother has been asleep for a long while. But I'm wide awake. This bed that I slept in as I grew up, this room that I spent my girlhood in, seems too large and empty now.

I think about our room and our bed and your deep breathing when you're asleep beside me. I think about our baby growing within me, and

I know that I belong somewhere else now, wherever you are. I've been wondering the last few days what I ever did to deserve such happiness, but I can't think of anything special. All I can say is that I know I was never meant to be anyone but the girl you love, the girl you met when you thought you couldn't be in love again, the girl with whom you helped make a new life grow. Our last months together have been the most wonderful that I've ever had. And I thought I was incapable of true happiness again. Thank you, my darling. If the world ended tonight, I've had more happiness than anyone has ever had. I'll be waiting for you when you get back Sunday. (I hope I haven't gotten too chubby in the week since you've seen me.) Wherever you are (since I can't mail this to you), I hope that God is keeping you safe for me. I'm yours forever. Be mine, too.

Lee

Rino folded the letter, put it away, and lay down on the bed again. What was he going to do? What was there to live for now?

It was 10 o'clock. He wasn't sure whether he had fallen asleep. And he thought he heard a knock on the door. It surprised him. The knock was soft, not like Jean's or Frankie's. He opened the door, and outside stood Libby in her pajamas.

"Grandpa, can I talk to you?" she said. She had been crying.

"Sure, baby, come in," he said.

She sat down on his bed, and he sat next to her. She hesitated for a few seconds, uncertain of how to begin. "What color eyes did she have, Grandpa?"

He stared at her for a few seconds. The face had changed in the few months since he last bothered to look. The slight thinning of the cheeks, the maturing of her eyes—she was becoming a young woman. And tonight, the troubles she felt made her look older than she really was.

"They were brown, Lib," he said softly.

"Those nights at the funeral home... like she was sleeping... I wanted to know... but her eyes were closed."

Rino took a deep breath when she said "sleeping."

Libby looked up at him. "I'll never be as beautiful as she was," she said plaintively.

"You're beautiful, Lib. You just look different than—"

"I'm cute, Grandpa, but I'll never look like her," she said, shaking her head.

"You can be as good as she was, Lib."

"But I'll never have someone love me the way you loved her," she said.

"Sure you will, babe. You don't have to be beautiful to have someone love you. Look at me." He smiled, hoping she would feel better. Instead, she lowered her eyes away from him, and they were filling with tears again.

"Grandpa, I'd change places with her right now if she could come back to life for you."

Her words frightened him. The thought of somehow losing Libby after Lee made his heart falter. But he also realized that what she had said was the fine, selfless wish of a child who thought more of others than herself. In simple love and caring, she was as good as her mother.

"Listen to me, honey. Life isn't like that. When bad things happen, you can't turn back the clock. All you can do is hope that when those people were alive, you were good to them."

She began to cry. He put his arm around her and held her close.

"Grandpa, please come back to us," she whispered. "I can't stand it when you're up here all alone like this. I know you miss her. Let us help you, please."

Rino held her away to look at her. The eyes and the face of every woman he cared about had been red and tear-stained lately, he thought.

He walked over to the dresser and took the folder of pictures of Lee out of the drawer. "This is the picture I'm going to put in a frame and keep there," he said, pointing to the top of the dresser. Mary's picture was no longer there; he had taken it away months ago and put it up on the wall.

"I can see why you loved her, Grandpa," she said.

"But I love you, too, honey." He took the picture from her, put it back into the folder, laid it atop Lee's robe, and closed the drawer. "Lib, if I come down, will you make me some toast and tea and have some with me?"

She smiled and hugged him. Then she took his hand and led him out of the room.

The next morning, Rino was sitting in the kitchen having coffee when he saw Lou's car pull into the driveway. Lou walked in, not expecting to see him downstairs. Lou looked at Jean, who simply raised her eyebrows to indicate uncertainty.

Things must be getting better, Lou thought. "Are you done with your coffee?" said Lou.

"Yeah. Why?"

"Get your coat. I have to go somewhere." Rino hesitated for a second. "Come on, man," Lou urged.

Finally, he got his coat and followed Lou out to the car. Lou drove down to one of the old mills, long since closed. "I'm glad you came out of your room," said Lou.

"It was time," Rino said.

Lou stopped his car at Pig Iron Bridge. "Come on. Let's take a walk," he said.

Rino got out of the car and walked with his brother. Below them were the mills that so many of their friends and family had worked in, loading pig iron and hauling glowing ingots of steel. The Mahoning River flowing through the dormant mills was still a dirty brown.

When they were children, they would run up one sidewalk of the long bridge, cross over, and run down the other side. Below them, the molten currents of steel used to splash into giant rectangular molds.

"I don't know why she was taken from you, Rino," Lou said suddenly as they walked. "Every time I think about it, it drives me crazy. But look: this girl gave you something I never had, nor your kids, nor the guys at the Tre-Sette... nor you, Rino, with Mary. Whatever she had for you was magic. Just think: the day she was born, you were out here working, playing cards, golfing, raising the kids. All those years, without you knowing it, she was turning into a dream come true... just for you.

"So your memories are better than mine, kid. And your pain is worse. But then, Lee gave you enough to keep you going. Remember that she and that baby are waiting for the man she held in her arms those nights, not some loser who blows his goddamned brains out. Hear me, Rino? It won't ever be right that way. Never."

Lou drove Rino back home and came into the house to have a cup of coffee. Jean was with them in the kitchen when Rino heard the mailbox lid slam shut outside. He went to get the mail, a single letter with the college insignia on it. Lou was standing in the doorway of the living room, watching his brother open the envelope and read its contents. Suddenly Rino's face contorted, and tears ran from his eyes. He crushed the letter in his hands and threw it across the room.

"What was it, for God's sake, Rino?" Lou asked.

"My letter of apology from Chandler."

Part II

The Malandrine

ON FRIDAY NIGHT, Rino played poker. The boys were glad to see him. And he won, not because he played well, but because he was lucky. Also, there was a subliminal nonaggressiveness among the gang at Agee's. They called his bets, when in prior times they would have raised him. Then they'd often drop when he would raise.

After the game, Lou walked Rino out to his car. "You can still come to the banquet, cowboy... sit at our table."

"No, kid, I don't feel up to it."

"Guarino, I know it still hurts, but it's been over a year, and you're getting worse instead of better. Lee wouldn't want this. You know that."

"A year Sunday, Lou," was all Rino said as he got into his car.

Lou held the door before Rino could close it. "Listen to me, Rino," Lou said. "So you didn't blow your brains out. Is this better? Don't you see it's the same thing, only it's taking you longer to die?" Rino closed the door and drove away.

Rino slept Saturday morning away. When Libby knocked on his door at 10 o'clock, he had been lying awake for only a few minutes. She came into the room and sat on his bed. "It's breakfast time, sleepyhead," she said.

"I'm awake," he said. "I was just getting up."

"God, Grandpa, you were up late last night. You must be whipped."

"Old people don't need much sleep, Lib," he said, smiling.

"Are you okay, Grandpa? I don't have to go to that game tonight if you want to talk."

"No, kid, you go to the game. I'll be just fine. We can talk later."

She smiled broadly. Libby and Jean had decided without ever discussing it that they would take care of Rino. There was something about what had happened to him—Lee's sudden death, the hurtful months afterward—that made Libby and Jean feel that somehow Rino had paid too much. There had been something about his story: the look on Rino's face when he and Lee fell in love and the disconsolate loneliness he felt at her loss that made them want to hover around him to see that he was content.

He had changed in the last year, had grown quieter and more pensive. He stayed at home more, spent more time with Frank's family and with Lou and Connie. His life had become more routine than it had ever been. He never worked full weeks anymore. And he missed poker often. He took long walks in fall and winter and golfed less in the summer. He kept busy reading, doing household chores, and talking to Lou.

Everyone gave him room. Yet Lou tried to keep him active and involved with life again, forcing cares and obligations and deadlines upon him.

On the other hand, it was the women in his life who tended to his quiet moments. Jean and Libby looked after him and made him comfortable. But most of all they talked to him, confided in him, appealed to his wisdom, and listened eagerly if he ever talked of Lee. And, with Connie's help, they saw to it that no one brought disorder upon the life he was sorting out so quietly.

The next Tuesday, Rino worked at Spring Common. It was all easy work. After he was done buffing the halls of the science building, Rino headed across the green to Crandall to fix the plumbing in the women's lavatory on the second floor. He stopped at the cafeteria on his break. The coffee tasted good on the cool November Friday afternoon. It was a football day, breezy and bright.

Rino sat, preoccupied, in the deserted cafeteria. He hadn't seen Connie for almost a week. He'd have to see her... maybe tonight.

Just then, Barly came into the dining room. He surveyed the room, spotted Rino at the corner table, and waved to him, motioning for him to stay while he bought his coffee. As Barly headed toward him, Rino watched him. He had a funny gait, almost as though one leg wanted to linger behind him on each step. "How you doin', man?" said Barly, smiling as usual as he sat down.

"Not bad, Bar. How about you?"

"I'm okay... Nice day, huh?"

"Yeah."

"Where you headed after this?" Barly said.

"I have to go fix some leaks on the second floor of Crandall."

"The women's john again?"

"Yeah."

"I told Sammy about that last week. When did he give it to you?"

"This morning when I came in."

"You're losing some weight, huh, Rino?"

"Yeah... some."

"You okay, man? Anything I can do for you?"

"No. Thanks, Bar. You've been a good friend. I appreciate the free time and benefits you kept going for me last year."

"All I did was lean on Sammy, man. It wouldn't have gone down if it weren't for him." Barly took another sip of his coffee. "Speaking of all that... did you know your friend Chandler was just chosen teacher laureate?"

"Chandler? Jesus Christ!" Rino said.

"Him and that Indian guy from Engineering—you know, the one with the turban?"

"He's supposed to be a decent guy, right?"

"Yeah, always real nice when you talk to him. But let me tell you a little scoop I heard. I think Chandler rigged his part."

Rino snorted. "I can believe it."

"You know Betty, that pretty black secretary in Education? She tells me everything she knows, and that's considerable. Word is that the blonde instructor that Chandler's been banging had a letter-writing campaign going. She contacted alumni by phone and asked them to write letters. Then she went around flopping her tits against the other profs—even the dean."

"And so it was automatic, right?"

"Yeah, but they're supposed to play that one straight, man. They aren't supposed to mention it to the students—no campaigns. This guy gave her time in class to make a pitch."

"So the fucker pulled another one off. Hell, you just might be talking about the next president, Bar." Rino sighed and then drank a sip of coffee.

"Well," said Barly, "I just wanted you to know that your boy is up to the same old shit again."

Rino couldn't get Chandler out of his mind as he walked toward Crandall Hall. Chandler had moved on to new conquests. Rino had been just one small hitch in an otherwise superbly executed career trajectory. Chandler had easily gotten over the setback he'd suffered at the hands of the College Affairs Committee and had lived down his letter of apology to Rino. He had been smart enough to react quietly to the administration decision that he apologize to Rino. He'd sent his letter and forgotten it. And now the administration, feeling guilty about the embarrassment of one of its young stars, was willing to make amends. The letter-writing campaign gave them just the opportunity. They'd named Chandler as one of the teachers of the year. It wouldn't do to have a custodian win a pitched battle against a professor. Chandler had been made whole again.

Rino worked the next day, Wednesday, again. Then he had a long weekend ahead. Sammy always tried to give him long weekends nowadays. He also never made Rino a full-time substitute for people who were on vacation.

Sammy was saddened by what had happened to Rino. When Lee died, he told Rino to take as much time off as he needed. He and Barly also worked it out so that Rino had a different kind of job now: no painting anymore, just wiring, plumbing, buffing, and some general maintenance work. Neither one wanted to lose Rino, either as a worker or a friend.

Even his younger fellow workers, who knew vaguely of some personal troubles in Rino's life—a death in the family—liked and respected him. And they also regarded him as a kind of folk hero for winning a grievance against a professor, especially one like Chandler.

On Saturday, Rino kept busy. He went shopping, put gas in both cars, checked the air in the tires of the Buick, and had it washed. Then he went to the Tre-Sette and watched the Ohio State game. He and Agee talked a little. Lou came in late in the game and asked him once again to come to the dance at the Cavour Club. Again, Rino refused.

That night he watched television and had some tea with Jean and Frank and Libby. They all knew what anniversary was coming with sunup tomorrow, but none of them mentioned it. Later, when Libby and Frank were upstairs, Rino said to Jean, "I'm not going to be here most of the day tomorrow."

"Where are you going?" Jean said.

"Canton."

"Dad, shouldn't you... Why don't you let us drive you? Frank and I can come and—"

"Not tomorrow," he said. "I have to go alone tomorrow."

That night Rino sat on his bed, ran his hand over the spread, and went to the drawer where Lee's blue robe and pictures were. He looked at each picture, longing for more than they could give him... memories being pale substitutes for life. He touched the robe and the tie that he had unloosened so many times, both in passion and in play.

It became harder to imagine her in the robe. It seemed so small, so devoid of the essence of life that had once filled it and made the robe seem magical. Finally, after about an hour, he fell asleep.

The sun shone through mottled gray clouds that rolled forward toward Rino over the horizon. The day was pleasant and warm for November. Route 62 was clear and dry, and the few cars he saw were around small towns he traveled through on his way west. He wasn't sure what he wanted to do or what he would feel when he got to the cemetery. He was also afraid.

The cemetery was smaller than the one he knew in Youngstown. This one was only for the Protestants of the town. The Jews and Catholics each had their own. As he entered through the large wrought-iron gates, he could see the chapel that was in his nightmares so many nights: Lee calling him from within the casket or sitting up and talking to him, telling him how she didn't want to leave him. He averted his eyes from the chapel and drove past it, intent on finding the cemetery office. When he went into the office, no one was there. In a few moments, a tall, light-haired young man in a cardigan sweater entered. "Hi, can I help you?" he said.

"Yeah. Can you tell me how to get to the Gallatin family plot?"

The man went over to a large book and paged through it. "They're in

Section 18, Plots 29 to 38." He showed Rino how to get to the gravesites by a large wall map.

Rino thanked him and went back to his car. The place was all beautifully landscaped, gentle dales and rolling hills. Very little of it was flat ground. There were trees everywhere. And the sunlight shone through the large old trees and fell on small marble and bronze grave markers that seemed to litter the ground. Small, numbered stones were set at intervals as guides through the lanes. Finally, he spotted section 18. He stopped and began to walk straight back from the road, as the young man had told him. There was a large oak tree about 50 yards from the road. That was where the young man had guessed the locations of the plots 29 to 38 were. Sure enough, he saw striking Roman letters carved into a large gray marble grave marker: Gallatin. As he stopped before the graves, he saw only three—Joseph, Hilda, and a single other grave with a smaller marker, Dr. Stephen, Lee's father, who died in 1978.

Maybe I missed one, he thought. He searched several other headstones. This was the only Gallatin plot, but Lee's grave wasn't there. Suddenly, Rino grew anxious. Not finding the grave disoriented him. Somehow, the least he expected was that she was resting somewhere near her family.

Hurriedly, he got back into his car and returned to the office. The young man seemed surprised to see him. "Anything wrong?"

"The Reese girl isn't in the family plot," Rino said.

"Reese? In the Gallatin plot?"

"She's a daughter," Rino said.

"What's her first name?"

"Leila... Leila Reese. Why wasn't she buried near her father?"

"Well, I don't know that," the young man said, smiling tolerantly. "But I think I can tell you where Leila Reese is buried." He again paged through the book. "She's in one of the new sections, plots 11 and 12."

"Two plots? Is someone else buried there?"

"No, one grave's empty. It's near a Japanese cherry tree on the hillside, one of the prettiest parts of this place." He showed Rino on the map.

Back in his car, Rino paused before starting again. *What's wrong with me?* he wondered. *Why does it bother me that she's away from the family? Why did I even come here? That chapel drives me crazy. I can't bear those dreams anymore. Now she's not where I thought she was this past year.*

He started the car and drove slowly around the lanes as the man had instructed. Around one curve was a hill on the left where he could see a terrace in the hillside. Near the terrace was a large tree. He checked the marker. Section 31.

Rino trudged slowly up the hillside. *He had never done anything to deserve this wretched loneliness*, he thought. He had never done anything to deserve this long walk up to the grave of the only woman in the world whom he had given his whole heart to. She wasn't too much to ask, out of all the women who had ever lived. When he found her, she was alone and unwanted. Then, when he fell in love with her, when she meant more to him than anything ever did, she was taken from him.

The gravestone was a small, wedge-shaped marble slab that lay upon the ground, slightly outside the reach of the cherry tree. He read the inscription: *Leila Gallatin Reese, 1955–1988*. Around the grave there was only grass, no other marker. The caretaker was right. It was a beautiful part of the cemetery.

Rino knelt down on one knee, made the sign of the cross, and said a brief prayer for the dead that he remembered from his childhood. Then, in his mind, he called to her: *Lee.*

But all he saw when he opened his eyes was a lovely, tranquil place beneath an old tree, overlooking a small lake at the foot of the hill. Somehow it seemed to bespeak Lee: the beauty, the serenity, the quiet remoteness.

Finally, he walked down the hill. *It won't be as hard to come back now*, he thought. *Maybe it won't be as hard.*

Out of the cemetery, he drove to a gas station to ask directions. He wasn't sure if he was doing the right thing, both for himself and for her, but he had to try. He needed someone who could talk to him; he needed someone who knew how much he had lost.

It took him a few minutes to get there, but he found it easily. It was a graceful, white frame house with a long lawn sloping down to the street. There was a portico in front where a walk led from the front to the side of the house. A drive curved up the hill, past the portico, and back down to the street. Rino parked his car in front of the portico and went to the door.

When he rang the bell, Lee's mother opened the door. She seemed startled for a second, as though she had never seen him before or had forgotten who he was. But after a few seconds, she simply pulled the door aside and stepped back, letting him walk in. She closed the door and led him to a small library room, bypassing a large living room, a dining room, and another sitting room. The library was smaller and more intimate. "We can talk in here," she said, smiling weakly.

"Am I keeping you from anything?" Rino said.

"No," she said, shaking her head. "Can I get you something to drink? Some coffee?"

"Coffee would be fine."

"I'll be back in a minute," she said.

While she was gone, he looked around nervously. There was a stone fireplace, bookcases built into the walls, a small Parsons table in front of a white-curtained bay window that overlooked a side garden. At one side of the fireplace hearth was a love seat, and on the other were two Queen Anne chairs. Between them on a coffee table was a vase of flowers.

She returned silently and sat down opposite him on the loveseat. She looked at him, surveying the drawn, troubled face, the weariness of his visage. "You've lost some weight," she said uneasily.

"A little. It's been a rough year."

"Have you been sick?"

He looked at her a moment and then shook his head. She took a deep breath, knowing what his response meant.

"Why isn't she buried in the family plot?" he said directly.

Toni stood and walked over to the fireplace. She lit a match and ignited the kindling set beneath several thick logs. Rino watched her curiously. She, too, had lost weight, and more than that, she had lost some of her refined beauty. In the last year, she had seemed to grow grayer and more pallid, especially about the eyes and mouth. She took a deep breath. "I didn't want her there," she said.

"Why?" he said, his voice weak and slightly rasping.

She turned away from him, looking into the fire, her hands joined together in front of her. How much she reminded him of Lee, Rino thought. "I thought she might belong somewhere else," she said, still not facing him. Then she turned toward Rino, and on his face she saw bewilderment. "There's a clause in my will that says she'll be moved if..." She stopped, frustrated, not wanting to go on. He didn't understand, and she couldn't say what she wanted him to feel. She was getting annoyed with herself. "Well, there are two plots there..."

Slowly it dawned on him what she had done. "The second one is for me?" he said softly.

"If you want it," she whispered.

"Of course I want it," he said.

She began to cry. He stood up and held his hand out to her. She took it and came into his arms. He held her until she stopped sobbing. Then he brushed his own tears away quickly.

Finally, she moved. "Your coffee," she said. "I'll be right back."

He suddenly had an eerie feeling. He was now waiting for Toni to make him coffee, just as Lee had done all those nights, barely two years ago.

Lee, too, had cried in his arms; Lee, too, had been nervous when they first met. And her voice. It was as though Lee was talking to him again. The voice, the mannerisms, the gentility... *I wonder if she'll bring some rolls on a tray*, he thought.

In a few minutes, she came in with a large, round ceramic pot and set it down on a trivet. Then, without looking at him, she walked back out of the room. She returned with a tray loaded with sliced sweet rolls, cookies, and cups. Rino took a deep breath. How many times had Lee done that? She had held his hand and poured the coffee. Toni just poured a cup and handed it to him. She handed him a small plate and then held the tray for him. He shook his head slightly and smiled. She had a quizzical look on her face as she looked down at him. He tried to explain. "The second time I met Lee, she did this very thing... the coffee, the rolls... and she held the tray while I chose what I wanted."

She smiled. "It's a part of us," she said. "My other daughter would do the same thing."

"Is she like Lee?"

"Not as vulnerable as Lee. She's as gentle and as loving... but not as playful."

"She sounds like my daughter-in-law," he said. She nodded and sipped her coffee. After a few seconds, Rino spoke again, "Why didn't you tell me about the grave and the other plot?"

"Because I didn't know if you would ever come to see me, or what your children would feel... and I didn't know about you... your feelings for your wife."

Rino took a deep breath. "My wife and I were happy... and faithful to each other. There was love, but it wasn't what Lee and I had."

"Then I'll put your name on the other plot." She hesitated. "Are you sure? What about your children?"

"My children have nothing to say about this," Rino said.

They talked a long time, well after darkness had settled, and tried not to talk about Lee, though often they couldn't help it. Once, abruptly, Toni asked him if he wanted to see Lee's room. He said he did, and he followed her upstairs. First, she showed him three other bedrooms and a small den. Then she brought him to Lee's room. Rino walked in, feeling strangely out of place, and looked around. Then he turned to Toni, gesturing toward the closet. "May I?" he asked.

"Yes," she said.

He opened the closet and looked inside. There were about a half dozen dresses. "Are these all her clothes?" he said.

"Yes, most of what I kept," she said. "A few others are in the drawers over there."

He touched the black-and-white dress she wore the night they went to Castorina's. Toni was watching him intently. He seemed to sense Toni's eyes at his back. "I had to come here," he said, not turning toward her. "You're all I've got. Do you know how much your voice sounds like hers?"

"People have told me that," she said quietly.

When they went back downstairs, Toni showed him the rest of the house. It was strange seeing the place where Lee had grown up. How joyful it must have been, he thought.

They sat in the living room this time, and talked a little more. Finally, Toni said, "What made you come here after so long a time?"

Rino thought for a minute. "To visit the grave... I've never done that. And to see you. I need someone to talk to about her. And when I hear your voice, I know she wasn't just a dream I had."

After about another hour, he said, "I'd better go."

She got his coat from a front hall closet and stood quietly while he put it on and buttoned it. "Rino," she said. He looked up at her, surprised to hear his first name. "If you want to hear my voice, I'll talk to you any time. And since we're the only ones who can share her now... will you come back to see me once in a while?"

He nodded. "I'll be back. You take care of yourself, okay? If you need anything at all, just call me. I'll be here in an hour."

"I'm glad you came," she said.

"I should have come sooner," he said as he walked out the front door and off the porch toward his car. She stayed at the door watching. Suddenly he stopped and walked back to the door. "You're just like her, you know. Lee would have done the same with those two plots if it were her daughter."

She closed her eyes for a moment in a gesture of gratitude and relief. "She belongs with you. You don't know how good I feel now that I know you want to be with her... when you could be with your wife."

"She was my wife," he said as he turned away.

The next morning, Jean was full of foreboding as she made coffee and toast for Rino. She dreaded seeing his face when he came downstairs. Last night, he had come home and simply said goodnight and went upstairs. Jean and Frank exchanged glances of relief just to see him walk through the door unhurt.

But this morning was a new day, a new time beyond Lee's passing, the beginning of life without her again. When Rino came downstairs, Jean hesitated to turn toward him.

"Hi, kid. Where is everybody?"

His tone surprised her. She turned and said, "Libby doesn't start school for an hour... delay because of fog... and Frank's just getting up."

Rino poured himself a cup of coffee. "Tastes good," he said as he sat down at the table.

"How do you feel, Dad?" Jean asked.

"I'm better, Jean."

"What did you do yesterday?"

"I went to the cemetery in Canton. Then I went to see her mother."

"Is that all? You got in late."

"I stayed there a long time, just talking."

His voice was different, almost the way it used to be, she thought. Maybe it was her imagination, but he seemed a little brighter. "What do you want for supper? I can make anything you like."

"How about stuffed cabbage?" he said. "Sauerkraut and all. That'll get it out of your system for a while." He was smiling.

"I'll have it at 5:30, with mashed potatoes and apple pie, okay?"

"Best offer I've had all day," he said.

At work, as Rino entered the locker room, there was a right-of-first-refusal list posted on the bulletin board. The list was according to seniority, and Rino's name, of course, was near the bottom, both because of his few years at the college and his part-time status. Someone had to volunteer for the faculty council awards banquet.

Barly and Joe were standing together talking, waiting for Sammy to arrive. "Man, the gentlefolk are here," said Barly, winking to Joe. Rino took off his coat, smirking but ignoring Barly's good-natured taunt.

"Hey, Barly," said Rino, "what are the chances of working that awards banquet?"

Barly seemed surprised, first because Rino wanted to work, and second because he wanted the odd hours. "You sure, man?" Barly said.

"Yeah."

"I can get it for you easy. People ain't too crazy about working Friday nights."

"I'd appreciate it, Bar."

Rino had to work in Stilton Hall, putting in new florescent light fixtures in a large lecture hall. They had canceled the class, so he had plenty of time to work. Joe helped him, and they were able to hang most of the fixtures they needed.

A few minutes after 11:00, Barly stopped in to see them. "You guys going to lunch at 12:00?"

"Yeah, we should be done," said Joe. Rino nodded.

"Hey, Rino, looks like one big party Friday night. You and me and Joe are working the banquet."

"Joe, too? Good deal, Bar."

"Joe told me, if you worked it, so would he. And since I have super seniority... hell, I can't let you guys have all the fun."

"After the banquet, I'll take you both out for a drink," said Rino.

At lunchtime, Sammy stopped at their table and said to Rino, "I want to talk to you after you do that job in Stilton. You gonna be done today?"

"Yeah," said Rino. "Maybe about 2:30, okay?"

"Okay. Don't forget."

When the job was over, Rino and Joe cleaned up. They tested the lights and a rheostat Rino had installed. "Everything's fine. You're one hell of a 'lectrician, Rino," said Joe in admiration.

"Thanks, kid. I'm not gonna take a break today. I have to go see Sammy."

Sammy was at his office desk working on timecards when Rino entered the workroom. The door to the office was closed. Rino knocked, and Sammy waved him in. "Hi, boss," said Rino as he settled down into an odd chair facing Sammy's desk in the small office.

"I understand you want some overtime," he said, eyeing Rino skeptically.

"Yeah. I didn't think anyone would want to work it," said Rino.

"Since when are you interested in extra hours? You know I'd put you on full time in a minute if you wanted it."

"I don't need any extra hours, Sam," Rino said weakly. "I just want to work the banquet."

"You know Chandler's gonna be one of the honored guests at that banquet, right?"

"Yeah, I heard that."

"Come on, goombah!"

"Okay, he's gonna get an award. So what?"

Sammy looked down at his hands, then looked back up at Rino and spoke hesitantly. "Rino, you're not gonna do anything dumb at this banquet, are you?"

"You mean like throwing a pie in his face, Sam?"

"I'm serious, goombah. You and I both know fucking well that the only reason you're going there is because of Chandler. I just don't want to see you screw up your life by going after that bastard."

"Don't worry about it, Sam. I won't cause any trouble."

"Rino, there's something more between you and Chandler, isn't there? It's not just the grievance?"

"I don't like the man, Sam," he said softly. "Look, I'm not gonna blow Chandler's brains out at the banquet, okay? All I want to do is watch the son of a bitch, to see what he says, to see how he acts. You know the word is that he rigged that vote somehow?"

"Does that surprise you, man? You know what he's like. And you know that we're only maintenance men—goddamned janitors—and there's nothing we can do about him. Hell, if we're lucky, this award'll get him a better job, and he'll move the hell out of here."

"You think he'll move?"

"He has to move. He wants to be a college president."

"Don't worry, Sam. No funny stuff. I'm just gonna watch, then do my cleanup like a good boy."

"Rino, I know you've been through a lot lately, and you know how I feel about you. Don't go off the deep end on me, okay?"

"When I start sucking blood out of people's necks, you'll be one of the first, Sam," Rino said, grinning, a ghost of his old self.

That Friday afternoon, Rino started work at three o'clock. He helped Joe and Barly move tables and chairs into the convocation hall, and, later, set up the speakers and microphones to test them. They adjusted the lighting and began to move flat loads of plates, glasses, silverware, and linen up to the tables.

"Well, man," said Barly, who stood beside Rino surveying all their work, "do you think he'll be aw-shucks and humble, or just his same old arrogant self?"

"Whatever it is, he'll be smooth about it," Rino muttered.

"Ain't no justice in this world, Rino," said Barly.

When the food service staff came to the hall, Rino and Barly and Joe were done with their work. All they had to do was relax until after the banquet and then clean up the big stuff. Monday, a fuller crew would return the chairs and tables and dinnerware to storage, and the center would be clean again.

The three men went to supper at a little bar just off campus that made good soup and hot dogs. Later they walked back to the center. As they walked, they could see the parking lot fill up with faculty cars. Other than graduation, it was the biggest event of the school year.

Rino watched the crowd come into the hall and take their seats at the large round tables that were set with elegant formal place settings, the best furniture and dinnerware the college had to offer.

Many of the professors looked rumpled and ill at ease in the formal atmosphere. Whenever the faculty assembled without academic regalia, they seemed a motley, almost shabby lot. It was a sedate crowd; they had come to pay homage, not to be rowdy.

The table of honor was a long, straight one, set perpendicular to the rest of the round tables. The protocol was very formal. After the rest of the dignitaries at the table of honor were seated, the two honorees were then escorted to their places, one on either side of the podium, by the president of the college, to the applause of the throng.

Rino and his friends stood at the rear of the hall, watching the guests as they assembled and talked. Barly said, "Rino, come on. Let's go get some coffee."

"No, Bar, I'm gonna watch this. I want to see what it's like."

"Okay. Look, Joe and I'll see you later. We'll be back in the kitchen," Barly said.

Rino found a chair at the side of the hall near a large, portable stainless-steel ice table. He was discreetly hidden away from the eyes of everyone at the head table, though he could see them all very clearly. The applause began when the president walked into the room escorting the two professors.

Chandler was dressed in a black tuxedo, glistening black shoes, cummerbund, and black bow tie. He outshone the other man as well as the president. He knew how to act his part: elegant, handsome, and obligingly correct. Rino envied him his ease in the limelight. He wore success so comfortably, so easily, that he convinced everyone that it not only became him; it was his due.

The head table was served first—by the best waiters and waitresses from the center. This began the evening. The agenda was simple: each man would be eulogized by the president and then presented a scroll signed by the board of trustees, the president, and the chairman of the faculty council. After each presentation, the honoree would address the group. At the end of the meeting, the entire assembly would sing the alma mater, and the ceremony would be over.

Rino sat watching the group as they ate their dinners. This was their night, the night they acted as professionals, honoring some of their own. They were enjoying the evening.

Joe carried a cup of coffee out to Rino. "Since you ain't coming back, I brought you something to drink, Rino. We're still back there..."

"Thanks, kid," Rino said. "Tell Barly I'm not coming back. I have to catch somebody's act here." Joe nodded and went away.

Rino sipped the coffee and quietly studied everyone before him. *This is just like any other group*, he thought. *It might just as well be the Cavour Club. They like to get together and have a good time.* He realized that he knew about three-fourths of them. Some were nice people, some were not particularly friendly but decent nonetheless, and some were either arrogant and pompous or foolishly eccentric. A few would do anything possible to wield power.

Rino studied Chandler throughout the meal. He wasn't shy or self-effacing; rather, he was self-consciously smooth and polished, as much at ease talking to colleagues as to the president and the board of trustees—a born college administrator.

He was always secure, always rested. Money was no object; that great burden had been relieved from his shoulders the day he was born. For him, all of life's lessons were rolled into one: gaining advantage. And he had learned that lesson well.

But Rino watched him further. Without the money, he thought, what would he be without the money? If it were all gone tomorrow?

Here was a man incapable of friendship. Ambition was all he fed upon. The Mercedes-Benz was there, no doubt a house to match. Yet he had been jealous of Ted Reese. Why Ted Reese?

Maybe he envied him Lee. But then, why didn't he try to take her from Reese? No, it couldn't have been Lee he cared about. Lee was a symbol, something clean and beautiful that Reese had and Chandler couldn't have.

But there was something else. Why should an ordinary man like Ted Reese go through life enjoying the blessings of existence with a good wife?

An existence that set Reese free, just as Chandler was free of his own burdens, to care about other things—probably to care too much about a career.

Yet Chandler couldn't keep a woman like Lee. Instinctively, he knew it. Instinctively, he feared her goodness as a vampire feared the cross. He didn't want to possess her, not the way most men would. What he wanted was to defile her, to spoil her for Reese. And Reese, to his own damnation, helped Chandler do it. The two of them—one through malice, the other through weakness—had hurt the best thing that Rino had ever known in life.

Rino shifted in his seat. The engineering professor, Patel, was about to be introduced. Rino had made it a point to find out about the ceremonies. Each honoree was expected to address the group for about 20 minutes. As the engineer began to speak, Rino studied Chandler, watching his eyes, the same eyes Lee had seen so closely that night when she was in his bed. Eyes hollow and menacing, Rino thought.

Yet when Patel spoke, Chandler made all the right moves. He applauded politely and mechanically at appropriate lines and nodded knowingly at others. But during it all, he drummed the table with his fingers. If it had to be a joint honor with Patel, a journeyman engineer, Chandler would settle for it this time. But someday soon the honors would come solely to him.

Rino watched as Chandler took the podium. *He was good at this*, Rino thought—gracious to Patel, praising the profundity of his remarks, thanking the faculty, administration, and trustees for the recognition bestowed upon him. He was proud to be a laborer in the same vineyard that Buddha, Socrates, and Aquinas had labored in. He smiled often during the polite opening remarks. But then his visage grew more serious as he began a discourse on the mission of the researcher, his obligation to seek the truth and to tell what he has seen. This is the nobility of our calling, he intoned to his comrades. This is reward in itself. Recognition such as this award was incidental to the pursuit—welcome, but nonetheless of little importance compared to the great quest upon which they had all embarked. Applause, applause.

Rino sneered at the uncritical, mindless acceptance of Chandler. What even the lowliest janitor could discern so clearly seemed to escape the learned professors. Maybe they judge people by other measures, Rino thought. But then... how do they allow themselves to be so deceived? To form judgments so superficially?

It had to be that Chandler's nightmares were made up of people wanting what he wanted, Rino mused... of competition or a fair fight. That had to be it, Rino thought. Take away the tuxedo and the car and the money, and he was yet fearful—maybe of the abilities of others... or maybe of his own. And stripped of his silk shirts, fine shoes, and tailored clothes, he might be just another mannequin of a professor.

Without his wealth, he might have to deal with life in a different way, with people in a different way. He might need people more than he does now, might have to fear them more than he does now, might not be able to manipulate them more than he does now. Stripped of all these things, he would be... ordinary.

That's it, Rino marveled. *The knowledge of that commonness beneath the looks, the money, the title, the image of a winner, the homage of the graduate assistants, is terrifying to him. He knows he's not a great researcher and scholar. Worst of all, he knows he's not gifted. That's why he hates; that's what he can't forgive himself; that's why he tries to cut down those who are more favored. That's why he cheats.*

Suddenly Rino's revelation had his heart pumping faster. He eyed Chandler as he ended his speech. This was the kind of man he was seeing. This was a malandrine.

Around midnight, Rino stopped to play poker at Agee's Tre-Sette. He stayed until the game broke up at three o'clock. Rino and Lou talked quietly on the way to their cars. "What was wrong with you?" Lou said. "You blew some sure winners. You kept folding when you probably had the pot."

"I don't know... just wasn't sharp tonight. Must've worked too hard."

"You feeling okay?" asked Lou.

"Jesus, you ask me that all the time, Lou. I'm okay. I'm just fucking old."

Lou chuckled. "Did you lose?"

"A few bucks. Not much."

"I'll talk to you tomorrow," said Lou.

The next day was dreary, with the wind chilled by icy snow. Rino had breakfast, then went down to Hugo's to get the antifreeze checked in his station wagon. Then he stopped to talk to Lou at his shop. Later, he stopped at Connie's, but she was gone. So he returned home for the day—to read a novel, put some logs on the fire, watch football on TV, and relax, maybe let Jean and Libby baby him.

But as Rino settled into his favorite chair in the living room, with logs crackling on the fire, with coffee and anisette beside him on the end table, he was thoughtful. Chandler. He had stripped him bare in his mind, the image from the reality. He had discovered the fear that motivated his every action. He had discovered his own malice and grown comfortable with it. He had also discovered a plan to bring about Chandler's destruction.

For the rest of the day, and for Sunday, Rino moved quietly around the house, reading, talking to the family, and watching TV. But he also thought about his own life and what he would do with the remainder of it. Rino enjoyed the quiet times during the dreary preholiday weather. He didn't have to seem so happy then; it was easier to endure melancholy and not be burdened by the spirit of the season.

The sign read, *Oren Glazer and Associates.* Rino walked in and met an attractive, young, auburn-haired woman sitting at a reception desk. "Rino Bellanca for Mr. Glazer," Rino said.

The girl picked up the phone and announced Rino to the other end of the line. "May I hang up your coat, sir?" the girl said.

Rino nodded and handed her his coat.

"Would you like some coffee? Mr. Glazer will be out in a minute."

"Thanks. That'd be fine. A little cream, please."

Rino sat sipping coffee in one of the easy chairs in the office. It was a small anteroom with thick, plush, gold carpeting and oaken wainscoting and paneling with indirect light and indoor plants. There were four beautiful chairs with smooth, beige fabric. The room had the appearance of a living room in the house of someone wealthy.

Suddenly, the door opened. "Hi, Rino. Come on in. Nice to see you."

"Hi, Orrie," Rino said, following him. Inside, there was a large central law library with an office at each of the four corners of the room. There were no file cabinets visible. The room was a throwback to the 1930s: oak furniture and large, glossy, oak library tables. There were two conference rooms, a kitchen, a file room, and two elegant lounges.

"To think I knew you when you were poor, Orrie," Rino said in admiration as he looked at the posh surroundings.

"Listen," said Orrie, "since I made you and Lou rich, I thought I'd like to try it myself."

"Try it? Hell, you must have written a book on it."

Orrie chuckled, leading Rino into his office and closing the door. "So what is it now, my friend? You gonna buy up half the town again? How's your brother doing? Haven't seen him in a long time," said Orrie effusively. It was his style. His mind was as quick as his mouth, but he kept secrets. That was why Rino liked him.

"Lou's fine, Oren. Look, I want to do a couple of things, one simple, the other one maybe not," Rino said.

"What's the simple one?" said Orrie, slowing down a little and concentrating more seriously on what Rino was saying.

"I want to change my will," Rino said.

"What's wrong? Any trouble?"

"No, but here's what I want. It isn't much."

"Okay..."

"A woman by the name of Toni Gallatin has bought two plots in a cemetery, one for her daughter who was killed last year, the other for me."

"Killed? Is that the girl you were going to marry?"

"Yeah," Rino said.

"I'm terribly sorry about that, Rino. I had no idea who she was; I never knew until several months later that she was special to you."

"I know, Orrie. Your letter was very nice," Rino said.

Orrie grew thoughtful. "Your kids know about this?"

"No. And I don't want them to—for a while."

"So what do you want in the will?" said Orrie.

"I want to be buried next to that girl in Canton. Her name was Leila Reese, and Antoinette Gallatin's her mother."

"You think your kids are gonna give you a hard time?"

"Maybe. But I'm in no mood to hear it. I've been good to them. Now this is what I want. For the first time in my life, I come first."

"How do you want to do it? Make sure you're buried next to the girl before your money and property can be disbursed?"

"Yeah. That's good."

"You own this plot already?"

"No. Her mother said she would change it over."

"Okay. But it would be better if you owned that grave outright yourself."

Rino shrugged. "I'll check on it," he said.

Orrie studied Rino. He went over to a liquor cabinet and said, "What'll it be?"

"Got any anisette?"

Orrie smiled smugly. "Sure I do. This bottle just sits in here and waits for you. It must be five... six years old."

Orrie poured himself a scotch and Rino the anisette. Then he sat down. "This is important to you, huh, Rino?"

Rino nodded. "Yeah, very important."

"Well, I'll draw it up. Anything else? Any changes?"

"Not in the will. Orrie, I want you to do something else for me."

"Sure, kid. Is this gonna make us some money?"

"No, it'll cost me."

"What is it?" Orrie said, always fascinated by what Rino and Lou did with their money.

"I want you to set up an award for me."

"A what?"

"I want you to call Spring Common and tell them that an anonymous organization has set up a two-year award—a research fellowship, Orrie, for a faculty member. Two years, no teaching, just research."

Orrie looked skeptical. He sat back in his chair and grimaced. "Rino," he said, "you have no idea how much these things cost."

"Do they go for two hundred thousand, a hundred grand a year?"

"Jesus, Rino, you aren't thinking of putting up that kind of money, are you?"

"Yeah, Orrie, that's the program," said Rino.

"But you can give them five or ten grand for a student fellowship, and they'd treat you like a king! You don't have to do this. Hell, Rino, I know how hard you and Lou worked for your money."

"Orrie, I have to. Understand? It has to go that way."

"Just think about it, okay, Rino? I can't let you throw away part of your fortune on a deal like this. Why do you want to do it, anyway?"

"Personal," said Rino.

"Personal?" Orrie said, nodding his head in perverse agreement. "I'm the guy that's been handling your money for 40 years, and all of a sudden you have secrets?"

Rino paused, collected his thoughts, and said softly, looking directly into Orrie's eyes, "Orrie, I swear, it doesn't have anything to do with not trusting you. You'll still handle my money. It's just something I have in my craw."

"Let me get this straight: Spring Common State, right? Two years at a hundred grand a crack?"

"Yep. A one-shot deal."

Orrie shook his head, still not believing Rino had all his sanity.

"Believe it, Orrie. This is all right. I've thought about it from all the angles."

"Did you say you wanted to be anonymous? How come?"

"Personal," Rino said weakly. "You have to handle the whole thing for me. No one can know I'm the donor."

"Rino, I don't like this..."

"You have to, Orrie. I need a go-between—and I trust you. You know how to keep your mouth shut."

"Who's gonna pick the winner? How?"

"Tell them to set up a committee of professors. They can select the top six professors who apply. Then you give all of it to me, and I'll make the final choice."

"What if the college doesn't go for this?" Orrie said, his voice beginning to show grudging respect for Rino's ideas. Rino had done some homework.

"Your office can have a cashier's check in escrow. The money gets released only after I get all the names and the applications. You certify it, and they'll eat it up."

"What about your kids? How will they feel about it?"

"They're never gonna know, Orrie. Besides, you helped me set Jerry and Nancy up; you know they're loaded. Frank has the house and most of the will, so he's flush. Lou and Connie are taken care of. There's a lot more to go around after the two hundred grand is taken out."

"This is really wild, Rino."

"I told you. Everything's gonna be all right. Look, I want you to write it up and have an announcement printed. Call it the Theodore Reese Memorial Fellowship—faculty members only."

"What made you think of this, Rino? Why not a student scholarship? Or an athletic scholarship? They would have been cheaper—and gotten you some season tickets besides."

"It's a long story, Orrie. I'll tell you about it someday. Meantime, no one knows about me but you, right? Let's use some sham organization."

"You don't want to think it over?"

"I've already thought it over."

"So who's Theodore Reese?"

"He's a kid who used to teach at Spring Common, the one who hanged himself a few years ago. I have some special memories about him."

"Reese? Wait a minute... that was the girl's name."

"Her husband... before I ever knew her." Rino knew he had given Orrie something to chew on.

"I'll write something up tomorrow afternoon and have it typed. You can stop in to read it, or I can mail it to you," Orrie said.

"I'll come in the day after tomorrow," Rino said.

"You're sure about this, now? I mean, the deuce? You could get by with much less. Most of those profs don't make even 50 grand a year. Why sweeten it so much?"

"Hell, I'm worried that I didn't sweeten it enough, Orrie. I want this to fly."

"Okay, paesan, it's your money," said Orrie doubtfully.

"Just call the president's office and set it up, okay?" said Rino.

Rino felt a sense of satisfaction for the first time since Lee had died. He was closing in on Chandler. If he could bait the trap right, if he could find some skeletons in his closet...

At home, he sat in the kitchen, drinking coffee. Jean came in from the living room. "Dad, a letter came yesterday for you. I thought you picked it up, but it's still on the buffet."

"It's okay, Jeanie," Rino said, taking the letter from her. It was from Toni Gallatin, written in a beautiful, stylized script.

Dear Rino,

This note is just to let you know that I've changed the name on plot 31 from mine to yours. I've enclosed the deed. If, for some reason, that gravesite is not used for you, then Lee's body will be moved back to the Gallatin family plot–that remains in my will.

Since your visit, I've felt better than I have in months. I guess I had to be reassured that your love had not diminished or lost that special quality that made it so beautiful. I'm certain now that it hasn't.

Please take care of yourself. And remember that you are welcome here always.

Affectionately,

Toni

Rino stood up after he read the letter. He turned away from Jean's puzzled face to hide his expression. The letter had moved him.

"It's from Canton, isn't it, Dad?" Jean said.

"Yeah," Rino said, looking away from her.

"Is everything okay?"

"Fine, kid. It's gonna be fine."

The next morning, Rino gave Orrie a call from a pay phone. "Orrie, that grave is in my name, so you can write that change into the will now."

"Okay, Rino. Listen, I worked on a first draft of the fellowship guidelines. Cindy's typing it now."

"Fine. I'll pick it up tomorrow and read it over the weekend. Did you check with the president yet?"

"Not yet. But I know he'll jump at it."

The next day, Rino picked up the draft of the fellowship guidelines. It was the day before Thanksgiving, his second one without Lee. Last year, she had been dead only a week, and the ordeal of living without her had just begun. Now, this year, though the pain of her loss was just as acute, he was able to handle it better. He still had Lou and Frank and Jean and Libby and Connie—all those special people who had come to his aid when he had almost fallen apart.

And he had something more: some part of Lee that he could see and talk to. In Toni, he had found Lee's voice, her mannerisms, her thoughtfulness, her goodness. And, somehow, knowing he would be buried in Canton made the wait more bearable, made the rest of his life worth living as Lee would have wanted him to.

Rino began to be more resigned to the life he had left. At night, he asked himself again and again, what had possessed him to go fishing in Canada? Why hadn't he stayed home and married her and kept her away from Route 62? What strange view of life induces an old man to parcel out the days as if there were no end to them? As though pausing and waiting and planning could make the world conform to his dreams rather than God's? Somehow, Toni's gift had eased that regret.

But there were other bitter memories that never left him all those lonely nights, the ugly side of a fond dream: the death of Ted Reese and the pain and shame of Lee.

Dale Chandler still lived to cause more hurt, still lived, knowing that he had shamed and degraded Lee. He had taken her best, misguided, honest intentions and turned them upon her with a smile. He had lived to be teacher of the year. In Dale Chandler, Rino could see a mockery of good memories; he could see a task undone.

Thanksgiving was hosted by Frank and Jean for Jerry and Nancy and their families, Connie, and Danny and his family. Lou was in Chicago for the week with his son, Dom, and his family.

The day was pleasant. Rino and most of the men watched a football game, and the women played cards. Then they ate the meal that Jean had cooked, a New England-style dinner.

When they were all gone that night, Rino thought over what it had been like. If he was no longer capable of fun, at least he was capable of quiet enjoyment. He had talked to everyone who had been there and had especially sought out Jerry and Nancy's children, his grandchildren, whom he seldom saw anymore.

He went out into the kitchen for some water and saw Frank and Jean sitting quietly, talking about the day. Libby was staying overnight at a girlfriend's house, and Larry had gone to a movie.

"Nice dinner, huh?" Rino said as he passed them.

"Yeah," Frank said. Jean had just nodded. She looked tired. The dinner had been two days in preparation, and Jean had had little rest and little sleep.

After drinking his water, Rino stopped before her and held one of her hands in his. "Thanks for all the hard work, Jeanie. You look like you could use some rest."

"I am a little tired now that it's all over, Dad," she said.

"It was a fine meal. I think everyone enjoyed it and had a good time." He bent over and kissed her on the crown of her head. Then he put his hand on one of Frank's cheeks and gave him a little nudge, a slight slap that is so often used as an Italian gesture of love and affection. As he started out of the room, Frank said, "Pop, would you be all right if we went to bed? We're both bushed." It was 9:30.

"I'll be fine, kid," Rino said. "I'm going to read a little, then probably turn in myself soon." Rino settled into his chair as Frank and Jean went upstairs. He tried to read, but his mind kept wandering. At 10 o'clock, the house was absolutely silent. Outside it was snowing lightly, and the sounds of the city were muted and still. He thought of Larry, wondering what time he would be home, since the snow was beginning to stick. Probably not for a couple of hours, he thought. At his age, common sense wasn't his strong suit.

He walked over to a buffet in the dining room and took out a small notebook. In it was Toni's address and phone number. He returned to the phone and dialed.

When she answered after three rings, her voice sounded anxious. Almost no one would call her at 10:30 on Thanksgiving night without a message of trouble. Her heart fluttered for a split second. In all her life, she had learned nothing that would prepare her for another of those calls like the one she had gotten a year earlier, telling her that her daughter had been in an accident and that she should come down to a small hospital just off Route 62. "Toni? This is Rino Bellanca."

There was silence on the line. Rino began to regret, that instant, that he had ever made the call. It occurred to him then, during her long silence, that perhaps she was unable to face him, because he conjured up too many painful memories she was trying to cope with and sort.

Toni, in her silence, became distracted. Rino was part of the last tragedy that had afflicted her life. Could a call from him mean something terrible again? Could that aura of tragedy that she sensed around him be just imagination? "Hello, Rino," she said finally in a soft voice.

"How are you?" Rino said.

"I'm... fine. And you?"

"Everyone's in bed here and I was thinking. Well, you said if I wanted to hear your voice—"

"Lee's voice."

He took a deep breath. "Look, I'm sorry. It's late. I'll call back some other time."

"No, Rino, please... I shouldn't have said that. It's just that I was thinking of her, too. How was your Thanksgiving?"

"Okay. Better than the last one. How about yours?"

"Okay, too. I spent it at Nicole's. Her husband Jim's parents were also there. I got home about an hour ago."

They were both silent, neither of them knowing what to say next. "I'm here alone," Rino said, "and I just wanted to talk to someone."

"I understand. Why don't you come to visit someday soon? Plan on coming for supper."

"That would be nice, Toni. I'm not very good company, I'm afraid. Maybe you feel worse after we talk."

"No, Rino, I feel better. It's just that I still can't get used to thinking what our lives would have been like if she had lived."

"Yeah," he said wistfully. After a few seconds, he said, "Some people have told me that time heals all wounds. I just don't believe it. Anyway, how about if I call you in a week or so and then come to see you?"

"Yes, that would be fine."

The following Monday, Rino went to Orrie's office with the fellowship papers. Throughout the weekend, he had carefully read the prospectus and decided on some changes that had to be made, especially in the autobiographic sketch required of each candidate.

"How was Thanksgiving?" Orrie said.

"Do hebes observe Thanksgiving?" Rino said mischievously.

Orrie chuckled. "Yeah, but we don't do it like you dagos. We slaughter a fatted calf, whereas you guys go out and slaughter a few dozen hoods."

Rino laughed. They had been conducting a good-natured ethnic war for many years. Both men liked each other and were comfortable with each other. Orrie had never forgotten that, many years before, when he was a young lawyer from New York who was just out of law school, spoke with a funny accent, and had few clients because young Jewish attorneys could get only Jewish clients, a young Italian millworker took a chance on him and let him process all the property transactions that he and his brother were involved in. It helped put food on Orrie's table in those early days, and it helped him gain access to gentile business. Rino and Lou both sent many millworkers, Cavour Club friends, and Tre-Sette buddies to Orrie. It was all house closings, wills, divorces, and automobile injuries, but it established Orrie as a proper breadwinner and allowed his natural abilities to flourish and his practice to be a success.

"I've read it," Rino said. "And it's good. But I want a few changes in the application. I want a complete list of where they've worked, what they've published, and where they went to school."

"You want a complete dossier—wives, mistresses, jail terms..." Orrie said lightly.

"If dossier means names and addresses, then that's what I want. Also, the proposal has to say what he's gonna come up with in the end. Remember, no one knows who puts up the money."

"Okay, I'll put it in. Anything else?"

"Yeah. I want it all by the end of January—sooner, if possible. As you get each one, mail it to me. Okay?"

"Okay."

"Just send me a bill when it's over, Orrie."

Orrie shook his head. "I wish I had a clue as to why you're doing this, Rino."

"I'll tell you after you retire."

"Hell, I'm never gonna retire. My youngest daughter tells me she wants to go to Yale and be a lawyer. Now I'll have to work till I die."

"Well, don't die on me yet, kid. How about the will? Did you change it?"

"Yeah." Orrie opened a drawer and took out a file and handed it to Rino. "Here. All I changed was the first couple of paragraphs. You own this thing for sure, right?"

"Yeah, here's the title," he said, handing it to Orrie.

"Now you have to have a witness. I presume it'll be Lou? And somebody else now that Paolo's dead."

"Yeah. We'll be up in a few days to sign it. I have to talk to him about it."

"Okay. When you get it together, call me."

Lou's shoulder had been stiff ever since he'd come back from Chicago. The weather had been damp and dreary all the time he was there. It didn't snow much, but the wind chilled his bones every time he was outdoors. The arthritis was slowing him down a little, he thought. *Getting old wouldn't be half so bad if you didn't get so damned many sore muscles and stiff joints.*

He wasn't busy all morning, but suddenly three pairs of shoes came in during lunch hour. He was glad to be busy. He worked hard all afternoon on the shoes. It still felt good taking an old, ugly pair of shoes and making them look good again—heels and soles and polish.

When he was done, there was just time to clean the shop and close it up. He hurriedly swept it and washed the inside front windows.

The meeting at the Cavour Club was at eight o'clock. There was to be a Christmas party for the club members and a food drive for families who were still struggling with life after being laid off from the mills.

Lou never ate much anymore. Connie was always scolding him about being too skinny, and Annie was always trying to fatten him up. On nights when he didn't go out with Rino to eat, or go to Connie's or Annie's or Jean's house, he would make himself a sandwich and a salad at home. Tonight, he'd settle for a bowl of soup and a cup of coffee. Later, he read the newspaper, cleaned up the kitchen, and went upstairs to shower and shave for the second time that day. He grumbled to himself as the razor irritated his skin in protest against the too-frequent shaves his lifestyle had suddenly forced upon him. Then he showered and began to dress.

He was beginning to feel good. It was nice being back in the swing of things at the Cavour Club. It had been years since he had been on a Christmas committee. Too bad he couldn't get Rino involved again. But Rino wasn't doing much these days. He put Rino out of his mind and tied his shoes. Otherwise, he would become thoughtful and depressed. He hated what had happened to his brother. It was something that he, for the first time in their lives, couldn't help him with. Not really. He could entertain and divert him, get him to do some work for Annie or Connie, but he could never take that look of lonely pain out of his eyes.

Lou was always early whenever he had to be somewhere. As he drove leisurely to the Cavour Club, he hummed accompaniment to the radio. At the club, he saw Pete and Marty, Agee, Hugo—all the gang. Annie would be there later. He drank a beer and wandered around, getting reacquainted with old friends before the meeting began. Suddenly, Andrea Manasseri came through the door.

"So, what d'you think?" said Marty. "The queen bee is gonna be on a committee, just like regular folk."

"Rich people are big on charity," said Lou cynically.

Andrea came toward them and nodded to Lou and Marty as she passed, heading for the coatroom.

That night Marty separated the committee into two groups, and Lou was on the food committee. They were to collect canned foods and solicit fresh fruits, vegetables, and meats from local grocery stores. Then, large shopping bags of groceries would be packed and distributed the week before Christmas. The objective was simple, but means to it were debated and confounded by people who enjoyed committees—and endless, fervent discussion, parsing of sentences, and scoring of points.

Lou was bored and tired. A few times he tried vainly to synthesize points of contention. Then once he offered a compromise that was rejected. But closure was not the purpose of a committee meeting, and Lou knew it. Finally, agonizingly, the agreement came. Andrea Manasseri was still there. A few times she spoke but did little to resolve the commotion.

Once, while Lou was sitting, quietly drumming his fingers on the table, he looked up and found Andrea watching him. Later, it happened again: she was staring at him. Lou wasn't impressed. He could never understand much of what she did or what would motivate her to reject a man like his brother after having been married to a pompous, friendless man like Jack Manasseri.

But after their food drive meeting was over, the other committee, the Christmas party committee, was still in session, so Lou and his group had to kill some time until both groups could reassemble and report. Lou talked to most of the people who were in the room. The large square array of long tables and folding chairs enabled him to walk from place to place to meet old friends. Then he went back to the coffee urn.

He put a little cream in his cup and poured the coffee in. *I'll probably be awake half the night now,* he thought. But the coffee did taste good. He stood a few steps away from the urn, surveying the people who were present. *They were a lifetime of acquaintanceship,* he thought. Yet he knew so few of them well. How could you come to meetings, dances, weddings, wakes, baptisms, and church with people for five decades and still not know, really know, them?

"Good evening, Lou," a voice said to his back. He turned to face it. It was Andrea Manasseri.

"Hello, Andrea," he said, not sure if he had taken the tone of surprise out of his voice.

"How are you? It's been a long time since you've been involved in a committee here, hasn't it?" she said.

"Yes, a long time. But Marty asked me to be on one this year."

"It's nice to see you participate again," she said politely.

Lou sensed nervousness in her voice, and that was unusual. She had her customary uneasiness when she was talking to certain men. But this was something else. It was what she had shown when Rino talked to her. Only this time it wasn't Rino who had approached her; she had approached Lou.

"Well, I should have been involved a little more often. I guess we get sidetracked sometimes," Lou said.

"Is Rino here tonight?" She reddened a little when she asked the question. Lou noticed it and wondered why she would ask. He was sure she knew Rino wasn't there.

"Uh... no, not tonight. He couldn't make it tonight."

"Has he been active in the club lately?"

"Not lately." Lou sighed.

"How is he feeling? He's lost some weight, hasn't he?"

"Yes... a little. But he seems to be feeling better now." *Jesus, this is strange*, Lou thought. Asking about Rino? Is that who she has on her mind?

She continued nervously, "Does he... does he..." She stopped, now fearful of losing her composure.

Lou tried to help. "It took him a long time to even get his bearings, Andrea. He just tries not to show it."

"I understand," she said. "I had a difficult time myself."

Lou almost snorted. Instead, he took a deep breath to avoid any reaction. *What the hell*, he thought. *Maybe she did have a rough time.*

"I was very sorry about the death of the girl," Andrea continued. "She was quite lovely and seemed... very much in love with him."

"Did you know her?" Lou asked, surprised.

"One night at Castorina's, Rino introduced her to me."

"Oh," said Lou, not knowing what to say next. Rino had never told him that Andrea had met her. It was probably the same night that he had first seen Lee himself.

"Lou..." She arched her eyebrows involuntarily and wrinkled her brow in discomfort. "Tell Rino... at the right time... tell him... uh, that he would be welcome in my house."

Lou stared into her eyes for a moment. She had swallowed a few times, showing how difficult it was to say what she had said. So he nodded to indicate that he understood. "I'll tell him that, Andrea," he said. "I'll tell him."

Andrea thanked him and walked away, glad that her ordeal was over.

"Damn," Lou muttered as he watched her go, "I will never understand people."

The next morning, Rino stopped at Lou's shop. "How are you, cowboy?

Jean said that you called last night," said Rino.

"Yeah, I have something to tell you. Sit down. Coffee?"

"Yeah. I have something to tell you, too," said Rino.

Lou headed back into the kitchen for cups. "What are you doing tonight, Rino?" he called from down the hall.

"Nothing," Rino called back. "Why?"

As Lou emerged with the cups and some anisette, he said, "Let's go to the Tucker for some fish. What d'you say?"

Rino pursed his lips in assent. "Yeah, that sounds good. Lou, before we start this, will you come to Orrie's office with me tomorrow?"

"Yeah. What's going on?"

"I need a witness for my will. I changed it."

Lou frowned and his eyes narrowed. "What'd you do, Rino?" he said gravely.

"Nothing much. I just changed something about me, about where I'm going to be buried when I die."

"What are you talking about dying for, Rino?"

Rino sighed. "Someday I'm going to die, Lou. It might even happen to you."

"That's not what I mean, Guarino," Lou snapped.

"Lou, Lee wasn't buried in the family plot in Canton. She's in another place. Her mother bought two graves together... and she gave one to me."

Lou shook his head. Never did Rino stop amazing him. It was as though he delighted in driving Lou crazy. "You want to be buried in Canton?" he said in a rasping, incredulous voice.

"That's where Lee is."

Lou set his coffee down and looked outside at cars passing. He was quiet for a few minutes, obviously disapproving of what his brother was doing. "What about Mary?"

"Lou, please, I've thought this all out. Long before—"

"Look. What you're doing won't bring Lee back. Everybody knows, deep down in their hearts, she meant more to you than Mary. But why rub your kids' noses in it now?"

"I can't leave her alone in Canton, Lou."

"Rino, she's dead. She's not in Canton; her body is. When you die, that's all of you that would be there, too."

"Lou, I want to be buried beside her when I die. Only a few people have to know. They can have a funeral in Youngstown, then take me there quietly."

"Rino, this is morbid, first of all. Second, it's gonna drive your kids crazy that you don't want to be buried next to their mother and your wife of 40 years. Jesus Christ!"

"Lou, that girl was supposed to be my wife, too, remember? Only she died a couple of days before the wedding. So what makes her different from Mary?"

"If I have to answer that, cowboy, then you're a lot worse off than I thought. You knew this girl, what? Not even a year? And you want your kids not to feel insulted when you want to be buried next to Lee instead of their mother?"

"Hey, Lou, none of my kids went through this, okay? None of them are me. All my life I treated Mary and them the best I could. Now, for once, I'm gonna do something for me—just because it's in my heart. Now, are you going to sign the fucking will or not?"

Lou sighed, still looking away from his brother. After a few seconds, he said, "Yeah, I'll sign it. But I think you're doing this all wrong."

"Luigi, the few people who ever see those two graves will know there's a story that ties us together. No one else will care. Mary's next to Jimmy and Mom and Pop. It'll be all right."

Lou muttered something about Rino being crazy.

"Now, what did you have to tell me?" Rino said.

"Forget it. It's not important."

"Come on, for Christ's sake. You thought it was important enough to call me last night."

"No. I'm not in the mood. I'll tell you later." Lou got up and walked behind the counter.

Rino followed him with his eyes as he walked away. "Lou, I'm sorry, but I have to do this."

Lou snorted. "I just never thought you'd be like this, kid." He threw a bad nail across the counter in angry frustration and set down the shoe he was working on. "Hell, Rino, what do I know? I never lost anyone like her." He looked up at brother. "I'll pick you up tonight after I close the shop, okay?"

"Sure," said his brother doubtfully.

Lou nodded as Rino left.

When they entered the Tucker, they met Pete and Marty and were seated at their usual table. They talked about Christmas shopping and whether they would be able to have a luminaria on Christmas Eve. They ate more fish than they had in a long time. Rino had stayed away from the Tucker most of the year he spent mourning Lee. Pete and Marty seemed animated by Rino's presence. It was like old times.

On the way home, Rino suddenly told Lou to stop at a small coffee shop near his house. "I have to tell you something else," said Rino.

"Let me tell you first," Lou said.

They both went into a booth in a quiet corner of the shop. "So what's on your mind?" said Rino.

"Well, the damnedest thing happened. I was at the Cavour for that meeting Marty roped me into, and who do you think I saw?"

Rino shrugged.

"Andrea Manasseri," said Lou.

"And that's what you wanted to tell me?" said Rino dryly.

"Rino, she came up to talk to me. And she actually told me that you'd be welcome in her house. How about that?"

"Lou, you probably had a few too many and dreamed she said that. There's no way that woman would invite a man to her house."

"Not 'a man,' Rino. You! You know damned well you've never seen that before."

Rino paused thoughtfully. "I can't, Luigi. I don't have it in me."

"Rino, this woman is not used to inviting men to her house. Just the fact that she did it means something special."

"I can't do it, Lou."

"You don't have to do anything but go see her. It would be nice to talk to her, wouldn't it?"

"No. Why should it be different now? All the other times I've tried to talk to her, we both ended up hating it." Rino's voice grew louder. "Enough with Andrea Manasseri, all right?"

Lou sighed. "All right. But just remember, no other guy ever got invited."

"I don't have time to think about her, Lou. Besides, I want to tell you about something else."

"What else?"

"I set up a two-year teaching fellowship in Ted Reese's name at Spring Common State."

"Reese? Lee's husband? Why?"

"Because he got a raw deal at the college... and from Chandler."

Lou was quiet for a moment. "This has more to do with Chandler than it does with Reese, right?" Rino sighed. Lou sipped his coffee nervously, knowing that he and his brother were going to be on opposite sides of something again. "How much is this gonna cost you, cowboy?"

Rino took a deep breath. "Two hundred grand."

"What'd you say?" Lou croaked as he slammed his cup down.

"You heard what I said, Lou."

Lou stared at his brother for a few seconds. "Rino, you've lost your fucking mind," he muttered, shaking his head in disgust.

"I know what I'm doing," Rino said.

"No, you don't," Lou said angrily. "How could you say that when you're blowing money you worked like hell to save on some screwball scheme?"

"I'm telling you it's okay, Lou."

"It's not okay, goddammit," said Lou, pounding the table. "You're letting your hatred make you crazy. Forget Chandler! Nothing you can do to him will ever bring Lee back. She's dead, Rino. And you have to learn to handle that."

"You know, Lou, I'm sick of all your preaching. When did you lose a girl a week before you married her? A pregnant girl? Is it so hard to understand why I want him? After he practically killed Reese and..."

"Hey, Rino, save the bullshit about Ted Reese. You know goddamned well why you're doing this, and it has nothing to do with Reese."

"I helped cut that kid down from the banister, Lou. You didn't see him with a rope around his neck–I did."

"Rino, if you want to lie to yourself about your life, that's your business. But don't come around lying to me."

"You bastard," said Rino, "when did I ever lie to you?"

"You're lying right now! You're trying to pretend to me that you want Chandler because he's the prick who shafted Reese. But you know fucking well that the only reason why you're doing it is Lee. And that's goddamn insane."

Rino calmed down slightly, trying not to alienate his brother further. "Lou, two hundred grand just doesn't mean that much. I still have plenty. And I'd still give all the rest of it just to have Lee back."

"But Christ, that's just it, Rino! Don't you see? Lee won't come back. So who are you avenging? It's over, kid. Leave it alone."

"It's never gonna be over until I get him," Rino said calmly.

"What makes you think you will? How can you outsmart a rich college professor? Hell, you've seen him. Mosquitoes don't even land on him."

"He'll outsmart himself. He's too arrogant to let this go by."

"You're gonna bet two hundred grand on the come, hoping to nail a guy who wears silk drawers, in a crazy scheme that's nothing more than throwing your money down a goddamned rat hole."

"I want him, Lou," Rino said.

Lou stared at him for a few seconds. "I don't know you, Rino. The last two years, I don't know what's in your heart, let alone in your head." Lou got up and walked away, leaving his brother sitting in the booth.

Slowly Rino drew himself erect, threw some money on the table, and walked wearily home.

For several days, Rino went quietly about his life, working, talking to Oren Glazer about the fellowship, and staying home. For a while no one noticed that Rino and Lou hadn't been together. But one night Jean and Frank began to talk about it. "Have you seen Uncle Lou recently?" she said to Frank.

"No... why?"

"He hasn't called or stopped by for about a week. Is he in Boston?"

"I don't think so. Did you ask Pop? He'd know."

Jean raised her eyebrows. "Do you suppose they've had an argument?"

Frank began to be more interested now, looking up from the paper he was reading. "You think they're not talking?" he said in amazement.

"I don't know. But Dad's been awfully quiet lately, and he hasn't mentioned Uncle Lou."

"I'll ask him tonight," said Frank.

Rino was edgy now that he had set his plan in motion. Orrie had contacted the college, and they were surprised but willing. The president wanted to announce the donation with a news release. Rino had revised the criteria Orrie had drawn up over and over again. There were to be letters of recommendation, a 1,500-word biographical sketch, a personal data sheet for quick reference, a research proposal, and a list of past research, with names and dates. The deadline was noon, January 31st.

A $200,000 gamble. Rino was counting on Chandler having one fatal flaw above all others: arrogance. He still remembered the words Chandler had spat at him and Lee at the Seidler Restaurant: "I always get what I want."

Rino shook his head. I hope he wants the fellowship, he thought. But then, why wouldn't he? It would bring great personal prestige and money—surely enough to energize other professors to want it. And though Chandler didn't need the money, the award would be a stepping-stone to a professorship at Penn or Cornell. But most of all—and this was what Rino knew would happen—Chandler couldn't live with the thought of another person having the award, whether he wanted it or not.

Rino sat reading quietly in the living room, sipping a glass of anisette occasionally. It was Christmastime, and though his shopping wasn't done, his work was done. He had put Orrie on task and had set his trap for Chandler.

"Hi, Pop," said Frank as he came into the room.

"Hi, Frankie," said Rino absently, looking up for a split second.

"How are you feeling, Pop?"

"Fine, Frank. Fine," said Rino, not paying much attention to Frank as he read his book.

"Jean thinks you look a little tired. You've been awfully quiet lately."

"I'm okay, Frank," Rino said. "What's on your mind?"

"Uncle Lou hasn't been around in a few days."

"I'm sure he has things to do," said Rino.

"He always has things to do, Pop," Frank said, sensing a hint of discomfort in Rino.

"Yeah." Rino sighed.

"Did you two have a fight, Pop?"

Rino stared at his book for a few seconds, and then, without looking up at his son, said, "Yeah."

"Jesus. And you aren't talking? What the hell happened? I don't ever remember you two in a serious argument."

"It happens sometimes, Frank," said Rino sheepishly.

"Why, though? What happened to cause it?"

"Ah... it was personal, kid."

"Personal? Come on, Pop, what the hell happened?"

"It was just a disagreement, something we didn't see eye to eye on."

"Jesus, Pop, it had to be something big," Frank said worriedly.

"We'll get over it, Frank. We always do."

"Pop, this is wrong. You and Uncle Lou are as close as I—"

"Frank, it's not your business," Rino said pointedly. "It'll work out without you."

Frank left the room, determined to find out from Lou what he couldn't find out from his father. But the next day, when he called Lou, his uncle was as reticent and evasive as Rino. Lou didn't want to talk to Frank and politely suggested that it was none of his business.

That night, he and Jean talked in their bedroom. "Do you have any idea what caused it?" Frank said to Jean.

She shook her head. "I don't know." She sighed. "And after all he's been through."

"How are we gonna get them back together if neither one wants to talk about it? 'It's personal?' Jesus Christ!"

The next morning was a Saturday, and as usual, Libby and Larry were up early and gone. Frank and Jean tried to sleep in, tried deliberately to start the day off late.

Rino had been up for a few hours. He had gotten up early to fill up his Buick with gas and have it greased and oiled down at Hugo's. When he returned home, he found Frank and Jean in the kitchen finishing a late breakfast.

"Where are the kids?" Rino said.

"Larry's working, and Libby's decorating the church hall for the teen Christmas party," said Jean.

"Good," said Rino. "I want to tell you both something."

Jean and Frank exchanged glances. Rino was going to finally tell them about his feud with Lou, they thought.

"Coffee, Dad?" Jean said.

"Yeah, thanks," said Rino as he settled into a kitchen chair.

Jean got his coffee. "How about some breakfast?" she said.

"No, I had a doughnut down at Hugo's," Rino said. Jean sat back down at the table. Rino continued talking. "I wanted to tell you that I've changed my will," he said.

They were momentarily set off balance. "How, Pop?" said Frank hesitantly.

"Nothing big... for any of you," Rino said. "It has to do with me... after I die."

"With you?"

"When I die, I want to be buried in Canton, next to Lee," Rino said.

Frank seemed to recoil from Rino's words. "But what about the family plot? What about Mom, for God's sake!"

"Jimmy's there, Grandma and Grandpa; Connie will be there with

Uncle Guy... Terry and Lou. There's enough there. She won't be alone."

Frank's face reddened with anger. "She'll be alone without you! How could you disgrace Mom like this? Jesus Christ, Pop, I think you've lost your mind."

Jean put her hand on Frank's forearm to restrain him from saying harsher words to his father. Frank shook her hand away.

"I mean no disrespect to your mother, Frank," Rino said softly.

"What you mean and what you do aren't the same thing. What will people think? After 40 years of marriage, you place some stranger you knew only a few months above Mom. My God, her grave'll be all alone in that plot! How could you do this to the family?"

"Frank, you don't understand. What Lee and I had was—"

"What you had was an old man's infatuation with an emotionally unstable young girl. Girls that age don't go around falling in love with men in their 60s—unless they're going to get something out of it."

Now Rino was angry himself. But he held his anger because he wanted to make some sense in the argument he was having. "You through, Frank?" he said.

"Through? Sure! What more can I say? I see my old man going around like a damned zombie over a girl he hardly knew and not giving a damn whether he shames my mother's memory in the process. Hell, I'm through. I just think you're getting senile, Pop."

Rino's anger evaporated, as his son's words hurt him. Slowly he mustered up the words to speak. "Frank," he said, struggling with feelings that were tightening his throat and shrilling his voice. "I don't owe you an explanation, but I'll give it to you one more time. I loved and honored your mother while we were married. We had good years. And I'd still be married to her if she didn't die, and I would still love her." He paused for a few seconds, looking away from his son and trying to choose his words carefully. "But she did die, Frank. And I was alone... and I met Lee."

"So you were so lonely that a kid a little older than Larry, that you knew not even a year, can make you forget almost 40 years with Mom, right? Your idea of a loving marriage and mine aren't the same, Pop."

"Who in the hell do you think you are, Frank? A wise man? I told you, all I wanted was to grow old with your mother. I never wanted her to die. I never wanted to be with anyone else. But she did die, and I did fall in love with someone else. And maybe you can forget Lee died a week before I was going to marry her, but I can't."

"I'm sick of hearing about Lee, Pop. All this family has done this whole year is worry about you because that girl died. But people die all the time. Mom died, and you never went off the deep end for a whole year."

"Life is full of surprises, kid," Rino said somberly. "And maybe you can always come out on top, but I can't. So I'm sick, too. Sick of taking a lot of crap from kids who never for a minute put themselves in my shoes."

Rino walked out of the room and went upstairs, leaving Jean and Frank standing motionless in the kitchen. When the door of his bedroom slammed, Jean walked silently into the living room and sat down heavily into a chair, the one that Rino usually sat in. Her choice of chairs seemed significant to Frank, who had followed her into the room. He stood a few feet from her as she stared ahead, avoiding him. "Don't talk to me now, Frank," she said.

"How can you say that? You know what I've said is true."

"What you said hurt him more than anyone has ever hurt him in his life, you dummy," she snapped.

"Baloney. All I did was try to make him see that what he was doing was wrong."

"Wrong to you, not to him."

"Whose side are you on anyway, for God's sake? Did you hear what he said? It's not your mother's grave that's going to be all by itself after forty years of marriage."

"Well, I'm not on your side. I can't believe you could say those things to him. He's lost two wives, and—"

"She wasn't his wife, goddammit!"

"She was his wife more than your mother was, and you don't want to admit it."

"My God, you're taking his part in this. You actually think it's okay for him to change that will."

"I actually think he loved Lee more... completely than he ever loved Mom. And I think she gave him more happiness in those short months than he ever had. Don't you remember how bright and young he looked?"

"Girls that age always make men his age feel young."

"Do you really think she didn't love him, Frank?"

"I don't see how she could. And I don't see how he could subordinate Mom to this girl so quickly."

"You don't know your father at all, do you? You really don't understand."

"I don't understand what you can see that Nancy, Jerry, and I can't see. We're his children."

Jean stood up and walked out of the room. Frank watched her leave and then went outside, got into his car, and drove around Youngstown for a while. Then he stopped at his school office and tried to do some work.

Jean drove carefully down the road to Lou's shop. It was a part of town she seldom visited anymore, the old ethnic millworker neighborhoods of the city. She found the shop, parked the car in front, and entered, hoping she would find Lou alone.

Lou looked up from his work as Jean entered, surprised to see her early on a Monday morning. "How are you, kid?" he said as she dusted light snow from her hair and sleeves.

"Not so good, Uncle Lou," she said.

"Why? What's wrong?" Lou hurriedly came around the counter and guided her into a chair as she burst into tears. "Honey? Is someone sick?" He had known Jean and loved her for two decades, envying Rino his luck in having her marry one of his sons.

"Oh, Uncle Lou, I don't know what to do. Frank and Dad had a horrible fight, and Dad hasn't been home in two nights."

"Rino? He hasn't been with me. Where's he staying?"

"That's just it—we don't know. Uncle Lou, I'm afraid for Dad. Frank said some terrible things to him."

"What'd he say, for God's sake?"

"Well… uh… he said that Dad had been… well, he told him his mourning for Lee went on too long. Frank was mad about Dad changing the will. He thought it would disgrace Mom. Oh, Uncle Lou, Frank didn't mean all those things. He was just hurt. But Dad was hurt, too. And, God, he hasn't come home. Libby's crying. It's such a mess. I need your help, Uncle Lou. I can't stand to see my family fall apart like this."

"Take it easy, honey." He handed her his handkerchief. "Will Frank be home tonight?" She nodded. "Okay. I'll be there about eight o'clock. Don't worry. I'll talk to your husband. Then I'll try to find my brother." Lou sighed. "He's not too crazy about me lately, either."

That evening, Frank and Jean sat in the living room saying very little to each other. Larry was working, and Libby was upstairs in her room doing homework with a girlfriend. When they heard a car roll into the driveway, Frank glanced at Jean and then bounded out of his chair and ran to the kitchen window, thinking it might be his father. When he recognized Lou's car, the flush in his face changed to disappointment and pallor.

Lou walked into the kitchen. "Hi, Frank," he said, somewhat grimly, not smiling as he usually did.

"Hi, Uncle Lou," said Frank wearily. Jean was standing in the doorway of the kitchen.

"Come on in here, both of you. We have to talk," said Lou.

Wordlessly, both Jean and Frank followed Lou into the family room. Lou sat down, himself betraying the weariness that seemed to afflict them all lately. "So what are we going to do about your dad, Frank? My brother doesn't seem to listen to any of us anymore."

"I thought he listened to you," Frank said.

"He hears me, but he doesn't always listen. You know, I've been trying to talk sense into him ever since your mother died. I wanted him to meet other women from the club; he met Lee. I wanted him to think twice about going with such a young girl; he fell in love with her. I told him that life was too short to plan for the future with her; he decided to marry her. And when I told him that marrying her would be too much of an adjustment, she died. You see, whatever I said was either wrong or it didn't make a damned bit of difference. And guess what? I tried to get him not to change the will; he did it, anyway."

"He's gone bananas, Uncle Lou. How can he do that to Mom?"

"I don't know, kid. I guess he thinks he's right."

Frank snorted. "There's nothing right about putting aside your wife of 40 years, who bore your kids and worked hard beside you—"

"How about you, Jean?" Lou said.

Jean didn't answer. Instead, Frank said it for her: "She thinks it's okay… only it's not her mother, right?"

"Why is it so impossible to believe they could be in love?" Jean said plaintively. "He couldn't help if she was born too late."

Frank shook his head in dismay, looking imploringly to Lou for help. "I said some bad things to Pop about Lee, Uncle Lou. I guess I can't believe that he would prefer Lee over my mother. And he does. All he ever thinks about is Lee."

Lou took a deep breath. "Kids, I'm gonna tell you something that only a couple of people know, and if you ever tell anyone else—even your brother or sister, Frank—I'll curse you till your dying day." He looked at them, pausing for a few seconds, wondering whether or not he should continue. "Lee was pregnant when she died—with your dad's baby."

Jean put her face into her hands. Frank stood up and walked around the back of the couch. "Shit!" he spat, throwing a knotted rubber band he had been nervously fingering into the wall. "Jesus, why didn't he say something?" he croaked desperately, his remorse becoming unbearable.

"You know your old man, kid. Would he go around talking about personal things like that before the right time?"

"Well, I want him back here," Jean said. "Who's going to take care of him? He's away from everyone he loves. God, Uncle Lou, he has to come back."

"I'll talk to him," said Lou glumly.

Orrie had talked to the president a few times, mostly at Touchdown Club meetings where the president would host a kickoff dinner prior to football season and extract pledges from the affluent guests for scholarships and building drives. The president was a handsome, aristocratic Protestant: white-haired and erect, one of those people who seemed born to be deans of colleges. He looked like a president, and people seemed to believe whatever he said about education, enough so that they opened their pocketbooks to him. And that was Dr. Miles Wingrave's greatest talent as an administrator—he got things built.

When he took over the presidency of Spring Common 24 years before, it was a small, two-building municipal college, a low-tuition institution designed to enable veterans from the Second World War and Korean War to afford bachelor's degrees. The student body was older than most, and part-time attendance was the rule rather than the exception. Where other colleges were concerned with housing for students, Spring Common was preoccupied with student parking for the commuters who overran the campus after the workday.

Now Spring Common was a state college with a master's degree program, a new library, 10 buildings—most of them new—and 14,000 students. The college still served the children of Youngstown, but now they were the middle class that had been forged a generation ago from the mostly European ore of Irish, Italian, Polish, Slovak, Jewish, German, and Lebanese millworkers. Only Puerto Ricans and Blacks made up any notable contingent of non-Europeans.

Dr. Wingrave would soon retire. He was a reasonably content man, not a great scholar, though he looked the part. He had yearned one day for the presidency of places like Dartmouth, Northwestern, or Stanford, but the calls never came. Then, in his middle years, he would have settled for Ohio State, Penn State, or Michigan. But now, in his old age, he was resigned to Spring Common. No calls would ever come again; he was sure of it. And, humble and ordinary as it was, Spring Common was clean, well kept, financially stable, and did not give out too many unworthy degrees. At least, Wingrave felt, the college had some integrity, and that was the font of his satisfaction. He hadn't done a bad job under the circumstances.

"Come in, Mr. Glazer. Nice to see you again," said Wingrave.

"Thank you, sir," said Orrie, feeling suddenly rumpled and uncomfortable in Wingrave's wainscoted office.

"Would you like tea or coffee?" said the president.

"Coffee would be fine."

The president pressed a button on his intercom, and a young secretary appeared. He ordered coffee for Orrie and himself. In a moment, she was gone. And when she left, Orrie and Wingrave exchanged pleasantries and talked about the second-place finish of the basketball team in the conference championship. In a few moments, the girl returned with a silver tray of coffee cups and saucers, cream, sugar, and a burnished silver coffee urn, obviously many years old, an heirloom of past presidencies. Orrie waited for the girl to leave. Wingrave, sensing Orrie's impatience, called to the secretary. "Tell Mrs. Collier that I don't wish to be disturbed," he said smoothly but with the aura of command he had acquired from being president so long. He was accustomed to being heard and obeyed. Mrs. Collier was his personal secretary, an elegant gray-haired, middle-aged woman skilled at fending people off from the president.

"Now," said the president, "you wanted to see me about a gift to the college?"

"Yes, sir—a substantial gift."

Wingrave became more animated. "How substantial?" said Wingrave, hardly able to conceal his pleasure.

"Two hundred thousand dollars," said Orrie.

The president sat forward on his chair and set his cup on the coffee table between himself and Orrie. "That's very substantial, Mr. Glazer," Wingrave said appreciatively in a low voice.

"The only condition is that my clients wish to remain anonymous—even to you. The award is to be a one-time thing, given to the professor who submits a research proposal through a faculty committee. My clients will make the final choice from among those candidates selected by the committee."

"I'm surprised, Mr. Glazer," said Wingrave smoothly. "The college has many ways to show appreciation for such bequests—honorary degrees, named chairs, buildings. Why do your clients not wish us to know their identities?"

"This organization is completely aboveboard; of that I can assure you. But... they are rather eccentric... and for reasons unknown to me, they want to remain unacknowledged."

Wingrave nodded. "All right. On behalf of Spring Common State University, I graciously accept your clients' gift."

"Fine," said Orrie. "I've drawn up a prospectus that details the contest rules."

"Contest?"

"Well, of those submitted, only one will be chosen. It is a contest."

"Ah. Perhaps we can use another word, Mr. Glazer. The word 'contest' sounds too... commercial."

"Whatever," said Orrie, going on with his explanation. "The award will be one hundred thousand dollars per year for two years. The professor would then only do research—the college providing facilities. The money is to be used only for salary. Do you agree with that proposal?"

"Certainly. The facilities of the university are always open to any faculty member. And as for relief from teaching classes, that will be no problem."

"One more thing," said Orrie. "My client has set a deadline: January 31st."

The president frowned but then quickly grew careful not to seem too contrary to Orrie's proposal. "But, Mr. Glazer, that's an impossibly short time in which to make a proposal."

"They want it that way, sir. I'm sorry."

"Well." The president sighed. "This is most unusual. These things shouldn't be hurried so..."

"Well, if it's impossible to comply..." said Orrie, his voice trailing off, knowing instinctively how the president would respond. Orrie was a man of the street, the kind of person the president was uncomfortable with. He was unawed by the tradition and the prestige of office. Orrie was attuned to money, power, and leverage—the real world. He had known stuffed shirts, phonies, and people who lived apart from the marketplace, where comfort and genteel manners, airs, and postures were media of exchange. Orrie used to sweat a lot in the presence of people like Wingrave, but as he grew older, he grew surer of himself and learned to wait. He would sweat nonetheless, but he would wait, after words, after glances, after hesitations. It was then that he became a negotiator. The gray hairs on his head had to come, it seemed, before Orrie knew how good he really was, and before his colleagues, unaware at first, grudgingly acknowledged his abilities. Wingrave never stood a chance.

"Oh no," said Wingrave, "I'm sure that several worthy faculty members would be able to meet the deadline."

Orrie smiled, as much to himself as to Wingrave. *A piece of cake*, he thought. He felt a strange exhilaration at being part of Rino's game. The excitement was in the blind guessing, the mystery of it, and the possibility of failure. He had to find out what Rino was doing, but he also had to keep his wits about him. All his life he had prospered by keeping his clients' welfare foremost in his mind. Instinctively he was an infighter; instinctively he liked causes, especially if he believed in the people he was helping. He believed in Rino.

"All right," said Orrie. "Here are the papers for you to sign. As I receive the last of the list of the six finalists, as soon before Christmas as possible, and once the winner is chosen, the final check will be sent directly to you. Here is also a draft of the ground rules. Ah, I've made some suggestions for a cover letter you could write... because of the nature of the gift and the secrecy. I hope you understand."

Wingrave nodded. "Fine, fine. I'll read the articles tonight and take them to our attorney and the board by Friday's meeting. My administrative assistant will bring a confirmation to your office late Friday afternoon."

Rino had been shopping two nights in a row. It was nice doing it again. Last year had been so desolate; the Christmas season was a painful blur in his memory. Now he was busy at least, busy enough not to think about what might have been. Big events were ahead of him, and they buzzed in his consciousness.

It was Thursday, and Christmas was two Saturdays away. Orrie had given him the news that the board of trustees of Spring Common had approved the fellowship, and the gift was officially accepted. Rino was satisfied, if not content. He drank some tea as he read the paper. It was dark so early in this late part of the year.

The condominium was almost furnished completely now. A few more deliveries, another bedroom suite upstairs, a love seat in the living room; soon it would be intact, and he could learn to live this strange new single life he had embarked on.

He walked to a small cabinet and took out his notebook. He read the number and dialed it. When he heard the greeting, his pulse quickened. He could never forget the magic of that voice. "Hi, Toni, this is Rino."

"Hello, Rino, how are you?"

"I'm okay. And you?"

"I've been trying to do some things for Christmas."

"Are you spending Christmas with Nicole?"

"Yes. I'm going to stay the whole week with them."

"Oh..."

"Do you think you can come for a visit?"

"Well, I was thinking about this Sunday if you don't have anything planned."

"Sunday would be fine. You'll stay to dinner, won't you?"

"If it isn't too much trouble."

"Oh, you just plan on staying. What time will you come?"

"Maybe about two o'clock. Is that all right?"

"That's fine."

He hesitated. "Well, I guess I'll see you Sunday, huh?"

When he put down the receiver, Rino had a strange, warm feeling in the hollow of his stomach. Here was a woman asking for his presence at her table. Funny, it had never occurred to him that he would be in demand... until Lee. Those nights he went to see her in that apartment, he had never doubted it. She wanted him to come; she wanted him to stay.

Now with Toni, he had the same feeling. Somehow mother and daughter were able to make him feel wanted and welcome. And they did it in an easy, natural way. The daughter had taught him all he ever knew about love and longing, and now he was learning from her mother about the preservation of dreams and courage in the face of mournful reality.

But was Toni nice to him out of duty to Lee, or did Rino mean to her the same peace, the same memories that she was to him? It occurred to Rino that he didn't really know what Toni looked like as Toni, as someone other than the embodiment of the spirit and beauty of Lee. Maybe he owed her that. He had to think of her as Lee's mother, not as a surrogate for Lee.

The next morning, at the Spring Common cafeteria, Sammy joined Rino for a coffee break. "How are you doing, Rino?"

"Not bad, Sam," Rino said.

"Your Christmas shopping all done?"

"No, not all of it."

Sammy paused, hesitating to say what was on his mind, but then deciding to go ahead with it. "You know, we don't have long talks together like we used to." He glanced at Rino, and Rino nodded in agreement. "Those were nice talks, goombah."

"Yeah, they were nice, Sam. It's just that..."

"I know. Things change, right?"

"Yeah."

"Look, I'm gonna need you on the third floor of Crandall today. Okay?" Sammy said.

"Sure. For what?"

"We're gonna put new thermostats in all the rooms up there. Guess who's elected?"

Rino chuckled. "When are you guys gonna spend some money and hire a real electrician?"

"Why do we need an electrician if we have you?"

"I'm getting old, kid."

"You'll be around a long time, goombah. Don't worry about it."

Upstairs, Rino, with Joe Potokar helping, started disconnecting and reconnecting thermostats in each room. The job was easy but tedious; the adjustments and trials required made their progress slow. Then, one of the new thermostats didn't work, so a new one had to be installed after several futile tries of the defective one.

During lunch, Joe said, "Things have been quiet around here, huh, Rino?"

Rino pursed his lips in agreement. "Yeah, nobody's been in trouble for a long time, huh? How's Barly like it?"

"Man, he loves it. No problems, no headaches. He's thinking of running for union president, you know that?"

"Yeah? You think our group's big enough to get him elected?"

"Nah. We need more votes... like maybe the guys at the courthouse. If they went with us, he could get in."

"Well, maybe between now and spring we can do a job on those guys," Rino said.

Back on the third floor of Crandall Hall, Joe and Rino began to disconnect and connect as they had done all morning. But this time, Joe had moved to the north side of the building, while Rino was installing the last thermostat on the south.

Rino hummed softly as he worked. The job was easy enough, and it was warm inside, in contrast to the frigid, darkening weather outside that the grounds crew faced. After two more trials, he was done. Then he had to go downstairs to the main box to wire the thermostats in. Sure enough, they were working when he came back upstairs. He snapped his fingers in a display of satisfaction. This end of the building was done.

Where was Joe? he wondered as he walked down one of the long corridors on that floor. Rino checked a few rooms, but Joe wasn't around. He had disconnected two old thermostats, Rino noted, but hadn't done the third or the fourth they were hoping to finish.

Just as he rounded the corner, he saw Joe being harangued by Dale Chandler. Almost childlike in his sincerity, Joe stood before Chandler, his face red and his shoulders slightly stooped, seeming confused by Chandler's wrath. Instantly, Rino's pulse quickened as he advanced toward the two men. "What's wrong, Joe?" he said, glancing at Chandler but then ignoring him.

"This stupid oaf just ruined my trousers; that's what's wrong," said Chandler.

"Joe?" said Rino, still ignoring Chandler.

Joe spoke painfully, hardly able to make his voice more than a raspy whisper. "He kicked the penetrating oil can, Rino. It was my fault. I set it there for just a minute."

"This is none of your business, Bellanca, so stay the hell out," Chandler snapped.

"I'll pay for it, Rino," said Joe.

"You most assuredly will, you witless... cretin," Chandler said.

As Chandler spoke, all Rino could sense was that another person he cared about was being humiliated by the same vicious creature. Rino grabbed Chandler's arm, swinging him backward and slamming him against the wall. Then he grabbed the collar of his shirt and drew

Chandler's face toward him. "You bastard! It was an accident. You're the witless one, walking into a work area. Pay for your own goddamned pants."

"Take your hands off me, you animal," Chandler hissed, and he slapped Rino's face with his free right hand. Rino roared from deep within his chest as he threw Chandler across the hall again, this time slamming him into the opposite wall. Chandler wasn't expecting the strength Rino could exert on him, but when he hit the wall, the pain that suddenly stunned him was transmuted into fear. In turning, he could see the look of hatred on Rino's face as the older man advanced toward him, his fist poised to strike.

Joe caught his arm just as he was about to hit Chandler, who stared dully at them with blood trickling from a split lip. "No, Rino! Jesus Christ, don't do this."

Rino held Chandler at arm's length, as if measuring him for a final blow. "Come away, Rino. You're better than this," Joe pleaded.

Slowly Rino put his measuring hand down away from Chandler's throat. Then, in another few seconds, he lowered his right arm and stepped back. "Malandrine!" Rino snarled at Chandler.

"God, you'll pay for this, Bellanca. It'll cost your job at least," Chandler mumbled through swollen lips as he lurched unsteadily away.

Only two students, standing at the lavatory door, had seen the end of the fight, watching in wide-eyed amazement as Chandler walked away, wiping blood from his mouth with a handkerchief. The girls quickly went inside.

Chandler went into the faculty lavatory and washed his face. He rinsed his mouth out with water and spat into the sink several times. Then he splashed water on his face again and patted it dry, cursing at the swollen lip he could see in the mirror. Something else about him looked strange.

He wasn't sure if his nose was broken, or if his face had puffed up after hitting the wall. But he looked put upon, swollen and blanched, with a vivid red blotch under one eye. His neck ached, too. And when he breathed, he felt soreness in the left front near his ribs. *God*, he thought, *how could this happen to me?* He had to get out of Spring Common. It was too low-life and crude—no tradition of scholarship and achievement, no refuge for professors who were attacked by errant custodians. He had to get out of Spring Common.

But then, he couldn't be seen looking this way. His only instinct was to leave, leave and not be seen. Quickly he returned to his office to gather his coat and put some papers in a briefcase. He would go down the back stairs and out into the parking lot. Three o'clock classes were still in session, so he would be able to get out before anyone saw him. As he closed his office door and started down the corridor, he was feeling better about being able to remove himself so quickly from the arena of his anguish. But as he turned the corner to the exit, he saw Earl Higley closing the door to his own office.

Higley glanced at Chandler, surprised to see him. Then with a second, closer look, he said, "Chandler? Are you all right?"

Chandler hurried past him, muttering an assurance that he was fine. Higley watched Chandler round the corner and could hear him as he hurried down the steps. Chandler was a mess, Higley thought, quite satisfied to see him so harried. He detested Chandler, and it was nice to see him looking out of sorts. His lip was puffy, too, Higley mused. Must have had a fight with one of the grad students he was screwing.

On his way to the car, Chandler lowered his head, hoping frantically that no one else would see him. Christ. Of all people to meet: Higley. He disliked Higley because of his attitude. Higley always pretended to be unawed by Chandler. A journeyman professor, a plodder with hardly any publications... but, amazingly, renowned by some to be a man capable of thinking on the very highest levels of analysis. Yet he was so drably ordinary and unimposing. He would die at Spring Common, a dumpy local, content to limit his dreams to the horizons of Youngstown.

Chandler, to his great relief, finally made it to the car, and, as fast as he could, maneuvered it out of the parking lot. His jaw hurt, and his lip and eye were swollen. He grimaced as he sighed in disbelief. Even his ribs hurt more as he took a deep breath.

Rino had stopped trembling as he and Joe sat in the locker room. Sammy had not taken the news well. He was worried that Chandler would try to have Rino fired, and Sammy didn't want that. Yet he didn't want another fight with the president's office, either.

"How are you, Rino?" Joe said. "You calmed down now?"

"Yeah, Joe, I'm calm now," Rino said, hardly believing it himself.

"You think Sammy'll back us?" Joe said.

"Yeah, he will. He just doesn't want another go-around with the administration."

One of the workers had brought them coffee from the cafeteria. Joe took one and handed Rino the other. When they were alone again, Joe said, "Rino? You okay now? Why'd you get so crazy just for me? I don't want you should lose your job."

"I don't care about the job anymore, Joe. I don't think I can stay away from Chandler in this place."

"But you don't have to be here in this building. You can work over at Stilton or the science lab… maybe the administration building."

"It's not that, Joe. I just hate the guy. And our paths keep crossing all the time."

"What'd you call him? That dago name as he walked away?"

"Malandrine. It's some evil spirit that goes around hurting people."

Joe was silent for a few minutes. "Thanks for fighting for me, Rino. I'm grateful."

The next morning, Chandler felt better. The swelling of his lip had gone down so that there was only a slight puff, mostly on the inner side of his mouth. He had had a shower, and his aching ribs felt better from the warmth of the falling water. As he dressed, he began to think about his last thoughts as he lay awake and smarting from bruises that Rino had inflicted on him. No one had seen the fight. No one had seen him cringing from a blow about to be struck by an older man, a blue-collar worker.

He was sick of Bellanca. This time he was going to get him and make it stick. This time that bastard custodian was wrong, and no union could save him. This time he would know what happened to people who crossed Dale Chandler.

As he shaved, Chandler grew eager to put his plan into effect. First, he would file formal charges; then, later, he'd tell the dean. The dean wouldn't like it, but this time he'd force him to have some backbone. This time he would finesse the dean.

He'd get Bellanca for good. Nobody could do that to him—smash his face against a wall, give him a fat lip, make him have to slink out of Crandall Hall for fear of being seen cut and bruised.

God, why in hell did he ever have to deal with Bellanca? He had to get out of this town. Just a few more publications, a few more accolades, and he'd be at the threshold of Dartmouth. And why not? He looked the part; he acted the part. Spring Common would not be able to contain his career. He had to move on.

He poured himself some coffee and ruminated about what would happen. He had total confidence in his ability to beat Bellanca. He had beaten others. He had beaten Ted Reese when he began to get too big for his britches... in the sweetest way a man could: at work and at home, in the racquetball court, in the tenure game at Spring Common, and in his own bedroom with Reese's wife. She stayed around all night for that second banging, and Ted Reese knew it. Totally. He owned them both. And he would own Bellanca.

Hell, it was only dumb luck that had kept him out of his clutches last time. But this time the union wouldn't be able to stop it. Bellanca had been unprovoked. He had lost it. That's it. He had lost it. He's too old to handle normal crises without losing control. Too old. He's lost it. Chandler smiled contentedly and sipped his coffee.

When Orrie approached the receptionist at the secretarial pool, he asked for the dean. The girl asked if he had an appointment. He told her that he didn't, but that he thought the dean would want to see him.

As he waited for a few moments while the girl left her desk, he noticed a bulletin board with a large poster on it. It was for the fellowship. Orrie pursed his lips appreciatively. Nice money.

Just then the receptionist returned with an older woman with a skinny, rather frail body, hollow cheeks, and white, tightly set hair. She had the look of a professional pleaser, an officious deflector of personnel—away from the dean. Her visage discouraged mere mortals. She seemed humorless yet timid, the dean's secretary by dint of many years of not making waves, of pleasing only him. "I'm sorry, sir," she said, "the dean is in conference. He's not seeing anyone this afternoon. If you'd care to leave a message..."

The woman irritated Orrie; he had never liked stuffy, humorless people. How many students and faculty had she turned away in her lifetime? All for the comfort and convenience of one man. "Madam," Orrie said peevishly, "I'm an attorney here on serious business. And you can tell the dean that he'd be very wise to see me."

She seemed confused for a moment. Here was something she dreaded: the outside world intruding on their domain with its own rules of behavior. She stood transfixed on Orrie's face. "Go get him," Orrie said to her sharply, finally registering into her consciousness.

In a few minutes, Orrie was following her down a corridor. She knocked on the closed door and went inside. A moment later, she reopened the door and admitted Orrie. *Conference, huh?* he thought as he looked around the room and saw only the dean. He turned toward the secretary, dismissing her with a haughty look. The dean nodded, and she closed the door behind her.

Orrie, in that instant, was sizing up the dean. He was a husky man with curly white hair receding at the temples. He was well dressed and was also one of those people who smiled patronizingly as a person talked, as though he knew that only nonsense could emanate from anyone who was his inferior, and almost everybody was. He was a man who needed secretaries and associates around him to insulate him from the world. He also had a little power over students and more over faculty.

"What can I do for you?" said the dean, not rising from the chair behind his desk.

Orrie settled into a chair without being asked. "Dr. Burnham, I'm here on a courtesy call," he said in his best used-car-salesman voice.

Burnham changed his expression. The bemused look he wore constantly had vanished, replaced by a peevish, perplexed frown. This "courtesy call" was something more than that. "Please continue," said Burnham.

"I suppose you're aware of the incident—the alleged assault upon one of your professors?"

Burnham began to show some strain. "No, I wasn't aware of it. When did it happen? To whom?"

"Yesterday. A Dr. Chandler, from this college, went to the police station and filed a complaint against my client, Guarino Bellanca. Do you know both men?"

"Yes," Burnham answered nervously, blanching at the mention of the two old antagonists.

"What do you think about it?"

"Well, I know nothing about it. And I'm certainly not going to comment on something before I get all the details."

Orrie pulled out a cigar and lit up, chuckling inwardly at the No Smoking sign displayed prominently on a bookshelf behind the dean. "Frankly, Dr. Burnham, this case puzzles me," Orrie said at his insincere best.

"In what way, Mr....?"

"Glazer," Orrie said calmly.

The dean was uncomfortable with Orrie. He mistrusted him and was annoyed at the cigar, his presumptuous manner, and his lack of awe or deference. And the dean was also fearful. With lawyers, one can be drawn into a whirlpool of conflict, none of it your own making.

Damn that Chandler, Burnham thought. This was the second mess he had gotten himself and the college into. And with the same custodian. A damned custodian.

"Well, this young man doesn't have quite the case he thinks he has—no witnesses, no motive..."

"Are you suggesting that he drop the suit, Mr. Glazer?" said Burnham.

"No, sir, that's his business. But Bellanca is a man in his 60s, an ordinary guy who has a solid reputation as a worker and citizen. Maybe this is just an old-fashioned argument, with one no more at fault than the other." Orrie paused to take a long drag on his cigar, eyeing Burnham coolly. "And maybe the newspaper will have a lot more fun with this thing than it's worth. They're not too crazy about the college, anyway."

Burnham was beginning to be very uneasy. Each point Orrie made impressed him, not only by its logic but by the specter of uncertainty that it conjured up, the thought that the comfortable life he lived at the college would no longer be under his serene control.

"Perhaps I'll have a talk with Dr. Chandler, Mr. Glazer," Burnham said finally.

Orrie knew he had done his job. He nodded contentedly, certain that he had saved Rino a mess of trouble. He stood up after a few more minutes of earnest reassurances, shook hands with Burnham, and left the building.

Rino cursed the sleeting rain as he drove. Every time he had to travel, it seemed to rain. God, he hated winter. His left shoulder ached, the muscles between his shoulder blades were taut, and his eyes, all of a sudden, didn't seem to be as good as they once were. He found himself squinting and straining to see, found himself crushing the steering wheel in each hand.

The ride to Canton seemed longer than it had before. He wasn't even sure why he was going. Seeing Toni only made him think of Lee. Yet he knew he would continue going—if only to talk to her.

"Hello, Rino," Toni said as he stepped across the threshold. She was smiling and seemed less drawn and tense than she had been in past times.

Rino followed her into the study. As he walked, he noticed the marvelous odor of something cooking. He settled into a chair as Toni sat on a couch.

They exchanged nervous formal greetings. Then she brought coffee and rolls. Rino had a warm feeling in his stomach as he settled back into the chair and waited for the peace and quiet of the house to envelop him.

"Have you done any Christmas shopping?" she said.

"A little, but I still have my daughter-in-law and son to do. How about you?"

"A little, too. Some for Nicole's children, and her husband, Bob. Not yet for Nicole, though."

"Are Nicole and Bob all the family you have?"

"No. I have a brother in Kansas City, but he's not well, and I haven't seen him too much lately."

Rino sat quietly, the two of them awkwardly trying to find words to say. But none came. *Strange*, thought Rino, *I never expected this to happen. Hell, I'm just like this with Andrea Manasseri.* "How do you spend your days now?" he asked finally.

"I visit friends, usually visit Nicole and her family once or twice a week. I volunteer at the hospital twice a week. I keep busy, I guess." She stopped for a minute, almost expecting him to have a follow-up question, but he was silent, drumming his fingers on the arm of the chair. "How do you spend your days?" she asked.

He grimaced involuntarily and shrugged. "I still work at the college a few days a week. I see my brother, Lou, and my sister, Connie, all the time."

She sensed unease in him that was different from the social awkwardness between them. This unease was something personal... and hurtful. "What about your family at home?" she asked, aware that she was probing.

He hesitated. "I don't live at home anymore, Toni," he said, struggling with the words.

She seemed surprised but didn't speak, allowing him time to collect his thoughts and tell her as much as he wanted to. "It's better this way," he said. "Now they can be themselves and run their lives the way they want." He looked at her and knew she sensed that he was apart from his family, and it was not a happy parting.

The look of her was one he had seen on Lee so many times, the skeptical but reserved doubt, unspoken but unmistakable. He continued. "It's better this way," he said again.

"Oh, Rino, it was an argument that drove you apart," she said regretfully. For some reason, she felt that it somehow involved her.

He shook his head. "It's something nobody could have prevented."

They finally began to loosen up, and talk came more freely between them. Outside, the sun went down, and soon the warmth of the day was gone. The glistening snow grew fine and crusty in the cold and sparkling to eyes that scanned the windblown dunes in the distance.

Toni studied him as they ate. There were lit candles on the table, and softly lit lamps on the buffet cast a warm glow over the dark wood of the dining room. She sensed his nervousness. What had Lee seen in him? What had she seen that changed her? He was nice looking but not very tall, masculine but not alluring. What, then? He was warm and unpretentious, but was that enough? Was it the honesty that Lee had spoken of so many times? Was it the easy manner, the quiet way he seemed to move through life? He also spoke with humor, often talking about himself in jest, making self-deprecation seem a gentle tolerance for life.

As they talked, she began to be conscious of the wind outside. Once, Rino stopped, instantaneously turned his ear to the sound of the wind, and then returned to what they were saying.

"Why don't you take your coffee into the library while I clean this? It won't take more than a few minutes," Toni said.

"I could help you," he said tentatively. "I don't mind. I'd like to."

She nodded. Without talking, they each carried some things from the table. Toni seemed nervous as he helped her. Hurriedly she put dishes in the dishwasher, trying to be done as quickly as she could. There was something about this strange man helping her that she couldn't get used to. All the while she worked, they said little. She was becoming disturbed by her reactions. Suddenly she was enjoying having a man talk to her and be polite and respectful. It wasn't Lee's husband whom she was responding to; it was Rino. She was beginning to feel warm when he spoke and happy when he laughed, bright when he talked brightly and somber when he talked of dark or painful things. She wanted to ask him how much he missed Lee. Had the pain and longing subsided? What would he do with his life?

When they walked to the library, they could both hear the sound of the wind again. As they settled into their chairs in the library, facing each other, Toni said, "Rino, the weather is getting bad outside. You can stay here tonight. There's a guest bedroom with a private bath."

He shook his head before she was done. "Thanks. If I leave in a few minutes, I'll be okay."

"But you haven't been here..." She caught herself. She was worried that there would be some reason for him not to come again. He had to feel the need to see her, a longing that she'd fulfill. She was there as a surrogate for her daughter whose voice she had, whose mannerisms she still possessed, whose looks she had in some pale measure.

Listening to the wind, thinking of the snow as he sat opposite her, Toni was reminded of another night of bad weather when Lee had left her and headed in the darkness for Youngstown. As the notion persisted, she became frightened.

Suddenly Rino stood erect. Toni stood up slowly, waiting for him to speak. "Can I have my coat?" he said.

She sighed and, without a word, turned toward the hall closet. Rino followed her.

She handed him the coat, and he put it on in awkward silence. The wind was still howling, and snow was beginning to accumulate. "Thanks for the supper, Toni," he said, looking away from her as he concentrated on the buttons of his topcoat.

"You know you can come here anytime, don't you?" she said.

He nodded. "Maybe someday... after the first of the year."

"You're always welcome here. I mean that."

He stood awkwardly for a moment. She looked behind him through a window at the snow. "Oh, Rino, you shouldn't be out in this weather. You can stay here."

"Thanks," he said, shaking his head.

"Will you call me when you get home?" she said, looking down at her hands as she talked. "I think about that awful road, the weather..." She paused. "How dangerous it is..." As she said the words, her voice cracked, and she raised her left hand to her forehead as if to hold the anguish within her from gushing out. She bit her lip and tried to keep back tears, but she couldn't.

He studied her as she talked, but he wasn't ready for the emotion she showed in her anguished face. As he looked at her, he sensed again the vulnerability of Lee, the softness, the manner, the voice—especially the voice. She was a paler version of Lee, lighter skinned, with straight nose and large green eyes, beautiful and fragile looking.

But as he read the helpless weariness and loneliness in her face, Rino felt the same stirring that he had so long ago as he'd watched Lee cry. He reached out to Toni and took her in his arms.

Without understanding what he was doing, without any way to sort the feelings he had or the senses that impelled him to act, he moved his head toward hers. She looked upward and met his lips as they came toward hers. At first, only for a split second, there was a shock at the strangeness of the kiss that made them both hesitate. But then the kiss continued.

Suddenly Rino stopped as gently as he could. For a moment, he held her at arm's length and gazed at her face as though unsure of who she was. "Oh my God, I'm sorry, Toni. I'm so sorry," he said as he turned and hurried toward his car. She called to him, and called again, but he wouldn't hear what she was saying.

Rino wasn't enjoying the Christmas season at Spring Common. School was over for the quarter. Most of the faculty was gone, and the custodians were left to work in peace. Sammy tried to cheer Rino a little, and Joe was his gentle, patient self, trying to assuage the hurt he knew was in Rino's heart. But it didn't work.

How could my life be like this? Rino thought as he was having coffee alone in the Spring Common cafeteria. *Every chance I had, I blew. Every dream I had was unfulfilled. Everything I try to do doesn't work out: Lou's mad at me, I've fought with Frank and Jean, I'll probably get fired for punching Chandler, I've disgraced myself with Toni, I'm probably throwing two hundred grand down a rat hole. What the hell more can I do wrong?*

Just then, he saw Lou come into the main entrance of the cafeteria. Lou looked over into the corner, saw his brother, and then went to the coffeepot. "How're you doing, cowboy?" Lou said as he drew near to Rino. Rino shrugged. "Where have you been sleeping lately?"

"I rented a condo in Torrence Park."

"Rino, that's crazy, and you know it. What the hell are you gonna do in a condo all by yourself?"

"The same thing you do. I'm gonna relax and stay out of everybody's way."

"Nobody wants you out of their way. Your kids, Connie... I sure as hell don't."

"You could have fooled me, Luigi. But regardless, it was time for me to make a move."

"The only move you should make is back to your own house. Look, Rino, you know Frank didn't mean what he said."

"You weren't there, Lou," said Rino.

"Rino, those kids are crazy about you, and this'll kill them if you don't go back. How do you think Libby feels? And Jean? You know she came to my shop? If you don't go back, that family will never be the same again."

Rino was silent for a few minutes, looking out at the heavily falling snow. "What'd Jean say?"

"She said she wants you back. You know, who's gonna feed him? Who's gonna wash his clothes? Who's gonna take care of him? Rino, those kids love you. Frank's always been your favorite. And I'd trade 10 daughters-in-law for one of Jean. You can't let this come between you."

Rino shook his head, and Lou began to be desperate. "Listen to me, kid. You've lost enough in your life. Do you want to lose that family of yours, too? They want you back. Jesus! When Lee died, they kept you going. You all need each other."

"They kept me going and then threw it in my face the other day, Luigi," said Rino grimly. "It was like they were waiting just for the right time, and then they could open up."

"Oh, for Christ's sake, Rino! You know your son. Is he like that? It just hurt him because he was thinking of his mother. He doesn't understand this thing with Lee. But I know he wants you back."

Rino changed the subject. "How about it, kid? You still willing to sign that will for me?"

"Yeah. I'll sign it. I told you that," Lou said.

"You and I haven't exactly been drinking buddies lately," Rino said.

"You know, Rino, I guess I'm just afraid that you might be getting too weird. Remember what it was like when we were kids, when we lost the house? Bread, bacon grease, and black coffee? Remember how long it took Mom and Pop to pay back three grand for a house? Money was so damned important because we went hungry a lot of times. So when I hear you spending two hundred grand just to nail one asshole prof, it made me think back to the days we ate beans and oil for days at a time. Do you blame me for thinking you flipped out?" Lou stopped to study Rino, who was gazing out the window. The cafeteria was totally empty. Lou's low, muffled voice rumbled in the corner. Workers were putting up chairs on tables so the floor could be scrubbed.

Rino looked back at his brother and smiled wanly. "Maybe I have flipped out, Lou. But there's something I have to do before I die. With the life I have left, I have to nail that bastard."

"I don't know if it's worth what it takes—or what it turns you into, Rino."

"Lou, all those nights I dreamed of Lee after she died, the worst of it was knowing what I'd missed. I wanted her, that baby. Jesus, it would have been wonderful. But then I'd wake up into the real world: Lee's gone, the baby's gone, my blood pressure's too high, my stomach cramps at night, and Chandler's flying to the moon, still lying, cheating, screwing people. There's no justice, Lou; there's only revenge."

"But how are you gonna get revenge? Where the hell's your program? You don't know if you can even do it."

"It's a gamble. But if I know anything about people, it's gonna pay off. Chandler wants his name in lights, Lou—and he couldn't stand having someone beat him out for that award." Lou shook his head. "But I need your help, kid. We've been together too long to fold it all now. If we were gonna hate each other, we should have started it years ago, before we owed each other so much."

Lou snorted in agreement with his brother. "Yeah, kid. You know, if you get off early enough, maybe we can talk Jean into making some coffee and muffins for us." Rino looked at Lou doubtfully. "Come on, for Christ's sake, man," Lou said. "Do you want to grow old and die all by yourself in some goddamned condo? You'd hate it."

"I can make peace, Lou. But I can't go back. I have a job to do."

Chandler came to the college feeling jaunty and self-assured. He had seen Higley again and had addressed him confidently, having no more bruises to hide.

What a comic figure he was, Chandler mused, driving those old cars to school each day. He looked like a welder or truck driver. And he made up in longevity for what others acquired by scholarly achievement. But the hell with Higley. This day, everything would fall into place for him. A hearing would be held to assess the assault charges. And then he'd finally have Bellanca by the balls.

He acknowledged Higley coolly, the way men who despise each other do only out of mere strained civility. Then he passed down the hallway toward his office. Abruptly he changed course toward the main office and the faculty mailboxes.

As he was scanning the mail that had been stuffed into his box, the dean's secretary approached him, officiously whispering that the dean would like to see him. *Here we go,* Chandler thought, *the dean's pouting and needs a little stroking.* "Tell the dean I'll be there in a few minutes," Chandler said.

Chandler went into his office, read his mail carefully, and returned to the faculty lounge to get a cup of coffee. When he arrived at the dean's office, the door was open. "Arlen? You wanted to see me?" said Chandler.

"Yeah, Dale, come in," Burnham answered uneasily.

"What's on your mind?" said Chandler.

"What do you make of this fellowship business, Dale?" said Burnham, trying to disarm Chandler and start the conversation on a positive note.

"Probably some eccentric who's getting on in years. You see some weird bequests to colleges nowadays."

"I presume you're going to apply for it," said Burnham.

"My work should stand up to the test."

"I heard Steinberg from Psychology, Evans from History, Patel from Engineering..."

"Patel? The laureate award must have gone to his head; he's not much of a researcher. I'm not worried, Arlen. I think my credentials will do it.

Only Steinberg has a book to his credit—and not very well received at that. And Evans is just a big wheel in the Mahoning Valley Historical Society—that and a dollar will get you on the bus."

Finally, Burnham thought he had massaged Chandler enough. "I had a visit from Rino Bellanca's lawyer yesterday, Dale," he said.

"So?" Chandler said archly.

"We talked a little about your assault charge."

"What about it?" said Chandler, his back stiffening to meet the dean's argument.

"He seems to feel that this thing is being pushed a little too hard."

"Well, he would, wouldn't he? He's Bellanca's advocate." Chandler was getting angry but showed it only by being more aggressive. "Are you in the habit of winking at physical assaults on your colleagues, Arlen?"

"Dale, I didn't even know about the assault until I learned it from someone outside the college."

"Listen, Arlen, this guy almost throttled me in the hallway. When was the last time you were in a college where a professor—a department chairman—had to suffer that?"

"Dale, I'm concerned about the fellowship. They're not going to award it to anyone who has a cloud of controversy around him."

"I'm just defending myself, Arlen," said Chandler, facing away from Burnham, pretending to be scanning the books that were arrayed neatly on one wall. Then Chandler turned back toward Burnham. "No one else seems willing to try it."

"Oh, come off it, Dale. I'm talking about your own welfare. There's a damned good chance that someone from this college—you, most likely—would get it." Burnham paused and changed the tone of his voice into a slightly mocking singsong. "But if you insist on carrying on a seemingly eternal personal feud with a damned semiliterate custodian, there's not much anyone can do for you."

Chandler softened a little. "I just can't rid him from my life, Arlen. He seems to turn up all the time, haunting me. I'm sick of it. No one has any respect for rank and authority around here."

Burnham sighed wearily. He was not someone who liked to be caught in any kind of crossfire, let alone one between an abrasive young academic and a blue-collar union member. "Dale, I can't even get them to clean the chalk trays without a two-week negotiation session. How can I do anything for you when you get embroiled in these dogfights with someone over whom I have almost no control?" Burnham took a deep breath. "Look, Dale, I'm going to be retiring someday, and you would be the logical in-house person to take my job—that is, if you don't get a better offer in the meantime. And if you want to teach at Penn or Dartmouth, then this fellowship could be the entrée into that position."

Chandler paused thoughtfully, weighing the dean's arguments in his head. "You think I should drop the charges, do you?"

"I've told you what I think, Dale. It would be a short-term loss for a long-term gain."

Rino had grown weary of life the last few weeks. He had made a tenuous, stilted peace with Frank and Jean, much to the relief of Lou and Connie, so Christmas had come and gone without much effort—or strife. He had only felt the pangs of hurt on Christmas night, looking at the small tree in the condo, quietly having tea alone, and being tormented by the same old questions again: What if she had lived? And had the baby? What if she were here with him this lonely night?

Lately, he couldn't even dream of her in his bed. The warmth, the unimaginable softness, the clean yet musky smell of her, the pliant body that held him against the night—they seemed all a vague fantasy. Almost as though they had happened to someone else.

The wind outside was blowing the January dampness, churning it into snow that would be thick and hardened by morning. Rino was off the next day, and he sat reading in the quiet of his family room. Sundays were days when he had little to do. His presence was mandatory at Connie's or Jean's for afternoon dinner, but after that he usually left for home, begging off early and leaving them all worried about his mental state. He seemed not just changed, but rather diminished, as though his spirit and personality had been cleft and part of him lost.

Suddenly his doorbell rang. He was startled for a moment, and then he went to the door. It was Lou. "Everything okay, kid?" Rino said.

"Yeah," said Lou, walking into the apartment. "I just left Annie's, but I know I won't sleep if I go home. Got anything good to drink?"

"I'll put on some coffee for some royals," Rino said. Lou nodded.

Rino went into the small kitchen as Lou threw his coat over an arm of the couch. Lou settled back wearily into a soft, stuffed, plaid-colored chair and draped an arm over each armrest. Neither man talked while Rino made coffee. Finally, Rino joined his brother, sitting opposite him as the coffeepot began to perk.

"This is really a nice place. Lots of room, huh?" Lou said.

"Yeah," Rino said.

"Your kids miss you, Rino," Lou said abruptly.

"They have their own lives to live," his brother said wearily.

"Not without you, cowboy," said Lou.

"Hey, Lou, did you come on one of those mercy missions again?" said Rino irritably. "If you did, save it."

"You made your point, Rino. They're miserable without you... and feeling guilty as hell."

"Refresh my memory," said Rino. "Aren't you the guy who's been telling me for five years to get my own place?"

"I was wrong about that. I didn't think the kids would take it so hard."

Rino huffed in disgust. "How's Connie? You see her this week?"

"She wants to know where you've been hiding," Lou said.

Rino snorted, then stood up to get the coffee from the kitchen.

"You have some new troubles, kid?" Lou said as Rino walked.

Rino sighed. "I did something crazy, Lou," he said, pouring half cups of coffee into two large, brown mugs and motioning to Lou to hold his cup until Rino could put a dollop of whiskey into the steaming dark fluid.

"What's so new about that?" Lou said, blanching slightly, trying to take the edge off his brother's depression.

"I kissed her, Luigi."

"Who, for God's sake?"

"Her mother... Toni."

"Well? So what?"

Rino didn't answer his brother. Maybe this wasn't the time to tell him, he thought miserably. But he couldn't put it out of his mind. "It wasn't a friendly kiss."

Lou sighed and set the coffee cup on an end table and stared at Rino for a few seconds. God, maybe this was his calling for the rest of his life: looking after his younger brother. All of a sudden, that sturdy, resourceful man had to be advised and comforted at every turn. The last many years he had been helping Rino weather storms, all of them involving women: first Mary's death, then Lee, then Lee's death, and now Toni. Yet his heart was moved to help Rino, for all the good his brother had done him, for all the pain he had suffered the last few years, for all the promises unfulfilled in his age. *I wonder,* Lou thought, *what the two of us would be doing today if Rino had never met Lee that summer? God, life would have been easier.*

"Did she kiss you back, Rino?"

Rino was almost startled by the question. He had never thought about Toni wanting a kiss. "I don't know, Lou," he said, shaking his head. "She didn't push me away. But what about Lee? How could I do that?"

"Look, kid, that woman looks like Lee, right?" Rino nodded. "And she acts like Lee, doesn't she?" Lou glanced over at his brother, who wasn't nodding this time. Instead, he was staring back. "And she sure as hell sounds like Lee." Lou paused and looked at Rino for several long silent seconds. "Rino, you were kissing Lee. Don't you see that?"

"My brother the psychiatrist," said Rino, half believing Lou but somehow not wanting easy expiation.

"Rino, that goodness is there in the mother, too. And maybe..."

"What?" Rino said, unnerved by Lou's unfinished statement. "What?"

"Maybe you do the same to Toni that you did to Lee. Hell, she might have all the same buttons that Lee had."

Rino snorted. "Christ. I wouldn't do that for all the tea in China." He poured more coffee and whiskey for them both.

"Are we ever going to have fun anymore, kid?" Lou said. "Neither of us has many more years left—at least that we aren't senile."

Rino sighed. "I'm sorry, Luigi. I never thought you'd have to be putting me back together in pieces all the time. I never banked on any of this. If you'd have told me five years ago that this is what I'd be like today, I'd have said you were crazy." Rino stood up and walked over to the mantel above the fireplace, which still had a few lingering embers. "I never realized how close we are to being basket cases, kid. I thought if I could get over Mary's death, nothing could touch me—I'd have life all figured out. Then I meet one little girl..."

"Well, you did meet her and... she's gone. So let's move on. Someday I'm gonna want to take you over to Andrea Manasseri's house. And you're gonna join the human race again. There'll never be another one like Lee, cowboy, but you won't dishonor her by taking someone to a Cavour Club party once in a while."

Rino now only worked two days a week at Spring Common. Sammy would have used him more often, but Rino was beginning to wean himself away from his job at the college. He had talked Sammy into classifying him as a contingency worker with irregular hours. Usually when Rino came to work, there were more maintenance jobs and fewer cleaning jobs for him to do. Rino still cajoled Sammy to train the young man who had been an electrician's mate in the navy.

On his way out of Stilton Hall, Rino waved to Joe and Barly from across the wide green around which the many college halls were arrayed. Then he headed for his car, which was parked in a small faculty-and-staff lot on the west side of the library. Rino didn't like the ice on cold days, or the heat on hot days, to assail him when he was ready to leave the college after a long day's work. So he found a little remote lot surrounded by trees and removed from the two larger faculty lots nearer the buildings on the oval green.

As he neared his own car, he could see another car in the lot with the hood open and Earl Higley bending over the motor. Rino had always liked Higley. He was reserved but friendly and easygoing. He was, it was said, masterful at internal faculty politics, but he was not ambitious or aggressive. His professional achievements were unspectacular, but he was a good professor and scholar whose only love besides his wife and teaching was cars.

"What's up, Dr. Higley?" said Rino as he approached the car.

"Aw, I can't start this goddamned thing. It's hard to start after it sits for a while, and I can't figure out what's wrong."

"This is a slant six, right?" said Rino.

"Yeah," said Higley, surprised at Rino's perception.

Rino reached in to touch the carburetor and found it very hot. "I know a man who has one of these, Dr. Higley," said Rino. "He used to have the same trouble: this gas line gets so hot, it heats up the fuel, and by the time it reaches the carburetor, it's so hot it forces the needle valve out of its seat."

Higley looked up at Rino. "I hadn't thought of that," he said in respectful tones. "I tried it all, but I never thought of the hot fuel unseating that needle."

"This friend of mine owns a garage, and he made some heat baffles and air ducts from scrap metal and mounted them behind the grill. That helps keep the carburetor cool."

"An ingenious idea," said Higley, nodding approvingly.

"I can have him make you a couple out of some scrap pieces. He'll do it for a few bucks."

"Uh... sure, I'd like that fine. You're sure it's okay?"

"It's okay," Rino said.

Later, Rino stopped at Hugo's to order the baffles for Higley. While he was there, Hugo poured him a beer. Hugo needed any excuse he could find to get a beer out of the old Kelvinator in the small room at the rear of the shop, a near facsimile to an office. As he grew older, he spent more time alone there and let his sons and hired men run the place. Hugo had some favorite customers that he had a paternal interest in, or at least in their cars. But still, anyone he had known for over 50 years, he would often admit to his hideaway. And for friends like Rino, he'd go to the Kelvinator.

In his apartment later, Rino did some things he had put off doing the last few days: cleaning and straightening up. His apartment was usually spotless, except for the daily messiness that Rino would cause. A cleaning lady came in once a week to do washing and ironing and bed linen and household cleaning projects.

He finally settled into a chair to read the newspaper, sipping coffee as he read. It was 8:30 and long since dark. He could hear fine misty snow hitting the windows occasionally. Suddenly, his doorbell rang. He started for a moment and then headed for the door. It was Libby, standing outside the door silently. She looked small, red-faced, and sheepish.

Rino was surprised and unresponsive for a second. Then he said, "Well, come on in; you don't want to freeze out there." Rino guided her gently inside, nudging her by the arm into the room. She was still silent. "Give me your coat. Everything okay?"

She nodded her head. "I'll put some tea on," Rino said.

He rose, feeling very awkward, and left to go into the kitchen.

"Mom's here, too, Grandpa," she said, walking toward the kitchen.

Rino turned back to her. "Where is she?"

"She's parking the car on the other side of the street. She'll be here in a minute."

Just then, there was a knock at the door. "That's her," Libby said, going to the door as Rino stood still, staring at the woman who appeared there. There were some strands of gray in the dark blonde hair. She looked paler and thinner than she usually did.

"Take off your coat," Rino said. "I've got the water on."

She came in silently and took off her coat. "We can only stay a few minutes, Dad. We just stopped by to... uh, see how you were doing."

"I was wondering how long it'd be before you came here," said Rino. "This is the first time for either of you."

"I..." Jean stammered and swallowed a few words that Rino couldn't understand.

"What?" Rino prompted.

"Nothing."

"Nothing or something?"

"Well, we were never invited."

"Invited?" Rino said irritably. "Since when do you have to be invited? What a hell of a thing to say!" Instinctively, after he spoke, Rino glanced quickly at Libby. He saw what he feared he'd see: a look of pain and confusion on her face at hearing her grandfather speak sharply to her mother. Immediately Rino softened his tone, looking back at Jean, who had much the same expression as Libby. He spoke calmly, trying to remove the sting of his last words. "None of you ever need invitations to this place. Remember that," he muttered softly.

He put their coats into the closet. "How's the old man?" he said, smiling uneasily at them both.

"Daddy's fine," Libby answered.

"What are you two doing out so late on a night like this?"

"We were shopping," said Jean. "Returning some gifts. We decided to see how you were."

"I'm okay," Rino said. "I can still take care of myself."

"Do you miss us?" Libby said.

"Of course I do."

The women looked at each other as if to confirm what their next response would be. "You don't have to," Jean said softly.

Rino shook his head, trying to avoid the insistent logic of Jean. Then he got up to get the tea. Libby followed him and stood next to him as he reached for the tea in the cupboard. Jean watched them both. As Rino started to parcel out the spoonfuls of tea into the pot, Libby grabbed both of his hands in hers. "I want to do this," she said.

Rino sighed and backed away from her. As he did, he could feel Jean's eyes watching the small scene that had just happened.

"You never had to make tea in our house," Jean said as he turned toward her, away from Libby. "We want to do those things for you, Dad."

As she spoke, Rino reached behind him and grabbed Libby's arm gently, pulling her around front of him and urging her toward the table. "Look, you two," he said with a sigh, "I know what you're saying. And it means a lot to me—a whole lot. But I can't come back. It's your house."

"It'll never be our house; it's your house," Jean said.

"But I want it to be yours. If it isn't, then sell it and buy a new one. You have to have a house of your own."

"But I don't want a house of my own without you! Don't you understand that?" Jean whispered. "As long as you're here all by yourself in this lonely place—and don't tell me you aren't lonely—I'm never going to be happy in my own house."

"I can't," Rino said. "Understand? I can't."

As they talked uncomfortably and drank their tea, the wind grew louder and blew more snow against the windowpanes. Finally, Jean said, "It's getting bad out; we'd better go."

Libby took their coats out of the closet, and Rino held Jean's for her as she put it on. "I'll see you tomorrow night," Rino said.

"Do you work tomorrow?" Jean asked. Rino nodded. "Come after work for supper, okay?"

"Okay," Rino said.

At the door, Jean opened it and turned back to Rino. "Please, Dad? You know we're all sorry—Frank is—you know that," she said.

Rino kissed her on the cheek. "I can't, kid," he said. Then he kissed Libby. "Say goodnight to your dad for me," he said to her.

As they stepped out the door and started down the walkway, Rino said, "Be careful. Call me when you get home so I know you're safe."

Just then, Libby came back to confront him. "Lee wouldn't want you to stay away from us, Grandpa. She just wouldn't." Then she turned and joined her mother as they walked to the car.

It was Friday, and midwinter snow outside was fine and cold and crunchy underfoot. Sammy came to see Rino as he changed the fluorescent ballasts in three rooms of Stilton Hall. "What's wrong now?" Rino said when he saw him, thinking that something had broken down and

Sammy needed a maintenance man.

"Nothing. Can't I come up and talk to you?" Sammy said, feigning hurt feelings.

"You? Mr. Company, come up just to talk?"

"Okay, okay. You got a phone call from some guy named Hugo—wants you to call him on your lunch hour. Your broker, huh?"

"No broker," said Rino, chuckling. "He's a mechanic who works on my car."

After a few more jibes, Sammy left Rino. Later, on a break, Rino called Hugo and found out that Higley's heat baffles and ducts were ready. "I'll come to get them now, kid. Maybe we can put them on this weekend."

About one o'clock Rino returned to the campus. Hugo had done a nice job. The pieces were shiny and well made.

As he walked down the hall, Rino could see Higley, slouched in an easy chair, reading intently. Higley had a habit of never closing his office door whenever he was in the building.

"Dr. Higley," Rino said, "I have your baffles."

Higley brightened when he heard Rino's voice. He took the large paper sack from Rino and took the piece out to examine it. "Damn, that's beautiful. The guy does nice work."

"It'll really help that car," said Rino. "You think you can install them without any trouble?"

"I should be able to." Then he paused. "Do you remember exactly how they were mounted on the other car?"

"I can help you put them on. Then, to double check, we can have Hugo look at them."

"That would be damned nice of him… and you. By the way, I'll call you Rino if you call me Earl. I can't have anyone doctoring me if I trust him enough to touch one of my cars."

Rino nodded. He liked Higley. It was funny that he had never had a chance to deal with him before. They were always friendly and polite, but they had never been close enough to get to know each other. "You busy Saturday? I can come over to your place, and we can fit them on."

"That'd be fine. My wife's visiting our youngest son in Indianapolis, so I'll be alone. How about if you come over in the morning, and I'll make us some Kentucky buttermilk pancakes?"

"You don't have to do that," Rino said.

But Higley brushed his comment aside. "I always want a man to have some country cooking in his belly before he does some delicate work for me."

"How about eight o'clock?" Rino said. "We should be able to get them on and checked out by noon."

Higley wrote his address on a sheet of notepaper and handed it to Rino. "The coffee'll be on at 7:30," Higley said.

Rino tried to find Orrie in his office, but he'd been in court all day. Later in the afternoon, just before he left for Jean's house for supper, Orrie called him at home.

"I have three names," Orrie said.

"Who are they?" Rino asked.

"Wu, Patel, and Chandler, your old friend."

Rino smiled slightly and snorted as he heard the name. "Did they rank them?" he asked Orrie.

"No," said Orrie. "They'll recommend the top two by the end of the month, when all the names are in. They expect about 10 more names coming."

"I want to see those first three files. How would it be if I stopped over for them tomorrow?"

"I won't be here, but I'll leave them in a sealed envelope with Jill. She'll have them when you come." He hesitated for a moment, feeling he owed Rino a reason for his absence. "I'm going back to New York to see my brother. My niece is getting married. Hell, I might even sneak out to a Knicks game."

"Safe trip, kid. When you coming back?"

"Probably next Thursday—about a week."

"Have a good time. Lay off the kosher vino."

The next day, Rino stopped to pick up the files at Orrie's office. He left them in his car while he was at Frank's house, but often, during supper or when they sat in the living room talking, Rino's mind would wander toward the envelope with Chandler's papers in it. *Funny*, he mused, *who would ever bet so much money on a gamble that could easily go wrong?* What if there's nothing in Chandler's file that rings a bell? Chandler would be free, Lee would still be gone, and nobody would be avenged. Nobody avenged. There had to be something somewhere in that file.

That night, after showering and getting into bed, Rino sat up, reading. Chandler was 39 years old—older than Rino had thought. PhD at 28, bachelor's at Saint Andrew's in Northern Wisconsin, doctorate at Eastern Missouri State near Saint Louis—not Harvard or Yale, not Stanford. He stayed in the Midwest, his own backyard. Then Rino looked at the pages of articles and books: pages with long, abstruse-sounding titles that he could barely decipher. Four books—all by the same publisher—books that were used at Spring Common.

Chandler used the words "educational research" in most of his titles, all variations on a few themes. He paged through a few of the other files to look for publications. Compared to the other profs, Chandler was a writing machine. But Rino noticed other names, too. Chandler had collaborated with at least half the profs in the ed school.

Then Rino read more carefully. There were only a few articles that he had written alone, and they were older ones. One early book—the rest were all joint projects.

Rino read through the proposal. Chandler wanted to direct a project on reaction and recall times of learning-impaired students, a sensorimotor skills study. Sounded okay.

Barly had said that most of them didn't publish anymore, especially the old-timers such as Dresner. Yet somehow they came to Chandler when they wanted to write things. Why? Why didn't they do their own? Yet Higley's name wasn't on that list. Was Chandler that good compared to everybody else? Could he be wired to that many publishers? A bastard like Chandler?

The next morning, Rino stopped at Lou's shop. As they both read the newspaper and growled about the weather, Rino suddenly said, "Hey, Lou, I might have to go away for a while. Want to come?"

Here we go again, Lou thought. "What the hell are you up to now?" Lou said warily.

"You know that fellowship I donated? Well, a few of the proposals are in. I picked them up at Orrie's office yesterday."

"Let me guess," said Lou sardonically. "Chandler's was one of them, right?"

"Right again, Luigi. Now do you want to hear me or not?"

Lou sighed. "Go ahead, but I know sure as hell I'm not going to like it."

"I might want to go to near Saint Louis. Eastern Missouri State's where Chandler went to school."

"Jesus Christ," said Lou in amazement. "I haven't been dreaming all this; you really have gone bananas, haven't you?"

Rino chuckled. It had almost become a way of life for him lately, boggling his brother's mind once or twice a month. "Even crazy people can have fun, Lou. You said we didn't have enough fun."

"But this is movie stuff, Rino. You want to go all the way to fucking

Saint Louis to do a gumshoe operation on a rich guy?"

"That's it, cowboy. Besides, there are lots of dagos out there. We could get some good food at least, so it won't be a total loss. Besides, you've got too much money anyhow. You can't take it all with you."

"You've got some balls, Guarino. Pop always said you were a little crazy."

"Pop never thought we'd be rich, either, kid." Rino knew that his brother would come. Lou had two ways of responding, one really meaning "no, and never ask again," and the other meaning "no" but was open to negotiation and cajoling and bribery.

Rino was up early, long before dawn. He dressed in old jeans, insulated work shoes, and a heavy hooded sweatshirt. He took his toolbox and lantern with him in the station wagon. He reached Higley's house a few minutes early, but Higley heard him and met him at the door. Already the smell of fresh coffee brewing was a warm welcome.

Higley took Rino's coat and ushered him into the kitchen. There was a cooking island in the middle of the room, and opposite the island was a large rectangular table that was set with two place settings. Higley poured some dark, steaming coffee into two cups at the table.

As Rino sat, drinking the coffee and listening to Higley talk about cars as he cooked thick, unsymmetrical pancakes on a griddle, he looked about the house. It was old but very nice. A big old house, full of rooms and memories, a bit more cluttered with books and magazines than his own. Messy but clean. The house looked like Higley.

The pancakes were delicious. Higley had strong coffee, cold milk, soft butter, strawberry syrup, and maple syrup. And they began a friendship. Higley, at first, talked of himself, almost as if to demystify himself for Rino. He talked of his long-suffering wife who tolerated his cars and his books and his books on cars. And he talked of his children, three men who had scattered themselves around the country, each seeming to find a life close to the spirit and personality each one had. So Higley and his wife were alone and enjoying the aloneness if it didn't come in stretches too long.

But then he began to ask questions of Rino, gentle ones that permitted evasion if desired. Higley wanted to know about this nice and surprisingly intelligent man who had suddenly come upon him.

Then, abruptly, Higley stood up to clear the table. In a few minutes, they were out in a garage that housed four cars. It was an old, converted barn. And Higley had a 1936 Overland, a 1939 Chevrolet, a 1980 Plymouth, and a 1983 Dodge slant six, the car that they were to work on.

Rino set his toolbox out and talked about Hugo's advice. Fasten the part near the carburetor first, because the cool air had to blow across the carburetor at a precise angle. The problem they had was that Higley's car didn't have any place to fasten the baffle, because the air-conditioning hoses were in the way. Finally, they had to bend it to fit. And the fitting was by trial and error, retry and refit. But they got them on. The other small duct was more compact and thus easier to fasten. The job had taken three hours to complete, but the ducts were secure.

"Let's take it out," Higley said. "Do you have time?"

"Sure, no hurry," Rino said.

After driving awhile, they stopped at Hugo's garage. "We'll see if the thing'll start now," Rino said.

Hugo was busy, but he needed a cigarette and coffee break, and he brightened as he saw Rino come into the gas station.

"This is the guy you made those ducts for," Rino said, motioning to Higley. "Earl Higley, meet Hugo Malatesta."

"Pleased to meet you," said Higley, extending his hand.

Hugo grabbed Higley's hand firmly. "You're the professor, right?" Higley nodded and flushed a little. "How'd it go? Did Rino do what I told him?

Millwrights always think they know better than anybody else."

For a moment, Higley wasn't sure how to respond to the gruff man who had clasped his hand. But soon he realized that Hugo and Rino were smiling and friendly antagonists. "I think he did okay, but I'd like a second opinion," said Higley, trying to remain provocatively neutral and watch the fun between the two men.

"It's okay if your car starts," said Hugo dryly as he poured two cups of coffee and handed them to Rino and Earl. "Did you have any trouble fitting them in?"

"Yeah," said Rino. "We had to bend and fit."

"It's a good thing Rino had those metalworking tools," said Higley. "Else we'd have still been there."

Hugo snorted. "Hell, he probably stole 'em all from me," he said as he threw a burned-out match at Rino.

"Well, let's go see, paesan," Rino said to Hugo. "I'll kiss your ass if that car doesn't start."

Hugo huffed and began walking through the station. He stopped and growled a command at one of his sons, then proceeded to Higley's car. He motioned for Higley to open the hood. When it was opened, Hugo took a screwdriver from his coveralls and rapped the ducts sharply with the handle of the screwdriver. The ducts remained firm. He tried to shove one of the baffles with the heel of his hand. It held fast.

"Come on, you bastard," said Rino. "It's a good job, and you know it."

Hugo smirked. "The son of a bitch has to start, paesan, or it ain't worth nothing."

"Start it up, Earl," said Hugo as he laid his palm across the carburetor and probed his fingers, feeling for heat.

It started easily—the first time. Rino closed his eyes in thankful smugness. He put one hand on Hugo's shoulder. "Missed your once-in-a-lifetime chance for an ass-kissing, kid," he said, chuckling.

Hugo looked up at Higley. "He does good work. But he'd even do better if he'd listen to me more often," he said, smiling broadly.

"Want some lunch, Hugo?" said Rino.

"Nah, thanks, cumpare. I've got too much to do. Maybe next time."

Rino and Earl left Hugo and went to a small bar near the gas station that served good soup and sandwiches. "I really appreciate this," said Higley.

Rino shrugged it off. "How's school going?"

"Good and bad. In one class, they're bright and inquisitive, and in the other, they're dull and lethargic. It's really amazing how the personalities of classes can be so different."

"I imagine so," said Rino. "How long you been a teacher?"

"24 years," said Higley. "12 years in public school and 12 here."

"You must be a working boy," said Rino.

For a moment, Higley was puzzled by Rino's comment, but then he understood. "My daddy drove a horse-drawn milk truck in Kentucky."

"So that's why it took you so long to become a professor?"

"Well, I went to school off and on all the years I taught. Then, when I finally got my doctorate, there was an opening here, and they hired me."

"You like Spring Common?" Rino asked suddenly.

"Pretty much, especially the teaching. But sometimes the politics are disheartening."

"So why do you stay?"

"Why do you?" Higley said.

"Because Youngstown's home."

Higley smiled. Rino had answered his own question.

"Are jobs that tough to get in colleges?"

"If you're a superstar, they aren't. But most normal teaching profs can't move so easily. We get lost in the shuffle. No one knows our names."

"So you stayed here?"

"Yeah. I'm tenured here. My kids grew up here. This is home."

Both men could sense an easy, honest relationship developing. "So why aren't you a superstar?" Rino asked.

"I don't know. Maybe if you have to ask yourself that, then you never will be." Higley took a sip of coffee. "I never had that magic, that drive. I enjoy teaching, and I'm not a bad scholar, but I'm not much of a researcher."

"Why not?"

"I don't know. I've been toying with an idea for a couple of years, but for some reason—inertia—I never could muster up that burst of energy needed to turn it into a book. You know all the excuses: wife, kids, softball games, church. And every once in a while, someone tells me about a 1936 Ford sitting in some old lady's barn..."

"Are you ever going to do it?" Rino asked paternally.

"Someday I'll run out of excuses; then I'll have to do it—or else hate myself." He paused to listen to himself for a moment. "I sound like a big screw-off, don't I?" he said, looking at Rino.

"Not to me, kid. I'm lucky to be out of high school."

"As I was talking, I realized how much I sounded like other profs from the faculty club who always say they're going to write that big book, or do that big experiment, and never do."

"You're young enough. Why don't you do it?"

"I wouldn't stand a chance. Jesus, I sound like one of my students."

"Who's the superstar at Spring Common?" Rino asked knowingly.

"In the ed school, it's Dale Chandler," said Higley morosely. "Practically everything he writes gets published, no matter how trivial. And he's the dean's boy. I could win a Nobel Prize and still come up second best to Chandler in that place."

"How is it that a guy like Chandler gets to be such a big shot? Is he that much smarter than anyone else?"

"Well, first of all, Rino, I don't like the guy. So you won't be getting an unbiased assessment out of me. But for what it's worth, I think he's a whore who'd sell his mother into white slavery just to become college president somewhere. He's not terribly bright or original, but he looks good and has the knack of meeting the right people. Plus, he's rich. His family owns some paper mills in Wisconsin. That never hurts."

"But the bottom line is..." Rino let his voice trail off.

"The bottom line is that he's done something, and I haven't. No one cares about wives, kids, church, and all."

"You know, Earl, I've heard a lot of people—profs, students, workers—say you're damn good."

Higley sighed. "And that and a dollar will get me on the bus, Rino. I'm a good prof, and I know enough about university politics to keep out of trouble. But still I'm an excuse, a promise unfulfilled."

"Why don't you try that fellowship that they have posted on all the boards?" Rino said after a moment of quiet.

Higley seemed surprised that Rino knew about it. At first, the fellowship had been a hot topic in the faculty lounge, but later, when it was learned that all the superstars would go for it, and when it became known that a faculty committee would make recommendations, the lesser profs, just by attrition of will, considered themselves ruled out of the competition. *How timid we all are*, Higley thought. "No balls, Rino," Higley said.

"I don't believe that," Rino said.

"The alternative is to realize that we're too comfortable learning the works of others and too afraid to create knowledge of our own."

After the meal Higley drove back to his house. "Do you fish?" he asked as Rino started his car.

"Yeah, once in a while," Rino said.

"Let's go fishing sometime. It won't be long before the weather gets nice."

"I'd like to go," Rino said, surprised that Higley wanted to continue their acquaintanceship.

Higley waved as Rino backed out of the driveway. *Amazing the fine people you see all your life yet don't know a damned thing about,* Higley thought. *That guy's got more wisdom and character than just about anyone on the ed school faculty, yet he sweeps floors. And all these years I never even knew him.*

The next day, Rino had a pleasant morning at work. But on his lunch hour, he went to the library. College libraries always intimidated him. All he saw were sober-looking kids quietly poring over books, all very serious.

"Can I help you?" said the librarian, a dour, middle-aged woman with incongruously stylish, short-cut gray hair and a nicely tailored suit.

"Yes," said Rino. "If I wanted to read a doctor's dissertation, could you show me how to find it?"

The woman eyed him skeptically. "Have you checked Dissertation Abstracts?"

"Uh, no, I didn't. Where is it?"

"It isn't an 'it'—it's a whole set of volumes." She sighed coolly. "They're over here." Rino followed her as she walked toward the shelf of bound, green volumes.

"Thanks. I'll find it now," he said, ignoring her but watching out of the corner of his eye until she walked away.

Quickly, he turned to the Cs of 1974, trying to find Chandler's name. It wasn't there. He tried to find the reason: maybe he had the wrong section. But there were only years and names and dates, all in order.

Maybe he was wrong, he thought. Maybe it's the wrong year. Quickly he pulled the 1973 volume off the shelf and looked for Chandler. There were two, but neither of them was named Dale. Wrong school, wrong year. Then he got 1975 off the shelf. No Chandler. He checked three years on each side of 1974 and found nothing.

Finally, he went to the front desk and found the gray-haired librarian again. "Are all the dissertations in the country in those books?" he asked.

"They should be," she said. "Can't you find what you're looking for?"

"No," he said.

"What was that name again?"

Rino tried to deflect the question, not wanting to name Chandler. "Does every library have dissertations in it?"

"The larger university libraries usually do, especially if they have doctoral programs. We have a dissertation section on the third floor, but it only has those of faculty members of this university."

Rino thanked her and quietly made his way to the third floor, feeling a flush of good luck. The librarian there was an older woman, dignified but smiling and friendly. When he reached the dissertation shelf, he was amazed by the differences between them. Some were three inches thick, and some were barely a quarter inch, only a few typed pages, as small as some of the term papers Libby wrote. But Chandler's wasn't among them.

Suddenly Rino's mind began to wander. *What the hell's going on here? Nothing in the book? Nothing on the shelf?* Quickly he went down the stairs, his heart now beating faster in his excitement. He went to the Dissertation Abstracts again, this time to copy down some addresses and phone numbers. He might try to buy a copy of Chandler's dissertation.

Later in the day, Rino read through Chandler's application again. His wife was named Katrine, and her maiden name was Eberle, and they had been divorced five years.

Lou was busy. His job was one of feast and famine, fits and starts. The heater was on, and the shop was warm, permeated with the fresh smell of brewed coffee. Rino came in, feeling as much at home there as he would in his own house. He greeted his brother cheerily and went back into the kitchen to hang his coat and pour some coffee. He noticed an unmade bed in the small, lower bedroom. When he returned outside to the shop, he said, "You sleep here last night?"

"Yeah," said Lou, trying to fit a small piece of leather to a heel.

"Was Annie here?" Rino asked nonchalantly.

"No, Annie wasn't here," Lou said testily.

"Just wondering, just wondering," Rino said as he picked up the *Cleveland Plain Dealer*. "The Browns gonna get a new offensive coordinator, you think?"

"They should, but they won't," Lou said, turning his back to Rino and starting the machine. After a few seconds of noise and rumbling, he turned it off, turned back to the counter, and faced Rino, who had settled in the bay to read the paper by the gray Youngstown morning light. "What are you feeling so good about on a morning like this? What the hell'd you do now?"

"I didn't do anything. I had a good night's sleep—not like some old men who go out partying and chasing women."

"You're into something weird again, aren't you, you bastard?" Lou said.

"When are we going to Saint Louis?" Rino said abruptly.

"What for?"

"Come on, Luigi. You promised you'd go with me. We haven't been out of this town in two years, since..." Rino brought his words up short, not wanting to spoil the mood he was in with remembrances of things past. "We can fly down one day, see the place, stay over a couple of days, have some good food, and fly back. We can be back in time for the Super Bowl party."

"I didn't think you were going to that," Lou said.

"I've paid my money for my ticket."

"Okay, okay... You really want to go to Saint Louis? When?"

"Thursday."

"This Thursday?"

"Yeah. You just tell Annie where we're going, so someone will know. Then we can get out and back before my kids or Connie'll know we're gone."

Lou took a drag on his cigarette and turned on the machine again. This time he was at it longer, going from wheel to wheel, from sander to polisher to buffer. Then, when he turned the motor off, he said, "Why Saint Louis?" knowing it had something to do with Chandler.

"You know when people go for doctor's degrees, they have to write books—they call them dissertations. And every dissertation is in some big catalog called Dissertation Abstracts. Well, Chandler's isn't in there."

"You already checked, right?"

Rino nodded.

"Then you're probably not looking in the right place."

"Lou, I'm telling you: the guy's name isn't in that book. There's something shady about the whole thing."

"He's been faking it. That's what you're telling me, right?" Lou said sardonically.

"The guy's a crook, Luigi, and a prick besides. He's faking something."

"And you think you can blow his cover," Lou said half in exasperation and half in resignation.

"I think I can cut his balls off," said Rino. "You coming?"

Lou stared at him for a moment. He had to decide just then whether he was throwing in with his brother. Excuses were available: the shop, Connie, lack of faith, fear of Rino's mind wandering...

"Fuck it, Lou," Rino said softly. "Let's have some fun."

"It won't be much fun if this costs you two hundred grand and you come up catching his wind," Lou muttered.

"Lou, there're some skeletons in this guy's closet."

"Hell, man, there are skeletons in everybody's closet."

"Little ones... but everybody doesn't operate like this guy, Luigi."

The next day was Tuesday, and Rino went to work early. He had not slept soundly all night, thinking of what he could find in Saint Louis and fearing that he and Lou would find nothing. He sat in a small chair in the workroom, drinking a cup of coffee quietly. Sammy came in, furiously brushing snow from his hair and his clothes and stomping the snow off his boots. He was surprised to see anyone, although he often found Rino there when he arrived.

"Goombah," he said. "Cold as hell out there. I must be crazy. I don't need this shit. I belong where it's warm, where girls wear only bikinis, and you can sleep outside at night."

"Ain't no palm trees in Poland. You should be used to this weather," Rino said.

"What're you doing here so early?" Sammy said, ignoring Rino's jibe.

"Well, I want your job, Sam. Just give orders, bitch about the help, drink coffee all the time, and walk around from Stilton to Crandall, trying to look busy. I think I can handle it."

"You get up this early just to harass a hardworking foreman, right, goombah?"

"Yeah. Plus, I need a few days off."

"How many?" Sammy said seriously.

"Thursday and Friday of this week. Maybe even Monday."

"Are we covered?" he said.

Rino nodded.

"Okay, just finish running that line today to the chem lab, and put that new fixture on the demo sink. That water sprays all over hell when you turn it on."

"I'll take care of it. If Barly knows which fixture to get me, I'll be all set."

"Barly put it in my office; it came yesterday. Just go in and get it if I'm not here."

Rino worked all morning in the chemistry lab running the line and fixing the sink. Then he headed to the cafeteria for lunch. On the way, he saw Earl Higley coming from the cafeteria. Rino waved to him from across the green. Suddenly, Higley changed direction and headed toward Rino.

"Hi, Earl. What're you up to?" said Rino jauntily.

"You ever been ice fishing, Rino?" Higley asked.

"No. Something I never got around to."

"Want to drive up to Erie some Saturday real early and try it?"

"Sure. When?"

"How's this week?"

"Uh... I'll be out of town this week. Next week okay?"

"Yeah. If I don't see you around here, I'll call you."

"That's fine."

"Okay, count on it. I'll drive my van."

Rino was amazed as he entered the cafeteria. He had actually become the friend of a professor. All the years he had worked at Spring Common, he had never thought of any of them as an equal. Yet Earl wanted him to go fishing—as a friend.

The flight to Saint Louis seemed long to both men. There was more air turbulence than usual, and the stewardess was preoccupied and unfriendly. The brothers seemed grouchy and disoriented until they got their rental car, a new maroon Dodge, and drove out of the airport. Rino had already booked a hotel room near the university.

It was still morning, even though it seemed they had been up all day. As they drove, they marveled at how the town had changed.

"40 years makes a hell of a difference in a town, huh?" said Lou.

"Yeah. I came through here just before I went to France," Rino said.

"Yeah. I came in... '42, was it? After boot camp."

"Look at that arch," said Rino. "Nice, huh?"

At the hotel, Rino handed the keys to the valet, and his car was driven away. The desk clerk was friendly and courteous, and it wasn't long before they were ushered into a suite.

"Jesus, you do good work, kid," Lou said appreciatively.

"We're too old to rough it. We paid our dues," Rino said as he hung his clothes in the closet.

"For once I agree with you, cowboy."

"Write that down, Lou—and the date. If you and I and Connie ever agree on anything, the world'll come to an end."

They dined at a restaurant they had seen in the hotel billboard sheet. They both wanted seafood. "Before we go home, I think we ought to plow into a couple of 16-ounce steaks, Luigi. How about it?"

"I doubt if I can still do that, you know?"

"How's the scampi?" Rino asked.

"Good. How's yours?"

The next morning, they were both up early. Rino awoke to the sound of Lou showering in the bathroom. He seemed to be singing softly to himself. After he was finished, Lou entered the room in his undershorts, toweling his hair dry. "How'd you sleep, kid?" he said to Rino.

"Not bad," Rino said, surprised at the brightness in Lou in contrast to his morose and moody behavior of the day before.

Rino slowly pushed himself erect and out of bed. "How about if we just call down for some coffee and rolls?" he said to Lou.

Lou knew that Rino was nervous about what he would encounter at the university that day. As Rino shaved, showered, and dressed, Lou read through the morning paper. Later, they drank coffee quietly. Occasionally Rino coughed nervously. "Well, let's go, kid. This is what we're here for, right?" he said solemnly to Lou, meeting his gaze and holding it for a moment.

As they drove to the university, Rino began to doubt what he was doing. Maybe Lou was right. What if he did get something on Chandler? Who would believe a janitor against a professor? And if so, what would he do then?

The library was bigger, older, and more ornate than the new one at Spring Common. It actually had the look of a great university library, Rino thought. Rino swallowed as they entered one of the four massive wood-and-glass doors at the front entrance. They walked slowly to the information desk. "Jesus," said Lou. "You suppose there's any book they don't have here?"

"Only one, I hope," answered Rino under his breath. He asked the clerk, "Where are your doctoral dissertations?"

"Upstairs on the fourth floor—the Dickenson wing." She pointed to the elevator as she spoke.

Lou had stopped to look at a newspaper that he had taken from a kiosk in the center lobby. "Come on, let's go," said Rino impatiently. Lou sighed and put his paper back into the rack.

The elevator was old and lit only by a small, dim light. The inside had been painted over and over again, many yearly coats to hide the obscenities that young collegians would scrawl on the sides of the dingy cubicle. The door opened to the third floor, but no one was waiting. The stacks were dusty, and the books all seemed a hundred years old. The light did, also. Everything belied the brightness and size and orderliness of the downstairs lobby. These floors were the haunts of young scholars in tennis shoes unfolding dark secrets for their professors.

"They all look so serious," said Lou as he saw a young man in a navy pea coat crouched down near the stacks, holding a large old book and reading intently. An Asian-looking girl in slacks and blue ski sweater was standing on tiptoes, peering at the titles of some books on a high shelf.

"They all want jobs out there, cowboy. The revolution's over," Rino said softly. Lou snorted in agreement.

When the door opened to the fourth floor, the lights were brighter, and the stacks were arranged in less cramped and dingy surroundings. As they stepped off the elevator, they read a directory that was referenced to a map with a red dot that said, "You are here."

Rino and Lou walked toward the east corner of the building, back behind the entry to the elevator on a far side. The dissertations were there—thousands of them, it seemed, all bound in the same monotonous beige with dark-black lettering. Both men were affected in the same way. It was somehow depressing to see all these long-titled books by so many obscure names, hidden in this remote corner. *Wonder how many of them are even alive now?* Lou thought. "They're in alphabetical order, Rino," Lou said.

"Yeah," Rino said. As they rounded the edge of one shelf, they came to another, just like it, full of beige dissertations. "Here are the Cs, Lou," said Rino.

Lou stood away from Rino for a moment, staring at him and being quiet. Rino scanned the books. "Well?" he said to Rino, who had crouched down to read the titles. Rino didn't answer.

Then, in a moment, he stood erect and faced Lou. "There's no Chandler here, kid," he said.

Downstairs, at the information desk, Rino waited for the librarian to finish advising someone else. He always held every librarian up to Lee's image, and all of them lost favor for being not quite good enough. Yet most were friendly and helpful, so he warmed to them, feeling ashamed for being so judgmental about people he didn't know.

"There's no dissertation upstairs for someone named Dale Chandler," he said to the librarian who turned to him to help.

"Perhaps it's checked out," she said airily.

"Maybe. Could you check for me?"

She sighed. "Yes, but it'll take a few minutes."

"I'll wait," said Rino.

The brothers went into a small canteen area that was adjacent to a library lounge. Lou got coffee from a machine for himself and handed Rino one as he emerged from a restroom.

"Let's go into the lounge," Lou said. Rino nodded.

They settled into comfortable, cube-shaped, vinyl-covered chairs that faced a view of the campus and the surrounding city through a wall of glass on the far side of the room. To their left was a flagstone veranda, now dirty and partially covered with snow. The day was cold but clear, and the smoke from the city spewed into the sky and seemed to crawl slowly toward the horizon.

Both surveyed the view for a few minutes. "You really think this guy's a phony, huh?" said Lou, still looking at the view.

"A fifth of Crown Royal says she doesn't have that book," Rino said, not facing his brother.

"And if she doesn't? What do you do about it, anyway?"

"I'll tell you again, Luigi: if I get something on him, I'll screw him to the wall with it."

"But where would we go from here?"

"To the graduate school."

When they returned to the information desk 45 minutes later, the librarian said, "Yes, well, we don't seem to have that dissertation. Evidently, it was never turned in through the graduate school."

"Isn't that unusual?" said Lou, suddenly seeming very interested.

"Most unusual," she said, turning toward him.

Lou glanced at Rino. "Graduate school?"

"Perhaps they might have information on how to obtain a copy. We have no record or card on it here. I'm sorry," said the librarian.

"Thanks," Rino said as he turned away from the desk.

They asked directions to the graduate school and crossed the campus mall, heading for a dark-gray stone building. The wind was colder now, and both men hunched their shoulders for warmth against the wind.

Inside, Lou asked a student the way to the dean's office. They walked through the door and met a receptionist in a small room. "Can I help you?" she asked pleasantly.

"Yeah, we'd like to see the dean," said Rino.

"Can you tell me about what?"

"It's personal, miss," said Lou.

"You aren't salesmen of any kind?"

"No."

She smiled, unoffended by their reticence. "I'll be right back. Please have a seat."

"I like girls like that," said Lou as he watched her walk away. "She's nice and never had to have any lessons for it. If this dean hired her, he's gonna be an okay guy, Rino."

Rino nodded and grunted in assent.

She returned. "May I have your names? So I can tell the dean who's waiting?"

"Bellanca," Rino said, "Rino and Lou Bellanca."

In a few moments, she returned and ushered Rino and Lou into the dean's office. He stood when they entered and walked around his desk to shake their hands. He seemed to be a smiling, friendly man. "Brian Selden," he said.

"I'm Rino, and this is my brother, Lou."

"Come on over here," said Selden, motioning to two couches set parallel in a corner of his office. There were two windows on the corner walls that gave a view of most of the campus. The two brothers sat on one of the couches.

"What can I do for you, gentlemen?" said the dean, seeming more serious.

"We're looking for a dissertation," said Rino.

"But the diss..." Selden paused for a second, his eyes searching the faces of both men, trying to read their intentions. Suddenly he realized why they had come. "And the dissertation you're looking for isn't on the shelf in the library, is it?"

Rino and Lou stared back at him, noticing him seem a bit more uneasy than he had been when they entered. "The author of that dissertation wouldn't be named Chandler, would it?" Selden asked.

"Yes, sir," Rino said, curious about how Selden had sized them up.

Selden sensed their surprise. "That's the only one I know that isn't in the library," he said. "Why do you want it?"

"We want to read it," Rino said.

"Are you doing research? You're not professors, are you?"

"No, just some private citizens," said Lou.

"Private citizens who just show up here one day looking for the only dissertation this great university doesn't have on file? Come now, gentlemen." Selden leaned back on the couch, slightly annoyed. "Who the hell are you guys?"

"Look," said Rino softly, "we're not trying to do a job on you. And we sure as hell don't mean any harm to anyone out here."

"But..."

"But we have to see that dissertation. Can you help us find it?"

"Are you two private eyes?" Selden asked.

"No," said Rino, "we're not." He sighed. "This Chandler guy's name is on a short list that's gonna get someone a two-year fellowship. We want to make sure that the wrong guy doesn't get it."

"What's in this for you?" Selden asked.

"We belong to the organization that's sponsoring. And we have some say over who gets the award," Lou said.

"You two 'private citizens'?" Selden said skeptically.

"It's the truth," Rino said.

Selden eyed them, staring back and forth at each man. The brothers calmly, but with some trepidation, watched him size them up. They didn't look shady. He didn't detect any pretense or airs about them; they didn't look like hoods. They seemed honest enough—he looked at each man again—and solid. "Are you guys reporters? I don't usually talk much about one of the grad school's more embarrassing moments," said Selden.

Rino and Lou chuckled nervously as they shifted in their seats, trying to ease the tension they both felt. "No, and not lawyers, either," said Rino.

"We're not too crazy about reporters or lawyers," said Lou.

Selden settled back again. He was about to unload. "Three deans ago—I've been here two years—somehow this Chandler got a doctorate without completing a dissertation. You can understand, I'm sure, why people here are reluctant to talk about it, especially those who let it happen. Mind you, his degree is legal, and he walked across the stage and was hooded. But the guy had finessed everyone on his doctoral committee. A few old-timers told me that the guy looked so good and talked such a good game that, somehow, he got through. But his old man was a big donor, too; I suppose that might have helped a little. And after the dust settled, it would have been too embarrassing for too many professors to admit that they screwed up. So, the guy was home free."

"So he managed to do something that no one else has ever done out here," Lou said.

Selden nodded. "You keep saying 'out here.' Where are you guys from?"

"Ohio... Youn... eastern Ohio," Lou said.

"Youngstown?"

"Yeah."

"Chandler's teaching at Spring Common?"

Rino and Lou nodded.

"I know that place," Selden said. "Hell, it's too small for an ego like his. He wants the big time."

"Do you know him?" Rino asked.

"Of him. I've seen him at a lot of conventions. He's a big gun—blue blazer, tan slacks, Gucci loafers."

Rino and Lou smiled. They liked Selden.

"Word has it—if you quote me on this, I'll deny it—that he cooks his data."

"What?" said Rino.

"Uh, he fudges some numbers so his research will come out the way he wants it to," said Selden.

"How can they get away with that?" asked Lou.

"The reporting of the results of experiments and research is a system supposedly based on the honesty of the people involved. If you're not honest, sometimes you can get away with an awful lot—unless someone decides to go through your stuff with a fine-tooth comb. This Chandler guy—no one has ever tried to replicate his experiments, so his reputation thrives on work that only he swears by."

Lou glanced at Rino, but both stayed silent for a moment. Selden sensed their perplexity. "You know, it wasn't a total bust for everyone here. The guy has written some things—passable work, I've been told—mostly articles and textbooks, but it got him into the Old Boy network."

"What's that?" Lou said, already having some idea of what it was.

"He's in a clique of people who are big guns in the National Educational

Research Group—we call it NERG. They take care of each other—favorably review each other's publications, that kind of thing."

After a little more talk, Rino and Lou left Selden at the door of his office. "That guy'll never know how much good he did me," said Rino as they left the building.

"So how are you going to get him? See how shrewd he is? Even an outfit like this couldn't get him—or didn't have the balls to do it. You expect more out of Spring Common than that?"

"He's a good gambler. He bets they don't have balls, and usually he wins. Listen, Luigi..."

"Now what?"

"You have to go home and alibi for us. I'm going up to Minnesota to see his wife."

"Rino, no one is going to believe some bullshit from me about these past few days—especially if you're not there. Can't you see me telling Connie or Frank that you decided to take a 'vacation' or a business trip by yourself?"

"Lou, I need some information on where to start. If I want to get this guy, I have to know him where it hurts."

"I'm coming with you."

The plane to Rochester was an hour late, and Rino and Lou squirmed in their seats waiting for it to land. The counter girl at the airport must have felt sorry for them, because she found them a place that was cheap and spotlessly clean. They loaded their suitcases into a taxi and headed for the motel.

While Lou unpacked his suitcase, Rino lay across his bed reading the Rochester phone book. "Are we gonna see the Mayo Clinic, kid?" Lou said. "Hell, at our age we may be one of their guinea pigs someday. Ever think of that?"

"All the time, cowboy," Rino muttered without looking up from the phone book.

"You want to go out there now?"

"Nah, let's eat first."

"You want to call her?"

"I don't think so. I'm afraid she'll hang up on me. Then I'd be screwed."

They ate lunch at a quiet, clean restaurant near the motel. The desk clerk had said the closer they were to the clinic, the more crowded the restaurants were. Neither Rino nor Lou talked much during the meal. Rino began thinking about Jean. He missed her and the kids. Even Frankie. It was nice having him around, watching him change as he grew older, resembling Lou and Mary at times... sometimes a younger Rino.

Jean and Libby. Somehow, they were the only ones who could offer what he longed for, that feeling of softness and warmth and delicacy that he didn't experience around Lou or his other friends—even Connie.

What if Jean or Libby were taken from him? What would he do? Could he live in that kind of desolate world? Could he endure one more loss? He shook his head, banishing the thought from his consciousness. Lou noticed the movement and knew Rino had been communing with himself.

"What's so hard to take today, cowboy?"

Rino snorted. His brother always came too close to reading his thoughts. "Nothing, kid. Just thinking about... something."

"About Lee?" Rino shook his head. Lou thought for a moment. "Jean? And Libby?" he said resolutely.

Rino cast an annoyed glance at the slender man across the table from him.

"Rino, you're crazy for keeping yourself away from them. They want you back."

"I can't go back now, Lou," Rino said. "Not while..." He shook his head.

"Suppose you did get him—tomorrow. What then? Would you go back home?"

"Maybe. Maybe we ought to build a new house," said Rino.

"That's better than throwing your money at Chandler."

The waitress came and filled their coffee cups. Lou lit another cigarette. "You're sure you have her address?"

"Yeah. I got it off Chandler's application. I just hope she'll talk to me."

Lou took a long sip of coffee and a drag on his cigarette. "Maybe I'll just wait outside for you. Drop me off at a place where I can read the paper. Then pick me up when you're done."

"Sure you don't want to come?"

"Nah. You'll be better off without me. Anyway, you know more how to talk to young girls than I do." Lou was smirking as he spoke.

Rino snorted in response. He looked at his watch. "Well, kid, I think it's time. Call us a cab. I'll take care of this," he said, picking up the bill.

After the driver dropped Lou off, he drove Rino to the Chandler woman's apartment building. The driver drove up the circular drive and let him out in front of the main entrance. Inside was a vestibule with two rows of mailboxes. On one, the name was Katrine Chandler. It was a setup where the inner door had to be buzzed open by the resident after she answered the call.

Rino pressed a button above Chandler's mailbox. In a few seconds a voice answered, somewhat muffled by the microphone. "Yes?" she said.

"Mrs. Chandler, my name's Rino Bellanca. I'm from Spring Common College, and I'd like to talk to you."

"Are you a salesman?" she said.

"No, ma'am. I work there."

A few seconds passed. Rino waited nervously. Suddenly, from the door came a loud buzzing noise. Rino opened the door and walked inside. The apartment was on the first floor. In the corridor there were flowered wallpaper, soft maroon carpeting, and brass plate sconces that lit the way down the hall. Rino paused before the door a second, then rang the bell. He was dressed in a V-neck sweater, white shirt, tie, and slacks, trying to look as unthreatening as possible. "Mrs. Chandler?" he said.

"I don't have too much time," she said, obviously regretting letting him call on her.

"I won't take long," Rino said.

"What is it you want of me, Mr...."

"Bellanca. I'd like to ask you a few questions about your... about Dr. Chandler."

Her expression hardened. "Are you a policeman or investigator?"

Rino shook his head. "No, ma'am. I'm nobody important. And I don't want anything from you except a few answers... nothing to sell."

"What do you do at Spring Common?"

Rino hesitated for a second, looking at her, straining to get out the truth in answer to her question. He exhaled softly and finally answered, "I'm a maintenance man at the college."

"Oh, really, Mr. Bellanca. I don't think it's appropriate to talk about my husband—former husband—to a maintenance man from Spring Common. Or anyone else, for that matter."

Rino held the palm of his hand up before him in a pleading gesture. "Please, just a few minutes, I swear. Then if you want me out, I'll go. And you can call the police if I'm not gone one minute after you give me the word."

"But what business does a worker from Spring Common have out here with me?"

"It's a long story, believe me. It's just that there's a big teaching fellowship—two years—coming up at Spring Common. And your husband wants it."

"That doesn't concern me, Mr. Bellanca."

Rino glanced up at her face. He imagined her anguish as she discovered her betrayal by Chandler as he was banging his latest round of graduate assistants. "Mrs. Chandler, I'm here because I have to learn a little about your husband."

"But why you? Why would a custodian..."

"I belong to an organization, and I have some say over who gets the fellowship. Your husband's name was recommended by a college committee, one of the top choices. But I have to know some things about him. And you're the only one who can help."

"How?"

Rino searched her face for rejection but didn't see any. "By helping me find out what kind of man he is."

"I don't really want to discuss what kind of man he is, Mr. Bellanca."

"Did he fake his research? Did he ever make up any phony numbers?" Rino said abruptly.

She was startled, surprised by what he knew, and lost her train of thought while reacting to his question. She didn't answer. Instead, she nervously wiped the back of one hand with her handkerchief, a quick movement that was meant to somehow buy time. But it didn't work; time brought nothing to say.

"Did he do it all the time? Or just when he had to look good?" Rino said.

She kept silent and held her hands clasped self-consciously in her lap.

"All the time," Rino said with finality, prompting the words for her.

"I don't know if it was all the time," she said softly. Then she looked up at him pleadingly. "Mr. Bellanca, we've been divorced almost six years. I don't want my life to touch his ever again."

"I'm going. You've told me enough," Rino said reassuringly.

"Mr. Bellanca, please don't involve me in what you're doing," she said, seeming more hurt yet more animated than she had been all through the interview. "I'm just getting over it. I don't think I could live through another confrontation with him."

"No one's going to hurt you, Mrs. Chandler. They're never going to know I came up here to see you."

She nodded, unconvinced.

Rino hadn't thought about how tall she was. She was taller than he, an attractive yet pale and brittle-looking woman, with blonde hair, cut short and full about her face, straight nose, hazel eyes, and thin lips. *She looks like a dentist's wife*, Rino thought. *She should have had three kids and been a volunteer at the school library. Instead, she's pushing 40, alone and hurting.* He turned to her at the door. "Do you know the names Vasquez, Teare, McCauley, and Tennison?"

"They were all Dale's research assistants," she said, wondering what he could be asking about them for.

"Did they help him rig the numbers?"

"Tennison did. He was Dale's first. He got a doctorate later and teaches somewhere out west. Vasquez and McCauley were women. They became Dale's... friends."

"Affairs, you mean?"

"It happens all the time, Mr. Bellanca," she said wearily. "There's always next year's crop of cute graduate assistants."

"How about Teare?"

"She was different... a little older, a divorcée. She stayed a year and left Spring Common. I don't think she liked helping Dale cheat—at school or on me. She was smarter than a lot of women."

The plane to Youngstown arrived late—after midnight—delayed six hours by a snowstorm in Minnesota. Winter had come back to the Midwest as harsh and fearful as it could be, and Youngstown was bitterly cold. The brothers trudged wearily through the snow to Rino's car, still waiting in the parking lot. The car coughed and ground to a start and then rolled haltingly over icy streets and intersections devoid of slag or salt for traction. Lou was glad to be home, and, as he had been for most of the trip back, was cranky and sullen in the car. The long ride from the airport was quiet: Rino lost in thought and care for the blinding reflection of the car's headlights off the driving snow, and Lou convinced that the whole trip had been a fool's errand with the weather a mocking and harsh reminder of his loss of good sense.

"Maybe we'd better go see Connie Sunday, cowboy," Rino said finally. "She's gonna wonder what's up—not hearing from either one of us all week."

"Yeah," Lou muttered as he opened the car door.

Rino got out of the driver's side and walked to the rear of the car to help Lou carry his bags.

"I've got them. See you tomorrow," Lou said curtly as he turned toward the back door of his house. He seemed very tired.

"Hey!" Rino called to Lou's back.

"What?" Lou said with a grimace as he turned back to his younger brother.

"You're all right, kid," Rino said. "I appreciate it."

Lou nodded and turned back toward his house.

Rino was relieved to let Lou off—he had been feeling guilty recently for imposing on his brother's time and tranquility. When he got home, he wearily left his suitcase at the closet door, took off his coat, and sifted through the mail that was crammed into his mailbox. Among the junk and bills and magazines was a letter written in that remarkably precise style with just a hint of flourish that could only have been Toni's. He stared at the return address and started to open it but then stopped. He couldn't handle it tonight. If it was any kind of censure, or some wistful regret that it would have been different, or something about Lee...

He set it down and looked out the window, rubbing a shoulder that had ached dully all day on the plane and on the drive back into town. The snow was piling up. He turned his television set on and scanned the channels. More snow tomorrow—and cold. It was time to turn in. Sleep would feel good and give rest and refuge.

Late the next morning, Rino awoke with a headache, a slight sore throat, and a stiffness in his neck and shoulder. Wearily he pulled himself erect, shaved, showered, dressed, and put some water on the stove. He got the newspaper from outside his door and read it as the water began to boil. The cold air outside had chilled him, and he sneezed several times, cursing at the malaise that came upon him just as he had gotten home.

Later, at the store, Rino seemed to feel a little better. The warmth of the store, the smell of bread baking in the deli, and the free hot coffee near the entrance gave him a slight flush. He ended up shopping for more than he had planned for, buying more goodies than he should have.

Maybe he wouldn't go anywhere, he thought as he drove home. The weather was getting worse rather than better, and suddenly, reading a book and having some tea and anisette seemed like the only way to spend the evening. He'd see Jean and Frank tomorrow.

At home, he put the groceries away slowly, wondering how Lou was feeling as he worked. Then, as he waited for fresh tea to brew, he thought of Lee. Lou was right; his whole quest for Chandler was, at bottom, a mission for Lee.

He turned toward her picture in the living room. He hated what time was doing. It was easier to go through the day and function without her.

It bothered him. It would be so different if he could see her just one more time to say goodbye. Just to see her, touch her. *Morbid*, he thought. It's not life. It's not real.

The door chimes rang once, sounding almost tentative. Rino stirred from his troubled reverie and went to the door. There, standing awkwardly, was Connie. "Well?" she said in annoyance to her amazed brother standing in the doorway.

Rino immediately stepped aside. "Come on in. What're you doing out on a day like this? Who took you here?"

"Danny gave me a ride over. I'll call when I want to go home."

"I'll take you home," said Rino emphatically, somewhat offended.

Connie shrugged out of her coat, and Rino did his best to take it from her. "Nice place, kid," she said, looking around the room.

"Come on. I'll show you all of it," said Rino, touching her arm and guiding her into the kitchen. Connie toured the condo, nodding approvingly. "Tea or coffee?" Rino said after they had come back downstairs again.

"Coffee. What are you gonna do with three bedrooms?"

"Nothing. You see all the junk in the odd one... the other one... You never know when someone needs a bed for the night."

Connie huffed. As they returned to the living room, the coffee had perked. "Is everything okay, Con?" Rino said.

"Everything's fine," she said testily.

Rino hesitated for a second. "Then to what do I owe the pleasure of your visit, Concetta?"

"Can't I come and visit my brother if I want to see him?"

"Sure. Every 35 years or so... through a blinding snowstorm. Why not?"

"What 35 years? I visited you at the old house all the time—you and Mary."

"Right. You and Guy, me and Mary," said Rino mockingly.

"Well, they're both gone, Rino. So now it's you and me, okay?"

"Good. You gonna visit Lou from now on, too?"

"Don't get smart with me, Rino. He doesn't need my visits. He's too damned mean and smartassed for me to visit," she said half-jokingly but with a small bite of truth.

"So what's up, kid?" Rino said. "You short on cash?"

"No, damn you. I don't need cash!" she hissed.

"So?" said Rino, grinning slightly over her discomfort.

"So how was Saint Louis, brother?"

Rino was struck dumb for a few seconds. "Who told you?" he growled, cursing Lou under his breath for letting their secret out.

"Lou didn't tell me, so don't worry about him," she said. Rino glared at her, angry because she knew his secret. "So tell your big sister what takes two old geezers on a secret airplane trip in the middle of the week to Saint Louis, of all places?" Connie knew she had the ultimate weapon against her two brothers, knowledge of the truth that they were hiding. It made her self-righteous and sure of her motives.

"I can't tell you." Rino sighed. "It's nothing bad. There's no trouble."

"Rino, are you and Lou okay? I mean you're not sick or anything, right?"

"No, kid, we're not sick. We wouldn't keep that from you, anyway. But this... this is different. It doesn't concern the family."

"Doesn't concern the family? Don't make me laugh!" she said, staring intently into his eyes.

"It's just something I have to take care of," Rino said.

Connie decided to change the subject. "You really like this apartment?"

"It's not bad. I'm comfortable."

"Wouldn't Jean and Libby make you more comfortable?"

"Uh, I don't think so," Rino said weakly.

"Don't hand me that, Rino Bellanca. There's not a night you stay here that you don't think of Lee... and then wonder what Jean and Libby are doing."

"I can't go back now, Con. Maybe someday."

"Someday when your goddamned little game is over? You know what? Frankie's not the only one tired of the lying. I am, too."

"So not telling you every damned thing I do is lying, right? Give me a break."

"Listen, you snake, when you sneak around the whole damned country and not tell anyone where you're going or what you're doing and then come back here whistling Dixie, just like you've been working a little overtime, that's a lie."

"Somebody knew."

"Oh, right! Annie, who's not even in the family, and not a damned soul else. That's supposed to make us all feel good, huh?"

"Jesus, how the hell did you find out?"

"Because I'm smarter than you two dummies. Haven't you figured that out yet? And what are you gonna say when Jean asks you where you've been? Just hanging around, right? Lies!"

"Damn you, Concetta. I've never thrown you out of my house in 60 years, but it's gonna happen soon if you don't shut up."

"How could you lie to her, Rino? I don't give a damn about me, but how could you lie to that kid? She thinks more about you than she does about Frankie."

"You're crazy."

"I don't know how it happened, but you found two women half your age who think the world of you. Now, with one of them gone, you're treating the other one like she has leprosy. You're the one that's crazy."

"Con," Rino said, defeated and weary, "I need some slack on this one."

"You damned fool! People have been giving you nothing but slack. You're just too dumb and selfish to notice. You're driving Lou crazy, me crazy; you're hurting Frankie and those girls, and you act like nothing's wrong. Bah!"

Rino put his head in his hands and didn't answer further. Connie watched him for a few minutes, and then she stood up and walked over to the love seat where Rino was sitting. As she did, she ran her hand gently up the scruff of his neck and through his hair. Then she turned him toward her and kissed him on the forehead. "We're not Lee, Rino, but we're all you've got. Remember that."

Earl Higley was having a bad morning. His head ached, and he knew that the sharp pain behind the brow of his right eye meant dreary weather coming. February wasn't his favorite month. And worse, it would be followed by March and April, months of damp rain or drizzling snow.

The faculty lounge would be a nice respite from his desk. This morning's class had been dull and lethargic. And if he could last the day, his two o'clock class promised no more than his worst fears: bored clock watchers who wanted degrees but were uninterested in any suasion that would change them into seekers of truth. All that mattered to them was the test—and the grade.

The coffee in the lounge was usually good. Today it would taste like ambrosia. Higley walked in after acknowledging a greeting from a student. He exchanged soft greetings to other faculty members he knew, poured his coffee, and greeted a friend who wanted to talk about a team teaching project for the next semester. Higley heard but didn't commit to his colleague.

Soon he backed into a soft leather chair and ottoman. It would only be a matter of minutes before he was asleep. Everybody knew that was the protocol. If you sat in one of the two big brown leather chairs, you would be forgiven for nodding off.

It was quiet in the room. A bridge game of serious consequence was being held. A couple of professors, both women, were quietly conversing on a love seat to the left of Higley; two male professors of psychology, one old and the other a young, were finishing a chess game. The young man seemed to bear the serene look of a likely winner. Two men were standing near the bay window. Higley knew one but not the other, perhaps a visiting professor.

The time was right for a few winks just to ease his tension. Gradually, he could feel a slight tingling in his cheek under his left eye. He was relaxing. Sleep would do the rest of the job the two aspirins had begun.

Higley could see the whole room from his remote corner but felt himself withdrawing from it as the rumor of voices and sounds began to grow faint.

Suddenly, the dark, four-squared wainscoted door opened, and Dale Chandler walked into the room. As usual, he seemed preoccupied and slightly hurried but never frantic or ruffled. Higley stirred slightly, sensing his juices flowing faster again but not wanting to become fully awake.

Chandler walked over to the two women and spoke to them briefly, charming them and leaving them easily. As he turned to the small serving bar to get coffee, he noticed Higley but didn't acknowledge him. Higley was just as glad; even normal workaday pleasantries between them were a strain. He began to settle again into that twilight sleep that brought him relief from the throbbing behind his eyebrows.

But Chandler had something to say. As he poured cream from a glass pitcher into his coffee, seemingly intent on his work, he said, "Earl, rumor has it that you've applied for the research fellowship."

The projection of his voice bestirred the entire room. The bridge game stopped momentarily; the other conversants turned toward Chandler's voice and then attended to Higley's response. Knowing Higley and Chandler, they instinctively understood each man to be on opposite sides, no matter which issue confronted them.

"Which one is that, Dale?" Higley answered laconically.

"Come now, don't be coy, Earl. There's only one fellowship of any consequence nowadays."

"Well, if you mean the Reese fellowship, then, yes, I've applied."

"Well, good for you. The more proposals, the better chance that some significant research will emerge."

"Exactly," Higley said, dismissing Chandler and settling into his chair more determinedly.

But Chandler wasn't finished. "But I must say I'm surprised. You've given no evidence that you've been on track of some important research. I've known you for years and have always been assured that teaching, not research, is your forte."

"Sorry I didn't live up to your assurances, Chandler. But, in fact, I did make a proposal."

People in the room were paying more attention now, sensing that the subtle needling of Chandler would cause some fireworks.

"But surely, Earl, with your track record, you must know that this is a major-league contest. I hope you can handle the rej—the competition gracefully. I'd hate to see any bitterness from the contest sully a... solid career as a teacher."

Higley could feel a flush on the back of his neck. "Now, now, Dale, this is a meritocracy, not a physique contest. Why don't you use this intimidation rap where it counts? Go after the judges, not me."

"I'm just thinking of your own good, Earl. Disappointment sometimes has a deleterious effect on motivation."

"Why, gracious, I'm touched by your concern for my welfare, Dale."

Chandler wasn't having the unsettling effect on Higley that he had thought he would have, and it angered him. "Earl, I'm not sure I've ever read anything you've written. You must have some publications, haven't you?"

"Really, Chandler," one of the psychology professors said, "this is not the place for this dialogue."

Both men ignored him. Higley was getting angry but straining to control himself.

"I've written a few—refereed journals, mind you—and I'll stack them against your bootlegged output anytime," Higley said.

"A handful of articles against my total output: books and journals?" Chandler sneered a slight smile, now sensing that he was winning the moment.

"Textbooks, Chandler? Is that your idea of significant scholarship?"

"It took work. Work you might have done—if you were capable."

"Did you ever think that some people don't want to foist their own books on hapless students? Every prof here can find a whorehouse publishing company if there's a guaranteed student sale for years to come. Who do you think you're kidding?"

"We'll see next time you submit a merit sheet, pal."

"Gentlemen, please!" one of the women said.

Higley was angry, and it showed. His face was red and his manner agitated. But Chandler was angry, and it didn't show. Higley knew he had lost the battle of composure. Chandler had goaded him into a fight and then was not blamed for it because Higley had joined in. *Gentlemen, please. Chandler was a superstar, and Higley was a rumpled, drab imitation of a professor. Gentlemen, please. Amazing. When you look the part, you've won half the battle before it starts. People are so willing to give the benefit of the doubt to the stylish rich. Gentlemen, please.* Higley was caught. For not turning the other cheek, the dumb ones blamed him, and the weak ones who understood didn't side with him. Chandler had lost and won. Higley had only lost.

Higley sat on the edge of the leather chair, both hands clutching the arm rests. He looked as though he would spring at Chandler any moment. Chandler, having gotten the better of the weak little group present, stood tense and defiant. But neither of them moved. In those few seconds,

Higley wondered what had happened to him. What in God's name had made Chandler come after him? How, of all people, did Chandler view him as a threat?

Suddenly Higley realized what motivated Chandler. Hate. Hate for any threat, any enemy small or large. But hate unfettered by common sense or tempered by intellect or strength. Then Higley spoke quietly to Chandler, slowly letting himself settle back into the big chair and speaking only loud enough for his antagonist to hear him, "You know, Chandler, you've got a goddamned screw loose."

Rino slept that morning until the phone rang at nine o'clock. It was Frank. "You still asleep, Pop?"

"No, kid. I was just lying here."

"Everything okay? We haven't heard from you. Jean called several times."

"Just a little busy. How're the kids?"

"They're okay. Larry's been working too many hours. He got two Cs last term. Libby has supper with us once in a while, just to remind us that she lives here." Rino chuckled. "The reason why I called, Pop... We'd like you to come over all day Sunday. That okay?"

"That's fine. I was going to come today, but, well... maybe later."

"Okay. We're not going anywhere. Jean took Libby to practice, but I hope they don't hold it. There's too damned much snow out there."

"You'd think they'd have sense enough to cancel it, huh?"

"Pop?"

"Yeah?"

"Where were you the last few days? Uncle Lou's shop was closed. He didn't answer his phone, and you didn't..."

"I had some stuff to take care of, Frank—private stuff. We just took a few days."

"Pop, what if something happened to either one of you?"

Rino was quiet for several seconds. He realized that his son was trying his best not to be upset with him. Frank had told him many times how sorry he was about the argument that had split them up.

Finally, Frank sighed. "Okay, Pop. Okay. If you can, come today, too. Want me to pick you up?"

"No, kid, I'll try to make it. Or else I'll call Jean and say hello. Okay?"

As he dressed, Rino looked out the window at the large flakes coming down out of a gray sky; the snow had piled up to six inches. He went downstairs to the kitchen to make coffee. As he did, he noticed Toni's letter on the table. He picked it up but didn't take it out of the envelope. Instead, he held it, staring at the handwriting a moment. Then he put it in the top drawer of a cabinet in his living room.

The week passed slowly, the snow and cold seeming that they would last until August. But by Thursday, the forecast was for cold but clear weather—the snow, for a while, had ended. Rino was working in Stilton Hall, installing new chalkboards with Joe. The work was tiring, because the seamless boards were long and heavy. Barly and Sammy came to help out.

But as usual, when all of them worked on such a project, there was an argument. Sammy wanted the boards perfectly level, and they couldn't seem to get it done right. Sammy was cursing and grunting as he and Joe and Barly moved the board in response to Rino's prompting. He studied a set of levels while astride the top of an eight-foot ladder. But when the board was level, they had to change it again, because both Rino and Barly insisted that it looked strange compared to the skewed and unlevel floor and ceiling.

Eventually, they went to lunch, still arguing about the right way to level boards. Sammy didn't always eat lunch with them, but today he did, and it gave Rino and the others a chance to torment and tease him.

Just then, Rino noticed Earl Higley motion to him as he entered the cafeteria. Rino excused himself and met Higley in the open area between the scattered sets of tables. "Thanks for coming over," said Higley. "I didn't want to discuss my fishing hole to a crowd. How about it? This Saturday okay?"

"Sounds fine," said Rino.

"Okay. I'll pick you up around six o'clock. That too early?"

"I'll have one coffee royal under my belt by then," Rino said.

"Good. We'll see how long we can take it. If we don't get any action, or if the weather gets too tough, we'll just have a good meal up there and drink some beer. What d'you say?"

"I'll be waiting."

When Rino returned to the table, Sammy had gone. But both Joe and Barly remained, waiting for Rino. They were only to get a half hour for lunch, but all of them took nearly an hour. They viewed it as a fringe benefit. Besides, they always got the jobs done for Sammy, and he could count on them to help him when he was in a jam.

"You and he are buddies?" said Joe in amazement as Rino sat down at the table.

"Not like you and me, or this guy," Rino said, motioning to Barly.

"I thought maybe you like him just because he hates Chandler's ass so much," Barly said with a sly grin.

"He hates Chandler?" Rino said, somewhat surprised. "How d'you know that?"

Barly raised and lowered his eyebrows consciously a few times.

"Yeah, I know. You know everything, right?" said Rino. "But why, Bar?"

"He and Chandler had a blowout in the faculty lounge. Some secretaries, all spies on my payroll," Barly looked at them with mock bravado yet still expecting some admiring nods from his friends, "heard some faculty talking about it at the coffeepot in Psychology."

"So?" Rino said.

"Chandler must have picked a fight with Higley. And Higley gave him good as he got."

"About what? Anybody know?"

"About this new two-year ride they're gonna give some prof. Chandler must think he's got it locked up, and he probably doesn't want Higley fucking it up for him."

"Jesus Christ," said Joe. "What a bastard!"

Rino snorted, but he didn't speak. So Chandler had picked a fight with Earl. And Higley must have applied after Rino's pep talk. Chandler's getting rattled, he thought. Anything outside the control of the college makes him nervous. Here he's mastered the politics to his advantage. He knows how to pull the right strings, how to massage the system. For game players, it's bothersome to play and not know if you're doing what it takes to win.

During that week, the weather was the same: occasional snow and bitter cold. Rino worked three days, played cards Friday night, and Saturday was up early, having coffee royal while he waited for Earl to pick him up.

They drove in the early darkness toward the misty ice of Lake Erie. Rino had never been ice fishing for all his experience in rivers and streams. Earl drove the car onto the rough, hard surface of the lake, and Rino took a deep breath, inaudible to Earl but seemingly loud to Rino himself. He seemed amazed that Earl's van was rolling across the crunchy snow of a lake whose bed was maybe 50 feet below them.

Earl selected a spot not far from shore, and he and Rino set out a canvas shelter tent, got a gas fire started, put out chairs, put on coffee, drilled through the ice, and fed lines through into the frigid water.

In the distance, through the heavy mist that hugged the surface of the lake, they could hear voices and the drones of car engines. They had company, but the protocol was one where people kept discrete distances from one another.

Their luck was good at first. Each man had many hits on his line, and the ice chests were beginning to fill up. Then, suddenly, it seemed the lines were still, and they sat for an hour without a bite. They talked of fishing, politics, football, and cars, but not about school.

Rino was anxious to find out about Earl's confrontation with Chandler, but he was reluctant to broach the subject with him. Finally, as the conversation turned toward Spring Common, Rino saw his chance to talk about what had happened. "What's it like between all of you, Earl? Are you all good friends, or is it strictly business?"

Higley snorted. "It's mostly business, Rino. We see each other at obligatory parties and big school events. But I don't have too many beer-drinking buddies among them—nobody I'd go ice fishing with."

Rino chuckled, pleased that Earl would make the comment.

"I like cars, Rino. And my colleagues like other things. We talk shop daily, but then I want to get away from it when I'm home. It's funny; to me, scholarship is something solitary. I just can't be a scholar in the bustle of the college." He paused for a minute and looked across the ice. "The college is the last place where you can do original thinking and writing. There are committees, endless meetings, foolish projects dreamed up by the administrators. Classes and students are what it's all about, yet they seem subordinate to meetings and make-work, which are almost always a waste of time."

Rino stood up, walked over to the coffeepot, and poured two full cups. Then he brought them back to his stool and handed one to Earl. As Rino sat down and unwound his line from the hook they had screwed into the ice, Higley said, "Y'know, Rino, I applied for that teaching fellowship."

"That's good," said Rino. "You should have."

"In olden times, scholars never published their work until they were sure it would advance knowledge," Higley said. "Sometimes they would sit on something for years and never publish it."

"Is that what you do?" Rino said.

Higley chuckled and shook his head, not looking at Rino but staring across the lake. "No. I wish I could say I've been mining gold all these years, but I haven't. You know, sometimes you get afraid—of ridicule, even of criticism. But I decided, after your encouragement last time, that I've been copping out. I've done a good job in the classroom, but I've been too timid to do anything else, to do what I should have done. But if you're a scholar, you have to say something, then take the heat. And I've been hiding."

"I've been hiding, too, the last couple of years." Rino sighed.

Higley continued, "I decided, let the sons of bitches come after me if they want. But I'm not going to make their job easy anymore."

"Anybody want to get you, Earl?"

"Yeah, a few, Rino. I've had some run-ins. Lately, I've had a confrontation with a guy, and I don't even know what the hell I did to wrong him."

"Who?"

"Some prof named Chandler. You know him?"

"Yeah, I know him. He's not too crazy about me, either." Rino took a sip of coffee, looking away from Earl.

"It was the craziest damned thing: I was sitting in the faculty lounge, dozing off for a few minutes, and Chandler came in. He'd heard through the grapevine that I'd applied for the fellowship—and he laid this intimidation number on me. Like I was some real threat to him. Hell, he's the superstar. And everyone knows damn well he'll get it."

Higley stood erect and walked back to the tent to get some pipe tobacco.

When he sat down, Rino said, "Is Chandler that much better than everyone else?"

Higley snorted. "He thinks he is. He's got a lot of style and polish. And the money helps, too."

"You profs are supposed to be smart. How's a guy like that put it over on so many people?"

"Some of the most gullible, unperceptive people I know are professors. Education is vulnerable to all kinds of smooth operators who huckster their way to the top."

"Is Chandler going to make it?"

"I wish that I could say for sure that he won't, but he's just the kind to do it. He's got all the superficial things that sell so well in education: he's a tall, lean, good-looking clotheshorse who plays good rounds of tennis and golf, and he has an undistinguished but nonetheless voluminous set of publications."

Rino cleared his throat nervously. "You know, Earl, I've heard that Chandler is dishonest as hell—fudges experiments and phonies them up when he does his writings."

Higley looked at Rino for a few seconds, seemingly startled. "You heard that before?" he said earnestly.

"Yeah, from more than one place."

"Are you serious? Of course you are. But who the hell tells these things?"

"Earl, you can bet if one secretary knows, then a couple of dozen know... plus all of maintenance and housekeeping."

"The staff all knows, and the faculty doesn't. Jesus! How little we can see of ourselves."

"So he is a crook, isn't he?" said Rino.

"Yeah." Higley sighed. "He sure as hell is. But he's so well connected at Spring Common that no one can lay a glove on him. A few years ago, one of my grad assistants came to me and told me Chandler was forging the data on an experiment he was running. All the grad assistants knew it, but none would say anything."

"Why not?"

Higley looked at him for a moment, amazed at Rino's naïveté. "Because a grad assistant is a serf bound to his department. And if one professor, especially a big shot, gets a hard-on for him, he's dead, and there goes years of study and work and, just maybe, a career."

"So Chandler published his research and became a star."

"Yeah. A few of the grad assistants replicated the experiments and came up with statistically different results. I told my department chairman about it, and we went to the old dean. The dean went to the academic vice president. But any story in the mouth of the dean turns to sawdust—you know, weasel worded and mealymouthed. Anyway, the provost wouldn't believe that a rich kid with a pedigreed family could do something so vile. So the story died.

"Meanwhile, Chandler's articles had made some journals, the college got publicity, and no one wanted to rock the boat. Ever since, it's been the same. If you're critical of what you feel is dishonest research or hack writing and trivial scholarship, it's because you're jealous—too untalented to do such work but, instead, content to hide in the classroom and carp at the achievers. It's a goddamned madhouse."

It was now noon, and the wind had picked up from the east across the lake, a sure sign of worse weather to come. They began to clear their little camp and load their gear into the van. When they were done, Earl said, "Come on. I know a guy who'll filet these things while we get something to eat. In the off season, he'll charge about a quarter a pound."

They stopped at an old general store and bait shop. Inside, a surly, grizzled man who knew Earl but who still eyed him with suspicion for his clear diction and old-but-clean clothes agreed through his grumbling that he would filet and pack the fish.

Then, instead of waiting, they went to an old bar on Route 531 near Conneaut. The bar was not crowded, so they sat in a booth and ordered bean soup, beer, and chili dogs. Anything hot would seem like a feast.

The waitress came with their order. The owner and bartender also came up to them and asked about the fishing, assuming from their looks and their appetites that they had been out on the lake. "Who's filleting them?" he asked.

"The guy down at McCoy's Bait," said Earl.

"That's good. He'll piss and moan about being busy and your fish being too small, but watch when you go back. They'll be in nice, clean bags and nary a bone in 'em."

When he left their table, Earl got back to Rino, suddenly curious about his story. "You know Chandler well?"

Rino huffed. "No, but I've had a couple of run-ins with him. He didn't like the way I worked in his office."

"Wait a minute. Are you the guy who filed a grievance against him? You sure as hell are, aren't you?" said Higley, answering his own question.

"Yeah," Rino said soberly.

"Well, I'll be damned. I knew there was something I liked about you." As Earl studied Rino for a moment, he said, "Why do you work at Spring Common, Rino? You don't need the money, right?"

"No. But I need the work. If I don't work, I'll get old too fast."

Higley eyed him coolly but then nodded in agreement and appreciation. Rino cleared his throat. "Earl, did you know that Reese kid who killed himself a few years ago?"

"Yeah, I knew him," Earl said glumly.

Rino was intrigued by his reaction, not knowing if he liked Reese or not. "What'd you think of him?"

"He was a troubled kid, tried too hard. I was his mentor—kind of like a professional big brother—the first year he was here."

"Was he a nice guy?"

"I liked him. He would never screw anyone. He just didn't know how to have fun—too driven. He wanted to be a full professor in five years because Chandler made it in that. They were buddies for a while, too."

"What happened?"

"There were a lot of rumors that he started losing it—getting irritable and moody, hardly ever talking the last few months. He didn't get tenure, much less his professorship. Chandler was on the committee that screwed him."

"Can anyone do something about that kind of thing?"

"Only the dean. But Chandler was his fair-haired boy, and he'd never cross him just to save Reese."

"How well did you know Reese?"

"Professionally, fairly well, but personally, very little. He wouldn't let anyone get close to him. All I can say is that he was ambitious and nervous and single-minded. He wanted to be a superstar."

"Did you know his wife?"

"Reese's or Chandler's?"

"Both."

"Well, Chandler's wife was a tall, cool blonde. Rather aloof but nice enough. Funny. She was so unlike the grad assistants he was banging at the time. He was married to a Nordic princess, but he liked the earthy, sexy ones to play with."

"How about Reese's?"

"I only met her a few times at some mandatory faculty events. She was quiet but friendly enough. I'll tell you one thing: she was a beautiful woman, sexy in a quiet way. But you always had the feeling that they didn't fit, that each would be happier married to someone else."

Rino was quiet for a few minutes, thinking about Earl's words. Finally, he said, "I can't believe they let him get away with it. And look at him now: teacher of the year. Why hasn't anyone stopped him, Earl?"

"You can call it whatever you want, Rino—cowardice, moral bankruptcy, old age. What happens is that you come here young and idealistic, always ready to fight the good fight. But then, despite the caring and extra energy, you lose—again and again. Yet, instead of all of us being bitter revolutionaries fighting for principle, some of us can't wait to get up in the morning to whore ourselves to the dean." Higley paused as if to ponder the echo of his words and found them distasteful. He reached for his glass and took a long draft of beer, avoiding Rino's gaze. "Rino, in a place like Spring Common, where the administration is all-powerful, it's a game of politics. And the ass-kissers are co-opted so easily that, after a while, you just learn it's useless to fight. At best, you're reduced to doing guerrilla warfare, cutting your losses and surviving."

"But maybe once in a while we get a second chance, Earl."

"I hope so, Rino. I could use some second chances."

Later that afternoon, Rino took his fish filets from the trunk of his car and carried them to the door of Frank's house. He knocked as he usually did since he had moved out. Jean came to the door. "Why do you knock?" she said irritably. "This is your house—and even if it weren't, you don't have to knock."

Rino ignored her comment. "Want some fresh fish, filleted and packed?" he said brightly.

Jean glared at him a few seconds and then sighed. "Yes. Thank you."

"Where do you want them?" Rino said.

"They'll have to go downstairs in the big freezer. There's no room up here."

"I'll take them down," Rino said, turning toward the stairs.

"No, Dad, I have to rearrange some shelves in the freezer to make room. I'll bring them down."

"They're heavy," Rino said doubtfully.

"Give them to me," she said.

She's not feeling well, Rino thought. She had seemed tired the past few times he'd visited. She'd been short with Frank, had snapped at the kids, almost brittle in her behavior.

"I'll put on some coffee when I come up," she said over her shoulder as she went down the stairs, still not smiling.

"I'll make it," Rino said as he walked to the cupboard. Suddenly, he heard a thumping noise and a soft shriek, and then another sound as if something fell on the stairs. He called her name frantically as he ran to the landing. He could see her sitting on the bottom two steps, holding her hands behind her neck and her forehead resting on her knees.

She was crying. The bags of fish were scattered around the bottom of the steps. Rino stepped over her to the basement floor. "Jeanie? Are you hurt?"

She hesitated for a second without looking up. "I'm okay," she said quietly.

"Come on, let's go upstairs," Rino said, urging her with his hand on her arm.

"I'm all right," she said, finally looking up at him but turning away again in an instant. He had never seen her look that way, red eyed and gaunt. "You go up; I'll pick up the fish," she said.

"Don't worry about the goddamned fish," he muttered. "Come upstairs. Is anyone else home?"

"No," she said as he almost lifted her erect. "I'm okay, I can walk," she said weakly, while at the same time shrinking from him and shrugging away from his hand that was offered to support her. They both walked upstairs, only because Rino had blocked her way downstairs.

She sat down in a chair at the kitchen table. When he did also, she sprang up, still not making eye contact with him, and walked over to the sink, keeping her back to him. "What's wrong with you?" Rino said. "Why are you acting like this?"

"Nothing's wrong. What's wrong with you?" she said back in a strangely belligerent tone.

"Jeanie?" He stood up and moved toward her. She avoided him again. "Why do you keep turning from me?"

"Because I don't want to hear any more of your excuses."

He advanced toward her, and she recoiled from him again. "I've known you since you were a young girl," he said softly. "You've never been like this."

"You didn't know me," she said, still not looking at him but trying to hide the tears that were streaking down her cheeks. "You only saw what you wanted to see."

He tried a new approach. "Is it the kids? Or Frank?"

"No, it's not the kids or Frank," she said insistently, stamping her foot slightly as she spoke. "It's nothing; you just caught me on a bad day."

He sighed. No mistake; he was the cause. "You know I only want what's best for you."

"How about you?" she said, turning to look at him. "What's best for you? Look at that shirt! Did you ever wear torn seams when you were here?"

"No," he said weakly.

"Answer me honestly. Did you take your blood pressure medication this morning?" He was silent. "See, damn you! You don't know what's good for you!" she said, crying again.

"You didn't need me here. You had your own life."

"And you have your own life, wearing torn shirts and forgetting your medicine..."

"I don't care about the shirt, the medicine—I'll take it when I get home."

"You don't care about a lot of things," she said.

"Not for you, right?" he said.

"Not for me," she said in agreement, still looking away from him.

This time, just as he had done with Lee years ago, he grabbed her and held her tightly against her stiffening resistance, forcing her to stand face-to-face with him. "Listen to me, you," he said. "I love you more than I do my own kids. It's not supposed to be that way, but that's the way it is, and I can't help it. So don't tell me about not caring for you."

She suddenly quit struggling against him and stared into his eyes. "Then why do you make me beg you to come back?" she said softly.

Rino released her arms and walked back to the table several feet away from her.

She spoke again, "I don't want you to get sick… or die, away from here in some strange place, Dad," she said in a softer tone than she'd been using.

"I thought Frankie and the kids would be enough," Rino said.

"They're not enough. I want you here."

"I could die here, too, kid," Rino said.

"But you'd be with me. It would be the natural way, and I could feel right afterward." He turned back to face her. "When you were with Lee, I knew you were going to be happy. But now I know you're not happy out there." She stopped and looked at him. "Are you?"

He shook his head.

"Then why?" she said plaintively. "Don't you miss us?"

"I miss Frankie and the kids," he said with a hint of a smirk on his face.

She waited for him to say her name, but he didn't. For a few seconds she doubted, but then she realized what he was doing. She rushed into his arms, crying softly. He cradled her head and kissed her. "So you don't miss me, huh?" she said.

"I don't miss anybody who gives me such a hard time," he said, his tone changing entirely from their earlier conversation.

She raised her head off his shoulder and looked at him. "I never missed my father very much," she said. "But you… I think about you all the time, and you don't deserve it."

"Jeanie," he said seriously, "I'm involved in something now that I don't want you or Frank to have any part of."

"Business?" she asked.

He shrugged. "Some."

"Dad? This isn't something bad? Something that could hurt you?"

"No," he said, still holding her. "And when I'm done, I'll come back if you'll still have me."

She frowned at him.

"Okay, okay. I'll be back."

"When?"

"I'm not sure. Maybe by summer." She looked disappointed. "Look, let's not let anyone know, okay? When the time comes, I'll come back real humble and ask Frank if I can move back in."

"I love you," she said to him.

"I love you too, kid," he said softly, those words echoing from his memory when he had said them so many times to Lee. *What a life*, he thought. How could he ever figure that two young women, two strangers, would ever illuminate the latter years of his life, and both mean more than family and friends?

Finally, he turned her loose. "I got up in the middle of the night and froze my ass to get those damned fish. Are you gonna let them rot downstairs?"

The February weather had none of the bitter wind of January but rather the calm, clear cold that chills to the heart the traveler who stands still. Rino stopped at Lou's shop and found him smoking while he read the *Telegram*.

Lou made two coffee royals, and Rino settled into a chair in the bay and savored the coffee as it warmed his gullet and banished the cold that he had carried in from the outside. Lou worked, and Rino read for several minutes, neither of them talking. Finally, Lou addressed his brother. "Rino, have you noticed how Jean's been looking lately?"

"How's that?" said Rino, knowing exactly what Lou meant.

"You have a way of irritating people sometimes, Rino," Lou said under his breath. Rino ignored him. "Dammit, man, didn't you notice how tired she's been looking. She's your daughter-in-law. Did you ever think to find out if she could be sick?"

"I talked to her. Don't get excited; she's not sick."

"You sure? How do you know she's telling the truth?"

"Jean, right?" Rino said in amazement, looking at Lou over the paper, which had crumbled in his lap. "Lou, she's fine."

"She's not gonna be fine until you move back in with them," he said.

"You know, Lou, if all I ever did was follow your advice, I'd be bananas. You were on me for years to get my own place."

"I didn't know Jean would take it so hard. I don't know what she sees in you. You must both be a quart low."

"I had a talk with her, Luigi, last Saturday. I told her I'd move back in."

Lou almost spilled his coffee in surprise. "Are you serious?" he said.

"I'm going back."

"When?"

"By summer."

"Why summer? Why do you always try to mess with her mind?"

"I have a job to do," Rino said, looking back at his paper.

"That's all you're waiting for?"

"That's all."

Rino decided to change the subject. "Lou, I'm going up to Rochester—New York, this time. I have to see some woman."

"Alone?"

"This woman was the one who gave Chandler the air. I want to see how much she knows. It's just overnight. And this time you have to be the only one to know. Annie has the body of a 30-year-old and the mind of an eggplant."

"She said she didn't tell anybody," Lou said lamely.

"Right. She sees Connie at the club and plays cards with her on Thursday nights."

"So? Why would she open up to Connie?"

"Luigi, you've seen Connie in action. In five minutes, she could find out every secret Annie knows."

"So she knew all along," Lou said, cursing Annie under his breath.

"Cowboy, she pistol-whipped me for an hour the other day at my place. She could probably tell us what we ate for dinner in Saint Louis."

Lou decided to change the subject, first by turning on the machine, then turning it off, buffing for a half second a shoe he had polished carefully an hour before, and then by taking several sips of coffee. "Rino, have you ever heard from Lee's mother?"

"Yeah. I got a letter a few weeks ago." Lou didn't flinch, didn't look up. Rino turned to watch his brother acting as though the shoe he was fixing was the most important job in the world. And, as if in a subliminal projection, Rino sensed what was on Lou's mind. "I didn't open it," Rino said as casually as he could.

"Are you going to?"

"Maybe... I don't know."

Lou took another sip of coffee and was quiet for a minute. But Rino knew he had something more to say. "Rino?"

"Yeah, Luigi." Rino sighed wearily.

"I want you to come to the Saint Joseph's dance with Annie and me."

"The three of us?"

"Of course not," Lou hissed in disgust to show his irritation. He waited a few seconds, watching Rino feign interest in the newspaper while avoiding his brother's eyes. "With Andrea Manasseri, Rino," Lou said, casting his voice over the newspaper.

Rino drew a deep breath. "You're never gonna give up on this thing, are you? If she's so wonderful, why don't you take her out yourself? You're a single man."

"Come on, Rino, don't play games. You know damn well I've got Annie. Besides, you're the lonely one."

Rino began wearily pleading his case. "Lou, the woman's made out of stone. Compared to Lee..."

"Compared to Lee, everybody's second rate," Lou said, finishing for Rino. "We've been through this before, cowboy. Lee's been dead almost two years. And Andrea has invited you, out of all the guys who ever put moves on her, to her house. Christ, you'd sooner get an audience with the pope."

Rino shifted in his seat and made more noise with the paper.

"Cowboy?" Lou said.

"Maybe. I'm not sure."

"Of what?"

"Of the dance, let alone Andrea."

"You have a month. I want you to come with me. I'm gonna tell Marty and Pete."

The plane trip to Rochester was delayed two hours in Buffalo. When Rino got to the motel near the university, he was weary yet hungry. He went to a restaurant in the motel and had a bland and tasteless meal, something that he would be unable to remember an hour later.

He bought a newspaper, went back to his room, and lay across the bed. He was worried about what the woman would do. So far, he had been lucky. Chandler seemed to be more and more vulnerable as Rino talked to his former associates, but still, there was nothing to use, no way to hammer him with what he had done. He needed some way to catch Chandler.

The next morning, he drove to Port Ontario University and found the office of institutional research. He located Doreen Teare's name on a list in front of the elevators and rode up to the third floor.

As the elevator door opened, he could see a long corridor with large, glass-walled, sequestered offices off an open aisle. The second one down the hall was her office. But upon entering, he was confronted with a secretary who asked his business.

He said that he wanted to see Dr. Teare but was told that she wouldn't be in until 11:30 that morning. Rino glanced at his watch—almost 10 o'clock. He thanked the girl and left the office to wander around the campus.

He headed for the student union. His feet grew colder as he walked. Students bundled in jeans, boots, and heavy coats were walking carefully across the frozen snow on the well-packed paths. They didn't look any different from the ones at Spring Common. Well, not too different. Somehow, some seemed to have a more serious, perhaps older look. This was a much bigger place, with doctoral programs in many academic areas.

In the student union, Rino got a coffee and doughnut from the line in the cafeteria and sat at a table so he could look at whoever came in. He noticed the workers, trying to decide who was maintenance and who was not. There seemed to be a more formal separation of job classifications between maintenance and housekeeping. At Spring Common those distinctions were blurred, mainly because Sammy had overall responsibility for both tasks. And Sammy fit the best man or woman to each job. It all worked because of his judgment and his charm and the quality of his crew.

Rino was getting accustomed to strange colleges by now. He'd seen the big ones, Jerry's Ohio State, and the little one, Nancy's Lake Erie College for Women. Plus Eastern Missouri State and now Port Ontario on his journey for Chandler.

He sat for almost an hour observing while drinking two cups of coffee. Only at these strange and isolated times did he yearn for the cigarettes he had given up so long ago. Sometimes Lou seemed so quietly pleased with a smoke and a coffee as they sat serenely, relaxed and unburdened with the day's toil. Rino envied that look, but by fear or inertia or both, he never quite picked up the forgotten habit again.

He made his way back to the research office, hoping to be relaxed and less flushed from the cold as Teare arrived. He sat in a small waiting area of four chairs in a small nook, with education journals resting on end tables. Rino picked up the *Chronicle of Higher Education*, scanned it, and then scanned it again. The topical news items interested him most.

Just then, a very tall woman came into the office. She was sandy-haired, attractive, and nicely dressed. She approached the secretary, who whispered to her of Rino's presence. He rose from his chair as she approached. When she stood in front of him, she was about two inches taller than him and coolly formal—with not a slight hint of a smile on her face. "Mr. Bellanca?"

"Hello, Dr. Teare."

"What can I do for you?"

"If you'd permit me, I'd like to talk to you about Spring Common College."

"Look, uh... Mr. Bellanca, was it? I'm terribly busy, and I have a dean's council meeting in 20 minutes. I'm sorry, I don't think I can see you today."

"20 minutes would be okay, Dr. Teare. I don't need much time."

"But what do you want to discuss? Are you a faculty member there?"

"No. Uh, please, could we talk in private?"

"All right," she said curtly. "But not all the way back to my office. Is 316 open, Cindy?"

The secretary nodded. When they entered the small conference room, she deliberately left the door open, a sign that her time was fleeting. There was a small table around which were set four brown Naugahyde plush chairs. "Now, what can I do for you, Mr. Bellanca?"

"Well, first of all, I'm not a faculty member."

"I knew that," she said coldly. She had an arrogance about her that could wither the backbone of anyone who had the least doubt about engaging her. Yet Rino had to get something painfully secret from her, a commitment to tell the truth that she had been hiding. It was going to be tough.

"I have something to say about who gets an award at Spring Common—my organization."

"What could that possibly have to do with me?"

"Dale Chandler is one of the front-runners."

She blanched a little but didn't lose her composure. She had a way of listening, an amalgamation of postures and airs, designed to intimidate speakers she didn't want to hear.

"Who is Dale Chandler?" she said, regretting instantly the lie.

Rino's attitude was starting to change. He sensed that politeness and deference weren't the way to deal with this woman. The haughty tone is usually a facade of something more complex and less formidable inside. He'd seen it before.

But he had to be careful. If he guessed wrong, the whole venture could be ruined. "You were one of his third set of graduate assistants, Dr. Teare—in 1980," he said calmly.

She was upset because Rino had caught her lie. "Oh, Dr. Chandler..." She searched for some rationalization for what she had done. "Yes, now I remember him. It was for such a short time... a few months..." She glanced at her wristwatch.

Rino expected a protestation of lateness. But she didn't say it. Instead, she waited for another question, still instinctively fearing him. Rino tried to ease her mind a little. "I'm on a committee that will decide who gets a fellowship, a memorial fellowship—two years—for Ted Reese."

She looked at him sharply and spoke quietly. "Is Ted Reese dead?"

"A few years ago."

"Mr. Bellanca, I can't think of a single reason why I should have anything to do with your deliberations," she said as she stood up, dismissing him.

Rino was angry then, but since he needed her cooperation, he decided to take a chance. "Dr. Teare, you know why I'm here. You were Chandler's assistant when he was making a name for himself."

"That hardly qualifies me as an expert. It was only two semesters."

"Chandler forged the numbers on his experiments, and you knew it."

"How dare you! This interview is over," she said angrily as she began to gather up her notebook from the table to leave.

Rino had to act fast. "Dr. Teare, I know all about Chandler's—"

"Fine, Mr. Bellanca. Then you don't need me, do you?"

"But you helped him, too, didn't you? So when he wanted you to be more than just a useful grad assistant, you smartened up and bailed out."

"What do you want from me, Mr. Bellanca?" she sighed, calming down a little.

"Just a few minutes of the truth," he said. "What I want is some help. If you don't help me, Chandler might win that fellowship—and you know damned well he shouldn't."

"If you think I'm going to help you in a personal vendetta against Dale Chandler, you're sadly mistaken."

"If you don't help me, and Chandler gets uncovered for dishonesty, whose name do you think will be dragged through the mud with his?"

"He's had dozens of graduate assistants," she said. "Others more eager to do his bidding."

"Eagerness has nothing to do with it. If they were crooks, and your name shows up on a list of cheaters..." He paused for a few seconds, looking directly into her eyes. "Isn't all that noise going to reach you up here and then take you down with him?" Rino said coldly. "And if he does, don't you deserve what you get?"

"That's a threat, Mr. Bellanca!"

"I have only two choices, Dr. Teare. Chandler or you. Save yourself." Rino paused for a minute. "You know Ted Reese committed suicide. A few months after Chandler's committee shafted him on tenure."

She grimaced. "There was an appeal process. The dean could have overruled the tenure committee."

"You knew the dean. Do you think that would ever happen?" She didn't answer him but instead looked away. Rino continued pressing, "Dr. Teare, I know he put the make on you, and I know you had sense enough–in a short while–to bail out of the mess you got into. But that's not what I care about. I want to know how you helped him fudge the data."

"Mr. Bellanca, I'm late for my meeting now. Maybe we can have this discussion at a more convenient time."

"I'm leaving on a 9:30 plane tonight. There's a place near my motel called Charly's Villa. Will you come? I'll buy you dinner."

"All right, I know the place," she said hesitantly. "What time?"

"Whenever you want."

"Six o'clock?"

Rino went back to his room, packed his suitcase, and put it in the trunk of his rental car. He rested for a few hours, dozing off while reading the newspaper. When he awoke, he decided to unpack just enough to take a shower. For some reason, he was sweating. It was the sour, nervous sweat that made him feel clammy. He showered and put on fresh clothes—casual slacks, white shirt, and V-neck sweater.

He checked out of the motel and drove the half mile to Charly's. It was a pleasant place, an old bar that served such good, basic food that it had become a restaurant, too. Rino settled into a booth and left word with the hostess that a tall, attractive, sandy-haired woman named Teare would be coming.

It was a quarter to six. When the waitress asked if he'd like a drink, he refused, saying he'd rather wait for his partner. At 6:30, he called the university. The receptionist said Teare was gone for the day. He called her apartment; no one answered.

He decided to wait longer, only this time with a drink. He called the university again and checked his version of her home number against theirs. The receptionist was reluctant to give him any information but did confirm that the number that Rino quoted her was the right one.

At 8:30, Rino left the restaurant. He had been stood up. He raged inwardly as he drove to the airport. He checked in his Plymouth and boarded the plane home. It was time to see Orrie again.

When Rino got home, it was warmer. March promised relief from the bitter cold but not much relief from snow. Wearily, he sank into bed and tried to sleep, but he was still awake at 2:30. The sleep of peace wouldn't be his for the night. He'd be lucky to get an hour's doze before morning.

He thought of Lee, got up, took out her pictures, and went through them one by one. How little pictures compensate for the real being—as though the shadow could be a substitute for the rose. But still, his life seemed to be all shadows lately. Phantoms in dreams terrorized him, leaving him suddenly awake and sweating, yet forgetting the substance of what he had dreamed.

He picked up her robe and opened it for the first time in almost a year. *How small she was*, he thought. He folded it again, and then, by reflex, put it up to his face. Maybe it was his imagination, but it still seemed to smell of her. Faintly. Not in his imagination, but faintly. He remembered untying it those nights they played together as a prelude to making love. He remembered the very first time, when he untied it and pushed it off her shoulders and saw the magical beauty of her.

It was the turning point of his life. From then on, he was never the same again. It was as though his prior life was sepia, and then, suddenly, he had magic lenses that brought color to his mind's eye for the first time. Lee. The white bathing suit lines against the tan skin, the brown hair with highlights of sandy gold, the nipples, the dark eyes, the full lips against white, glistening teeth, the white of her eyes against the dark-brown pupils. But colors in memories pale over time, and other dreams make them over.

He knew Lou was right. He had to try something. Had to try Andrea Manasseri. He had to go out of the bedroom that held such hurtful memories that he endured almost every night. He had to go back to Frank and Jean and Libby. But back to Toni? Back to life. Back to Andrea Manasseri.

Rino worked Friday, and on Saturday he read some of the mail he had accumulated. Orrie had finally sent all the applications, and one of the last two was Earl Higley's.

At least it was coming to an end. Soon, with his choice, he would drive the stake into Chandler's heart. Rino went down to Hugo's to get gas late in the afternoon. He had played poker without Lou, who had driven

Annie to see her son in Columbus, and had won, something he was sure to tell his brother when he saw him again.

Earl Higley's proposal was given high praise by the committee. As Rino read it, he thought of Earl. It was less florid than Chandler's, less academic. And the goal of the research was sensible and would help ordinary teachers. The others seemed more boring to read, ponderous and dense, without imagination and without interest. It would be easy now.

When Sunday arrived, Rino lay awake in bed and read the newspaper. Then he made some breakfast and finished rereading the three top proposals. Then he reread the notes he had made to himself. He wanted to make sure he could give reasons for his choice. At least Orrie might want to know. Somebody had to believe it was something other than Rino's liking for Higley and dislike for Chandler.

Dinner was at Connie's, and it was a big one. Most of the family in Youngstown would be there. Rino was feeling both good and bad. His trip to Port Ontario had gotten him nowhere, but the applications were complete, and he was closer to what he had to do. Also, there was something pleasant about knowing that Jean secretly knew he was finally going home and that she cared so much to have him back.

When Rino got to Connie's, he kissed her, joked about her food, and tormented her about her weight. He said hello to Danny and the whole family. Everyone was downstairs in the recreation room watching a fight. When Connie came downstairs, Jean was alone in the kitchen. Almost no one was upstairs; Danny had fallen asleep in the large easy chair in Connie's living room.

Rino went up to the kitchen. He spoke softly to Jean, careful that someone would hear him. "Hi."

"Hi," she said, smiling.

"You still mad at me?" he said.

"Yes. Until you keep your promise," she said. "If you don't, I'll show you just what a gargoyle I can really be."

"What promise? I don't remember any promise."

"Dad," she said reprovingly, ignoring his taunts, "did you take your medicine today?"

Rino nodded. "Yes, Nurse. You know, you must be part Italian, to act the way you do."

"Funny. Just the other day, I was thinking that you had to have some German blood in you."

"Maybe so, maybe so." He chuckled. "How's your husband, kid? You and he doing okay?"

"Sure we are. He's just like you: a head like granite, but otherwise a doll. And I can handle that."

"He's a good guy. I still owe him for bringing you and Libby into the family."

She giggled slightly. "Don't I get any credit for Libby?"

"I was thinking you must have had something to do with it," he said, smirking.

Just then Lou came up from downstairs. "Aunt Connie needs some advice, Jean. She sent me up to find you."

Jean went downstairs, and Lou poured himself some coffee from the large stainless-steel pot that Connie had on the kitchen counter. "I notice your daughter-in-law looks a little better today," he said.

"I told you I talked to her," Rino said.

"What'd you find out in Rochester?"

"She's the one to crack, but I couldn't do it."

"Now what?"

"Now it's Orrie's turn. He's got to scare her. Profs are pretty skittish about their reputations. It might work."

"And if it doesn't?"

"If it doesn't, I find another way. Even if nothing happens, it'll do him in to know he didn't get picked. But bet the house I'm gonna get him."

Monday, Rino called Orrie from Spring Common to set up an appointment. He was in court all day, but his secretary said he was open at four o'clock. It was almost April, and Rino and Joe were doing their first outdoor job of the year—in the tower of Crandall Hall. They had to put a new set of wires in the bells so the carillon would play again. It had been silent for six years. The cold wind, far above the ground, numbed the bare fingers that Rino had to use to wire up the job.

Rino was tired as he entered Orrie's office. "Hey, paesan, how about a belt?"

"Best offer I had all day," Rino said as he shook Orrie's hand.

"Anisette?"

"What're you having?"

"My drink's a martini. Shall I make two?"

"Yeah, I'm in the mood for something strong."

Orrie went to the small wet bar in his office. It had paneled doors and a dark marble counter. Inside were several bottles of good whiskey. Next to them was a small refrigerator that made ice. Orrie mixed the drinks with the practiced ease of an experienced martini drinker. He handed one to Rino and sat with him on the opposite end of the couch. If it was to be a business call, Orrie was glad it was with an old friend with whom he could drink and relax as he counseled him.

They talked sports, weather, children, and health. Orrie growled about his doctor's harassment of him, his weight, his high blood pressure. Finally, they both sensed that it was time to talk about Rino's business.

"What's up, kid?" Orrie finally said.

"Thanks for getting all those applications to me so soon," said Rino.

"No problem. My secretary does all the work, and I still charge your brains out," he said, chuckling through a sip of martini. "That's not all you want to talk about, right?"

"No. I want you to write a letter for me."

"Okay... what about?"

"Orrie, I want you to do something... on faith."

"Oh, shit," Orrie muttered, setting down his drink.

"It's not crooked, Orrie. I just have to lean on somebody, and I need you to do it for me."

"So who're you leaning on?" Orrie said.

"There's a woman professor at Port Ontario. She used to be a grad assistant to one of the guys who applied for the fellowship."

"What do you want me to tell her?"

"She has to be scared enough to give me some information I need. See, this guy's name is Chandler—"

"The guy who pressed charges against you?"

"Yeah. Chandler not only tries to screw his female grad assistants, but he also gets them to do some dirty work for him."

"What kind of dirty work?"

"Fudging data on experiments and research. That's serious stuff to those profs. And Chandler uses these kids to make his experiments come out all right. They change some numbers so he looks good."

Orrie got up and made two more martinis in the pitcher. He was silent as he stirred and poured. He turned and looked back at Rino, who had remained seated on the couch. He handed him another drink, studying Rino as he reached for the glass Orrie was offering him. Suddenly his sober visage betrayed amazement. "My God! You're doing a setup," he said in awed tones.

Rino didn't answer him.

"That's what this fellowship is all about, isn't it?" Rino calmly took a sip of his drink, not speaking, knowing that Orrie had finally caught on. "Two hundred grand?" Orrie continued, more for his own benefit than for Rino's. "A real son of a bitch..." Suddenly Orrie sat down, his eyes wide with wonder. "Chandler!" he said, turning to face Rino. "You've set Chandler up!"

Rino finally answered. "You know, Orrie, back in the old days, Lou and I used to watch you in court. When you started working, some people would fight you, and some would be putty in your hands. But sooner or later, you got them. Remember those people you were holding by the balls? You could have smashed a lot of them on that stand, but you only went as far as you had to go. And I never saw you hurt someone just to make them squirm.

"But Chandler does, Orrie. There was a young prof at the college who trusted him and looked up to him as a friend. You know what Chandler did? He shafted the kid so he wouldn't get tenure. He screwed his wife and ruined the kid's career. So a couple months later, the kid hanged himself." Rino raised his eyebrows and pursed his lips in a gesture that indicated that his case was made. Orrie shook his head in wonder. Rino continued. "You know, Orrie, Chandler's still there, riding tall in the saddle. He's gonna be a college president someday, and Ted Reese is in a box six feet in the ground."

"Reese? That was the name of... Whoa! This is too heavy for me, Rino. I think you have to be a dago to do this."

"You have to hate, Orrie. That's all—hate and keep your wits about you," Rino said coolly.

Orrie shifted in his seat and studied Rino. He took a sip of his martini and looked again. "I thought I knew you, Rino."

Rino sighed. "Will you write the letter? I need what that woman has."

"What does she have?"

"Knowledge. She was there when he rigged the numbers. Those experiments put him on the map."

"Rino," Orrie drawled in anguish, "I'm your lawyer and your friend, and I have to tell you this is dangerous. You—"

"There's not one damned thing crooked about this, Orrie. That's why I wanted a faculty screening committee. I'm not on the take; I'm giving something."

"Rino, you're out to destroy somebody. You have to be careful."

"Orrie, I've lost a wife, a son, some good friends, and the girl I was going to marry in two days. I'm 64 years old and take blood pressure pills. I could check out tomorrow. Don't talk to me about being careful."

"Rino, you know this isn't your style. This could... change you."

"His own greed is going to do him in, Orrie. All I'm going to do is offer him his poison."

Orrie thought for a moment. "Rino, I don't like this. You gambled a fortune just to try to get some guy—"

"Will you write the letter for me, Orrie?" Rino said softly.

"Yeah, I'll write it." Orrie sighed. "Somebody has to keep you from screwing up your life."

"Say that there are some questions about experiments Chandler used as a recommendation for the fellowship... and that the organization you represent would like to see some data. Say her name came up, and ask if she'll help."

"What if she says no?"

"If she says no, then I'll have to go talk to her again—and then you write a nastier letter, talking fraud and lawsuit and spreading her name all through it."

"Rino, if this woman's smart, she'll just stonewall it and tell me to go fuck myself."

"Scare her, Oren. She may be smart, but she also has ambition. And that means more to her than anything else."

Orrie shook his head and whistled in a low, drawn-out burst. "God, I don't believe this."

"Kid, you knew it wasn't always going to be title transfers and trust funds. Sooner or later, it was going to be something that hurt a little bit."

Orrie nodded, understanding but not placated.

"There's something else," Rino said.

"Yeah?"

"I've narrowed the list. It's down to Chandler and Higley. Write them a letter and send a copy to the president. Tell them the organization says they have this last chance to add something to the proposal—whatever they want. Tell Chandler the first experiment was very interesting. We'd like to see all the data."

"My God, you think he's gonna submit something else?"

"Bet your ass he will," Rino said.

Rino worked three straight days at Spring Common. The weather was foggy and dreary, but the snow did not accumulate very much. It was a pleasant time. Rino was feeling better, and Joe and Barly were in especially good spirits. All three conspired to torment Sammy, each in his own way. It was the kind of carefree work that Rino had done in the days before he met Lee—before he realized how much he could still lose out of life. But it was fun, and Sammy was in a good mood all week. There wasn't much to do, and what there was, was easy—a good way to end the work week.

After work, Rino went home and fell heavily into an easy chair, savoring the warm coffee he had made. He would play poker tonight. And eat lightly now. Agee's brother would cook steaks for them after midnight. He closed his eyes, dozed a half hour, and then took a shower. Orrie had sent him a copy of the letter to Doreen Teare. Rino admired Orrie's skill with words as he reread the letter. It had just the right tone—an implied warning, an implied threat, an overt request for help, and a subtle hint that she could come out clean and unmentioned if she would cooperate. He had to wait to see if Orrie would get a response.

Later the next week, Rino saw Earl Higley in the cafeteria. Rino was sitting with Joe quietly drinking coffee after their meal. The cafeteria was not full of people, as it had been during the noon break. Earl came over to Rino's table, and, as he did, Joe greeted him and said he had to use the men's room, politely leaving Rino alone with Earl.

"Rino, the damnedest thing just happened. I got a call from the president. I'm one of the two finalists for that fellowship. Isn't that something?"

"I knew you'd do it, Earl," Rino said, motioning for Higley to be seated. He sat down quickly, almost missing one of the chairs that ringed the table.

"Well, it's nice to know I'm at least a finalist," Higley said. "I owe that to your encouragement."

"I think you've got it," said Rino matter-of-factly.

"No, my friend, some things just aren't in the cards."

"Why not?"

"Because the other guy's Chandler."

"So? Why him and not you?"

"It's called 'star quality,' Rino. I'm a country boy trying to jump above my station. Chandler doesn't have hairy arms and a spare tire around the waist. He's just the blow-dried, tailored type that looks good in university recruitment brochures."

"And you think Chandler's got it locked up?"

"I've gotten used to seeing Chandler lock things up, Rino," Higley said softly. "Then, too, this just might be the one time when the son of a bitch wrote a better proposal than I did." He chuckled. "And that's the story of my life."

Four days later, Orrie called Rino. "I think I got a bite from our friend in Rochester," he said.

"When? What'd she say?"

"She got the letter today and called me from her home, not from the university. She says she wants to talk—that means deal, to me."

"You tell her I'd see her?"

"Yeah. I said you'd be in Rochester tomorrow or Wednesday... and you'd look her up."

"You're a good man, Oren."

"You be careful, Rino. I don't want this thing blowing up in your face."

Rino's plane ride to Rochester was different from the last one. Then he didn't know his quarry or what she would be like. This time he was not begging her to cooperate. This time she had to deal, and she knew it. This time he wouldn't hurt her, but he didn't have to be all that nice to her, either. She was arrogant and ambitious—plenty to dislike. And plenty to relieve him of the obligations of gentility.

From his hotel room, he called her at home. "Dr. Teare, this is Rino Bellanca. When can we meet?" Rino hadn't been so cold and steely eyed in years, and in a way, he enjoyed it. It was vicarious retribution: her for Chandler.

She hesitated a second. "Well, not at the university, surely," she said, recapturing her haughty tone.

"I don't care where, Dr. Teare. Just when."

"Perhaps in the same restaurant where we agreed to meet the other night."

"The night I waited almost three hours? I'll tell you something, Professor. I won't do that again," Rino said, trying to sound as threatening as he could.

"I'll be there, Mr. Bellanca." She sighed.

Rino snorted. "If you aren't, the whole damned world is going to know that you used to be a numbers cooker for Chandler."

She was silent for a few seconds. Then she spoke in a weak, resigned voice. "I'll be there."

She was a very imposing, tough woman, easy to fear. Yet Rino didn't feel very good about her capitulation. He still didn't trust her, but he didn't like himself for having been hard on her. Rino packed his few clothes again. All he needed was her information, and he could take the late plane home. If not, he'd leave on an early flight the next day. It all depended on what Teare could give him.

As before, Rino was at the restaurant a half hour early. This time he ordered a whiskey and soda and savored the cool taste of it while he thought of what he would say when Teare arrived. If it all went well, in a few hours he'd be rid of her.

She entered Nick's restaurant precisely at six o'clock. The place was still not crowded, so they would be able to talk and negotiate in peace. "Hello, Dr. Teare," Rino said, standing as she approached him. She nodded grimly. "Would you accept a drink?" He motioned for her to sit down on a chair opposite his.

"No, thank you," she said, her eyes avoiding his.

He sat calmly, waiting for her to get settled with gloves and purse. She was reddened by the cold. "Are you sure you wouldn't like something?" Rino said again.

"Perhaps a cup of tea," she said, smiling weakly.

Rino motioned to the waitress and ordered tea. "Why didn't you come last time? We could have saved us both a lot of trouble," he said finally.

"Because I don't want anything to do with Spring Common or with Chandler. I thought that part of my life was behind me," she said without looking at him. She shuddered slightly. Occasionally, as she spoke, her breath escaped in the middle of a word, as though her heart was beating arrhythmically, and she couldn't draw enough air to speak.

"I didn't come here to hurt you," Rino said.

She looked up at him then, as though surprised. "I have no way of being sure of that, Mr. Bellanca."

Rino nodded. "All right. I guess you don't."

"But what do you want from me? Why me? I was only there—"

"You were there with Chandler at the beginning—when he became a big wheel."

"So?"

"So I want copies of all the work you did for him," Rino said abruptly. "Especially those where you changed the data."

She was startled that he seemed so sure of his information. "I'm not sure. I don't have any copies," she said.

Rino's tone softened. "That's why you left, wasn't it? You had to have something to protect yourself. You wouldn't throw that stuff away."

"You have no idea why I left," she said.

"You knew that he'd use you up and throw you away—like he did all the other girls who worked for him. And you couldn't stand being the crook he turned you into, so you left. He did use you, didn't he?"

She looked down at her tea and was silent for a moment. "He used me," she sighed.

"Anything you have would help," Rino said. "Anything."

She thought for a moment. "But what are you going to do with it? I want no part of a... vendetta against Chandler."

"Well, for openers, Chandler won't get the fellowship. After that, I don't know. There are a lot of grad assistants who didn't have the guts or brains to leave the way you did. He's still using them."

"Mr. Bellanca... please, I don't want to be involved in that."

"If you give me everything you've got, I swear your name won't come up," Rino said. "Only one other person knows about this but me." He paused a few seconds to emphasize his next point. "But if you give me garbage that I can't use and waste my time, then you're tying a noose around your own neck, and Chandler takes you down with him."

"God, I hate this!" she said, forcing her fist against the tabletop as though straining not to pound it in frustration.

"I told you, I'm not here to hurt you," Rino said. "And if you help me... well, then you can finally bury it. No one will be coming after you like I am, ever again."

"But most of that material is on IBM cards. They don't even use machines like that anymore."

"Give me the cards and the printouts. I'll get them taken care of."

She paused. Then she finally looked up at him. He was staring back. He really didn't seem contemptible. He was blunt and direct—not easily fluent like a professor, but rather like a businessman. "All right. I'll give you what I've got. But then please don't contact me again." She crumpled a napkin. "God, how did I ever get involved like this?"

"You were young, and you wanted to be somebody—and Chandler's a smoothie. I'll bet it didn't seem like such a bad thing at the time," Rino said casually.

She seemed surprised at his tolerance. "Do you really believe that?" she said.

"I believe it." He sighed. "Hell, it's easy to do dumb things when you're young and somebody colors them pretty for you."

For the first time since he had met her, she smiled and nodded, both in acceptance and appreciation. "Can you wait another day? I can't get it all until tomorrow. Especially the data cards. And I'll indicate the ones that are the most egregious cases."

"Yeah. I can wait."

"Well, you come to the university at lunchtime. I'll have all the information then. You can just take it."

"To the university? Are you sure?"

She nodded.

"Are you going to make copies?" Rino asked.

"No," she said. "When you're done with them, throw them away. They only represent pain in my life."

The next day, Rino went to Teare's office at noon. She seemed placid and almost cordial. She also seemed relieved. When Rino picked up the box, he looked at her for a moment. "Thanks," he said. She nodded silently.

Rino got home from Rochester and rested the next day. It was Friday. He intended to play poker, but first he had some business with Agee Mancuso at the Tre-Sette. When he arrived, it was about seven o'clock. A light rain had started to fall. Only two people were in the bar. The poker players would soon be ambling in.

Agee passed Rino a coffee and side of anisette. "Listen to that cold rain and wind," he said to Rino as he poured. "Ain't this weather a bitch?"

"Your son-in-law still works at the *Telegram*, doesn't he, Gee?"

"Yeah," said Agee.

"I have a little story he might be interested in."

"What's it about?" said Agee.

"Something's going on at Spring Common. It might make a good article."

Agee wiped the counter reflexively. "He'll be in tonight. He usually comes in when Jenny bowls."

"Okay. You know where I'll be."

During poker, Rino lost consistently. But after an hour his luck and his concentration changed, and he began to win. At nine o'clock, Agee came in the back room and bellowed, "Rino, phone call."

Lou looked at Rino questioningly, but Rino indicated with a slight wave of his hand and a grimace that the call was unimportant. Rino folded, excused himself, and went out into the bar.

By now the bar had become busy with basketball fans who had braved the weather and the noise of the game and now sat celebrating a victory of Thornhill High School. The shuffleboard game was rowdy with easy money being bet and arguments erupting between teams. Loud rock music could be heard only in muffled waves that ran through the noise of the crowd. "He's back in my office, Rino," Agee said.

"Thanks, Agee," Rino said, following him.

"Tim, you know Mr. Bellanca, don't you?"

"Sure. How are you, Mr. Bellanca?" Tim said, extending his hand. "You're Frank's dad, right?"

"He's an old friend," Agee said simply, his tone conveying the admonishment that Rino was to be treated with courtesy. Agee did not always approve of Tim's jaded aggressiveness and was scornful of his naïveté in dealing with the people of the East Side—his neighbors.

"How's Jenny?" Rino asked, a familial courtesy among the Italians that Tim considered quaint.

"Oh, she's fine. Her bowling night's my night to prowl. I come over and play shuffleboard and tend some bar. You never know when you might need a job."

"He's a lousy bartender," said Agee, chuckling.

"Cheap, too," Tim said as he winked at Rino.

"Okay, you guys, I'm leaving. No one will bother you in here," said Agee.

"What'd you want to talk to me about, Mr. Bellanca?" said Tim, suddenly changing his tone, sounding more like a professional newsman.

"I'd like to know if you've heard about any scandal at Spring Common?"

Tim shook his head. "I haven't heard anything. What's the story?"

"I think one of the profs is writing up phony experiments. He's a big wheel, so it would be a real scandal."

"Look, Mr. Bellanca, I know you work there, but I have to tell you: a prof cheating isn't much of a story. Not too many people give a damn about such things."

Rino was anxious. He had to interest Tim in Chandler, or the story might be hushed up and forgotten. "I guess I thought if a big shot gets caught doing something crooked, then that's a story."

Tim tried to mollify Rino. "We specialize in scandal, Mr. Bellanca: who's screwing whose wife, which politician's a homo, who stole what, who bribed who. Personal tragedy, a Shakespearian fall from the heights, just doesn't read well unless the guy's a real wheel."

"Okay, Tim," Rino said dejectedly. "Sorry I wasted your time."

"Well, while we're here, you can at least tell me what you've heard."

"I thought you might fill me in on some of it, Tim," said Rino.

"I haven't heard a thing; I swear. You know, Spring Common's not such a hot beat. So, what have you heard?"

Rino hesitated. Tim was a professional cynic. Nothing surprised him, and consequently nothing affected him. He had lost a moral perspective, had become incapable of being shocked—or, much worse, had become incapable of indignation.

Tim sensed Rino's reaction to him and didn't like it. It was a cross his personality and his profession caused him to bear. "Come on, you've got me curious now," he said.

Rino told Tim the outline of the story.

"But if he goes, what will that do?" Tim asked. "I mean, how will things have changed?"

"A boy wonder will bite the dust. He's screwed a lot of people to get where he is—department chairman, teacher of the year, author."

"And he's a prick besides?" Tim said, suddenly seeming more curious. Rino nodded in assent. "And most people are gonna love it when he crashes? How will this go over at Spring Common?"

"It'll shock the hell out of everyone. The guy's a superstar."

Tim thought for a minute. "All right. This time of year, we get some slow days in local news. Maybe this will play." He reached for a business card in his wallet and handed it to Rino. "If this thing ever blows, I'd appreciate a call. But early enough. I mean, I don't want to hear it on all the goddamned TV and radio stations in the town first."

"You'll know as soon as I hear. It'll be early."

Tim paused, surveying Rino. "Why are you telling me all this? What's in it for you?"

"Satisfaction. Sometimes when you screw people, they have friends who remember."

The next day, Orrie called Rino early. "If you want the additional stuff, I've got it. I'll drop it off at your place before noon."

"Did they both send something?" Rino asked.

"Not Higley. Just Chandler—just as you said he would."

"Did you read it?"

"Some of it. If you can show any of this is crooked, you've got him by the nuts."

Rino went over to Lou's shop in the afternoon. The weather had warmed into the forties, and Lou was working contentedly on the only pair of shoes he had in the shop for repair.

"One pair?" said Rino. "When are you gonna fold this place?"

"When I die, just to spite you and Connie," said Lou curtly. "Next question?"

"Okay, okay. Have you seen Connie this week?"

"Yeah. We had lunch together Wednesday, and I called her last night."

"How's she doing?"

"She thinks you're bananas… and I'm at fault."

"Bull. She's just being herself, Lou."

"We have to start acting a little more conventional in our old age, Rino. We're starting to seem like a couple of… eccentrics."

"Like what? Does she think we wake up in the morning and try to be weird?"

"Like having normal relationships. Like escorting nice women to the Saint Joseph's Day dance."

"Lou, I know just the thing: you marry Annie and quit all the sinning and fornicating, and Connie'll be delirious."

"And you'll take up with a woman near your age, like Andrea Manasseri, right?" Lou said.

"I don't bother anybody, Lou. Hell, I even gave up smoking," Rino said in a jibe at his brother, who had just lit up.

"I'll see her this Wednesday at the committee meeting. What should I tell her?" Rino was silent. "Cowboy? What do I say?"

"Propose to her for me," Rino said.

"Come on, bastard. When do I tell her you'll come to call?"

"Christ," Rino grumbled under his breath.

"When, Rino?"

"I don't know, Lou. Whenever my work—" He stopped abruptly, then continued after a second. "Whenever you want, Lou."

"Jesus, Rino, why does this have to be like pulling teeth? I don't want you to marry her. Just ask her to a dance—in front of God and everybody."

Rino sighed deeply. "Tell her... no. Ask her if she would mind if I called on her."

"Mind? She's the one who suggested it, remember?" Lou said.

"Just ask her, Lou. Maybe she's changed her mind."

Lou continued to work on the shoes that he could have finished an hour earlier. This time things were going to work out his way. And Rino was going to be the better for it.

Orrie had brought Chandler's new material. Throughout the weekend Rino looked at it. The proposals were almost readable, except for the statistics. All Rino could determine was that Chandler's experiments always resulted in something "significant." He wondered if Chandler had ever done something insignificant. Doreen Teare's notes pointed out where most of the fudging of the numbers came in. If some experiment doesn't become significant, then you redo the numbers until it all comes out fine. Then you write your article.

Rino dated and numbered the experiments on a notepad. The first ones were the ones he paid most attention to. Later, on Sunday night, Rino looked at the cards and the printouts that Doreen Teare had given him. These were five double packs of IBM cards, all neatly labeled and bound with rubber bands. And there were ten printouts. One set had yellow highlighter markings scattered throughout the long rectangular arrays of numbers. The second set was done in green highlighter in the identical points of the array but with different data entries—the forged data. And finally, there was a clean sheet of numbers unmarked but with entries identical to those highlighted in green. Rino smiled in satisfaction. He finally had his poison.

The weekend had been quiet. Rino had gone nowhere for dinner Sunday, begging off from Jean and Connie. Lou had called him, but even he couldn't entice him to go out anywhere. Rino was strangely troubled. All his machinations to get Chandler did not weigh as heavily on his conscience as his commitment to see Andrea Manasseri. How would he be able to do it? To talk to a woman who in the best days of her youth would pale beside Lee? It wasn't even fair to Andrea, to be compared to the memories of love that Lee still evoked whenever he sat quiet and undisturbed a few minutes. He could never love this woman. At best, it would be cordial. At worst, it would be tense and overly polite... and careful. Careful not to offend her... or to seem uninterested in her. Careful not to compare her to Lee. It was going to be an ordeal.

On Monday morning, he worked in the halls of Stilton, helping Joe buff the floors. It was a season of slush and mud and salt tracked across the floors of the college. He had to see Earl soon, maybe later in the afternoon.

Sammy came up to Rino and asked if he would work overtime that night. "That Puerto Rican kid's wife's in the hospital having a baby."

"Yeah, I'll work it," Rino said.

Sammy's expression changed. "Will it be a problem?"

Rino smiled. "But I want a lunch hour."

Sammy nodded. "Why do I ever hire goddamn troublemaking greasers?" he mumbled to himself as he walked away. "Puerto Ricans and dagos."

After his work was done, Rino went to Higley's office. Higley was there in bifocals, reading a set of term papers. "Hi, Rino," he said as Rino approached the threshold of his office.

"Hi, Earl. You have a class tonight, don't you?"

"Yeah. 7:00 to 10:00," Higley said.

"Have you had dinner yet?"

"No. Are you gonna be here?"

"Yeah. I'm working overtime—a double shift. How about if we go out for a pizza about 4:00? I'll drive."

"Best offer I've had all day. Will we be back around 6:00?"

"Yeah. I'll see you downstairs, okay?"

At four o'clock, Higley was waiting at the back door of Crandall. "Look at that snow," Rino said upon approaching Higley from the rear. "Looks more like January than March."

"Want to cancel? We can go to the student union."

"I had my heart set on pizza. I know a place nearby."

The Tre-Sette had a good dinnertime crowd in spite of the weather. Higley and Rino settled into a booth, and Agee's waitress came over to them. "Hi, Rino. What'll it be?"

Rino ordered pizza for them and a pitcher of beer. While they waited for the pizza, Earl poured two glasses of the pale, cold light draft that Agee had served in frosted mugs from time immemorial. They made small talk and relaxed, warmed by the friendly familiar faces, the beer, and the cozy warmth of the building. "This is such a nice place," Higley said.

"These are my headquarters," said Rino as he waved a greeting to Agee, who had just emerged from his office.

"Earl?" Rino asked. "I have a question. If you knew a guy was cheating—you know, cooking experiments—would you testify against him?"

"At a hearing? Yeah, I suppose so. This is Dale Chandler we're talking about, right?"

"Well, what if it was Chandler?"

Higley chuckled. "For Chandler? Hell, I'd enjoy it." Then Higley stared at Rino thoughtfully. "What's going on, Rino? Do you know something I don't know?"

"I've been hearing things..."

"It won't happen to Chandler, Rino. This fellowship'll propel him into administration at some eastern college."

"I told you you're gonna get that fellowship, Earl," Rino said matter-of-factly.

"Thanks for the confidence. I wish the whole of academe was made up of people like you. You've never screwed anybody in your life, have you, Rino?"

"I try not to," Rino said. "But neither have you, right?"

"Couple of swell guys." Higley chuckled.

"Earl, what do you have on Chandler? Could you nail him if you wanted to?"

"I have some strong circumstantial evidence, Rino. Some printouts, some changes that he made to get significance from his treatments. But the people who'd corroborate my story are long gone, and Chandler's a big fish now. I'm afraid it's too late."

"Could a sensible person be convinced Chandler was a crook?"

"You would. But that might not be true here. The old dean never was convinced. They all see what they want to see, I guess."

"Yet you never threw that stuff away?"

"I never throw away something that I might use someday against a prick and a back-shooter."

That night, after Rino went home, he showered, put on his robe, and read quietly. *It was almost time*, he thought. He had read Chandler's data and compared it with Teare's again. He had read it so many times that he could almost find the changed data entries on an unhighlighted sheet.

Lonely. He wondered what Jean and Libby were doing; he wondered what Frankie was doing. It was too late to call. Lou was out with Annie.

These were the times when he would call Lee and have a quiet talk that filled his mind with dreams of the future. But not anymore. Lee had left such an imprint on his heart that he couldn't stand these quiet moments. He had to find something or someone to take the pain away. *Lou's right. I have to go on*, he thought.

The next day, Rino saw Sammy early. "Hey, K'bossy, why don't you give that PR kid a few days off to be with his wife and new baby? I'll work nights the rest of the week for him."

"Well, I'm covered on the weekend. Why don't you just work second shift through Thursday night? He just goes around spot checking, changing broken lights, ballasts, fixtures. It'll be easy, Rino."

"Okay. Tell the kid I'll work it for him."

On his break, Rino sought out Barly. "Let's go get some coffee, huh? I want to talk to you."

"Sure," Barly said. At the student union cafeteria, the two men sat in the workers' corner alone. "Lay it on me, Rino."

"How about if you work second shift tomorrow night—with me?"

Barly seemed puzzled and surprised at the same time. "What's going on, man?" he said softly.

"I'm working second for Diaz this week, and I'm gonna be up on third floor a while. I need a friend on the other end of a walkie-talkie."

"Say what? What the fuck you gonna do?"

"Nothing crooked, man," Rino said, trying to calm the excitable Barly.

"Nothing crooked, but you want me to be ride shotgun on second shift?"

"Barly, there's not a goddamned thing in this place that I couldn't buy if I wanted it."

"I know that... but nothing stole, nothing crooked. So what do you want?"

"I want into Chandler's office. I want to check around in there."

"Man, don't fuck with him. Chandler's bad meat. You know he's gonna get this fellowship, don't you?"

"I heard the word, but I don't believe it. You gonna hold the walkie-talkie?"

"You ever do anything like this before?"

"I've never been a second-story man, if that's what you mean."

"I mean doing something that ain't in your soul just to bring down a dude that's getting bigger every day."

"Barly, pricks like him leave footprints if you know where to look." Rino was uncomfortable speaking in metaphors, but he really didn't want Barly to be part of his operation. For one thing, he didn't want to cost Barly his job if the operation failed.

"You gonna do this no matter what?" Barly asked.

Rino nodded.

"Well, I guess I should help you, just so you don't fuck up everything more."

"Thanks, Bar," Rino said, slapping him gently on the shoulder. "I'll see you tomorrow night. Oh, I'm gonna need the master keys."

"File cabinets, too?"

"File cabinets, too," Rino said.

Barly groaned in dismay. "Man, I'm too old for this shit. Now I'm gonna have to give Sammy some half-assed kind of story about how I can't work days tomorrow."

The next night at Spring Common, Joe Potokar was surprised to see his old friend show up on second shift. "Rino? Why you working second?"

"For Diaz. Because of the baby."

"Oh, Barly asked Sam if he could work second, too. Wonder what he's doing?"

Sammy saw Joe and Rino talking and approached them. "Rino, we need some help in the big lecture room on the fourth floor. See if you and Barly can fix that new blackboard—it's leaning too much."

"We'll take care of it, Sam," said Rino.

"Sure you will. You two bastards are gonna drink beer and fuck off the whole night. I know it," Sammy said as he walked away.

Later, Rino saw Barly in the locker room. "Bar, what time do they turn out the lights on third floor?"

"They don't turn them all out, man. They turn 'em down and leave one square on every forty feet—just enough so you don't bump into anything."

"What time?" Rino said.

"It's on automatic—about quarter after 10:00."

"Anybody around then?"

"Nah. Dresner stays late sometimes on second floor. But he'll be gone by then, too. And Housekeeping does Crandall early, so everybody'll be gone by nine o'clock."

"Then it's just you and me?"

"You and me and two walkie-talkies. Now, I'm not gonna talk unless I have to. We don't want anyone listening in on our frequency from another building. The security guys don't come around until about midnight, so you have about an hour and 45 minutes. If anyone comes, I'll call you. You just get your ass out of his office, understand?"

"Yeah," Rino said. "Remember, I don't want to get caught, either."

Barly snorted. "Here's the master chain. His file's probably an MJ-28, so try this key with the triangle hole in it first."

"Barly, is there anything you don't know about this place?" Rino said in amazement.

"Nope," Barly said, grinning. "28 years. I know every goddamn brick and cubbyhole in this whole college. I make it my business."

At nine o'clock, Rino and Barly left the lecture hall and went down to the third-floor offices. Crandall Hall was dark except for a few scattered lights. Rheostats had dimmed them, and the automated switches had shut most of them off. It was strange hearing the creaking of wood and steel as the building contracted from the cold outside and expanded from the heat within. The joists and rafters would occasionally produce a hollow boom that sounded eerie and haunting in the quiet darkness.

They walked down every hallway in the building. The lights in the offices were all out, and the building, except for Barly and Rino, was empty. The cold, wind-driven sleet and snow had convinced everyone that it was a bad night to be outside.

"We can do it now, Rino," Barly said. "The parking lot's empty except for our cars."

"Okay. I'm looking for something. If I find it, it'll take five minutes; if I don't, a little longer." For a split second the thought occurred to Rino that nothing would be there in the office, that there would be no way to find what Chandler had done.

"What are you looking for, Rino?" Barly asked, his curiosity finally getting the best of him.

"He made some mistakes, kid. He did phony experiments and has been getting credit for them for years. That crooked stuff is up there in that office on computer cards and printouts. Without it, he's got some trouble showing he's honest."

"So you're gonna steal something after all," Barly said somberly.

"No, Bar. I'm gonna replace the phony cards with the real ones. He's never gonna know. See, he—"

"Okay, okay," Barly said, not wanting to hear any more reasons to increase his doubts. "I'll be down here so I can see both entrances and the parking lot. If you hear me come on and say, 'Rino, the coffee's ready,' you get the fuck out of there, understand?"

"I understand," Rino said. "But don't call my name. Call me Harry, and I'll call you Bill."

Rino found the key to Chandler's office easily. But he had to be careful with his flashlight. Odd night flashes might make campus police come over to check them out. Rino shone the light on the shelves, on the desk, and on the counters and bookcases. He couldn't see any cards. They had to be in the big upright cabinet or the three-drawer chest cabinet. Rino opened the big file cabinet first. His heart sank when he saw the dozens of stacks of cards, all neatly labeled and bound by rubber bands.

Slowly and laboriously, he began reading each label to see if they would represent the experiments of his cards. FORTRAN STATEMENT was written on some cards, and some were blank. Rino's cards were blank. He wondered whether there was a real difference. *No,* he thought, *there couldn't be. They were only cards with holes in them. The holes mattered, not what was written on them.*

But he didn't find the dates he was looking for. Suddenly, Barly called to him on the walkie-talkie: "Rino, you finish that job yet? You're taking a long time." Rino didn't answer for a few seconds. His concentration was causing him to sweat—above his lip and on the back of his neck. Barly came back: "Rino? The coffee ain't ready yet. You have time."

"Okay, Bar," Rino mumbled into the microphone. He stopped for a moment, thinking he had heard someone. No one was there, he reassured himself. He stopped again, trying to keep his wits about him.

His search wasn't going well; it was taking too long. And what if he was caught? What if there was no way he could find Chandler's cards? These cards? He paused again, looking around the small room. Chandler was neat, thank God. On the bookshelves, there were no file boxes, only books. The file cabinets! He would try them. He checked the key code: MX415. Frantically, he searched Barly's ring of keys. In a moment, he found the key and opened the first cabinet. There were only files, no cards. Hundreds of file folders, each with its own label, were tightly packed into each drawer. He started to panic. All his effort, all his hopes could be gone if he didn't succeed. He took a deep breath again. He opened the second file cabinet. No cards. Finally, he searched the third cabinet. Nothing.

Rino prayed that Chandler had kept the cards just as Teare had done. He turned back to the large open cabinet behind him. It had to be in the stack of cards on the bottom shelf. He started again, searching, careful not to disturb some possible categorizing scheme. They seemed arrayed by subjects. But then he found one deck with the same date as Teare's cards. He carefully pulled it out of the cabinet to look at it. They were the same. He replaced the pack with Teare's deck and took off the label card and replaced it, arranging the rubber bands in perpendicular lines around each side of the deck. *This is taking too long*, he thought. He looked at the other shelves. They did not have packs of IBM cards. The most recent were bound sheets of computer paper and a few boxes of floppy disks. Only the bottom shelf held cards, now becoming obsolete in the new computer technology.

Rino was sweating now, laboring over each sheaf of paper or deck of cards. He found another deck on his list. Quickly he replaced it.

"Rino?" Barly called. "You okay?"

"I'm okay," Rino said.

"The coffee ain't ready yet."

"This job is hard, Barly. I'll be a little longer."

Slowly he lifted each deck out and replaced it again. Once he scraped a knuckle on a shelf brace, and he cursed. It began to bleed, and he quickly wrapped his handkerchief around the cut. The last thing he wanted was to spill blood on those cards.

Again, he began the agony of examining and replacing. The light was not as strong as it first had been, but it seemed that it would last. Finally, he came upon two decks of cards labeled separately but bound together by another rubber band. They were the ones he needed. Slowly and carefully, he replaced them and put the others in his box. They were identical decks, control cards arranged in exact order. Teare had done a good job of copying. One more. He continued for a few more minutes. He was tired, and his hip muscles ached. He wiped his face with the bloody handkerchief. He found the last one and breathed a sigh of relief. Each one was labeled in the same handwriting. Chandler had been fastidious to the last.

He examined the file cabinet. It looked fine, just as it had looked before, when he entered. He shined the light around the room. Nothing out of place. He was careful to keep the light low, toward the floor and away from the long horizontal window at a man's eye level. As he turned, he backed into a chair, which upset a stack of books and a few bound papers. He cursed, angry at himself, and stood for a moment in speechless rage in the center of the office. He set the books back up and slid the papers into a pile. If anything was amiss, he reasoned, Chandler would think that the housekeepers had done it. He went back to the cabinet, looked at it, and then dusted the door handle with a clean handkerchief. No one would find his fingerprints if they tried, he thought.

He gave the room one more look. Then he had a second thought. Once again, he opened the cabinet, stooped down to the last shelf, and shined the light on the cards. They looked the same. Chandler wouldn't see anything different if he opened the cabinet tomorrow. He closed the cabinet, locked it, and wiped the handle. This time, he carefully made his way to the door, locked it from the inside, wiped the handles, and closed it behind him.

He decided to take the stairs rather than the elevator. His footsteps echoed through the silence, and Barly's heart froze as the sound grew nearer. Finally, Rino opened the glass-paned stairwell door. "Man, why didn't you call me?" Barly said frantically.

"Every step I took, you could hear. Why should I go on the air?" Rino said.

"You do it?" Barly asked.

"Yeah. Let's go. I want to buy you a drink."

They stopped at a bar near the place in town where their paths would diverge on the way home. It was an old place, once a busy neighborhood watering hole for mill workers but now a sleepy, middle-aged bar kept open only until the owner's retirement.

"Thanks for being there with me, Bar," Rino said.

"No sweat," said Barly.

"You still don't know what I did, right?"

"I figured you'd tell me if you wanted me to know," Barly said, looking down at his drink.

"I switched cards on him, Bar. And he doesn't know it. If he tries to lie his way through that fellowship, he's gonna get caught."

"How'd you get those cards? They don't even use them anymore."

"An old grad assistant. See, he used to make some of his grad assistants change the numbers on those experiments so he'd come out looking good."

"And some of those kids told you what they did?" Barly said with a hint of skepticism.

Rino nodded. "Even his wife said it: he tried to turn those kids into crooks like himself."

"Why do you want this cat so much, Rino?"

"You know he and I go back a long time, right? Remember the grievance? Remember what he did to Ted Reese?"

Barly nodded. "Chandler screwed him bad."

"But he got away with it, right? He always gets away with it." Rino took a sip of his drink. "And that's why I hate him, Bar."

As he listened to Rino, Barly mused about the day he ran upstairs in

Crandall Hall to find the ambulance crew zipping Ted Reese into a body bag and Sammy and Rino nauseated and horrified for having cut him down. Barly had heard an echo of the truth in the whispers and rumors of intramural office gossip, and he knew enough about the story to understand that it was not only Ted Reese who was Chandler's victim, but also the wife of Ted Reese, the girl who had meant so much to Rino.

Weren't the stories all true? Of Reese's wife, the phantom beauty: small, shy, seldom seen in the social whirl of Spring Common? And wasn't Rino crushed and pale almost two years ago? Illness, Sammy said at first. But what illness? Heartsickness maybe, but not heart trouble.

Barly knew that Rino had done something strange upstairs tonight. This wasn't the old sensible, reliable Rino who had a solution to all the maintenance problems of the college. But it wasn't a crazy, vindictive, harried man bent on a frenzy of revenge, either. Rather, it was a quiet, lonely man, possessed of a fury within that made him into a stealthy, almost sinister, plotter. Who, with slow, deliberate singleness of purpose, had stalked his victim and laid a trap that, when sprung, would earn Rino satisfaction as cold and pitiless as that of any inquisitor wreaking judgment upon a heretic.

Chandler had made one too many enemies and had met someone who would sell his soul just to destroy him. "So you switched the cards. How do you know it's gonna mean anything?"

"Those cards put him on the map. What if someone finds out that he rigged them?" Rino said coolly.

"If someone finds out, you say?"

"Sometimes, when you go for a prize—like that fellowship—the people that you screwed on the way up are laying for you. They just might have time to reconsider some old experiments." Rino paused and looked directly at Barly, who had looks of fear, amazement, and admiration on his face, all at the same time. "This isn't crooked, Barly. All I did was put a little truth back into the game."

Rino was a substitute bowler, sixth man, on the team sponsored by Agee's Tre-Sette Bar. Lou was a regular, and so were Pete, Marty, Hugo, and Agee, the old baseball players from Barkley field. Pete, the best of them, was captain.

Rino and Lou decided to go out to supper alone Thursday night, before they bowled. They ate at Anson's, a small steakhouse and bar on the outskirts of the city. The atmosphere was quiet and unhurried, a place to relax and talk. "I'm not going to eat too much now," Rino said. "We'll end up going out after the games, and then I'll be too full to eat."

"Okay, how about just a steak sandwich? I'll buy," said Lou.

"Best offer I've had all day," his brother said.

After the waitress took their orders, each of them had a whiskey and water before the meal. It tasted soothing to Rino and brightened his palate and made his juices flow. He was getting hungry.

"Long time no see," Rino said, taunting his brother.

"You bastard," Lou said. "I called you twice this week and came by your place last night, and you weren't home."

"I went to see Connie."

"I'm not defending you to our sister anymore, either," Lou said. "It'll do you good to get your ass chewed by a real pro once in a while."

"Once in a while? How about twice a week? She's getting more like Mom every day, you know that? Remember how Mom used to be after Pop died? If you didn't call her for two days, she thought you were mad at her."

"She's the same with me. She just worries about us." Lou sighed. "Although I don't know why. You're the crazy one."

Rino chuckled. "Not one dead brain cell in your head, is there, cowboy?"

"Not me. I'm loaded, have a nice girlfriend, straightened out my slice—"

"I'm doing okay, too, kid," Rino said.

Lou snorted, remembering the money Rino had spent on the fellowship, Orrie's fees, and the cost of the trips and other schemes of entrapment.

"How about girlfriends?" Lou said.

"Jean, Connie, and Libby all look after me like mother hens. I have all the female companionship I want," Rino said.

"I'm talking about the other kind of companionship: affection, attraction, maybe even making love once in a while."

Rino shook his head as if to prevent the sound of Lou's words from reaching him.

"You know, Rino, you can cut the bullshit anytime. Don't tell me you couldn't get it up if the chance came your way."

"I don't know," Rino said glumly. "Boy, talking to you sure has been a barrel of laughs lately."

"Things are tough all over," Lou said unsympathetically. "About the girlfriend... when should I tell Andrea anything? I'll see her a few times before the Saint Joseph's Day dance."

"I'm almost ready," Rino said. "Maybe a week or so. What do you think?"

"I think if someone else asks her first and she accepts, I'm gonna cut your balls off."

The following Tuesday, Orrie made his way to the president's office at Spring Common. The receptionist greeted him, took his coat, and ushered him into a small, dark-paneled anteroom next to the president's office and prepared a cup of coffee for him. Orrie took big sips of coffee as he tried to figure out how he would work his strategy.

In a moment, the president walked in and greeted Orrie warmly. After a few pleasantries, Wingrave ushered Orrie into his private office. The president was effusive and content. "Do you have some good news for us, Mr. Glazer?" the president asked, to open the business part of their meeting.

Orrie was a good play actor, particularly when he was about to shove a knife into someone. He paused, gave the president a weak smile, then grew more serious. "Good news and bad news, Dr. Wingrave."

Wingrave seemed startled by the unexpected trouble conjured up by Orrie's grim visage and tone. This was the kind of deal where everyone was a winner. How could there be something wrong?

"We've chosen our fellowship winner. That's the good news. The bad news is more important, however," Orrie intoned.

"Does it involve funding the project?"

"No. Fortunately, money is no problem; it's still there." Orrie paused again, in a pensive pose he had masterfully played in court over many years of combat. "As you know, sir, there was a thorough investigation of all nominees by my client—especially the two finalists. And on all of them, the investigations were happily positive and confirming—except one."

"What's the bottom line, Mr. Glazer?" said Wingrave impatiently.

"What I'm trying to say, with all due respect, is that one of your professors has altered the data on some of his experiments in order to change the outcomes—that is, to be able to assert statistical significance where there was none."

Wingrave took a deep breath. "Who was it?" he said in a soft, strained voice, looking away from Orrie.

"Dale Chandler," said Orrie.

"How do you know? What proof do you have?"

"We have data that was altered. And we know that his normal conduct was to instruct selected graduate assistants to alter data so that statistical tests would come out as he wished them to."

"But could you have replicated those experiments so quickly? There was no way..."

"Well, I suppose it depends upon how many instances of dishonesty it takes to convince an open mind. My clients have viewed certain—but by no means all—of his earlier experiments, especially the ones where he first distinguished himself as a researcher, and found dishonesty. By the way, if you'll check the dissertation shelf of your library, you'll discover that his is the only one not there among all the professors. And if you check his alma mater, you'll find that there is no dissertation on file in the graduate school, either."

"Which may verify nothing more than a bureaucratic snafu," Wingrave said.

"He reported a dissertation on his application," Orrie said. "That was what first raised our suspicions. It was enough to question other things he had done, other people who... ah, worked for him... and all the data he had submitted to us."

"I still don't see how you could have found all this out so quickly," the president said stubbornly.

"Do you think my client can afford two hundred thousand dollars and yet not afford to investigate a questionable fellowship application?"

Orrie's logic seemed persuasive. "What should I do?" Wingrave said.

Orrie shrugged. "Don't you think you'd better talk to Chandler?"

"Yes. I'll do that immediately."

"Sir, these were mostly old experiments with data on IBM cards. Today, data is more easily altered. If I were you, I'd impound those data cards and have them run off. Perhaps then you'll be convinced. I can also then show you the coordinates on the data grid where changes were made."

Orrie had completed his mission with frightening efficiency, enough for his own heart to be troubled. Wingrave was shaken, pale, and tremulous of voice. He was being forced into a dreadful confrontation with one of his professors. And if all that Glazer had said was true, he had to fire him. He could not even turn it over to a faculty committee to diffuse the responsibility for Chandler among them like a deadly fog.

Orrie stood up. "I regret the unpleasantness, Dr. Wingrave. But I'm sure you'll handle this thing. We'd like to go public with the award to Higley soon."

Wingrave also stood up as Orrie folded his notebook and put his pen in his suit pocket. The pen was Orrie's version of a security blanket; when he was working, it was always out, ready to jot down any scrap of information that might, in a moment of revelation and synthesis, be the key to a case or an argument.

"Tell me, Mr. Glazer, did Higley win the fellowship outright, or did he win it by Chandler's default?"

"No, sir. He won it by himself. His was clearly fresher and more original than Chandler's, and the outcome was more promising."

"The reason why I ask is that Chandler has always been one of our most prolific writers, with a fine future. Higley was not reputed to be... well, a first-rate researcher."

"But on the basis of the screening committee's findings and the quality of his proposal, doesn't it seem like Higley was somewhat underrated?"

Wingrave grimaced. "You know, Mr. Glazer, I must confess I don't know Higley very well."

"Or perhaps Chandler, either, Mr. President," Orrie said, looking directly at Wingrave.

Michael Bettencourt had been provost of Spring Common for four years. He was in his early 40s, likeable, lean, and muscular, with almost no hair on the top of his head but with a robust, tan face and distinct, youthful features. He strode across the mall and nodded to two students he met coming in his direction. He dreaded his unpleasant mission. He knew Chandler socially—they had often played tennis together on the courts of Spring Common—and was as friendly toward him as Chandler would permit.

Chandler impressed him as someone who felt he, himself, deserved to be provost by divine right, and Bettencourt always resented that presumption. He didn't like ambitious men who, in one great stride, might accomplish what had taken him 18 years of steady, careful plodding to become.

The secretaries all nodded and straightened a little as Bettencourt walked off the elevator and up to the receptionist at the secretarial pool. There was the buzz that Bettencourt could always hear as he walked into an academic area. *That buzz, those murmurs, was what it was all about*, he thought. *When you hear it, you know you're on your way.*

The receptionist directed Bettencourt toward Chandler's office. As he approached, he could feel his heart pump stronger than usual. Yet Bettencourt decided, after hearing what the president had told him that morning, that he would say as little as necessary to Chandler. "Hello, Dale," Bettencourt said as carefully as he could, trying to seem casual and free of serious concern.

"Mike? What are you doing in this neck of the woods?" Chandler said, surprised to see Bettencourt.

"Well, I'm on my way to a Policy Council meeting, and I thought I'd stop by."

Chandler permitted himself a moment of speculation and smug satisfaction. The provost was coming here to talk to him. What wonders a fellowship works, that even chief officers of the university make a path to his door—if not for homage, then for politics and coalitions? For a moment, Chandler thought Bettencourt was there to announce his selection as the winner. But since he hadn't done that, then Bettencourt was there to make points.

"And you just stopped by?" Chandler said.

"Well, actually, I had to see you about some business, too."

"Oh? What's that?"

"I need the data on these experiments." Bettencourt took a small sheet of paper and presented a list to Chandler.

"Mostly older ones?" Chandler said, puzzled by the list. "Why? They're on old IBM cards. Do we still have a card reader?"

"Yeah, over in the computer center, but I'm not sure if they're even going to run them. Maybe they just want to read them. Anyway, if you have them handy, I can take them now."

Chandler was curious but not anxious. The reward of the fellowship was too sweet, his progress through academe too fluid and effortless for him to feel threatened. "They're right here," he said, opening the file cabinet and choosing the decks quickly. Chandler handed them to Bettencourt in a large paper bag. "I still don't understand why they want those particular experiments," he said. "We could transfer the data electronically to a remote terminal. Then we wouldn't have to fool with all those cards."

"Well, who knows why they want them?" Bettencourt said, trying to seem disinterested. "All I know is that Wingrave told me to stop by to get them. I suppose we should humor him."

"Well, how about it, Mike? What's the word on the fellowship?"

"Well, your odds aren't bad at all, right?" Bettencourt said with a halfhearted smile.

Chandler seemed satisfied. In contrast to Higley, everyone knew him as writer and researcher. It looked good. He couldn't imagine them giving a lightweight like Higley the nod over himself.

"You should know soon. They want to announce it by Friday. Try to relax. Maybe we can play some handball or half-court if you're over at the gym."

"Yeah... fine, Mike," said Chandler.

Orrie called Rino to his office on Wednesday. "What do you want me to do now?" he said. The puzzle was beginning to resolve itself for Orrie.

"Are they gonna run the cards?" Rino said.

"Yeah. I told him to call me when they did," Orrie said.

"When he calls, show him where the changes were made on the grid. You're going back, aren't you?"

Orrie nodded.

"Okay. I counted 37 cards that had to be changed to get significant F-ratios on that one 1980 test."

"And after they run the cards the second time?" Orrie said, checking to see if he and Rino were of the same mind on the job ahead.

"No. Before they run the cards, you predict what the new F-ratio will be, and tell them it'll be significant. Also, let them know that all the others are going to be the same."

Later in the day, the president summoned Orrie. "Damn, this is fun," Orrie muttered to himself as he walked to the main entrance of Spring Common.

The president looked grim and pale. "We've run all five decks, Mr. Glazer. Now, what do you want to show me?"

Orrie opened his briefcase and unfolded a section of computer paper, the one with the changes Doreen Teare had made for Chandler in green highlighter markings. "If you change the numbers where I tell you and print up new cards, you'll get an F-ratio of 7.96, and that will be significant," Orrie said.

"I suppose you have such sheets for the other experiments?" Wingrave said.

Orrie looked up at him for a quiet second. This was the moment Orrie had bided his time for. "You know he's been doing this all along, don't you? The man's a fraud."

Wingrave took a deep breath and said nothing for several seconds. "I'm sorry I ever became involved in this, Mr. Glazer. That money has been like a curse for this institution."

"Well then, Mr. President, let's talk about the nice part. Higley will be the new fellow. A fresh face. And more prestige for this place. Next year... well, you never know, do you?"

"What about Higley? When can I let him know?"

"This whole timetable is up to you. Higley's our choice—that's official—but what are you going to do about Chandler?"

Wingrave pushed his chair back slightly from his desk. He looked away from Orrie for a few seconds as he weighed the consequences of what he had discovered. Chandler had to go. If the papers ever got hold of Chandler's story, it would cause great damage to the school—and to the administration that Wingrave had led for so many years. Chandler had to go, but it had to be quiet. "I'll have to deal with it, Mr. Glazer."

"Good. When you're ready, let me know. I'll have the cashier's check drawn up for you. By the way, I'm sure you're planning to be discreet about Chandler. It's a good idea."

Wingrave's secretary let Mike Bettencourt into his office. When he entered, Bettencourt seemed nervous, especially when he saw Wingrave's ashen face.

"Well?" said Bettencourt, knowing he would hear something unpleasant.

"It's the worst," said Wingrave dryly. "Bring the decks over to the computer center and have these cards rerun. If the test shows significant F-ratios, then he's been forging data."

"But how do you know?"

"They ran the tests on some of his experiments and found nonsignificant F-ratios. Yet, in all the articles he wrote, he reported significance every time."

"So where'd they get their information?"

"I don't know. The organization sponsoring the fellowship must have done some kind of investigation. Somehow they got hold of the original decks. They know exactly which data points Chandler fudged. That lawyer pointed some out to me right here on this desk."

"What in the hell possessed Chandler to do that? With his style and charisma, he'd be a president someday—easily."

Wingrave shook his head. "I don't know. But that damned fool has put this whole college in jeopardy. Can't you just hear Jay O'Connell at the next board of trustees meeting if this gets out?"

"They'd roast our asses over a slow fire," said Bettencourt grimly.

"And the fund drive for the physics lab would be dead in the water. Damn that Chandler! How could he do this to us?"

Later in the day, Rino and Barly met in Crandall Hall. An air vent needed cleaning or replacing. Barly had come to have coffee with his friend. They stood outside an alcove where the coffeepot was placed for faculty and staff. As they drank and talked, Rino surveyed the secretarial pool. "What do you think, Bar? Which one of these women would I talk to if I wanted to start a rumor?"

"Are you getting crazy on me again, man?" Barly said.

"Come on, Bar. Who?"

"Depends on who you want to know and how fast it's gonna be spread."

"Fast."

"See that old broad back in the corner?"

"You mean Catherine?"

"Yeah. Since the old dean left, she's been on the outs. The younger faculty around here hate her. Back when she was the dean's secretary, she used to talk to them like they were dogs."

"So she's the one?"

"If you want secretaries and staff to know, she's not it. But if you want the faculty to know, she'll do the job for you just fine."

"Thanks, Bar," said Rino. "See you later."

The vent was easily replaced with a new one. As Rino worked, he studied Catherine, waiting for her to move to the coffeepot. When she didn't, he lingered on the job, trying to look busy.

A few people spoke to him briefly as they passed. He knew most of the secretaries, but not all of them spoke—there seemed to be as much snobbery among the secretaries as there was among the professors—and some of them felt themselves to be further up the caste system than the maintenance and custodial crews, even though their wages were far lower. The nearer they were to power, the more the power captivated them.

But time has a way of making people beholden to those who keep the house. Sooner or later, everybody needs maintenance—and then they have to talk.

Finally, Rino pulled the ladder noisily toward Catherine's desk. He climbed a few steps, pretending to look at a molding above a door and acting as though there were something important to do. When he came down the ladder, he turned toward her. She looked up from her work, seemingly annoyed at his closeness. Rino knew he had to hook her quickly. His opening line had to be a good one. "Sorry for the noise. But I guess it'll be even busier up here in a few days, huh?"

He knew she didn't like being addressed by a custodian, but her curiosity made her take heed.

"Busy?" she said, trying to seem half interested.

"Word has it there's gonna be a party," Rino said nonchalantly, bending over to his toolbox.

"What kind of party? I haven't heard of—" She stopped suddenly, knowing she had seemed too eager and curious.

"The celebration for Chandler," Rino said, "for the fellowship."

"But how do you know? No one has mentioned who had been chosen."

"Word's been out," Rino said. "Haven't you heard anything over here?"

She was excited now. She had turned directly toward Rino and was looking right at him. "I doubt you're right, or surely we would have heard of it," she said.

"Well, I don't know. Maybe you're right. All I know is that people in other buildings have been saying that Chandler's won it. It's been sewn up from the beginning, but the president just wanted it to seem like a fair contest."

"I'm afraid I wouldn't believe everything I hear," she said with a sniff. "Excuse me." She stood up and walked toward the coffee alcove and poured water for tea.

Rino watched her walk away from him in the weird mincing gait she had affected through years of practiced kowtowing. He had accomplished his mission. Soon a reluctant believer would sound more positive as she propelled her story into the pipeline.

The weather was cold and cloudy despite a forecasted warm spell. Dale Chandler shaved slowly and took a long, leisurely shower. Out of the shower, he dried himself off, stretching as he dried, seeing himself in a clear full-length mirror that covered part of the wall of his bedroom. He'd be tough in tennis this spring. He'd stayed in shape the last few years, had gotten rid of his lackluster wife, Katrine, and had adopted a winning attitude.

He walked over to a dresser to put on cologne and powder. As he pulled out one of the dresser drawers, looking for cuff links, there among some other old papers, was a letter from Katrine. He dried his hair with a blow dryer. The fine, sandy-colored hair had not changed a bit in ten years. The hairline had receded slightly, but only Chandler knew it. Otherwise, the slight hint of winter tan that he had picked up in Acapulco lingered just enough to give his face that faint, healthy reflection of the sun.

He combed his hair through with a styling comb. He looked at his body again. Still long and lean. He chuckled, satisfied with himself. Maybe 10 pounds more of muscle, he thought, knowing he was still satisfied with the 180 pounds he carried. And maybe a thicker cock, just to be able to make that first insertion more memorable for them.

He picked up the letter addressed in Katrine's thin, florid script. He shook his head—abject surrender. *How could people degrade themselves that way? At heart, they're whores*, he mused. *They all want something. They want to be seen—with me, as I rise to the podium at the NERG convention in Chicago, and beside me in the publisher's suite when I'm introduced as one of their headliners. And they want that Dale Chandler dick in them when we come back that night to the VIP suite.*

The middle-middle class, the intelligent but untalented, the beautiful but unintelligent. It was hard to give up their kind of life. Yet all they could barter for it were their bodies, some of them overly ripe. That was why they were so pathetic when they wrote the heartfelt love notes asking why he had grown cold and aloof. But what could he tell them? The world of ideas, the world of publishing, the metalevel of academic promise was too rarified for dull sentiment. It was a survivor's game. And if the coolness came, if the staleness came, if he noticed wrinkles and sags on her body, then it was a sign that the coupling didn't take. She wouldn't be the one to attend faculty council parties with him at Cornell or Penn. But surely she should have known her limitations. Her promise to read more, to take more courses in the arts, was... pathetic.

But now he had other things to think about. All the phone calls last night, all the plans he had to make, had exhilarated him almost to the point of giddiness. He had to be magnanimous toward Higley. He had to be a graceful winner. He had to wait a mere two years, and then he'd be dean of faculty somewhere.

Mike Bettencourt walked into the president's office late in the afternoon. "Well?" said Wingrave as soon as he saw him.

"Bad news and more bad news," Bettencourt said grimly. "The guys at the computer center ran them off. And Glazer was right. Chandler had changed all the data."

"What else, for God's sake?"

"The word's all over campus that Chandler's been chosen for the fellowship."

"Oh, Lord!" Wingrave rasped and closed his eyes. It had been his last hope of avoiding an open confrontation with Chandler. "He must have been doing it all along—all those articles, all those convention speeches..."

"Teacher laureate," Bettencourt said.

Wingrave stood up and walked to a window overlooking the campus mall. "If he has sense enough to go quietly, maybe we can keep a lid on this, Mike," he said.

"And if he hasn't?"

"Then I'll make certain that he doesn't take this college or this administration down with him. I'll make damned sure that it's his character that's the issue, not Spring Common, and that he doesn't teach in a good college ever again."

"He hasn't been in his office all day. His secretary said he was at a one-day conference in Columbus," said Bettencourt.

"Well, as soon as he's on campus tomorrow, I want him here. And I want you to be in on this, too, Mike."

Bettencourt nodded. It was going to be unpleasant but bearable. He really didn't mind seeing a smug and arrogant superstar brought down.

On Thursday, Rino stopped in to Lou's shop. As usual, Lou was reading, smoking, and drinking coffee. "How many shoes have you fixed this week?" Rino asked.

"Not many," said Lou contentiously as he went to pour coffee for his brother.

"How many is that?" said Rino.

"Three pairs. What's it to you? You sound like Connie."

"Don't get excited," Rino said. "I'm just thinking that you spend a lot of time here for so little work."

"Do you need those few bucks you make at Spring Common every week? So what do you tell Connie when she asks you why you keep working?"

Rino nodded in capitulation. Then he tried to change the subject. "Did you read the paper last night?"

"Yeah," said Lou. "What about it?"

"They finally settled the probate on our old Mennonite friend."

Lou seemed surprised. "Jesus. Hosea? Did he die?"

"The end of November. Where have you been, Lou?"

"I don't know, Rino," said Lou, shaking his head in sad amazement.

Hosea was an old friend who had sold them peppers for decades. Not a beer-drinking buddy, but a big, hardworking, likeable man.

"I guess they're gonna sell the farm," Rino said, feeling a bit more somber now, catching on to Lou's mood.

"I just completely missed it," Lou said.

"You must have been in Boston or Pittsburgh, cowboy. I didn't know for a few weeks, either. Hugo told me."

"Things are starting to slip by us, aren't they, Rino?" Lou said quietly.

"Some things, kid. Maybe we just think so much of our own troubles that we don't notice."

Dale Chandler's morning had been pleasant despite the dreary weather. He had dark-charcoal wool trousers on, black tasseled loafers, a camel sport jacket, a white silk shirt, and a paisley tie. He had stopped for breakfast and had read the paper at his leisure. His lecture was already prepared, and he felt relaxed. As he drove his maroon Mercedes into his usual spot in the parking lot, two secretaries smiled brightly at him. He walked into the ground-floor lobby of Crandall Hall, again acknowledging the greeting of a colleague. Lately, as he walked about the campus, he felt a flush of achievement and contentment akin to the satisfaction of the victory walk on the final hole at Augusta National, born of the adulation of the throng, and graciously acknowledged with a restrained wave of the hand.

He took the stairs quickly and made his way up to the third floor. On the landing, he met Dresner, who came over quietly to congratulate him—discreetly, Dresner would say—so as not to seem in any way improper. It was the academic equivalent of wolves in a pack lying belly up before the leader as a gesture of subservience and submission. Only this time it was done quickly: a knowing look, a hurried clasp of the hand, and a furtive sideways glance to see if another colleague would have caught them in the little ritual of homage. Dresner had surrendered completely. His academic future was gone. All he had was his tenure at Spring Common. He had finally come to terms with Chandler's presumption of superiority.

Chandler walked down the corridor to his mailbox. Several secretaries smiled at him as he walked by, but now as they smiled, it was with the beaming adoration and awe they felt in the presence of someone gifted both by nature and by fate. A few other colleagues greeted him politely but effusively. But he had not yet seen Higley. And he wanted Higley.

Suddenly, at his back, he heard the voice of his own secretary. "Dr. Chandler?"

"Yes?" said Chandler, turning toward her and eliciting a smile, to which he responded sanguinely.

"President Wingrave's secretary called a few minutes ago. She left a message to have you come to his office as soon as possible."

"Fine. Call his secretary back and tell her that I'll be over in a few minutes."

Rino, after leaving Lou's shop, feeling slightly depressed by Lou's dreariness of heart, went down to the Tre-Sette. It would be lunchtime, and Tim Moorcock might be there. He came to Agee's for lunch a few times a week. *If he's not there*, Rino thought, *I'll have to call him.* But he didn't want to do it. He didn't want Tim to ponder the obvious questions: Why is he doing this? What's his interest in this man?

But Rino wanted this story in print, so he made his hopeful trek to Agee's. When he arrived, Tim wasn't there. So, Rino talked to Agee, had lunch, and then stationed himself at the big cigar showcase at the front of the bar and read the paper. But after some talk with old acquaintances and an hour-long wait, he went home to his condo and called the *Telegram.* When Tim answered, Rino began his story. "Tim, remember I told you something was going to happen at Spring Common?"

"Yeah," said Tim in a bored, lethargic tone.

"Well, they caught a professor forging data on experiments."

"Who told you this?" Tim said, seeming slightly more interested.

"I just know. A lot of people know."

"Just knowing won't be good enough for me, Rino. What's this guy's name?"

"Chandler... Dale Chandler. He's a former teacher laureate, full professor—big man on campus."

Tim conjured up his coolly patronizing professional voice. "Rino, are you sure of this? This kind of thing could destroy the reputation of a professional scholar."

Rino was getting angry. It was hard to like Tim, but it was even harder to deal with him when he had something Rino wanted. "I thought reporters were supposed to check out stories, Tim. All I can tell you is what's happening. And I don't have any proof. If you're worried so much about the guy's reputation, maybe you can catch the story on TV. I'm done."

When Rino hung up the receiver, he wasn't certain if Tim would follow up on the lead. Yet Tim seemed to be doing a little too much posturing this time. Hell, it was a scandal. And Spring Common had made some sensational headlines in the past. He couldn't be that uninterested.

Chandler walked across the mall to the president's office. When he entered, the president's secretary smiled politely and asked him to have a seat in the inner waiting room, one of the small den-like rooms where VIPs were kept while the president finished business in his office. Chandler waited, confident and relaxed. He drank a cup of coffee that a receptionist brought in and paged through a magazine. But he began to fidget as time passed. It seemed unusual to be kept so long. Suddenly, he heard Mike

Bettencourt's voice in the outer room, talking to the president's secretary. A few more moments passed, and then Bettencourt came into the waiting room from the president's office. He smiled weakly at Chandler and appeared to be formal and somewhat stiff in his movements.

As he came into the beautiful, darkly paneled office, he saw the president sitting behind his desk. Chandler sensed an incongruous uneasiness that he couldn't understand. Wingrave did not come around to the other side of the desk, never extended a hand of greeting. Never smiled. Finally, he addressed him. "Dr. Chandler, please be seated."

Chandler began to get a hollow sensation in the pit of his stomach. *My God*, he thought, *could it be that I didn't get the fellowship?* He shuddered slightly; the muscles in his stomach shivered.

Bettencourt sat in front of the president's desk, beside Chandler.

"What's this all about, gentlemen?" Chandler finally said, trying to defuse several minutes of awkward silence. His voice was hesitant and weak, but he got the words out.

"I'd like your resignation," Wingrave said solemnly.

The words seemed to strike Chandler in the chest, taking his wind. He looked at Bettencourt, then back to Wingrave. "This is some kind of joke, isn't it? This is about the fellowship?"

"It's not about the fellowship," said Bettencourt.

"Listen to me: I've been getting telephone calls for a day and a half congratulating me on that fellowship—all from faculty. Now what the hell's going on?"

"You didn't get the fellowship. I don't know where those rumors came from, but they didn't come from this office," Wingrave said.

"So what's all the nonsense about resignation?"

"You have no idea, do you?" Wingrave said.

"No. Suppose you enlighten me." Chandler was trembling visibly now.

"Damn you, Chandler!" said Wingrave, banging the heel of his hand on the blotter on his desk. "Don't you be coy with me."

"I think you two have lost your goddamned minds," said Chandler in amazement. "Do you really think you can fire me? I'm a tenured full professor."

"You're a fraud who alters data in experiments to make them turn out to be significant. You're a seducer of graduate students to get them to do your dirty work for you. You're an exploiter who writes articles based on false research," Wingrave said.

"You're crazy, Miles. Who the hell have you been talking to?" said Chandler, trying to appear composed.

"We have evidence, Dale," said Bettencourt. "Remember those cards I picked up? They were the original data—unaltered."

"No, you're wrong," said Chandler. "They only—"

"They only show the changed cards? On the contrary, they showed the original data, prior to the changes. You screwed up somehow, Dale, misfiled the cards."

"I made no such changes," said Chandler quietly.

"We have before and after results on at least five experiments, all of which show alteration of data. We haven't even begun to look at your more recent work," said Bettencourt.

"What kind of fucking railroad job are you two trying to pull?" said Chandler. "I'll have your asses in court for defamation of character, for—"

"The fellowship people investigated your data and interviewed your former assistants," Bettencourt said. "We have original and corrupt data. We know what you reported in your papers—claims at variance with the results of your experiments. What more do you want? Each of those things would have gotten you fired at any university in the country."

Chandler sat silent for several seconds—staring, touching his forehead, brushing his thighs, straightening his tie, preoccupied with the fit of his tie bar, acting almost as if the other two men were not in the room. *Jesus, it's like he's waiting for a train*, Bettencourt marveled.

As Wingrave watched the sudden withdrawal, he tried to analyze his own feelings toward Chandler. Knowing him, this was probably the only reaction Chandler could ever have to a tragedy: total denial. Yet one couldn't feel sorry for him; he was hurt, but not pathetic or pitiable. The wreckage of his past conquests and exploitations had been legendary at the faculty club for years. His hair was never mussed; his ties always color coordinated with his suits. And he always covered his tracks. The next morning, he was always back in his office, charming the secretaries, chairing committees, lecturing and commanding graduate students. *Chandler is at home nowhere else but here*, Wingrave thought. He had mastered this environment, had thrived on academic distinction, the awe of graduate students, the deference of colleagues. Outside the academic world he was an alien, a user, a hostile wanderer bent on conquest and striking first before being smitten by others.

But here he was, sitting quietly, hoping they would tire of their game and tell him that he had in fact won the fellowship. This was too strange. He had learned nothing in life to prepare him for this moment. He had been caught, and it would be public humiliation. He who had promoted himself endlessly. He who was the scourge of junior professors both at colloquia and in private committees. He who knew just when to smile, just when to frown, just when to nod, just when to touch.

Wingrave wasn't the kind of man to totally crush someone; unlike Chandler, he had no killer instinct. But this was a terrible mess. Events had proceeded in a way that removed Wingrave's control over them. The fellowship had changed everything, had made all the normal rules of passage different. This mess could not only forge Chandler's destruction; it might, in some remote happenstance, bring about Wingrave's own. He did not want to be known as the president of a college that had permitted systematic, deliberate fraud upon the academic community. He had never, in his later years, harbored ambitions beyond Spring Common. It was a lovely place—not a rat race, but, rather, a quiet, competent, average Midwestern college that turned out fairly literate graduates. It was a nice place from which to be president emeritus. He could retire in winter to his condo in San Diego and return east in spring, attached to something like the Carnegie Commission.

Slowly Wingrave slid a single sheet across his desk and motioned to Bettencourt to hand it to Chandler. Chandler took it and read it. It was a simple statement of resignation. Chandler was about to speak, but Wingrave spoke over his words: "You have, at most, until the end of the semester. Sign it now, and perhaps we can do enough damage control to keep this thing quiet."

"You're not going to announce it?" Chandler said.

"You fool!" Wingrave said. "Do you think a blatant case of academic dishonesty is something an administration would be proud of? Can you imagine some kid working on a master's degree and using your journal articles in his research only to find out they were all a sham?" Wingrave paused for several minutes, trying to regain his composure, trying to breathe normally again. Finally, he spoke again softly. "I want this thing to go away quietly, and I'll do everything I can to ensure that it does. But that must mean that you go away quietly, too."

"But why not give me till the end of the year? By then I can have another position." Chandler hesitated, realizing the presumption of what he was saying. Suddenly he sensed a weakness in Wingrave's strategy. Chandler might drag them all down with him. "In fact, I must have that time. I'll get a lawyer to handle it for me otherwise."

Bettencourt huffed in grudging appreciation. This crook was plea bargaining. "How can a lawyer do anything about phony articles published in national journals that have your name on them, Dale? You may not have until this afternoon, much less the end of the quarter. Other people know about you, and we have no way of knowing who all of them are."

"Sign it, Dale," said Wingrave, "and do your damnedest to come out of this with some vestige of a future left."

Chandler, in a quick, fluid motion, took a pen from Wingrave's desk set and signed the resignation. He handed it to Wingrave, reaching it across the desk and ignoring Bettencourt.

"I'll sit on this as long as I can. If you're lucky, you've got six weeks; if you're unlucky..." Wingrave paused and looked at Bettencourt for help.

"If you're unlucky, you'll get a call from one of us to tell you that there's no grace period left," Bettencourt said.

"Should I tell the dean?" Chandler said, still seated.

"Mike?" said Wingrave.

"We should tell him, Miles," Bettencourt said.

"We'll handle it, Dale. Maybe we can impress upon him the need for secrecy."

Wingrave stood up, and Bettencourt rose with him. Chandler pulled himself erect and took about five seconds to orient himself. "Are you all right?" said Wingrave.

"Of course I'm all right," said Chandler angrily. "Do you think this little kangaroo court is going to do me in? You'll be hearing from me."

Bettencourt raised a hand toward the door, ushering him forward, out of the room. "I have a suggestion, Dale," said Bettencourt. Both other men seemed curious. "You can say you resigned in protest over not getting the fellowship. It might not fly for everybody, but it'll cloud the resignation just enough to make it plausible."

Chandler glared back at both men, and then he turned and walked silently through the door.

Friday morning, the dean of education walked into his office and greeted his secretary as he hung up his coat in the closet in his office. There was only one message: the president wanted to see him at eleven o'clock. Burnham was elated by the news. Chandler was the fellow and would probably be gone after a two-year hitch, to bigger and better things. Both prospects were pleasant.

Burnham had a busy morning. He had to soothe the ruffled feathers of Dresner, who had been voted out as chairman of yet another faculty committee. He had also had a strange call from a reporter from the *Telegram*.

At eleven o'clock, Burnham sat dutifully in the small anteroom of the president's office. When Mike Bettencourt ushered him in, he seemed surprised.

Bettencourt offered him a seat, in the same chair that Chandler had sat in the day before. "Arlen, we called you here to discuss something very important," said Bettencourt.

Burnham flushed slightly. It was a good feeling, knowing that the two final choices for the fellowship were both from his own college. He smiled and settled comfortably into a chair. Both the president and the provost noticed the contentment in Burnham's manner and in unison, as if on cue, decided to awaken him to the reality of Chandler's fate.

"It's something not very pleasant, Arly," said Bettencourt.

But still, Burnham didn't understand. His mind was only on the fellowship and Chandler. Unpleasantness would only come about from having to deal with the loser, the one not chosen.

"But before we tell you the purpose of this meeting, we want it understood that under no circumstances will what we have to say be made public—not even to your closest friends, Arly, or I will hold you personally responsible," said Wingrave.

Burnham was startled by the tone Wingrave used and suddenly emerged from his pleasant languor. The threat in the president's last words was unmistakable.

"We've just asked for—and received—Dale Chandler's resignation... for fraud, academic dishonesty, and conduct unbecoming a professor at Spring Common," said Wingrave.

Burnham hesitated for a moment and then said, "This is some kind of joke, isn't it?"

"It was all unraveled by the fellowship people, Arly," said Bettencourt. "They checked his research, discovered falsification of data points in order to influence outcomes of experiments, talked to former grad assistants..."

"Did he admit all this to you?" said Burnham, still astounded.

"Not at first, but eventually," said Wingrave. "It's all true, Arlen."

"Do you know that he had never written a dissertation?" said Bettencourt.

Burnham frowned. "Is his doctorate not real, then?"

"It's real. He just managed to somehow wrangle a PhD out of them without one," Bettencourt said dryly.

"Are you surprised that he did it—or that we caught it?" asked Wingrave.

"Not that he did it. I'd heard rumors about his conduct before."

"What?" said Wingrave, beginning to show anger, his face reddening. "You mean you suspected Chandler of cheating before?"

"Well, before I became dean, when Silberton was here, one of the faculty—I think it was Earl Higley, as a matter of fact—came to the dean and told him that there was evidence that Chandler had cheated. But Silberton never pursued any of the charges beyond the old provost. And I don't know why."

"Let me get this straight: You mean that a faculty member discovered fraud and brought it to his dean's attention, and I wasn't told about it, for Christ's sake?" Wingrave said.

"When I came here, all this was at the rumor stage."

"And you never felt you should follow through on it? My God, Arlen, this thing could set the college back decades. How in hell am I supposed to raise money out of the state board if I have a suicide and scandal the dimensions of which are totally unknown to me?" Burnham was beginning to wilt. "Why in God's name didn't you at least go to the provost?"

"I was in no position to resurrect something that occurred before my arrival. I had no evidence. I didn't know the parties involved. I..."

"You copped out, that's what you did," said Wingrave coldly.

"Chandler's star was rising, Miles. He'd just made full professor, had gotten a second book published, had written articles. Was I supposed to tarnish the reputation of a rising young scholar based upon a spurious investigation?"

"Spurious? Do you see what your neglect has brought us? This scandal could engulf the university, your college, and all our careers. If you would have done your job instead of playing politics..." Wingrave banged his fist sharply on the desk. "Damn you, Arlen," he said in low, malevolent tones, "if I lose the new physics building or the gym because of this thing, you'd better be looking for another job."

Burnham reflected for a few minutes. "There's something more I should tell you," he said weakly. Wingrave snorted, and Bettencourt shifted nervously in his seat. "I received a call this morning from the *Telegram.* I didn't understand what it was all about at the time, but some reporter wanted to know if any of my faculty had resigned lately. Of course, I told him no. I had no idea about Chandler."

"Jesus," Bettencourt mumbled.

"You see, Mike," said the president, "I knew it was too good to be true. We've lost it."

Barly was sick with flu, so Rino was called out to work. He suggested several small jobs at Crandall Hall that had to be done, so Sammy gave him leave to do them all.

Word was out: Chandler had resigned, and there was a stunned, morose group of secretaries carrying on the usual business of the college. Rino was up on the third floor several times that day. Twice he saw a light in Chandler's office, but the door was closed. Twice the office was closed, but the light was out.

Rino was angry with himself for not being there to see Chandler. Twice more he checked his office but saw no one. But finally, in late afternoon around four o'clock, he saw Chandler step off the elevator. Chandler went to his mailbox and called a secretary to him to give her further instructions. He was beginning to set things in order for his departure. He looked grim and tired but still immaculately dressed.

Rino hurriedly left the electrical switch he had been working on and went to the corridor to Chandler's office. He waited, his heart beating heavily, counting the seconds as though they were hours. In an instant, Chandler appeared from around the corner. He was reading something he carried in his hand, a single sheet pulled from a freshly torn envelope. He didn't notice Rino standing farther down the corridor. As he approached his office, Chandler turned slightly toward the door and began to reach into his pocket for a key.

"Malandrine," Rino said softly, projecting his voice just enough so that Chandler could hear him. "It was no accident. I did this to you... for Lee, for Ted Reese, and for all the others you screwed and abused. You're finished."

Chandler stared blankly at Rino as he turned the key in the lock. It would be just like Bellanca to be a parasite upon another's misfortune, to claim credit for his undoing, to speak of things fantastical as though they were true. And yet... he had seemed to turn up at every embarrassing and painful moment in his life the last few years, as though he needed Chandler's pain to subsist. But could he have done all this?

When Chandler was inside, he closed and locked the door. Only a few more things to do, and he would be on his way. His other things could be gradually packed and put into storage. He had to take his most personal writings and just a few books.

Suddenly the phone rang. "Hello," Chandler said nervously.

"Dr. Chandler, this is Tim Moorcock from the *Telegram*. I've been told that you've resigned your position. Is that correct?"

Chandler's mind and heart both raced. He had to placate the reporter, yet give him a plausible reason that would look good in print—that he left Spring Common over principle. "It's no secret that I've resigned," said Chandler coolly.

"But under duress? There was some talk of your falsifying experimental data. Can you speak to that? Is it true?"

"I've resigned because I was not offered a fellowship despite my accomplishments as a researcher. A great deal of money was involved, and in the end, the administration chose politics over principle. And I can't live and work under those conditions. The man who won was a well-known faculty operative, an insider whose only skill is political machination. At best, someone of questionable research accomplishments."

"Anything more you care to add about the other allegations?"

"They're false—just unfounded rumors. That's all I've got to say. If you want anything more, contact the president's office."

Outside, Rino had stopped because he had noticed Earl Higley's door open. All he did was stop to shake his hand. Higley stood up and came to greet Rino.

"I just wanted to congratulate you on the fellowship. I knew you'd win," Rino said.

Higley grimaced. "By default, Rino. That's what everybody'll say."

"You know you won it all by yourself, Earl. Don't worry about what anyone else says."

"Yeah. You got your fishing tackle ready? There'll be some running soon."

"I'm ready whenever you are."

"Also, I just bought a new car, a 1936 Cord. Cost me a fortune. How about coming out to see it soon?"

"Okay. I'll call you."

Just then, Chandler, who had left his office, came around the corner into the small corridor that led to the rear stairs. He was angered to see his two nemeses talking together.

"Well, Earl, I won't congratulate you on a fair fight, because you and your guinea friend there did your best to make it dirty."

"Chandler, the last thing you were looking for was a fair fight," said Higley, surprised for a moment at the hatred that Chandler seemed to bear not only for him, but for Rino.

"Well, if you don't turn out to be much of a researcher, you can always go back to your first love—character assassination."

"You keep telling yourself that, Dale. Only it wasn't I cooking my data and writing up bogus experiments," said Higley, calming a little.

"My work can stand on its own. And I'll make sure that what you produce is exposed as the drivel of a lightweight hack."

"No one will listen to you, Chandler," said Rino, breaking into the argument. "Where are you going to teach now?"

"He's lucky he can get a job as a book salesman, Rino," Higley said coldly.

Chandler, facing the two sneering men, reddened, scowled, and then walked past them hurriedly. "Fuck you both—two slimy second-raters."

That night, Rino and Lou found another restaurant on the outskirts of Youngstown, another quiet bar and steakhouse that served fine, simple food: steaks, potatoes, salad, and French bread. Both men had several drinks during the meal, not their usual custom. Rino slowly related the story of Chandler's fall to Lou, who listened in awe of his brother's singular determination and cold destructiveness. "I've known you from the day you were born, and I never saw this in you," Lou said.

Rino shrugged. "If it was in me, cowboy, it fed on Chandler."

"You know all of this was because of Lee, don't you?" said Lou. "You were getting revenge for her, not for Ted Reese or anyone else."

Rino nodded. "Let's talk about something else," he said. "I have a proposition for you."

"Jesus Christ," said Lou softly, taking a big swallow of whiskey.

"Come on now, Luigi, this isn't crazy. It's just a business deal."

"Okay, so what's the business deal?"

"I want to buy that pepper farm—you and me."

Lou shook his head as he laughed softly. "Hell no, that's not crazy at all, Rino. Who would ever think that?"

"I'm serious, Lou. We can do it. The price is two hundred eighty grand, and Orrie thinks we might get it for two fifty."

"You talked to Orrie about this already?"

"I've been talking to Orrie every day for two weeks," said Rino. "He was worried about how this thing with Chandler would shake down. So yesterday, when it was all over, I told him about the farm."

"A pepper farm?" Lou repeated incredulously, grimacing as though he had just swallowed something strange.

"Lou, I'm done with Spring Common. I don't belong there anymore, and you're tired of fixing shoes—I know it."

"Who told you that?"

"You don't average two pairs of shoes a goddamn day, Lou. You don't enjoy it anymore."

"So for that I should go out and buy a farm?"

"Look, how many years did we help Pop in the garden? Is there anything you don't know about peppers?"

"There's a hell of lot I don't know about 26 acres of peppers," said Lou.

"Well, goddamn, I suppose you're going to have to learn something. You might even have to work."

Lou paused. "This is no joke, right? I mean, you're not having one of those waking dreams again?"

Rino shook his head. "I'm dead serious. It'll be interesting. We work March through October, and then we'll have the rest of the year to take it easy. We know the work; we know a little about the retail business. And Pop would be proud of us."

"Pop would have given you up as crazy a long time ago—and me for listening to you."

"Come on, Luig'," Rino said in the old family dialect that he had learned from his parents and used whenever he was plying his brother or sister. "We can't lose, and it'll be fun. If we make some money, so much the better. We'll have real work to do again, and it'll be just for us."

"You're serious?" Lou said, eyeing him coldly.

"I'm serious, kid. There's a little house on the place that we can fix up, use it on some nights when we don't feel like driving home into town."

"Where into town?" Lou said suddenly.

His brother knew immediately what he meant. "To Frank's place. I'm going back," Rino said.

"When?"

"Now. The job I had is done. Now I can move back in and leave it all behind me."

"Does Jean know?"

"Yeah. I'm going over this weekend to ask Frank if I can go back."

"Ask him? You and I built that place one brick at a time," Lou said.

"It's his house now, Lou. I have to ask. Besides, I've given that kid a bad time the last few years."

"You did all right by him, Rino," Lou said softly.

"Still, he's a good boy, and Jean—"

"Oh yeah. And Jean..." Lou said.

Rino frowned. It was annoying to have someone think he knew every motive for every move one made in life—even if he did know most of them. "It'll just be nice to be back," he said, fending off his brother's comment. "So what do you think, kid? Are you up to it?"

Lou took a sip of whiskey. "It's crazy, you know that? Everybody's gonna think we've lost our minds."

"What's so new about that? Just tell them that I'm senile and you're taking care of me."

"Hell, they already think that," Lou chuckled. "We'll be greenhorns, you know."

"We'll manage," said Rino. "Hell, it'll be fun. We can still golf sometimes and go see the Browns play once in a while."

"How much again?"

"About one twenty-five apiece, and if we get tired of it, we can sell it."

"I have to see it first. You sprung this on me after I've had three drinks. I have to have a clear head when I let you play with my money."

Rino smiled. He had found his brother in the right frame of mind. Lou had grown tired of the shop. He knew it was an anachronism, yet he couldn't part with all the memories it held.

Since they would work until they died, the pepper farm would be just the thing: seasonal, concerned with life, productive, and usually financially rewarding. The Mennonite, Hosea, had raised a large, happy family on what he earned selling peppers—and he worked the farm until he died.

Rino knew that he and Lou could do the same.

"When are you moving back?" Lou said abruptly.

"Soon. I have to sell off some of my stuff first," Rino said.

"And when are you quitting Spring Common?"

"Right away. I'll tell Sammy Monday that it's time to go. That Puerto Rican kid will handle my job just fine. And Barly will break him in right."

"Okay," Lou said, "how about tonight?"

"What about it?"

"It's time to go see Andrea."

Rino groaned.

"Rino, this isn't going to dishonor Lee's memory any more than Lee didn't dishonor Mary's memory."

Rino snorted. "A lot of people tried to spin it that way, Luigi."

"You don't have to marry her, kid. All I want you to do is take her on a date."

"All right," said Rino. "When we're done here."

"The dance is next week. You should have asked sooner."

For several minutes they were silent, both thinking of things that had troubled them in recent days and both giving fleeting thought to the future. Lou, who had been having more ponderous thoughts lately, was still troubled. Now it was he who grew uncertain and reflective, just as Rino had begun thinking lighter thoughts of pepper farms and going home again.

But suddenly Lou became aware of their silence. And in his reawakening, spoke a revelation to Rino. "You were the malandrine, Rino."

"What?" said Rino, bewildered.

"You. You were the malandrine."

"Right. Thanks, kid."

"Rino, the day he was born, the day he got his first Rolex watch, his first Mercedes, you were lying in wait for him."

"Lou, all I did was bump into him—and just give him enough rope to hang himself."

"His malandrine, kid. Only his. Even now, he probably doesn't know what hit him."

"Vivid imagination, Luigi."

"Rino, the day you made up your mind about the fellowship—and you didn't even flinch; two hundred grand, Orrie, Saint Louis, both Rochesters—he was finished."

Rino reflected on what Lou had said as he took a sip of coffee. "I think of Lee in his bed, how he smiled when he hurt people. When she died, those memories were too much for me. Chandler was just too much evil in the world."

An hour later, Lou drove slowly back to Youngstown while Rino sat beside him, nervously looking out the window. When they drew near Andrea Manasseri's house, Rino took several deep breaths. Lou had stopped two houses away, in order not to be seen. He looked at his brother. "You know you have to do this, don't you?" he said.

Rino nodded.

"Just go up and say hello. You should know by now how to make conversation with a nice woman."

Rino glanced at Lou and then silently walked up the three flights of stone stairs leading to the front porch of the house. His heart was beating as much from the excitement and trepidation as from the upstairs climb. On the porch, he could see Lou's car, partially obscured by the tall bushes that grew along the front edge of the yard.

Rino turned and took a deep breath. It was as though he was at the doors of a great temple with a cavernous roof and eerie, forbidding aspect. He rang the doorbell. As he waited, he felt a strange sensation come over him. The fast heartbeat, the sweaty palms, and the harsh intake of breath—they were there as they had been those early nights when he stood uncertainly before the door of Lee's apartment. Only this time, when he rang the doorbell, there was, somewhere in the recesses of his soul, a longing... to respond again, to hear the soft, "Hi," to see the gentle, unforced smile, feel the warm, soft touch, breathe the perfume of her existence.

His heart beat so fast his breaths became half drawn. For a moment, he felt dizzy. Suddenly the door opened, and he heard Lee's voice call him. He seemed to be facing into bright sunlight as he saw Lee standing in the doorway, her hand still resting on the doorknob as it always did. The smile, the smooth, unhurried grace, the soft brown hair pinned up off the nape of her neck, the blue bathrobe tied loosely and revealing no nightshirt beneath, the bare legs and feet. Again, he heard her voice call, "Rino."

The light was growing brighter, leaving her face shadowed against the backlit glare behind her. She didn't move. She didn't take her hand away from the doorknob. Again, he heard her call his name, that same voice that had soothed and thrilled and enchanted him through so many happy days. "Rino?"

He felt the dizziness again, the weakness of every sinew of his body. It was as though he was dreaming, yet this was real: the noise of the city behind him, the car horns, the trucks, the factories, and her. She was there. He would know that shadow anywhere: the hair, the slightly cleft chin, the glistening dark-brown eyes. She was there. Lee was there, calling his name again.

He seemed paralyzed. But he could speak. "Lee?" he called to the form now shadowed away from him. "Lee?" The noise of the city was growing louder, the light in the doorway blinding to his eyes. He was struggling to hear against the crashing, then waning noise. Once more he heard the voice call his name. This time he cried her name aloud, calling over the noise, calling against the searing brightness.

And suddenly all he heard was the echo of his own scream. The noise had stopped; the light had become softer and less glaring. Again, he heard his name, now called in a different voice, Andrea's voice, as she stood in the doorway, lit from the hallway behind her. "Rino, are you all right?" she said.

Rino knew where he was now. The strange world he had just encountered, where yesterday was today and light and noise were frightening, was gone. "Andrea?" Rino said.

"Yes, Rino, won't you come in? All you all right?" she said.

He started to take a step, but the step wouldn't come. He couldn't go in. Lee had changed his heart... and changed his future. He wasn't going in.

Once, in another time, Andrea would have brought new light into lackluster days. But now she paled against what life had become for Rino, even in his pain. Rino shook his head. "No, Andrea." He shook his head again. "This is a mistake," he said, stepping back from the door. He turned away once, then turned back. "I never meant hurt to you. I'm sorry." Before his voice had finished the words, he was on the steps, going downward.

Lou watched helplessly. At first, he thought of driving over to his brother and giving him a ride. But then he realized that Rino had seen him waiting in the car and had turned away from him, walking alone. Lou started the car, still watching Rino, but made no other move. He knew Rino was heading for Frank's house, heading toward his son and Libby and Jean.

Lou realized that it was too late to talk any more about Andrea. Rino's fate was bound up in special women who came his way in life. There seemed to be no choice about them: not Lee, not Jean, not Libby, not Connie. The one choice he could have made was Andrea. And that was the difference, Lou thought, as he watched Rino recede from his sight. Love for Rino had never come by choice; it came uninvited.

Andrea Manasseri stood for a few moments at her doorway as Rino fled down the stairs. She was stunned but hardly showed it. Looking at her, one could sense the reserve, the hatred of display, of emotion, of public witness. But as this man left, the one man she would have welcomed into her house since her husband died, she was aware of what she missed. She missed someone who might have wanted her and might have needed her. She missed what might have been her awakening, her chance to feel it and share it, the closeness that comes from love.

Slowly she backed away from the door, closed it, and stood silently behind it, facing the inside of the house. She took a deep breath. In those few seconds, her brief encounters with Rino passed before her mind's eye: the times she had avoided him or needlessly embarrassed him, the times he had come open-hearted and honestly to her and spoken in his simple, direct, and guileless way, the prodigal times she was not her best self, not doing what others would do so easily, not letting herself be attracted—or honest with her own feelings.

In those few seconds, she remembered the look that had passed between the lovely young woman and Rino that rainy night at Castorina's. It was not a cloying, fawning look of infatuation; instead, it was that natural look between two special people belonging in love, belonging to each other. She had seen it in a split second. She had heard it in the soft, halting words they spoke when he returned from outside with her lost purse. It was something she had recognized instantly and easily, something she understood and longed for—something she had never had.

Andrea Manasseri wiped her eyes, ran her hand across her forehead, and walked into her living room alone.

Rino walked a long, convoluted route to his condo. At first, he thought of Jean and Frank and Libby. But this was not the night to calmly have tea and talk easily of mundane things. This was the night he had to walk away the madness. His mind wasn't all his to control any longer. He had always felt it was, but tonight he knew there were memories and feelings over which he had no control, that could haunt him in his waking moments as they tormented him in his sleep.

When he returned to his apartment, he sat exhausted in the big chair in his family room. After a long while, he poured himself a whiskey and soda and then sat down again, savoring the calming taste of the drink, letting feelings and memories wash over him like a tide that cleanses and renews a beach.

It was 11 o'clock, and the temperature had grown colder, and the wind outside grew noisy and rampant. Rino walked over to a window and stared silently at the grim weather for several minutes. Finally, he went to the cabinet in the living room and took an envelope out of a drawer, Toni's letter that he had never opened. He sat down again, took a sip of whiskey, and then read it:

Dear Rino,

Since I haven't heard from you, I know you must be upset about what happened here the last time you visited. I know that although you kissed me, I was only a reflection of Lee and whatever you saw in me that reminded you of her.

It seems at times that I've been lonely much of my life. Not only was my husband, Steve, taken from me early, but then, after seeing Lee's unhappy marriage and having such fond hopes for the promise of new love and happiness that you brought to her, she was also taken–from both of us.

I guess I'm willing, anymore, to take happiness wherever I can find it. I'm not sure what lies ahead–life can be so harsh and unpredictable–but I know that in whatever days I have left, I want to choose happiness over sorrow and hope over despair. If what I've said makes any sense to you, then you must know that I'm not sorry or resentful of anything that happened between us. I don't know what our friendship will mean, but I know I don't want to give you up. I've lost too much already.

With affection,

Toni

Rino put the letter down and finished his drink. Amazing how much like Lee her thoughts and feelings were. So what would he do now? How would he ever know that it was Toni rather than Lee that he was responding to?

He picked up the phone, dialed a number, and waited. It rang two times, and then a quiet voice answered that made him shiver slightly. "Hello, Toni, this is Rino," he said.

"Hello, Rino," she said softly.

"Were you asleep? I hope I didn't scare you."

"No. I couldn't sleep. I was just reading," she said.

It was strange hearing that voice again and feeling the mood it created. She seemed to speak hesitantly on the phone, with no art or brightness, with only the calm and careful reserve that Lee also had. *It was almost eerie,* Rino thought. Both mother and daughter had that same reticence about speaking. They never said too much. Rino often wondered, especially in the beginning, just what Lee was thinking when he called her. She seemed to say only enough to get them together again. Their emotions were so open, so unguarded, so simply trusting that they never had to seem boisterous or forward. They were soft of speech, of manner, of looks, of style. They both responded best in person and warmed and brightened only in intimate times.

"I got your letter," Rino said abruptly, "a while ago."

"Yet you haven't called?"

"I just read it a few minutes ago. I've kept it."

"But why didn't you read it?"

"I was afraid of what would be in it," he said.

"Oh, Rino..."

"I'm so sorry, Toni. I didn't mean any disrespect," he said.

She sighed. "Rino, you were never capable of disrespect, either to Lee's memory or to me."

"I've been thinking about what made me do it. What... I don't know, Toni. I think that the happiest moments of my life were when I was kissing Lee, and somehow I wanted the world to be like that again, like trying to turn the clock back."

"I know that, Rino. That's why I wrote the letter." She was silent for a few seconds. Then she tried to change the subject. "How have you been?"

"I'm okay... mostly okay. How about you?"

"I have good days... and some bad ones." She was silent a few moments again. "Rino," she said, struggling with her words, "I'd have better days if you would come to see me." She paused, not wanting to make it seem as if she was pleading. "I mean, well, if you don't come, I want it to be only your choice. I don't want it to be because you're feeling guilty or self-conscious."

Rino snorted to himself softly. Toni's feelings and sentiments were so reminiscent of Lee, it unnerved him. "Your letter means a lot to me, Toni. You have a way of making people feel good. And Lee had that from you."

"Rino, maybe you don't realize it, but somehow, part of Lee is in you. That's why when you come here, I feel better, too."

"What are you doing Saint Joseph's Day?"

The voice changed slightly, a small, barely perceptible hint of music in it. "Lutherans don't know about such things, Rino. When is it?"

Rino chuckled. "Shows what a local boy I am, huh? It's this Saturday, the 19th."

"Will you come then? That would be fine."

"I can come. Midafternoon, okay?"

"Okay," she said. "I'm glad you called, Rino."

The Wisconsin Upland was still caught in bitter winter. The drive had been exhausting from the moment he set out that morning, and he wouldn't make it to Ashland by daylight if the blowing, dusty snow got worse. His stomach cramped from time to time. The food he had eaten so long ago still seemed lodged at the base of his gullet.

As he drove in the dark, he thought of his father, retired long since but still an advisor to his brother, now president of the family mills. People would find it strange that he was home, especially his family. What was he going to say?

As he headed north, the lighter sky above him seemed to be swallowed by the yawning darkness ahead. Lights from distant cities could be seen from the tops of hills as he traveled, but they grew more blurred and faint as time passed. What was he going to do?

He banged his hands against the steering wheel and moaned softly in his throat. Somewhere he had to find a place that would hire him. But how could he be given a full professorship? Or tenure? And if not tenure, how could he live through that ordeal again, the weighing and parsing, the constant evaluation by his peers, the constant unease born of the fear that somehow, somewhere, he had inadvertently offended a colleague who now bore a silent grudge against him? And how would he face colleagues at conventions, people who once admired him? God, he'd end up being another Dresner—hanging on, superserviceable, apple polishing, blending into the gray mediocrity of the untalented.

But worst of all, there would be the sneers of younger colleagues. No longer would his style, his grace, his future make him their idol. Now he would be patronized or, worse yet, pitied. And never again could he produce anything that would not be suspect.

His stomach churned. He would have to lie to his parents: he had resigned because of the fellowship. But his father would reflect on it and then begin to doubt. And then begin to ask him questions. What if he were to get hold of a *Telegram* article and read of forged data and invalid experiments? What if he already knew?

The road ahead was glazed hard by the cold air coursing over its darkened surface. His shoulder muscles ached as he drove. Only once in a while would he see a solitary car passing. All through the long ride, images returned again and again to torment him: Higley, Wingrave, Ted Reese, Bellanca. Could it really have been Bellanca? But how? And why? Just because of Lee Reese? God, what he would give to have that out of his past.

He stopped at a roadside rest area. He stepped out, looking up at the tall trees that shielded the rest stop from the wind, their bare branches seeming like dark veins against the murky night. He walked from the car a few paces and looked around again, startled by the brittle night sounds of cracking limbs and lonely animals calling to the sky. The trees would whisper quietly in the illusive wind that came and went. He shivered slightly, took a deep breath, and walked back to his car.

In the middle of the night, a Wisconsin state patrol car rode down the slippery highway, dusted pale white by the blown and powdery snow. Two young men in uniform were inside, not speaking, each lost in his own thoughts; by instinct, one driving, the other watching, alert subliminally for any trouble in their way. The radio was silent as usual on the remote stretches of Wisconsin highway in the early morning.

As the car lights illuminated the road and reflected patches of ice on the roadside, the other officer started for a second and craned his neck back over his shoulder.

"What's wrong?" said the driver. "What'd you see?"

"I don't know. Maybe there's a car back in that rest."

"Lights on?"

"No. The place is empty and total dark. Come on, go back."

The driver turned the car around and reflexively switched on the flashers. As they entered the roadside rest, the car lights revealed a parked car ahead—a large, maroon Mercedes-Benz sedan.

"Jesus," said the driver, "that's a damned expensive car to be abandoned way out here. You suppose it's stolen?"

"No one's in it, huh? What are those, Ohio plates? Mahoning County?"

"Yeah. Call it in. For some reason, I think that's over near the Pennsylvania line."

As his partner called in the license number on their radio, the driver got out of the police car, put on his cap, and unleashed his holster strap. Then he turned on a large flashlight and came up carefully behind the car from the driver's side.

The other partner waited for the computer check on the license plate, he watched the driver shine the light in one window, then go quickly to the opposite side to look again. Suddenly, he turned the flashlight off and walked back through the light of the patrol car, opened the passenger door, and leaned down to talk. "Better call another unit and the local sheriff," he said dryly. "There's a guy up there with a bullet through his head."

Dear Reader,

Thank you for choosing this book and, more importantly, for taking the time to read it. In a world full of distractions and endless options, the simple act of sitting down to read is something truly meaningful, and I don't take that lightly.

Every page you've just read was written with the hope that it would resonate with someone like you. Whether you found it to be thrilling, entertaining, or even just a moment of escape, I'm deeply grateful that this book is a part of your library.

Books are never complete without a reader. Your willingness to engage with these words is what brings the story to life. And in that way, you've been a part of this work too.

Amazon reviews are important to me as an author, because I trust your perception, and the reviews provided are important to Amazon.

Thank you again for your support, your time, and your trust.

With sincere appreciation,

Donald Greco

About the Author

DONALD GRECO grew up in Youngstown, Ohio, and has lived in Ohio all his life, fulfilling a career as a fifth-grade schoolteacher, a high school geometry teacher, and later as a professor of mathematics. He always dreamed of writing stories, so in his spare time, he wrote novels throughout his adult life. The only one who knew of his secret passion was his beloved wife, Angie, who sadly passed away. He is still a resident of Ohio and is the father of three sons and five grandchildren.

He published his first children's book, *What Ever Happened to the Smooth-Tongued Cats?*, in 2022. He also has five adult novels as part of his *Youngstown Quintet Series*. These books include: *Abramo's Gift, Tommy the Quarterback, Dracaena Marginata, The Malandrine,* and *The Ghost Hawk.*

greconovels.com
dongreconovels@gmail.com

www.ingramcontent.com/pod-product-compliance
Lightning Source LLC
LaVergne TN
LVHW041056080826
845145LV00007B/1599

* 9 7 8 1 9 7 0 4 7 1 3 0 4 *